THE BEGINNING

going
HARD

STEELE RIDGE
www.SteeleRidgeSeries.com

Print Edition, October 2016, ISBN: 978-1-944898-07-6
For more information contact: kelsey@kelseybrowning.com

CONTENTS

Steele**RIDGE**

THE BEGINNING

KELSEY BROWNING
TRACEY DEVLYN
ADRIENNE GIORDANO

CHAPTER ONE

Late January

IF JONAH HAD TO HEAR one more fucking word about who had authority over the truck's radio dial, he would pull out Reid's concealed carry and shoot all three of his brothers point-blank.

"It's a ten-minute drive into Canyon Ridge," Britt, the oldest, said in his calmest peacekeeper voice. "We could probably turn it off and, you know, talk to each other."

Grif snorted a laugh. "You? Mr. I-live-in-a-cabin-in-the-woods wants to talk?" He hit the down button on the window and stuck his head out as if looking for a lightning bolt. Unbelievably, when he pulled his head back inside the cab, his hair still looked, as their sister Evie would call it, artfully tousled.

"It's my truck and I say we listen to Merle Haggard." Reid hit the button on his steering wheel to change the music from alternative to classic country.

"Y'all should know better than to try to negotiate with a primate," Jonah said. "Besides, he'll just keep switching the station until we're all suicidal."

Reid grunted, reinforcing his image as a big gorilla of a guy. Granted, his size probably came in damn handy in his line of work.

They cruised down the North Carolina back road from their mom's house toward the park where, thanks to Mother Nature and her generosity in granting them with above average temperatures, they'd be celebrating her sixtieth birthday. Up ahead, a vehicle tore out of a gravel side road, stirring up a billowing cloud of dust and shielding the make and model from view. A pair of faint brake lights appeared when the shithead fishtailed too close to the ditch.

"What the hell?" Jonah asked.

Reid's face was serious, grim even. "You see that?" He pulled a Richard Petty and shot down the gravel drive.

"Son of a bitch." Britt stretched over the front seat to peer out the windshield.

Jonah spotted the line of smoke trailing from a big building that had recently been built on the old Tupelo Farm, where the Tupelo family had raised hogs and Christmas trees for as long as anyone could remember. At least before the city bought their twenty thousand acres and built a state-of-the-art sportsman's complex. And from what his mom said, that complex had cost the city twenty million dollars.

"We need to call nine-one-one," Britt said, always the reasonable one.

"Already on it." Phone in hand, Jonah tapped out the emergency number. But as they drove closer, he noticed no one was streaming out of the building. "Won't the sprinklers and alarms go off? Where is everyone? Why aren't they evacuating?"

"Everyone, who?" Britt said.

"Like the people who work there and the people who play there."

"It's empty."

"On a Saturday?"

"On every day."

Jonah braced himself against the dashboard as Reid shot into the lot and screeched to a stop a fair distance from the expansive glass and gray stone building. His truck was the only vehicle around.

"Dammit," Jonah said, "we're gonna have to do something about this fire."

"No shit." Reid piled out of the truck and everyone else followed. "Or did you think we'd just let it burn to the ground."

"Maybe it's not as bad as it looks," Jonah offered up, even though he knew that was pure BS. They might need to pick up extra flowers for their mom before heading to the party though, because it was clear they would be late.

Grif looked down at his high-end khakis and hand-tailored shirt. "I hope to hell not."

Reid, never missing a step toward the building even though he was limping slightly, cuffed Grif on the back of the head. "I'm sure you have a hundred other pair of those fancy duds in your closet back in LA, Pretty Boy."

As they jogged closer to the building, it was clear someone had broken one of the front windows and that this thing was picking up steam. Flames were already licking their way up what looked like a reception desk.

Reid jabbed a finger at them. "You three stay out here, and I'll—"

"No fucking way," Jonah cut him off. He'd been underestimated his whole damn life, first by his big brothers, then by kids in school, and eventually the big game-development moguls in Seattle. But he'd damn well shown them all. "You're screwed in the head if you think we're going to let you go in there by yourself. You'll get yourself killed on Mom's big day and we'll be the ones who have to tell her. Not enough flowers in the whole world to make up for that kinda news."

"He's right," Britt said. "This looks like a four-man job to me."

Reid's face was a study in stubbornness, but Grif, using his master negotiator tone, said, "Do you want this fire put out?"

"Hell, yes."

"Are you willing to wait for the firefighters to get out here?"

"Hell, no."

Yeah, Jonah hadn't expected anything else from his older brother. After all, Reid was all about anything that would get his adrenaline pumping. So Jonah gave his brothers a big ol' grin and said, "Then let's get in there and fight this bitch."

Britt Steele's protective instincts flared to life. The past five minutes had set off shrieking warning bells in his head. The hightailing vehicle, the burning building bankrupting the town, the broken front window, and now his brothers were about to enter the fray with no personal protective equipment and no way of knowing what other surprises lay inside.

"The sprinkler system's failed," Britt said.

Reid's head swung back and forth like a curious owl's as he studied the three-by-three gaping hole with Etch-a-Sketch lines of cracked glass zigzagging out in all directions. "So has the alarm system."

"If we bust out the rest of that window, we can hop through and hit the flames with fire extinguishers." Grif jabbed a thumb over his shoulder. "There're leftover cinder blocks in that pile of construction debris. One of those should do the trick since it was probably what the first guy used."

Glass shattered, and Britt whipped around to see the three-by-three hole was now large enough for his little brother Jonah to crawl through.

"Guess you were right about the cinder blocks," Britt said.

Reid grinned. "I didn't know the Baby Billionaire had it in him."

"Then you haven't been paying attention," Britt said. "Half the stuff you get in trouble for with Mom is the billionaire's handiwork."

"Are you shittin' me, Tarzan?"

Britt hated the nickname. Not that he'd admit the fact to his dipshit brother.

"Let's get in there before I forget there's a fire and kick your ass."

"The electricity is out," Jonah said.

"Probably a tripped breaker," Britt said. "Reid, Grif—fire extinguishers?"

The two of them looked around, scanning the walls and the hallway just beyond the reception area. Then Grif started running. "Found one."

"Jonah," Britt said, "let's find the electrical panel. If the extinguishers don't work, we need the sprinkler system operational."

"Basement?"

"Most likely. I got a chance to see the plans for this place during the conceptual phase. Let's hope it hasn't changed much."

Like an explorer following a treasure map, Britt used the design layout still embedded in his mind to navigate the hallways. He had a knack for remembering the smallest detail and hoped his gift didn't let him down now, when he needed it most.

He paused at the door adjacent to the staff restrooms, felt the door for heat just in case, and found it room temperature. He ripped it open and a well of darkness yawned before them. Without a word, he and Jonah took out their cell phones and clicked on the flashlights.

"Who do you think set the fire?" Jonah asked.

"Probably bored drunk teenagers."

"I never committed arson as a teenager."

"That's because you were a vampire. You actually would've had to leave your room—and computer—to commit a crime."

"Not necessarily. Tons of havoc can be wreaked

with the touch of a keyboard." Jonah's hazel eyes danced.

A familiar weight wrapped around Britt's chest and squeezed. "Don't we know it."

"Sorry, Britt. It was a stupid thing to say."

"My fault, not yours." He released a hollow chuckle. "Now you know why I spend my time working alone or walking the woods."

Britt made his way to the electrical panel and found the breaker labeled Reception Area. The switch was set to ON. He looked at all the switches. None of them had tripped to neutral.

"It's not the breaker. The electricity is off."

"Thanks for pointing out the obvious, genius."

"No, I mean the electricity is *off*. As in no power running into the building. It's turned off, completely."

"Who would turn off the building's juice?"

"Would have to be the city. Only the property owner can shut it down."

"Maybe the city didn't pay their electric bill."

"There's that, too."

"Come on. Let's go make sure Reid's using an extinguisher rather than an accelerant."

While Britt and the Baby Billionaire searched for how the hell to get the sprinklers working, Reid stood in the vacant lobby, eyes scanning the giant circular reception desk. Beside him, Grif let out a low whistle at the growing flames quickly engulfing the desk and carpeting. And, hell, good thing the place was empty or this fire would be a whole lot nastier. The lack of furniture helped.

Aside from the now toasted desk.

And the fire extinguisher mounted behind it.

He hustled to the wall, his right knee groaning from the damned brace hidden under his jeans. "Hey, Louis

Vuitton, you gonna hold that fire extinguisher or use it?"

Ignoring the dig about his clothes, Grif got to work reading the instructions on the fire extinguisher—*God help us all*—as Reid snagged the one from the wall, pulled the pin, and—*whoosh*—unleashed that baby. A cloud of fine yellow powder shot free as he doused the whipping flames.

Hot damn.

And yeah, if this was the only action Reid had to look forward to after a knee injury blew his Green Beret career out of the universe, well, he had big problems.

Twenty feet to Reid's right, Grif hit the lever on his extinguisher and more yellow powder flew. His brother's face lit up and Reid grinned, knowing all too well the adrenaline rush, the battle high, had fired his older brother's system.

"Don't shoot me with that crap. Do you even know what you're doing?"

At that, Grif laughed. "I read the instructions. It's not that complicated, you flaming asshole. Pun intended."

Side by side, they stayed with it, knocking down the fire while Reid worked on the desk and Grif concentrated on the flames crawling across the carpet. They needed to get this shit under control.

Fast.

Britt and Jonah, fire extinguishers in hand, appeared at the end of the hallway.

"Good idea," Reid said. "Work it from that end. If we don't get that carpet out, the whole place'll go up."

Britt and Jonah unleashed the mother of all fire extinguisher sprays and Reid let out a whoop. Frickin' wicked. Something about it, the partnership, the working together, reminded him that spending time with his brothers, no matter the reason, wasn't a bad thing.

The flames died down, slowly relenting as more of the fine powder pounded them. Still spraying, Reid took a second to check the window behind him, the one with the hole in it. A cinder block sat on the floor and, if Reid guessed right, some kind of fire-inducing element—a Molotov cocktail, maybe—had been launched through the broken window.

Britt, Jonah, and Grif released the handles on their fire extinguishers, and everything grew eerily quiet.

"Son of a bitch," Grif said.

"What happened?"

"My shoes." He stared down at his feet. "Fucking mess."

Good old Grif. His hoity-toity sports agent brother had spent way too much time out in California with all those models and slick athletes.

"Dumbass," Reid said, slapping him on the back. "You've gone soft on me. I should tie your ass to the bumper of my truck and drag you around some. Scrape all that pretty off you."

Grif eyed him, his gaze shooting over the jeans and T-shirt and black biker boots he'd taken to wearing whenever he wasn't in uniform. Which was now permanent. *Goddammit.*

"Hey," Grif said. "We're on our way to our mother's birthday party. It wouldn't kill you to put some effort into your clothing choices."

"Pfft. Mama doesn't need me in church clothes to know I love her." He smiled at his brother. "She knows."

"Plus, now we stink. I hope you're happy."

Happy? That was debatable. But Reid didn't put too much stock into that word. What the hell did that even mean? Are you happy? When? Right now? Putting out this fire, doing some good, yeah, that made him happy. Washing out of the Army, sitting around their hometown trying to figure out what the hell he'd do with his life?

Not so much.

Sirens wailed and two fire trucks and an ambulance screamed up the long drive of the property. Maggie—Mags—his cousin on his mom's side and the sheriff of Canyon Ridge, trailed behind, her cruiser kicking up dust as she hauled ass.

"Well, they're a little late," Grif cracked.

"Yeah, but they'll have to hose this shit down. Douse any hot spots."

Jonah and Britt disappeared. Most likely they'd gone out the emergency exit at the other end of the hallway. Grif and Reid backed up, made room for the firefighters, then slipped out the door behind them. Maggie hopped out of her cruiser, slammed the door and—*ooohhh-eeee*—when his cousin got mad, look out.

"She's pissed," Grif said.

Really? Hadn't noticed. "Yep."

Mags rounded the front of her cruiser, her uniform pants and shirt sporting more than a few wrinkles. Being the sheriff meant working Saturdays. And any other damned day if required.

She faced them down, eyeballing each of them. "What the hell happened?"

"No idea," Grif said. "We were on our way to Mom's party and saw the smoke. Stopped to check it out. The desk and part of the carpet were burning when we pulled up."

Mags glanced at the building, the broken window, and the firefighters now hosing the place down.

"Window's broken," Reid said.

"I see that. Did you see anything on the floor? An accelerant of some kind?"

They both shook their heads. "But," Reid said, "I was focused on the fire. And Grif's clothes getting trashed."

"Oh, fuck you," Grif said.

Mags rolled her eyes. "Don't start. Did you see anything else?"

"Shit," Reid said.

"What?"

He turned to Grif. "Remember the vehicle tearing out of the drive?"

Mags cocked her head. "What vehicle? Did you recognize it?"

Reid thought back, pictured it in his mind. Too much

dust to recognize the make and model. Based on the height, probably a car or one of those midget SUVs. "Could've been a car, or maybe a small SUV."

His cousin stared up at the building, shook her head. "I hate this place. Nothing but a pain in the butt since they broke ground. Now we're wasting emergency resources on it. Damned thing is slowly sinking us."

CHAPTER TWO

FORTY-FIVE MINUTES LATER, GRIF climbed back in the truck, sharing the backseat with Britt. Dammit, his favorite Gravati loafers now looked as if they'd come off a thrift store rack. Between that and the way Reid had taken over—as usual—during the fire reminded Grif why he'd gotten the hell out of his hometown years ago. Crazy that it had been so easy for him to become a high-impact player in a place the size of LA when he'd been overshadowed by either Reid or Britt every day of his life in Canyon Ridge.

"You look like you're in mourning," Britt commented. "They're just shoes."

"Italian leather."

"You ask me," Reid said, "Italian sausage is a better deal."

"Pretty sure that's why you're known as meathead."

One side of Britt's mouth quirked up, about as much of a grin as he ever wore. "But that streak on your shirt? Now, that's something you should probably cry about."

Grif twisted, trying to see his own back while his brothers snorted like a bunch of wild hogs. "Dammit, I must have bumped something. And, hey, in my line of work, looks and clothes matter. I can't walk into a hundred-million-dollar contract negotiation wearing board shorts and a Billabong shirt." Reality was, he was damn lucky to be doing any negotiations after Madison Henry, heiress to the Henry hotel fortune, had fucked him over a few months ago.

Reid shot a sly look Jonah's way. "I think he's so pretty because Mom really wanted her second kid to be a girl. We should probably just be happy he rarely wears lipstick."

Grif couldn't even bring himself to raise a halfhearted fuck-off finger at the back of Reid's head.

When they pulled up at Barron's Park, the place was already covered up with people, and they were running close to an hour late. "If Mom's already cut the birthday cake, you know it's all gone."

"Dammit, we deserve that cake," Reid grumbled.

"Carrot's my favorite," Jonah said like a six year old denied candy.

"You're a first-class pouter, you know that?"

"That's what happens when you have the kinda money he does," Reid said. "You get used to having everything you want."

"And I damn well want carrot cake."

They got out of the truck, each with a different offering in hand. Wild-looking flowers of every color from Britt. Handmade chocolate truffles from Reid. A fancy e-reader loaded with e-books from Jonah. And Grif held a silver box with a silk Natori nightgown and robe inside. The crowd parted and Grif watched their mom, one of the most beloved people in Canyon Ridge, stroll toward them in a seemingly casual manner with their sister Evie at her side.

"Oh, fuck," Reid muttered.

Yeah, Mom wasn't happy. That strained smile on her face was the one they'd all seen a thousand times. When they broke curfew, when they brought home subpar grades, when she found Betsy Cochran hiding in Grif's closet after a particularly educational game of Truth or Dare. When Grif Skyped with her right after ESPN broke the news about Madison's accusations.

"My darling boys," she said. "Did you get lost between my house and the park? Or did you simply forget this was my birthday party?"

Grif half turned toward Reid, who'd always been fast with a get-out-of-jail-free line, but before he could make eye contact, his mom grabbed the back of his shirt. "Griffin Fletcher Steele, what have you been into? You have a black streak all the way down your back."

Grif shot Britt a death stare and got an eyebrow waggle in return. So he hadn't just been yanking his chain.

Then she turned her face up and sniffed. "And why do you all smell like you've been roasting hotdogs?"

"Might as well come clean," Britt said. "It's not like she won't hear."

"What in the world have you four been up to this time?"

Evie tossed her dark hair over one shoulder and raised her chin. "And why wasn't I invited?"

Jonah looped an arm around her neck and ran his knuckles over her hair. She tried to bat him away, but he just danced her in a very awkward circle. "Because you're the baby."

When she was able to squirm away from him, she jammed her hands on her hips, which only showcased that their baby sister was stacked. A fact Grif damn well didn't want to acknowledge.

They were all still having trouble accepting that she was out of grade school, when she was twenty years old and a junior in college. If her older brothers had it their way, she'd never grow up. And definitely never have sex.

Britt stepped forward. "There was a fire out at the sportsman's complex."

"And you decided to all become firefighters?"

"We were driving by," Reid said, "and happened to see smoke."

"You wouldn't have wanted us to ignore it and have

the place burn down, would you?" Grif asked his mom, giving her his best charming smile.

"Of course not."

"But they have come up with this amazing new service," Evie drawled. "You just use your cell phone—you know what that is, right?—to punch in three numbers." She tapped her chin with her index finger. "I think they're nine, one, and one."

Reid, ever the hero, puffed out his chest. "We actually put it out before Mags and the rest of the emergency services crew arrived."

Their mom sighed, the sigh of a woman who'd given birth to six kids who'd nearly driven her batshit. She waved them toward the pavilion. "Why am I not surprised?"

Rescuing Evie from Jonah the evil tormentor, Grif put his arm around her and strolled in the direction of the covered area packed with people, presents, and enough helium balloons to give James Earl Jones a squeaky voice for eternity. "How's it going, kid?"

"School, you mean?"

"What else would I be talking about?"

"Maybe my love life?"

Grif winced. "Lower your voice. If Britt gets wind of the fact that you're an adult, you'll never hear the end of it."

"God, don't I know it."

As people shifted, Grif caught a glimpse of golden red hair. Long and lush.

Interest flared low in his belly.

He knew that hair. Knew it? Hell, he'd had his hands tangled in it years ago.

While he slid inside the woman. Even fifteen years later, the memory of the night he'd spent with Carlie Beth Parrish made his blood hum. Sure, it wasn't as if he thought of her often, but when he did?

Well, it was a damn good memory.

His old Ford Taurus, a couple of cheap beers, and a

prime parking spot at Deadman's Creek. He smiled, remembering what he'd done to her on his hood.

"What are you grinning about?" Evie asked him.

Oh, he might recognize his baby sister was, in fact, of age, but he wasn't about to share those details with her. "Just feeling a little nostalgic about home."

"You missing Canyon Ridge?" She went on tiptoes and laid her hand across his forehead. "Do you have a fever?"

"I'm allowed to have good memories of this place." And he did. But it just didn't fit him anymore, even if he longed for the comfort of it from time to time. It was like shrugging on an off-the-rack jacket after years of wearing custom suits. That didn't mean he didn't want to say hello to Carlie Beth.

Hell, this was the South. They wouldn't do the shake-hands-and-air-kiss-on-the-cheek thing. Here, people hugged. Good ol' breasts-to-chest kinds of hugs. And having his chest against Carlie Beth's breasts would not hurt his feelings one damn bit. "Hey," he said to Evie, "I think I see an old friend. Mind if I…"

"Be my guest."

He walked away from his sister, his stride a little faster than he'd feel comfortable ever admitting, and homed in on that beautiful hair. That spun gold had clung to their sweaty naked bodies when he'd laid her back on his car and made her scream. More than once.

Grif shoved away that little tidbit. Sporting a boner at his mom's birthday bash wasn't exactly good party etiquette.

When he was within a few feet of her, he called out, "Carlie Beth, it's great to see you."

She whirled around, her pretty brown eyes like those of a deer that couldn't get off the center line fast enough to avoid the semi bearing down. Her mouth also formed a little O. And that sure as hell didn't make him think of any type of wildlife. It made him think of—

And just that quick, she gave him a little I-don't-think-I-know-you wave, turned around, and fled. God, this must be Grif's year of shitty luck with women.

Micki stood next to her father, Eddy Steele, under the heavy shade of a hundred-year-old oak at the edge of the park. He was holding his portable police scanner, listening to some nonsense about a fire at the old Tupelo Farm.

Had to love Canyon Ridge, where a small fire drew all kinds of speculation.

Every town should have this level of problems.

In Vegas—land of sin and debauchery—a tiny fire would be a dream come true for first responders.

Her brothers, Dad's pride and joys even if he hated to admit it, stood around, messing with each other like they'd been doing since they were kids. Britt laughed and shoved Reid back a step while Grif looked down at the front of a white shirt that had probably cost him a thousand dollars. He picked something off of it and stared down at whatever piece of lint dared to litter his clothing. He always did have a hankering for the finer things.

She glanced at her long-sleeved T-shirt. A black one with a skull and crossbones splashed across the front. Combined with her black jeans and boots, she wasn't exactly the belle of the ball her mama always wanted. On the contrary, she'd been the disappointment, and watching the boys make their way into the party, Micki felt…lost.

Alone.

Because she no longer had the kinship her brothers did. That sibling affection that meant cutting up on each other and hurling insults they all knew were only meant in jest.

Except when they weren't and someone got bloody. Still, they loved each other.

Unconditionally.

Just then, Jonah stopped walking, his instincts clearly alerting him to something. He glanced left, away from her, and she made a move to duck behind the tree, but...too late. Her twin swung back, his gaze, even from the distance, connecting with hers.

Jonah.

She'd missed him. Fiercely. And seeing him now, joking around with the other boys, the fissure inside her grew. Just a slow, torturous expansion that left a giant crevice inside her.

He took a step toward her. No. She couldn't face him. Not yet anyway.

She shook her head and inched closer to the tree and Jonah hesitated.

Please, don't come over here.

Dad held up the police scanner. "Fire's out."

"That's good," she said, distracted by Jonah's stare.

"Yeah. We'll get the update from the boys. I heard Maggie say they put it out."

"Who?"

"The boys."

Figures.

The can-do-no-wrong boys.

One of whom stood staring at her. Three long seconds passed before Grif grabbed hold of him and pulled him away. That fissure in her chest turned into the Grand Canyon.

Micki tapped one booted foot. Tucked her hair behind her ears and licked her lips. No lipstick, only lip balm. Her mother would have an effing fit. A good Southern girl always had lipstick.

But Micki hadn't been a good Southern girl for going on ten years now.

Sorry, Mom.

Dad gestured to his carousing boys with the handheld

radio. "I'm gonna head over there. See what happened. You coming?"

Again, Micki glanced down at her black jeans, her tank top, her unpainted and chewed fingernails. *I so don't belong here.*

Vegas. That's where she should be. Where she fit. In Vegas, no one judged her. In Vegas, she was a rock star, a master in front of her beloved laptop. Tomorrow, she'd head back home. To Vegas. Not here. She'd simply come today to celebrate her mother, a woman she barely knew anymore.

Still, Mom had requested it and for all the mistakes Micki had made, all the stupid decisions that had caused her family hardship, this one seemed like a fairly simple—and grantable—request.

Even if she did stay hidden beneath a giant leafy oak tree.

"You know…" Britt said.

Oh, crap. Reid hated when Britt said "you know." "You know" was always followed by some kind of do-good lecture that would half turn him to stone.

Britt style.

And coming off their father peppering them with questions about the fire, Reid wasn't in the mood for a lecture. Thankfully, Dad had gotten distracted by one of the locals asking about the pros and cons of a rifle he'd been looking at.

"Huddle up, boys," Grif said, joining the group. "Big brother has something on his mind."

Britt waved a hand. "Everyone who is anyone in our town is at this party."

"So?"

This from Jonah, who probably didn't get his requisite twelve hours of sleep last night.

"*So,*" Britt said. "We should walk around, listen. See if the gossips know anything about that fire. Maybe someone heard something."

"Great," Grif said. "Now we're investigators?"

"I didn't say we're investigators."

But, hey, Britt had a point. With all the folks here, it couldn't hurt to ask around. Maybe dig up some dirt. Something Reid had always enjoyed.

"He's right." Reid waved two fingers. "Forget listening. Fan out. *Talk* to people. Keep it casual. Just shoot the shit."

His brothers, after some grumbling that Britt stifled with a single raised brow, moved off and headed into the crowd.

Scanning the packed picnic area, Reid broke it into quadrants. He'd start at quadrant two. See how far that got him.

I got this.

He sucked at a lot of things. He didn't have a problem admitting it. Mainly because for every one thing he sucked at, there were two more he excelled at.

And the thing he could ace the shit out of, hands down, was talking.

His entire life his mama had been trying to get him to shut up. He might not have been slick à-la-Grif, but he had other ways of getting information. And it usually worked.

He tromped across the park toward Mr. Greene, a man who'd been ancient fifteen years ago when Reid was a freshman in high school and got caught trying to slip his hand under Mr. Greene's granddaughter's shirt.

Lucky for Reid, he'd seen the old man coming and snatched his hand back before he'd lost the sucker in the absurd amount of cleavage between Christy's extremely ample tits.

Jesus, that rack. He still dreamed about it.

Reid cleared his throat, rid his mind of tits, and marched the last fifteen feet to Mr. Greene.

The old man swapped his cane to his other hand, leaned in heavily, and held his right hand out. "Reid, how're you, son? Heard you were back home."

Thanks for the reminder. "Yes, sir." He shook the man's hand and pointed to his knee. "Blew out my knee so I didn't re-up."

Not altogether a lie. Yes, it had been time for him to reenlist and yes, he had blown out his knee. What he hadn't said was that the bum knee had earned him a spot at the spectators' table. The big, bad Green Beret, after years of training and gut-shredding missions that would send a weaker man to a fetal position, couldn't pass the fucking physical fitness test that qualified him for service. At least not the kind of service he wanted to provide. A desk job, for a guy like him, a boots-on-the-ground guy, would shred him.

And now he had to figure out what the hell to do with his life.

Mr. Greene lifted his cane, pointed it at Jonah, wobbling enough that Reid itched to hold on to him, but didn't dare. Sometimes a man would rather fall over than receive help standing.

At least that's how Reid saw it.

"I heard you fellas saw the fire over at that eyesore sports complex."

"Yes, sir. We were driving by. News travels fast around here."

The man snorted. "Not much has changed."

Wasn't that the truth?

"Yeah, we saw a car hauling ass outta there."

"You see the driver?"

"Nah. But I'm wondering if whoever was driving set that fire." He looked down at the old man with his gnarly, arthritis-ridden fingers. "It wasn't you breaking speed records outta there, was it?"

The man howled and it kicked off a harsh coughing fit that had him smacking his chest and clearing the phlegm.

"Boy, even if I could still drive, I wouldn't be stupid enough to try that. I'll tell you what though, I don't blame the idiot who did. That goddamn thing cost us taxpayers. I almost had to move out of this town because of the tax hike. And now it don't even bring us any tourism. Yeah, half this town is mad enough to set that fire."

A brunette sauntered by, wearing snug jeans over her curvy hips, a clingy turtleneck and high-heeled boots that sank into the grass, forcing her to work her feet free as she walked. Who the hell wore those heels to a party in a park?

He didn't know her, but—holy titties, Batman—she made Mr. Greene's granddaughter's rack look like amateur hour. And the ass? He wanted to bite it. Yep, just sink his teeth right into that juicy bottom.

"Well," Mr. Greene said, "would you look at them titties?"

Reid swallowed hard, fought a wave of nausea as he glimpsed his future in Mr. Greene. If he didn't figure out something to do with his life, that'd be him. Old, decrepit, horny, and blurting out inappropriate comments about tits.

One of his brothers would have to save him from the nightmare. Where was Jonah? He'd be the one who'd actually enjoy putting a bullet in Reid's head.

Horny old bastard or not, Mr. Greene had a point. "No kidding," Reid said. "Who is she?"

"That's Brynne Whitfield." He paused, pursed his lips. "Whitfield? Yeah, I think that's it." The man shook his head. "Hell, I don't know. She owns that fancy shop in town. The one next to the Triple B."

Brynne. Nice name. Nice everything.

Reid cocked his head, watched her move across the grass to a picnic table filled with Canyon Ridge residents all coming out to wish his mama a happy birthday on an unseasonably warm January day.

Brynne Whitfield.

Wasn't she something?

His coming home just got a whole lot nicer. Even if he'd struck out with Mr. Greene on any possible suspects.

Britt scanned the partygoers, for what, he didn't know. This wasn't the first time he'd gone along with one of Reid's crazy ideas. Well, it was actually his own crazy idea, sort of, but he hadn't expected they'd be questioning people. He figured they'd walk around and eavesdrop on some conversations. Then Reid decided they should play Columbo.

If nothing else, this would force him to mingle, not one of his favorite activities. He sucked at small talk. Never knew what questions were okay to ask and which ones would be considered nosey. So he avoided chitchat as much as possible.

Even though he'd lived here his entire life, Britt kept his social circle small, intimate, limited to those he trusted. It wasn't that he disliked people. He simply didn't have the time to build meaningful relationships.

But for his mom, he'd do anything, even chitchat. Besides, she would expect him to make their guests feel welcome and comfortable. Two birds with one stone, and all that. He never understood that old saying. Who the hell coldcocked birds with a stone?

His gaze landed on Barbara Shepherd, and the tension bear hugging his chest loosed its grip. He couldn't think of a better place to start than checking in with his mentor. For the past couple of years, Barbara had been teaching him things about wildlife management that no classroom could replicate. Especially online classes, the only college coursework he could manage after his dad became a hermit, spending more and more time at the family cabin, and leaving him to father his brothers and sisters and take care of his mom.

Having worked for International Wildlife Conservation for over twenty years, Barbara knew more than most of the biologists in the North Carolina Wildlife Resources Commission and U.S. Fish and Wildlife Service combined.

"Are you enjoying yourself?" he asked her.

She sent him a warm smile. "I'd much rather be hanging over the bluff's edge, observing our pack."

Late last fall, during a floral survey of Barbara's property, they'd come across a canid track. The paw print appeared larger than a coyote's or medium-sized dog's. Curious, they followed the canid's trail along a creek bed until they heard a series of excited yipping. They'd almost turned back, believing they'd found an unusually large coyote. But something kept them moving forward.

Thank God they had. A once-in-a-lifetime sight met them at the end of the trail.

Wolves.

Not just any wolves. Endangered red wolves.

No one had seen a wild red wolf in this part of North Carolina since the late nineties.

The find was almost too good to be true. He and Barbara had made a pact that day. To keep the pack's location a secret until they could confirm they were full-blooded red wolves and not a wolf-coyote hybrid. They'd been studying the pack ever since.

"I thought I might head out there tomorrow." Out of the corner of his eye, Britt caught sight of a familiar face, though he couldn't come up with a name. A shame, because he would've made that beautiful, long-haired blonde in the show-your-assets jeans and blue form-fitting sweater his next stop.

"Would love to join you," Barbara said, bringing his attention back around, "but I'm off to San Diego in the morning."

"Give me a holler when you return. The wolves should be mating soon."

"Is that smoke I smell?"

Britt sniffed his shoulder. "Yeah, someone set fire to the money pit."

"You helped put it out?"

"My brothers and I saw the smoke on the way here and stopped to give a hand."

"Kids tagging the building first and now someone's setting it on fire. Any idea what caused it?"

"Molotov cocktail and boys with nothing better to do would be my guess. Though I know this town is pretty upset about the steep taxes, so it could be anyone."

"It wouldn't make much sense to burn it down. The city needs the revenue, and the taxpayers need the city to turn a profit."

"Any thoughts on who might have lit it up?"

"Desperate people aren't the wisest. Even though burning the complex to the ground might not be in the town's best interest, there are those who'll act before thinking." Her gaze swept over the crowd. "If I had to guess, I'd say Johnny Gillis. As I recall, he had an affinity for setting fires as a child. He's turned into a rather unpleasant man. Always spouting nonsense about Big Brother and his rights being violated."

"Anyone else?"

"No one comes to mind."

Something over Britt's shoulder caught Barbara's attention. Her spine snapped to attention like a bowstring springing back to the home position. She smoothed her hands down the front of her cardigan and dampened her lips as if her mouth had gone dry. Britt angled his head around to see what had put his mentor on the defensive and saw the gorgeous blonde.

Their gazes caught, and Britt's chest constricted against an overwhelming pull. He stared and kept staring. If he'd been at a bar, he would have approached her, bought her a drink, attempted a kiss. At least, he thought he would have if his legs had cooperated. Britt had never been gobsmacked before. He disliked the loss of control, yet he didn't want the moment to end.

She broke eye contact first. "Hello, Mom."

Mom? Shit.

"Miranda, have you met Britt Steele?"

"Not officially." She held out her hand. "Call me Randi."

Britt's large, work-worn palm engulfed her small hand. In moments like this, Britt wished he had the uncalloused touch of his gamer brother rather than his rough, impossible-to-get-the-dirt-from-beneath-his-fingernails construction grip. But Randi didn't flinch away. She gave him two firm shakes before withdrawing.

"My daughter owns Blues, Brews, and Books on Main Street. The shop's been there a little over a year. Have you been?"

"Haven't had the chance." Or the inclination.

Blues, Brews, and Books had never appealed to him before. He preferred run-down, whisky-serving watering holes where a man could put his boots up on the table without getting yelled at. But now he'd have to reconsider her place.

Britt tried to judge Randi's age, always dangerous. He guessed her at thirty-ish. Could someone so young run such a complicated business? From what he'd heard, Triple B was a coffee shop, bar, and restaurant, operating at all hours of the day and night.

Then again, his brother Jonah had started and sold a video game business that had made him a freaking billionaire before he'd reach twenty-seven.

"I can't stay to chat," Randi said, not meeting her mom's eyes. "Gotta get back to the bar."

Before either he or Barbara could say a word, she was off.

The odd pressure around his chest eased once she disappeared from his sight. Britt's body felt roughed up, as if he'd taken the beating of a lifetime and barely survived.

"She's single."

Frowning, Britt said, "Pardon?"

"You'll never find a more hardworking and loyal woman."

"Are you trying to set me up with your daughter?"

"I couldn't think of a better match for her." Barbara's smile faded. "I…haven't been the best mother. She needs someone solid in her life."

He found her statement hard to believe. The Barbara he knew was generous with her time and would praise the smallest success. She had a wicked sense of humor and a kind heart—second only to his mother's. But, obviously, something had gone wrong with her relationship with her daughter. Something they kept between the two of them.

Britt excused himself from Barbara's company and trudged his way around to a few more townsfolk before joining his brothers again.

"Any suspects?" he asked.

"Every damn person we spoke to," Reid grumbled.

"Same here." Except for one stunning blonde. Perhaps he'd need to stop by Triple B and question her more. "What do we do now?"

"Keep our ears open," Grif said. "If the arsonist is stupid enough to tell one person, we'll hear something within a few days."

"So much for stirring up a little excitement," Jonah said, digging his phone out of his pocket and sinking into his cyber world.

"If I were you," an aged female voice said behind Britt, "I'd focus on Bobby Ray Benton."

Jeanine Jennings shuffled on by, not bothering to explain herself or even make eye contact. She didn't have to. The eighty-something baker's assistant had an uncanny ability to *know* things. If she thought they should turn their attention to Bobby Ray, that's what they'd do.

"Well, boys, are you up for a little snooping?"

Chapter Three

"WHO THE HELL IS BOBBY Ray Benton?" Grif asked while trailing behind Britt on the way to the parking lot. "And where are we going?"

Britt waved a hand. "Bobby Ray's car is in the lot. It's a black Prius, but this is bad."

"What's bad?" Reid had a scowl on, the one that shouted he was about to go kick some serious ass.

"Bobby Ray is the guy Mayor Hackberry hired as city manager. He spearheaded the entire sportsman's complex project. Was actually the driving force behind it."

"Then why would he—" Reid started.

"Probably insurance money."

"What a fucking bozo," Jonah muttered. "Did he really think the cops wouldn't figure out it was arson? That tends to screw up an insurance payout big time."

Reid's scowl had turned into a sharkish smile. "If he's our guy, he just earned himself an all-expenses-paid trip to a cell."

Grif hustled over to a black Prius and checked the license plate. SWAGRR. Jesus, he saw twenty of these things a day on the freeway, but this was the douchiest yet. "Britt, is this Benton's car?"

"Yeah."

"The windows are cracked," Jonah said. "Weird for January, even on such a nice day."

They surrounded the car, peering in the windows.

"Oh, hello," Reid said. "You boys see those rags on the floor?"

Yeah, they looked just right for building a Molotov cocktail.

Jonah put his nose close to the open window. "Smell that?"

The others followed suit. Grif hoped no one had a camera on the four of them sniffing Bobby Ray's vehicle.

"Definitely an accelerant," Reid said.

"Think he has the empty cans in his trunk?" Jonah asked.

Reid strolled around to the back of the vehicle, his intent obvious. "Don't even think about it," Grif said. "Mom will beat us all bloody if you wind up in jail on her birthday."

Britt, always one to take charge, pushed off the car. "Let's talk to him. See what's what."

All four of them advanced on the guy Britt pointed out by the dessert table. The dude wore slacks and a turtleneck sweater sporting an argyle design. Hell, he should've been arrested for the sweater alone. Once they walked closer, Grif could see the city manager's shoes were dusted with a gray powder. Gravel dust, if he had to guess. *You're going down, SWAGRR.*

Britt held out his hand to the guy. "Bobby Ray, I don't think you've met my brothers."

Poor SWAGRR had to crane his own neck to look up at them. "Great to meet y'all." If there was one thing Grif hated, it was someone who wasn't from the South pretending to be from the South. It always came across as condescending bullshit.

Yeah, he and the pretender were about to get down to business. "So Britt tells me you're the brains behind the sportsman's complex."

The guy's eyes darted here and there as he obviously thought about whether or not to take credit for the complex in its current state.

"Pretty impressive project."

SWAGGR's gaze settled on Grif. "It's state-of-the-art."

Huh. *Was* state-of-the-art. "Damn shame it's sitting empty."

"With the electricity shut off," Britt added.

"Uh…" Yeah, those shifty eyes started moving again, never landing long on one brother or the other. "Well, that place in Asheville really knocked our feet out from under us and—"

"As city manager," Grif said, "wasn't it your job to perform due diligence?"

"Yeah," Jonah said. "Must've been a real blow when it all fell apart. Kinda surprising you still have a job."

"I…well—"

"Let's cut to the damn chase here," Reid said. "Where were you before this party?"

"I was at my house. Alone."

Jonah made an obnoxious game buzzer sound. *Naaaaaah.* "What kind of car do you drive?"

Turtleneck's face scrunched. "A Prius."

Reid just rolled his eyes.

Grif smiled. "Can you tell me what those taillights look like?"

"Why?"

Grif cocked his head. "Because I asked you so nicely."

"Uh, kinda up and down. You know vertical."

"With a sort of curve to them?"

"I guess."

"Yeah," Jonah said with a definitive nod. "He's our dude."

"Who's your dude?" Maggie elbowed her way inside the circle they had the city manager trapped inside.

"Take a look at ol' Bobby Ray's vehicle. Betcha you'll find a gas can in his trunk to go with the shop rags in his back floorboard."

Bobby Ray gawked, his face turning three shades

whiter. "Wha...what? Every person in this town has gas cans."

Maggie cut him a sharp look and then let her gaze touch on each person in the group with the last name Steele. There was no mistaking her message. *Stay the hell out of my playground, you sand kickers.* Then she said, "Bobby Ray, did you try to burn down the sports complex?"

"I...no...I..."

"Don't lie to me," she said. "I found glass shards behind that desk and the neck of the bottle. I can get prints off the bigger pieces. So, if you threw that thing, you'd better fess up now."

His gaze darted over each of them and his throat bobbed with panic. Oh, yeah. He was caving. *Come on, buddy. Give it up.*

Boom. His shoulders slumped and his head went down. "I thought it would be for the best."

"To commit arson." Maggie's laugh was sharp and disbelieving. "Yeah, that's often the case." Grif could hear her unspoken words. *You dipshit.*

"You boys," she pointed a finger—one, two, three, four—at each of them in turn. "Go wish your mom a happy birthday and I'll take care of our friend here." Then she discreetly put the cuffs on the city manager and walked him toward the outside of the pavilion as if they were simply having a friendly chat.

That's when Grif noticed a dark line snaking its way down the inside of the city manager's pant leg. "I'll be damned. Take a look at that."

Reid's grin went wide. "I thought I smelled piss."

"Maggie should swear us in." Jonah shoved his hands into his front pockets. "We tracked down an arsonist and it's not even dinnertime yet."

"We had a bit of help from Jeanine," Grif said.

"Maybe she should be deputized, too."

"The old bat freaks me out," Reid said. "Have you read the chalkboard signs outside the bakery? I swear they're prophetic."

"Don't be so damned paranoid," Britt said. "She's the town's biggest gossip. That's all."

"No way, Tarzan. She knows things that have never made it to the gossip mill."

Britt shook his head.

Jonah stared at Reid. The dude wore a look as if the Grim Reaper had whispered in his ear.

"Let's hope the town can find a buyer for the sports complex," Grif said. "I can't imagine what'll happen to the property taxes next year if the town continues to lose money on the place."

"People have already been packing up and leaving," Britt said. "It's only going to get worse."

"Canyon Ridge will be a ghost town in five years," Reid said.

Jonah listened to his brothers' conversation while his gaze traveled around the gathering. Although he'd been away for several years, making his mark on Seattle's gaming world, Canyon Ridge would always be his true home. Despite Britt's reference to him being a vampire, he'd made memories—good and bad—all over this town. Made lifelong friends who still treated him like the Goth he used to be and not the billionaire he was now.

He studied his brothers. All thriving in their own way, yet miserable beyond measure.

Canyon Ridge, its residents, and the Steele clan had all helped mold Jonah into a freakishly wealthy guy. A guy who could fix a broken town and help a lot of people. A guy who could make a difference and not even feel the impact. A guy who could begin the process of healing his family's deep wounds. Wounds he'd helped create.

"All we can do is make sure our family and close

friends ride out the worst of it," Britt said, his voice grim.

"Let's start by making Mom's sixtieth the best party ever," Grif said.

"Amen to that, bro," Reid said.

His brothers started to disperse.

Decision made, Jonah raised a staying hand. His gaze caught each of his brothers' before dropping the bomb that would change all of their lives forever. "I've got an idea, but not a damn one of you are gonna like it."

KELSEY
BROWNING

To my readers who enjoy a good small-town story.
I hope you'll find Steele Ridge has it all—
quirky characters, a great setting, and a little deception…
along with a handful of hot heroes and the sassy women
they come to love.

CHAPTER ONE

IF HIS PHONE BUZZED INSIDE his suit pocket one more time today, Grif would be happy to lob it into the Pacific and watch it float toward Hawaii.

"That damn thing ever stop ringing?" his brother Jonah asked as he unfolded his lean body from the car.

"Every third Sunday between two forty-eight and three oh-two." After years of getting a complete surge of energy each time his smartphone rang, sometimes he now fantasized about grinding it to bits beneath his heel. But then he remembered it was his livelihood. Remembered it was a symbol of all he'd accomplished.

Remembered it was his pathetic security blanket. Even if that blanket was ragged at the edges and full of holes after what had happened last fall.

Thankfully the constant calls from reporters had finally stopped, which made resisting the urge to drown his phone a little easier.

Besides, that was impossible today since he was in North Carolina instead of California. Outside his hometown's redbrick city hall, he shut the door of his *blu passione* Maserati, Louise, and gave Jonah a chin lift over the roof. "Gotta get this before we go inside."

"Be my guest."

He hit the accept button. "Steele here."

"Grif, we got problems." By the man's panicked tone

and flat Midwestern accent, the caller was clearly Dean Lindstrom, the Houston Hurricanes star forward.

"Well, that's pretty clear since you never call me when things are all sunshine and daisies." And Grif wasn't known as the Steele Shark throughout the pro sports industry for nothing. "What's up?"

"The team's head trainer is pushing for me to have that ACL surgery, made it mandatory for me to see a surgeon before I can get back on the ice. And I'm afraid the general manager is actually listening to that crap."

Grif doubted it, but he couldn't be away from his clients for two days without some shit hitting the fan. Something he'd had to risk because he'd needed a break from it all so damn bad. He scanned Main Street, backdropped by the Smoky Mountains on one side and part of the Pisgah National Forest on the other, and inhaled a deep breath of western North Carolina air. "Look, I'm about to walk into another meeting, but this deal will take me all of ten minutes to close. After that, I'll talk to the trainer."

"I need this handled today."

"Dean, do I tell you how to out-deke a goalie in a shootout?"

"Are you crazy?"

"Then get off my ice and go do your own job."

"When will I hear—"

"You'll hear back from me when I have something worth saying." Grif hit the end button and pocketed his phone. Took a second to straighten his suit coat and shoot the cuffs of his Carroll & Co. shirt.

"Problems in paradise?" Jonah was lounging against a parking meter in his normal uniform of tennis shoes, jeans, and lewd T-shirt. This particular one boasted a picture of two pigs doing the deed and said *Make bacon, not war.*

"Sometimes being a sports agent is like having a daycare full of two-hundred-fifty-pound toddlers."

"At least you don't have to shove them in high chairs and feed them creamed spinach."

At that image, an internal shudder worked its way through him. "I don't really understand kids."

"Have you forgotten you were one once?"

"Back then I didn't have to feed myself or wipe my own ass."

With a nod toward a young mother toting one kid on her hip and holding another by the hand, Jonah said, "I think kids are kinda cool."

"Well, you hang around Canyon Ridge long enough and maybe you can score yourself a Suzy Homemaker." He glanced around the small downtown area again. Not a lot shaking on a Friday afternoon. Nothing like Los Angeles, where some deal, some hustle, was always going down. One car drove past and an older lady in a faded pink cocktail suit crossed at the light and moseyed into Highland Bank & Trust. "Y'all can get to work on pumping out the next generations of Steeles."

"I'll keep that in mind after the mayor hands over the keys to the city." Jonah headed for the door to City Hall and Grif followed.

Yeah, that was the reason Grif was back on this coast for a few days, to help his baby brother bail out a town that would otherwise sink under the weight of debt and bad decisions. Good thing Jonah had big buckets.

But Grif still thought the whole thing was a sucker's deal.

A half hour later, as he signed the stack of papers in front of him, Mayor Gene Hackberry looked as if he'd recently eaten a mess of chili-cheese fries and desperately needed a handful of Maalox or a big-ass belch. The older man pushed the contract across his desk, and Grif reached for it.

Jonah blocked him with a strategic elbow. "Dude, leave it alone."

"You don't sign anything I haven't read." After all, that was his superpower, negotiating multimillion-dollar contracts and making sure his clients got the best—the very best—end of the deal. Jonah might not be on Grif's roster, but he was family, and no one screwed over one of the Steele brothers.

Grif skewered Jonah with a glare that had made major-league team owners piss themselves, but he just barked out a laugh. "You've read this damn thing so many times you can probably recite it like a nursery rhyme. Get off your tuffet, Miss Muffet, and let's get the fuck on with this."

"You're about to sign away a lot of money."

Jonah turned a grin on him, the sly I've-got-it-all-under-control one that had made him very popular among the ladies in Seattle. "I've got it to burn."

True. Since Grif had helped him with the sale of Steele Trap Entertainment, his mega-successful video gaming company, Jonah could bathe in a different stack of hundreds every day and never run out. "But do you really want to be the owner of a small North Carolina town?"

Not to mention one that was flat-out belly-up.

"No, but I want to save our hometown," he said. "And I count myself lucky to be able to do it."

It was Grif's job to steer guys with too much money and too little sense away from deals like this, and here he was, watching his brother hand over bags of cash. But Jonah was obviously bored, and a bored Jonah was a dangerous Jonah.

Frustrated with the whole thing, Grif shoved at his hair and leaned back in one of the mayor's fake leather visitor chairs.

With his scratching scrawl, Jonah plowed through the pages in front of him, signing one after the other. When he finished, the mayor looked even more dyspeptic, but Jonah was grinning so wide Grif would swear on a stack of Mount Shiloh Baptist Church hymnals that he could see his brother's wisdom teeth.

"We never should've built that damn sports complex." The mayor pushed himself to his feet and held out a hand to Jonah. "Not sure what we would've done if you hadn't approached the city council about helping out Canyon Ridge—"

"Not Canyon anymore." Jonah stood as well, but he didn't return the man's gesture. "The contract says the town will be renamed. Steele Ridge."

"Son, that name change is gonna take a little getting used to, so why don't we just ease everyone into—"

"Sir, I'm not your son." Jonah's smile never wavered, but it took on an edge as he picked up his set of the contract papers and slid them into an envelope. "So why don't you get the post office on that change right away? No use in dragging it out."

"I see." The mayor shifted his focus to Grif and tried the handshake thing again. Least Grif could do was follow through when his brother hadn't. "Grif, it'll be great to have you on board."

On board? What did that mean? But Grif never let the other side see gaps in his prep work, so he just said, "Thank you."

Jonah caught Grif by the suit coat sleeve and yanked. "Great doing business with you, but we have another meeting to get to."

Oh, once they made it outside, little brother was gonna pay for that stunt. He damn well knew not to fuck with Grif's wardrobe. Grif removed Jonah's fingers from the fabric, smoothed his sleeve, and calmly walked out of the mayor's office. But once they were through the lobby and outside on the steps, Grif rounded on Jonah. "Steele Ridge? We never talked about renaming the damn town."

One of Jonah's shoulders did a casual up and down. "I figure if I'm throwing down several million dollars, we should get something out of it."

A nerve behind Grif's right eyeball pulsed. "Jesus, you're getting plenty out of it." Plenty of pain in the ass as far as he was concerned. "You basically own a town of eight thousand people, twenty thousand acres of western Carolina land, and a belly-up sports complex."

Yeah, that complex was what had done in the town.

They'd gambled big on attracting folks to Canyon—hell, Steele—Ridge and lost when another facility had been built forty miles east in Asheville. Who was going to mosey out to Podunk when they could get their rock climbing and Zumba-ing on inside the city?

No. One.

Jonah wandered over to a nearby parking spot, checked out the sign in front of a boring midsized sedan. "This should do, don't you think?"

"If you're looking to buy a new car, you can do better than that."

"Nah, man. I asked for a parking spot for Mom. Figured this one's right in the middle of everything. Perfect."

So this was the reason Jonah hadn't been hot for Grif to read through the contract again. He'd slid in a few bullshit stipulations. Fine. If getting his way, having a little control, made him feel better, then Grif would let it slide. This time. "If you want my help in the future, don't ever screw around with my contracts again."

"You got it." Jonah slung an arm around Grif's shoulders. "But there's no need to since I got everything I wanted this time."

Grif's gut roiled like it did when a team's management was trying to lowball him during negotiations. Didn't happen often anymore. But early on they'd tried because he'd been the youngest hot-shit sports agent in Los Angeles. "What else did you demand besides a parking spot and a new town name? And what the hell was Hackberry talking about when he said it would be great to have me on board?"

"Well," Jonah drawled, his country accent coming out. "I got Mom that parking space. And you? Hey, I got you a new job as city manager."

The temperature was only in the high fifties, normal

for early April, but Carlie Beth was sweating like a hog being led to the butchering table. Wearing thick gloves, goggles, a full helmet, and dark coveralls, she was absorbing the heat, making the temperature inside her welding gear a good fifteen degrees hotter.

"Hold that pipe steady." Her instructions to her apprentice Austin Burns were muffled by the plastic shield protecting her face, but he nodded his understanding and adjusted his grip on the length of black steel.

He shifted his weight, what there was of it on his lanky nineteen-year-old frame. "You heard about the new jam sessions over at Pisgah Brewing Company?"

Keeping up with stuff the neighboring town's brewery hosted was outside her daily to-dos. She shook her head, and a trickle of sweat slipped its way from under her do-rag and down her temple. Twenty bucks. That's what she'd give to wipe away the irritating distraction.

But doing that while holding a welding torch was an excellent way to become both blind and bald.

Like it would really matter all that much. It wasn't as if her long strawberry-blond hair and brown eyes were reeling in eligible bachelors these days. Usually she didn't care because men her age tended to have marriage on the mind, and she'd scratched that off her bucket list when the only man who'd asked had up and disappeared on her.

She seemed to have that effect on men.

So she'd reconciled herself to handling her responsibilities on her own, but a little discreet, mutually beneficial *adult time* wouldn't hurt her feelings. But instead of giving that too much airtime in her head, she concentrated on the task before her, a patch job on a cattle guard she'd spot-welded a couple of times before.

"Thought I'd take my guitar"—Austin's voice muted behind his protective gear, too—"and sit in on some songs."

"Bet you'll have a great time and the girls'll love it."

Other people were thinking of their weekend plans at four o'clock on a Friday afternoon, and here she was surrounded by cows and sweating over a cattle guard. Sexy on steroids.

Fixing cattle guards wasn't flashy, but it paid the bills, unlike her artisan blacksmithing projects. If only she could make as much money for a hand-forged door knocker as she did mending fences and gates. Maybe if she kept selling well through the gallery here in town, she could approach others. And then—

Stop daydreaming about art and deal with what's right in front of you.

But before she could bend over the joint again, Austin said, "I thought maybe you could...that you might want to—"

"Carlie Beth!"

She spotted someone in her peripheral vision and idled down the welding machine. It gave her the perfect excuse to lift her visor and attack that damn sweat. She wiped at her face and turned toward the cattle farmer she was doing the patch job for. "Hey, Dave."

"You almost done there?" His ever-present baseball cap, embroidered with the Black Horn Ranch logo, bobbed when he nodded toward the cattle guard.

She squatted down and pointed out the joints where the cross pipes joined the frame. "I know you only mentioned this weak spot on the right-hand side, but I went ahead and checked everything. I don't know who originally made this guard for you, but either the soldering was shoddy or your cows have been gaining weight."

"I've run some heavy stuff over it lately." The way Dave's face bloomed with a dull pink made her wonder exactly what type of stuff he was talking about. A commercial crane? A tank? A T-Rex?

Seemed like he was always having some issue with his fencing and pens.

"Well, another fifteen minutes and you should be in

good shape." She started to flip her visor down and return to her work, but Dave reached out. His fingertips came within a couple inches of her elbow, but never actually made contact.

"I...um...I was wondering if maybe you'd like to go out with me tonight. We could head over to Maggie Valley to that new sushi place. I'm not much for raw fish, but Yvonne mentioned you like it, so..."

Dammit it to Georgia and back. Here she'd just been bellyaching about her lack of social life and then this.

Thanks, God.

"Oh, that's really nice of you to offer, but—"

"She's going with me to listen to music."

Carlie Beth did a quick double-take at Austin's interruption, his presumption, and the way he squared his shoulders. His fists were clenching and releasing at his sides.

With an almost undetectable lip curl, Dave ignored the younger man and asked her, "You got more welding jobs after mine?"

"No, but I have to work tonight. I promised Randi I'd fill in at Triple B." The locals joked that Blues, Brews, and Books was too long to remember, so they'd given the restaurant and bar a nickname.

Dave's face lost all animation. "You know what men go to bars for."

Carlie Beth's mental eye roll did a swimmer's turn in her head. One of Dave's Black Angus meandered over and nibbled at the sleeve of her coveralls, and she scratched its broad forehead. Suppressing a smile, she said to Dave, "Beer?"

He huffed in disgust and yanked off his cap, giving Carlie Beth a glimpse of his receding hairline. Bouncing the hat against his thigh, he shot a quick glare at her apprentice. "No, they go looking for hookups."

And Lord, a temporary hookup sounded just right to Carlie Beth's long-neglected girl parts right now. But Dave wasn't a one-night kinda guy, and Carlie Beth had no interest in developing anything more with him. Truth be told, she wasn't even attracted to him. And that was downright pitiful because he was a nice man even if his looks were average. But she'd learned there was no explaining what set off a spark between a man and woman.

Austin shoved his helmet back so far that it flew off and hit the ground with a bounce. His dark hair was as sweaty as hers and had curled against his forehead and neck, making him look like a boy-band lead singer after an energetic concert. His chest bowed out and he advanced on Dave. "What're you trying to say? Carlie Beth is a nice girl and you're talking to her like she's some—"

"Hey, hey. I think this whole conversation took a sideways turn." With some quick footwork, Carlie Beth stepped in between them. She wasn't a girl, nice or otherwise. And all she'd wanted to do was get this job done and get paid. She certainly hadn't expected some strange pissing contest between her apprentice and one of her best repeat customers. "Thank you both for your kind invitations of dinner and music, but I'm not available tonight."

"Maybe some other time." Dave jammed his hat back on his head, but the movement couldn't disguise his scowl. He gave Austin another shit-on-my-shoe look, then glanced at Carlie Beth. "You seeing someone else?"

He damn well knew she wasn't. Gossip in Canyon Ridge flowed faster than the upper Nantahala River when they opened the dam each year. "No, but—"

"Then expect me to ask again." Dave strode toward his waiting crew-cab truck, and the driver's side door shut with a definitive slam.

"He's a dickhead," Austin huffed, glaring at Dave's truck as he pulled away. "He should know you're way above him. Too pretty for an old balding guy like him."

Carlie Beth flipped down her visor so Austin wouldn't see her squeeze her eyes closed. She'd been taking care of herself and her business since she was her apprentice's age. While he was thinking of bands and beer, she'd been worried about raising her baby. And she'd made a life—a good one—and she damn well wasn't a dog treat to be growled over by a man she wasn't interested in and a boy who worked for her.

She'd committed to training Austin to be a blacksmith and she would do that to the best of her ability, which meant she had to throw a blanket over whatever ideas he had about her being more than his boss. "Not that it's any of your concern," she told him. "But if I want to date Dave, that's my business."

And as for Dave, she needed these soulless welding jobs. They were what put food on her and Aubrey's table. She might just have to say yes to a dinner if that's what it took to stay on his good side.

Jesus, what a world she lived in.

A place where a blacksmith had to resort to sushi prostitution.

CHAPTER TWO

CARLIE BETH'S ESTIMATED HALF HOUR stretched to a full one when she checked the cattle guard's wings only to discover weak joints there as well. If she hadn't already done such a good patch job on the thing, she might've felt obligated to advise Dave to buy a new one.

Hmm…maybe she could start fabricating guards and gates herself. At least then they'd be quality. Which would also reduce the opportunity to fix them in the future. Her work was not shoddy, that was for damn sure. Plus, projects that size would take all the room in her forge, something she wasn't willing to give up.

She checked her welding machine to make sure it was secure on the trailer, swung herself up into her old but beloved SUV, and headed back into town. Thank goodness Austin had his own wheels so she didn't have to deflect any more invitations. But she still didn't have time to swing by her house and get cleaned up if she planned to be at Triple B on time. Randi'd had enough of a struggle lately without worrying about her staff's punctuality. Carlie Beth would just have to make do with a quick shower in Randi's private bathroom at the bar. If Carlie Beth went in looking—and smelling—like this, she wouldn't score a tip all night. And Aubrey's next orthodontist bill was coming due.

She parked in the almost empty lot behind the building

and grabbed her boots and uniform of jeans and a white T-shirt embroidered with Blues, Brews, and Books over the right breast. When she opened the back door, she was momentarily blinded by the change from bright spring sunshine to the stockroom's darker interior.

Although Randi would kill her a hundred times over if she waltzed into the bar looking like this, Carlie Beth would die of dehydration if she didn't get something to drink. Right this second.

Her eyes adjusted now, she hung her clothes in the storage area and eased open the door into the bar. A quick glance around revealed no sign of Randi or anyone else.

Perfect. A quick in and out with a glass of Cheerwine, and she'd be home free.

A vee of sunlight splashed across the wood floor, signaling someone coming in the front door. Carlie Beth bolted behind the bar and crouched down. Maybe she could snag a drink and get out before whoever it was saw her. She grabbed a highball glass and quickly filled it from the soda gun. The sweet scent from the soft drink was too much of a temptation and she gulped down several swallows, making her head contract in a painful brain freeze. "Ugh," she moaned but went back for more, draining the glass.

"Dean," a male voice said from somewhere disturbingly close by, "I talked with the GM and straightened out the misunderstanding about your surgical consult. Believe me, he wants you back on the ice as much as you want to be out there."

At the man's rumble above her, every tiny hair on Carlie Beth's body did a Don King imitation. She hadn't heard that voice in years, not until his mom's sixtieth birthday party a few months back. He'd called out to her, his smile just as charming and sinful as she remembered. Panic had swamped her, and she'd hightailed it out of there, leaving her best Pyrex bowl in the middle of the food table.

But one night fifteen years ago that voice had whispered the smoothest dirty talk Carlie Beth had ever heard directly into her ear. While the man himself was sliding inside her.

"Yeah, this is exactly the reason you pay me the big bucks." His low laugh shimmied through Carlie Beth. "I'll check in with you when I get back to town."

His Carolina Boy drawl had matured into the intoxicating smoothness of expensive artisanal whisky. And she knew the risks of bingeing on it.

"Anyone here?" he called out. "Because I could sure as hell use a drink."

An arm came over the bar top to snag a glass and she squeezed closer to the shelves. The next time she had a craving for a Cheerwine, she would stop at the Sack & Snack before coming in here. But for now, she was trapped.

"Hope you don't mind, but I'm making my own." His words were accompanied by the sound of liquid being poured.

She could pretend she was in a bubble, unable to see or hear anything, and just waddle her butt back to the hallway. But she wasn't a timid little girl. She was a grown woman. A strong woman, who didn't hide from things. Okay, so maybe she'd *hidden* a thing or two, but she had to face the man she knew was on the other side of this bar.

Carlie Beth filled her lungs with air, then lifted her head.

He was leaning over the wood expanse, staring down at where she was crouched next to the extra shot glasses. Every molecule she'd just inhaled whooshed back out.

He shouldn't impact her this way. He couldn't impact her this way.

His eyebrows drew in over his nose. "Carlie Beth, what are you doing back there? And why do you look like you just lost a mud-wrestling match?"

Griffin Steele was one of those men born on a day

when God was in an excellent mood. Artfully mussed golden-brown hair and eyes the blue of titanium welded too hot. A face that made angels break out into The Whip and a smile that made women like Carlie Beth lose their panties.

Fifteen years ago, those laugh lines around his eyes and mouth hadn't yet put in an appearance. Now, they hinted that he was a man who'd been around the block. Probably in a Mercedes Benz with a number of beautiful women riding shotgun. At that thought, something that felt oddly like jealousy sparked inside her midsection.

No, that was just her stomach growling from missing lunch. Because one look at Grif and she'd realized he was the masculine version of the Mad Batter Bakery's sinful hazelnut cream cheese puffs. Delicious, but so dangerous. Few women could resist that kind of temptation.

You can. You have. And you will.

With Grif staring, uneasiness swarmed over her. The sweat on her skin was cooling, making her shiver. Her hair was half stuck to her face, half a bedraggled tail hanging limp on her shoulder. No makeup. Not a speck. Seven-year-old jeans and a Canyon Ridge band booster T-shirt from Aubrey's drawer.

This was what happened when Carlie Beth put off doing laundry. Her face went hot because although she was a mere bra size bigger than Aubrey, that shiver had woken up her nipples, now clearly visible against her snug shirt. "I...uh...wait tables here. I was just grabbing a soda before getting cleaned up."

She tried to get her legs to work, but the damn things were apparently just as affected as her lungs. *Get your shit together, you two.*

"Looks like yours is empty." Grif leaned farther over the bar top and held out the glass he'd already filled. "Here. Take mine."

She couldn't tear her attention away from his hands. Those long, talented fingers were able to finesse a curveball *and* a woman's curves. Tan and obviously strong, they did more for her than seeing another man's naked body. "No, I couldn't—"

"I insist."

So he was still a gentleman, something she'd found hard to resist years ago and couldn't seem to hold out against now, either. Her hand was shaking as she reached up and took the lowball glass. She tried not to touch him, but it was impossible. Her fingertips grazed his knuckles, shooting heat up her arms and into her torso.

Grif's gaze dropped to her chest, held there for long enough to make the soft fabric of her bra feel scratchy and binding, almost unbearable against her tight nipples. When he finally looked up, his eyes had darkened to navy.

She knew that color.

It was the color of sex.

"The waitstaff isn't supposed to drink while working," she said, trying to keep her voice steadier than her knees. Unable to stand being at such a disadvantage for a single second longer, she gave her thigh muscles a pep talk and drew herself up to her meager five-foot-three height.

But her legs were still unreliable and she desperately needed whatever was in the glass she was gripping like it might grow wings and fly away. Bracing a hip against the bar, she took a deep swallow.

Son of a monkey!

There wasn't a drop of soda or water in that glass. If she had to guess, it was a double shot of high-end Glenlivet. She inhaled, and the air burned all the way down her throat and lit a brushfire in her stomach.

"Not what you were expecting?" Grif's wide smile dazzled her, making her head reel with the effect.

"Nope." She wheezed through the pain. "But just what the doctor ordered. Now, if you'll excuse me, I need to go get cleaned up." With as much dignity as possible given her disheveled appearance, she flashed a smile at him and turned toward the hallway.

"Carlie Beth." Grif's whisky-tinged voice came from behind her. "Aren't you going to give me my drink?"

Not a chance in hell. Rather than answer, she gulped the rest of the liquor and tossed the empty glass to him.

Twenty minutes later, Carlie Beth was headed back toward the restaurant and bar, feeling moderately in control after coming face-to-face with Grif Steele. Hot water, a ponytail elastic, and Just Peachy lipstick could do that for a girl. Still, she practiced a little yoga breathing before pushing open the door into the bar.

B. B. King was playing softly on the jukebox and the first person in her path was Randi, eyebrows raised. Her hair was a golden waterfall down her back, highlighting her enviable green eyes. "Drinking on the job, huh?"

For Pete's sake. "How did you—"

"I can see how those two might make a girl very thirsty." A smile lit up Randi's face, and she gave a head tilt toward the men sitting at a barnwood table in the corner. The light from the rustic silver pendant above highlighted their handsome faces.

Hmph. Grif must've said something to Randi about needing a refill. Carlie Beth tried to ignore him and instead studied the man who'd joined him while she was showering. Jonah Steele had dark shaggy hair that looked as if it hadn't seen the sharp end of a pair of scissors in months. He happened to glance up and grin at her, pleasure clear in his hazel eyes. Oh, that one had a mischievous streak when he was a kid. At ten years old, he'd hacked into the school's computer network just before report cards went out. Strangely enough, every student in Canyon Ridge made honor roll that term and had been given an unexpected school holiday. From what she heard around town, Jonah's propensity for trouble mixed with fun hadn't changed one bit.

But even through his smile, she could see his face was now shadowed with seriousness, something that made her think he'd suffered damage he couldn't quite erase.

Carlie Beth nodded at him, then grabbed a short

apron from behind the counter. Tying it in a perfect bow around her waist, she kept her attention on a vintage Lance crackers sign on the wall. It promised *just right...right now!*

Ha. With Grif sitting across the room, there was nothing right right about now, that was for damn sure. "Not interested," she said cheerfully to Randi.

"You'd have to be dead not to be interested."

Then drop her six feet under, because she had no plans to get close to anyone in the Steele family. It was too dangerous, not only to her mental state but to her complete state of being. "Which station am I taking tonight?"

Randi checked the plastic clipboard where she mapped out the waitstaff assignments in erasable marker. "Looks like three."

Carlie Beth's head popped up, but she didn't look at the table situated smack-dab in the middle of station three. "You did that on purpose."

The purple marker tapped against Randi's bottom lip. "Why in the world would I do that?"

"I have no idea," she snapped before she caught herself. *Not the way to treat a friend, Carlie Beth.* So she let out a deep breath and smiled. If she made too big a deal of this, Randi would get suspicious, and she didn't need anyone poking around in her history with a certain Steele brother. "Sorry. Just a tough day."

"You'll be the first one I send home tonight."

"Thanks." For a second, Carlie Beth gave a fleeting thought to asking another waitress to trade tables, but quickly nixed the idea. She could handle serving Grif Steele beer or whisky or whatever else he wanted to drink. No sweat off her brow. No water off her back. No...no...yeah, she had nothing else.

Might as well get this over with.

She grabbed a serving tray and headed directly for Grif and Jonah's table. "Gentlemen, can I get you a refill?"

"Hey there, Carlie Beth," Jonah said.

Grif propped an elbow on the table and leaned in, his grin never faltering. "That was some quick cleanup work."

She set her teeth in what she hoped looked like a smile instead of the lockjaw it was and stood there undergoing Grif's slow scrutiny. His scan started at her feet, covered with her favorite cowboy boots, bad-ass black with a red flame stitch and toebug. They were from a custom boot shop in a little Texas town called Prophecy. She'd splurged on them when she sold her first commissioned blacksmithing project.

His perusal was slower than pouring molasses in January, and it took every bit of Carlie Beth's self-discipline to keep from shifting from foot to foot. He took in her bootcut jeans and checked out her white vee-neck T-shirt as if it was the most interesting fashion to come off a European runway.

Do NOT respond. She mentally chanted the three-word command to her nipples. And good Jesus, she'd talked more to those two sluts in the past half hour than they'd been touched in the past two years. And they listened about as well as her childhood pet, a golden retriever, had when he'd been on the scent of something.

Which was not at all.

When Grif finally made it to her face, Carlie Beth was about to jump out of her skin. She'd never understood that phrase until this moment. But if her bones and muscles and nerves could find a convenient exit, they would leave her epidermis lying on the bar floor like a bear-skin rug.

"A testament that Ivory soap can work wonders." His eyes sparked with amused interest.

Carlie Beth casually braced a hand on an empty chair to shore up her wobbly knees. "Now that you two have checked behind my ears, can I get you something else from the bar?"

"Oh, ho." Jonah chuckled and shot a look at his brother. "Now that sounds like a challenge."

No, no, no, no.

But of course Grif smoothly rose to his feet, his elegant dress shirt hugging his chest and tapering into obviously expensive gray slacks. He'd hung the matching jacket over his seat and turned back his shirt cuffs in two precise folds. He rounded behind her, taking his sweet time with deliberate steps, and Carlie Beth's body responded to his nearness as if an epic thunderstorm was rolling in, electricity sparking all over her skin.

His fingers trailed lightly over her ponytail, and its weight was off her back only to land on her left shoulder, where the strands teased one of her apparently deaf nipples. Then Grif touched her ear, just a stroke of his fingertips along the outer rim, but the shock that zipped through Carlie Beth left her breathless.

Lord have mercy, he smelled so good. Like a stack of new hundred-dollar bills being fanned in front of her nose. Fresh, crisp, and with the indescribable undertones of success.

Why had she ever thought she could handle waiting on this man? Correction, waiting on his table. Because she'd never waited *for* him. She'd been smarter and more independent than that.

"I'd better get a damn good tip from you two." She pushed the words out with sheer will. And if they were slightly froggy, to hell with it.

Grif laughed and his breath caressed the back of her neck.

Date. She needed a date. And she was damn well going to get serious about it after this.

A sliding step to the left pulled her out of Grif's orbit as she tried to think of something both intelligent and polite to say. "Tell you what, to celebrate Grif's visit back home, why don't I bring y'all a bottle of Randi's best scotch?"

"That would be nice"—his smile was slightly tilted, both ruining and highlighting the perfection of his angel-blessed face—"but apparently I'm back in town for much more than a visit."

CHAPTER THREE

WELL, HELL. GRIF DROPPED BACK into his chair. He might need something even stronger than scotch after that little face-off with Carlie Beth Parrish. Jesus, his hands were shaking from touching a woman's ear.

Or maybe he was just still pissed at the way Jonah had dropped the city manager bomb on him. That had to be it. Afterward, Grif hadn't said a word even though his insides had been on fire. He'd simply walked away, strolled down the sidewalk as if being manipulated didn't make him want to do permanent damage to Jonah's face.

"She's even prettier than she was fifteen years ago," Jonah commented.

Yeah, he'd noticed that earlier even through the cockeyed ponytail and dirty clothes. Her neck was slender, her skin a pale gold. And that hair—the perfect combination of red and blond. He'd never seen anything like it until he met her, never seen anything like it since. Sometimes he still dreamed of her hair.

When he'd leaned over the bar and spotted her sitting there, all messy and sweaty, she'd stolen his breath.

Normally he preferred his women put-together and almost ice cold. But Madison Henry had cured him of that. After what she'd pulled, he couldn't help but wonder what kind of lies were hiding behind those polished faces.

But damn if he hadn't enjoyed the way Carlie Beth stood up behind that bar and wrapped her dignity around her. Met him head-on, word for word. He knew that scotch had burned like hell when she swallowed it, but he admired a woman who knew how to hold her own even when she'd been thrown off balance.

Between her take-no-shit attitude and the way her nipples had pressed against her T-shirt, he'd wanted to lean across that bar and put his mouth on hers.

Which pissed him off because it was the first time he'd felt that temptation in months.

"No ring on her finger," Jonah commented casually.

"Doesn't mean anything."

"I know for a fact that she's not married."

That surprised him. When he first moved out west, he hadn't returned home for close to five years, waiting until he'd made something of himself to visit his family. He'd been curious about Carlie Beth, but by that time, he'd assumed she'd settled down. Nothing could've come of him asking about her, so he'd left well enough alone. "If you think she's so hot, why don't you ask her out?"

Jonah's grin went sharp and tight like a steel trap that had just closed around Grif's leg. "Why would I do that when it's obvious you still have a thing for her?"

A thing? A *thing*? Sure, he and Carlie Beth had gotten busy—very, very busy—the night before he took off for LA when he was eighteen. Just because he'd tried to talk to her at his mom's birthday party earlier this year didn't mean he had a thing for her.

But his detoxing-from-a-bender hands said something different. "I don't do hometown girls."

"She's not a girl. Looks like a real woman to me."

Grif knocked back the last of his drink, then made a sound low in his throat. "She doesn't exactly meet my cup-size requirement."

"Your what?"

"I've decided to trade up in bra size and down in brain size." After all, those women were infinitely less dangerous. "Bet Carlie Beth struggles to fill up a B cup." Yeah, he was being a complete prick, but he didn't want to admit he remembered exactly how big Carlie Beth's breasts were.

"You gotta be shitting me. I'd rather have a hundred of Carlie Beth than a single double-D filled with all that pumped-in crap. I thought Madison Henry would've taught you something about messing with fakes. Glad I figured out that kind of woman wasn't what I wanted."

Madison's dishonesty had been on an entirely different level from super-sized tits, so Grif ignored Jonah's jab and waved a hand at the bar's interior. "And this is what you wanted? You sold your company and came back to play emperor in your hometown. That's messed up."

Jonah's fist came down on the wood tabletop. "No, this town is messed up and I'm fucking fixing it. That's why I had the city manager clause written into the contract."

"Without saying a word to me. I don't know what the hell you were thinking. I have no interest in being a public servant." He grabbed his phone from the edge of the table and typed in a Google search. "You have any idea what the average city manager makes?"

"No," Jonah sighed. "But I have a feeling you're about to tell me."

The figures Grif was already scrolling through were pitiful, and the city managers were basically slaves to the town's citizens. "Looks like about eighty-k a year, and that's for a city. If you figure this little burg is ten times smaller than the average midsize city, you're looking at something like—"

"Yeah, yeah. I passed math," Jonah said. "Eight grand. Like the money really matters."

"Look, Baby Billionaire, some of us still have to work for a living." Grif leaned over the table and made a gimme motion. "Now, hand over the contract."

"I could remind you that your bank account isn't exactly anemic." Jonah reached into the chair beside him, then slapped the thick envelope into Grif's palm.

Grif thumbed through the paperwork, rapidly looking for an amendment. Back when he'd put himself through business and law school, he'd taught himself how to speed-read. It had been his ace in the hole for finishing a six-year BA to JD program in three and a half years. Once he found what he was looking for, it took him all of twenty seconds to read and absorb it. "This just says the Steele family will provide a city manager. It doesn't name me specifically."

Thank Jesus. It would've been humiliating if word had gotten out that the Steele Shark had been bested by his own brother.

Jonah's left eyebrow went up. "You know anyone better for the job?"

"You can't afford me."

"Wanna bet?"

No way in hell was he going to be a kept man, especially kept by his little brother. "I have a business, a real life, back in LA." One that had recently cost him both emotionally and professionally.

"You call that real? Lying heiresses, entitled athletes, and a city full of plastic tits are not a life. At least not a real one. Now, what Carlie Beth has under her T-shirt? Those are real life."

"Excuse me?" The real-life Carlie Beth stood not a foot from their table, a full bottle and two clean glasses on her tray.

"Damn." Jonah covered his eyes with his hand. "That wasn't what it sounded like. I was just…"

"Yeah, Jonah, why don't you tell the lady what you were just saying?"

Carlie Beth set down the three items, each with a definitive clink. "I really don't want to know."

"We were having an argument and—"

"About my boobs?" For whatever reason, Carlie Beth turned her glare on Grif when his brother was obviously the one at blame here.

So Grif tried the smile that had once gotten him out of everything from speeding tickets to unwanted advances by a three-hundred-pound defensive end's wife. "You have to admit they're worth talking about."

Her glare only flared hotter. "If it wouldn't get me fired, I would dump that whole bottle on you."

And if Grif was reading her right, she'd then break the damn thing over his head. All those years ago, he hadn't quite realized how fierce this little bit of a woman could be. And he was perversely turned on by it. Maybe spending a little time in Steele Ridge until he could find Jonah a city manager wouldn't be a total loss. "Rather than that, why don't you let me make up for my idiot brother's unfiltered mouth by taking you out to dinner?"

Her nose flared, and it was about the cutest thing Grif had ever seen. He half expected her to paw the ground with her cowboy boot and charge. "No, thank you."

Oh, she'd thrown it down now. And he would sure as hell be picking it up. But he was a patient man, so all he said was, "Suit yourself."

She calmly turned away. No whirling, no stomping. But her clipped stride and the sassy swing of her hips communicated her anger.

Jonah stared after her like a puppy that had been swatted with a rolled-up newspaper. "Mouth, meet foot. I should do something to make up for—"

"Don't even think about it, little brother. You may have temporarily backed me into a corner with that city manager shit, but you're not going to screw me over by making a play for my woman."

"Your woman?" Jonah's head shake was slow as if he were trying to understand someone whose picnic basket was not just shy of a few sandwiches, but completely empty. "That sure happened fast, and somehow, I think Carlie Beth might disagree."

"You screwed me into sticking around town for a little while, and I deserve a distraction."

"What's a little while?"

"Until I find you a city manager willing to work for the kind of chicken feed this town can afford. Max of two weeks and not a minute more."

"You can't ignore them," Randi said, standing near Carlie Beth's left shoulder. "They're your customers."

The rag she was using to viciously scrub her drink tray wrapped around her fingers and cut off circulation. "If that bottle doesn't keep them happy for a while, I don't know what will."

"Which is exactly the reason you need to get over there and offer them food. Hot wings, potato skins, those new pork belly fritters. I don't care what, just something."

Before Carlie Beth could make an excuse that would keep her away from the man who'd just crashed back into her world, the bar's door opened and in strolled Roy Darden, chest puffed up and chin jutting out as if to say *try me, asshole.* Carlie Beth grimaced and focused on Randi to avoid catching Roy's attention.

"What?" Randi asked.

"Roy just walked in."

"You know what sucks about being a business owner?"

"The fact that some customers are jerkwads?"

"Bingo." Randi took a quick peek over her shoulder at the man who worked at a local auto repair shop. "I can't believe you ever went out with him."

Carlie Beth bristled at having her judgment questioned. "Have you looked at him?"

"He's gorgeous, I'll give you that. But everyone in three counties knows he knows it and uses it."

Yeah, with his thick dark hair, country-boy smile, and ripped body, Roy turned his share of heads. He'd turned

Carlie Beth's. Something she'd regretted for the past year, ever since they'd gone on their first and only date and he'd assumed a steak dinner and a glass of cheap wine entitled him to shove his hands under her skirt. He was lucky she hadn't marched down to the sheriff's department and reported attempted rape.

Roy sauntered over to the one empty table still left in Carlie Beth's station. It was like the man had a secret sense. He unerringly ended up in her area. Every. Damn. Time.

"Kris can take that table."

"No." Carlie Beth sighed. "I wouldn't do that to her even though she's management. I can handle him." Maybe.

She slapped a smile on her face and headed in his direction. If she kept having to fake her expressions like this all night, she'd need a chisel to get them off her face.

Before she could make her way to Roy's table, someone else reached out and caught her by the elbow. Dave. Holy bejesus, were all the men she'd ever dated or who'd ever wanted to date her planning to come in tonight? If so, Austin should show up any minute.

In a low voice, Dave said, "Roy Darden is trouble."

Her cheeks trembled with the effort of keeping them lifted. "He's also a customer."

"Tell Randi—"

"Dave"—his name came out sharper than she intended—"I'm not telling Randi anything. I'm doing my job. So please let me get back to it." She stared down at his hand until he released her arm.

She slipped away and approached Roy's table. "Evening, Roy. What can I get you?"

His once-over didn't feel anything like Grif's had earlier. This perusal felt slimy and black, making her skin ripple as if she'd stepped in week-old roadkill. "How about two little tits with a side of sweet ass?"

Carlie Beth bit down on her tongue so hard the taste of blood bloomed in her mouth. *Remember you owe the orthodontist.* "How about an Ass Clown ale or a Dirt Bag IPA?"

"Guess that'll do for now," he said with such a good-natured grin that Carlie Beth knew the subtext had flown right over his head.

She nodded and strode away, trying not to trip over the toes of her boots as she made a quick getaway. The front door opened again, and this time the person walking in was more welcome.

"Hey, Yvonne," Carlie Beth called. Her friend was in her mid-thirties with midnight black pixie-cut hair and had a good six inches on Carlie Beth. Yvonne was also the owner of Triskelion Gallery and first person who'd given her a chance to sell the jewelry and art she really loved making in her backyard forge.

Yvonne waved and made her way over. "I didn't know you were working tonight. Looks like a good crowd." She scanned the room, but there were no tables left, only a couple of stools at the bar.

"I was just on my way to check on a table, but if you want to grab a stool, I'll make sure Grady gets you set up."

Yvonne looked beyond her. "Now those are two handsome Steele brothers."

"You went to school with Britt, right?"

With a laugh, Yvonne said, "Yep, but it's not like any of them could go unnoticed."

She spoke the absolute truth. "Then why don't you come over while I check on them?"

She and Yvonne approached the table, where the bottle of scotch was half-empty, but neither man seemed sloppy drunk. Or even buzzed. She said, "Jonah and Grif, I don't know if you remember—"

They both came to their feet and Jonah reached out to wrap Yvonne in a bear hug. "Yvonne Winters. I've been meaning to come by and check out your gallery."

She poked him in the side. "What's keeping you? I've got lots of art and other goodies that are just looking for a good home." He released her, and she embraced Grif. Carlie Beth would swear Yvonne lingered in Grif's arms longer than she had his brother's. "Well, if it isn't the handsome sports agent. You know the last time you were in town and I shoved a handful of business cards at you?"

"Yeah?"

"Well, a couple months later, Ian Brinkmann bought several pieces from me, including one of Carlie Beth's."

"One of Carlie Beth's what?"

Great. She'd forgotten nothing about this man, down to a birthmark shaped like a hawk in flight on his inner thigh, yet he couldn't remember what she did for a living. The night they'd been together, she'd just returned from her two-year blacksmithing apprenticeship in Spartanburg. Only nineteen, she'd been so high and excited about her future that she'd not only thrown caution to the wind, but she'd tossed her good sense after it.

Why else would she have done something that had accidentally changed the entire course of her life?

"She crafts some of the most beautiful ironwork you've ever seen," Yvonne told Grif.

"I'll be sure to come in to the gallery and look for myself." He gestured toward an empty chair. "Would you like to join us?"

Although Carlie Beth had been hoping they would offer, the way Grif was behaving toward Yvonne rubbed at her like a rasp. "How about some appetizers? The pork belly fritters are fabulous and we have some dynamite habanero hot wings." Maybe they'd give Grif indigestion for days.

"Sure," Jonah said. "Bring one of each for the table."

"You got it."

She tried to skate her way past Roy's table, but he held out his arm like a railroad crossing. "What about me, sweetheart?" he asked with just enough edge to raise the hair on Carlie Beth's arms.

"Were you ready to order food?"

"How about you and me heat something up after you get off work tonight?" Lord, if he thought that droopy-eyed look was sexy, he needed a better mirror.

"Sorry, but I need to get home."

"Just a little ride and I can make you change your mind about that."

He couldn't make her change her mind about him if he suddenly produced a new triple-width gas forge out of thin air. "I'm not dating anyone right now, but thanks for the offer. Why don't I put in an order of pulled pork sliders for you?"

She made a show of jotting on her notepad even though she rarely needed it. Then she turned toward the kitchen. Before she could take a full step, she felt a sharp sting across her right butt cheek. Not a love pat but a full-out smack on the ass. Mouth open, she looked back at him to find his palm still in contact with her posterior. "What the hell—"

"You better get your hand off the lady's ass before I permanently remove it from your arm." How Grif had made it from his table to Roy's that fast, Carlie Beth had no idea. But he was standing there, mouth flat, his fist wrapped tight around the other man's wrist.

"Who the fuck are you?" Roy took in Grif's suit pants and pricey dress shirt. "Look like a pussy to me. Your mommy shine your shoes for you? Or maybe your boyfriend?"

A vein in Grif's temple throbbed. *Boom, boom, boom.* Something about that hard pumping did a number on Carlie Beth's hormones. Anger shouldn't be sexy, but Grif's cold fury was. "I doubt it'll matter much to you who buffed my shoes when I have one wedged up your butt all the way to your lungs."

Roy rose from his chair, slowly drawing himself up to his six-foot-plus height, forcing Grif to release his wrist. Roy didn't tower over Grif, but he was thickly muscular, while Grif was a sleek package of power. "You threatening me?"

One side of Grif's mouth quirked up in a fuck-you expression. "I don't need threats because I only make promises I can keep. And I promise you that although these Tom Fords look slick, they're still gonna hurt like hell when I insert one into your ass."

The taller man went for Grif, but didn't even make contact with his shirt front because Grif smoothly sidestepped and nailed Roy with an uppercut to the chin.

Carlie Beth was yanked back from the fray, and she glanced up to see Dave had once again attached himself to her elbow. Swear to Jesus, if she didn't need that arm so much, she'd hack it off and just give it to him.

"Enough!" Randi stood behind Roy holding her favorite Louisville Slugger. "This is a family establishment. If you two bozos want to tear up something, do it somewhere else."

Grif's edgy smile and chin lift told Roy it was his call, that he'd just as well beat his ass outside as inside. But Roy rubbed a hand over his chin and grunted. "This little dick-lovin' asshole ain't worth my time." He shot a venomous look Carlie Beth's way. "So you can cancel that beer order for now, but you and me? We ain't finished by a long shot."

They all watched him stomp out. Then Grif reached into his pants pocket and drew out a handkerchief, an honest to goodness square of what looked like real linen, and wiped his hands. He asked Carlie Beth, "Good friend of yours?"

It was none of his business, but she found herself blurting out, "We went out once. But it wasn't a good match."

"I take it he'd like to try again."

"He hinted."

"Shortcake, an ass slap isn't a hint." He did remember something about her, that he'd teased her, calling her Strawberry Shortcake as an affectionate reference to her hair and her height. He skimmed a finger under her chin, forcing her to look up at him. "It's an assault."

She sighed. "Did you forget we're in small-town North Carolina?"

"I don't care if we're in fucking Timbuktu. A man who hits a woman should be taught a lesson." And with that easy pronouncement, he sauntered back to his table.

CHAPTER FOUR

432 BALSAM DRIVE. ALL IT had taken was a quick Google search for Grif to find out where Carlie Beth lived. Last night after he'd gotten rid of that douchebag at Blues, Brews, and Books, Carlie Beth had given him a curt thank-you, but something about her tone had told him she was less than happy with him stepping in and solving the problem.

But no way in hell was he going to sit there and watch a man smack a woman without doing something about it. Not ever, but especially not after what he'd been accused of. Carlie Beth should've appreciated the restraint he showed by not following the guy outside and finishing what the asshole had so idiotically started.

Instead, she'd avoided their table for the rest of the evening, apparently assigning them to another waitress. Regardless, they'd left a generous tip and asked the other woman to share with Carlie Beth.

And since he'd decided Carlie Beth was the perfect distraction for his two-week stint in North Carolina, it looked as if a little sucking up was in order. So he navigated Louise down the wide expanse of Main Street in the direction of Balsam.

He noticed a few people drifting into the Mad Batter, but as taste bud thrilling as the bakery's pastries were, a line should've been snaking its way around the chalkboard sign that always sat on the sidewalk. Heck, the prophetic messages Jeanine Jennings, baker's assistant and sandwich sign soothsayer, carefully printed on there each day were reason enough to visit the bakery, whether or not you believed in them.

Today's read: *Home is where the hazelnut cream cheese puffs are.*

Grif shook his head at that obscure bit of wisdom and a flash of golden-red caught his eye on the other side of the street. And there Carlie Beth was, strolling along in front of the shops, wearing jeans, a baseball shirt with olive green sleeves, and what looked like heavy-duty work boots. She stopped at the Triskelion Gallery and went in.

Perfect. He could have a word with her and check out a little of the local business climate. Not that the shops and entrepreneurs had anything to do with him. He wasn't really Steele Ridge's city manager, much less in charge of economic development. But it wouldn't hurt to see what Jonah would be dealing with in his new fiefdom.

Unfortunately, it was all too easy to find a parking spot, which didn't bode well for a mountain town on a beautiful Saturday morning. Tourists should be swarming this area.

The town needed a hook. He needed a special reason for people to visit and spend their money here.

No, *he* didn't need anything. Jonah needed to figure this shit out for himself.

Before Grif could stroll into Triskelion Gallery, he was waylaid by one of his favorite cousins, Maggie Kingston, wearing her sheriff's uniform. He held out his arms for a hug.

"I'm on duty, Grif."

"So?" He pulled her in, giving her hair a little tug like he used to when they were kids. "When did they start making cops so pretty?"

"Shut up. You'll undermine my authority."

"Nah." He laughed. "You want me to undermine you, I'll tell people that time we were down at the creek and you—"

"I have a loaded gun, and you know I know how to use it."

Sheer joy swelled inside Grif. Few women in his LA circle would ever utter those words. People in that city were more likely to freak out when they discovered you owned a gun. Damn, he sometimes forgot how much he loved his family and how much he'd missed people being upfront and honest. "Fine, now that I've been threatened by police brutality, I have no choice but to—ooph."

Maggie's fist connected with his ribs, but she squeezed him once more with her other arm before stepping back. "Seriously, I'm working. Hey, I heard a crazy rumor that Jonah asked to change Canyon Ridge's name."

"Not a rumor. Certified fact. You're now living in Steele Ridge, North Carolina."

"Someone needs to do an ego-ectomy on the whole lot of you. Does he have any idea how much that's going to cost taxpayers?"

"Pretty sure he's got it covered." Grif laughed. "What're you up to this morning besides harassing people about progress in this town?"

"Actually, I was about to drive out to your mom's."

"You know she's already started moving stuff into the old farmhouse at Tupelo Hill, right?" Grif had no doubt Jonah's decision to spend a crapload of money on a sports complex had more than a little to do with their mom's lifelong yearning to live in the house that also sat on the massive piece of property. "In fact, I'm due back to help haul furniture in an hour. Wouldn't surprise me if everything is in by nightfall and she sleeps there tonight."

"I heard she rented y'all's old house to the Garvey family starting next Saturday."

Well, that screwed up his plans to stay in the house

he'd grown up in. Looked like he'd be joining his mom at Tupelo Hill for the next couple of weeks. Apparently Jonah had already been squatting out there from the beginning of the year because he'd been so sure the city council would go for his crazy-ass plan.

He'd been right.

"Mom in some kind of trouble with the law?" As if. Joan Steele was the definition of upstanding citizen. She loved this state, loved this town, loved these people.

"I don't know that *anyone* is in trouble, but I was coming out to talk with you. Then I spotted you and saw Carlie Beth walk into the gallery. Figured I'd get a two-for-one and chat with you both at the same time."

An uneasy feeling snaked through him. "What do you need to talk with us about?"

Maggie nodded toward the gallery. "Why don't we do this all at once?"

Jesus. He hadn't been in town long enough to stir up shit. Besides, that wasn't his MO. He was the one who dragged his clients out of the crap they created, which was why it had been so tough when he'd needed help digging out from under his own problems.

He held the door open for his cousin and followed her into the gallery. Inside, it smelled of patchouli smoke and apples.

Carlie Beth and Yvonne were bent over something spread out on the countertop, but looked up when he and Maggie entered. Carlie Beth's eyes widened, just enough for him to catch it, and the spark he felt when he'd touched her neck last night seemed to arc across the room between them. Yeah, something was there. Something he wanted to explore.

Because she was definitely a what-you-see-is-what-you-get kind of woman. Just what he needed in his life right now.

Yvonne opened her arms in welcome. "Two customers at once. Can't remember when I've been so lucky."

Another reminder that his hometown was seriously hurting.

"Sorry to say, I don't think either of us is here to shop," Grif said, softening his words with a smile.

But Yvonne just lifted a shoulder. "You don't know how persuasive I can be." She asked Maggie, "What can I do for you?"

"I need to ask Grif and Carlie Beth a few questions. Do you have a place where we can have a little privacy?"

"Stockroom, but it's a mess."

"That'll do."

Carlie Beth shot Grif a what-the-hell look, and he returned it with a your-guess-is-as-good-as-mine shrug. They followed Maggie, their shoulders brushing as they walked toward the back of the gallery. Rippling with awareness, Grif's nerves reacted as though he and Carlie Beth were skin to naked skin. One subtle sniff and he discovered the source of the fruit scent. Carlie Beth smelled like a just-baked apple pie with a scoop of homemade vanilla ice cream slowly melting on top.

Grif's stomach growled.

"Miss breakfast this morning?"

Hell, no. Even as busy as she'd been, his mom had insisted on cooking a full country spread—eggs, grits, biscuits, gravy, bacon, and fresh sausage from a local farm. If he kept eating like that, he'd have to buy a whole new wardrobe when he got back to LA.

But damn, it had been delicious.

"The mountain air does things for a man's appetite."

She slid him a suspicious look, as if she suspected he was no longer talking about food.

And hell, he wasn't. Since he always asked for what he wanted, and sometimes a little more, he said, "Hey, I heard there's a good sushi place over in Maggie Valley. I'd love to take you tonight."

"What is it with sushi these days?" Her lips turned up in a secret smile. "And is the high-powered Grif Steele asking me out on a date?"

Something about her teasing tone made his face heat. Completely ridiculous since he'd once dated much more beautiful and much less approachable women. "This is how it's usually done."

"Grif, I can't—"

"Both of you, take a seat, please." Maggie used her normal pleasant drawl, but it didn't disguise that her words were an order. She pointed to a table ringed by cardboard boxes, some sealed and some open.

"Maggie, what's this—"

"Sheriff Kingston."

"Right. Now, what—"

"Griffin Steele, sit your ass down and shut up." She pointed to the chair behind him, and Grif sank into it, anger starting to bubble its way through his system. "I'm not one of your hotshot clients. You are not in charge here. So if you'll just shut it for an ever-lovin' minute, we can get through this."

She sat on the opposite side of a small café table and said to Carlie Beth, "I hear you had some trouble with Roy Darden last night."

Carlie Beth shook her head and huffed out a breath. "Nothing more than the usual."

Grif swung around in his chair to stare at her. "Are you telling me he's hit you before? My God, Carlie Beth, what are you think—"

Maggie mowed over him. "Explain what you mean by *the usual.*"

Slumping in her chair, Carlie Beth sighed. "Roy and I went out, and since then he—"

Grif said, "I still can't believe you would—"

"He what?" Maggie asked.

"He just won't accept that I'm not interested."

With her stylus, Maggie jotted something onto her tablet. "From what I understand, that was his habit with women."

Grif's entire body went still at the seemingly innocent statement. "Was? You said *was.*"

Maggie jabbed the stylus his way. "I'll get to you in a minute." She turned back to Carlie Beth. "Did you have any other contact with Roy last night?"

"No, luckily he left after…"

"After his run-in with Fancy Shoes here," Maggie finished for her, shooting a look at Grif. "Did Roy have a habit of hanging around Triple B until you got off?"

"A couple of times, I found him loitering in the parking lot after my shift. But I was always able to wiggle out of a long conversation."

"Jesus." This whole thing disgusted Grif. Did people around here have no concept of personal safety? And they thought LA was dangerous.

Maggie gave Grif a look as sharp as his dad's favorite fillet knife. "What about you, Mr. I'm-Gonna-Put-A-Loafer-Up-Your-Ass? Maybe you decided running the guy off wasn't enough last night. Had another pissing contest with him or maybe you tracked him down early this morning."

"Earlier this morning, I was helping Reid tighten all the grips on the sports complex's climbing wall so I can get some damn exercise while I'm here. But now that I know all this about Darden, I sure as hell wish I'd gone after him and yanked his intestines out through his nose."

Carlie Beth choked out a laugh.

"What?"

She waved a hand at his pressed chinos, Sea Island cotton shirt, and polished shoes. "It's just that you look more like a lover than a fighter."

Oh, he could definitely be both. Most of the time, he was able to take out his aggressive impulses across a negotiating table, but something about Carlie Beth, a woman he'd slept with *once*, made him want to pound his chest and club all the other cavemen away. *Je-sus.*

A thud came from outside the stockroom door, and they all turned in that direction.

Yvonne called out, "Just dropped a box. Sorry about that!"

Maggie returned her attention to Grif. "So you're saying you didn't go after Darden?"

"No." He glared at his cousin. "Jonah and I left Triple B at about ten o'clock. I dropped him out at Tupelo Hill, then headed for Mom's."

"And I suppose you were completely sober?"

He raised his brows. "I would never drive Louise drunk. She deserves better than that."

"Louise?" Carlie Beth asked.

"Men." His cousin snorted. "Some name their cars and some name their pric—"

"Louise is your penis?" Carlie Beth's attention was suddenly one hundred percent on him.

"Hell, no." The heat from earlier returned to Grif's face, but he beat it back through sheer will. "There's something inherently wrong with a man giving his dick a woman's name."

"So Louise is just your car."

"No," he snapped. "She's not *just* a car. She's a Maserati Quattroporte."

"Back to the original question," Maggie said. "You and Jonah went straight home?"

"Yeah. Mags, what's going on here?"

"I just needed to make sure what looked like an accident was, in fact, an accident. Because it appears Roy got pretty lagered up last night and fell down the stairs outside his apartment."

"Ow," Carlie Beth said. "Did he break anything?"

"You could say that," Maggie said wryly. "Just his neck."

CHAPTER FIVE

"DEAD?" GRIF ASKED.

"Yes."

So that's why Maggie had waylaid him outside. Grif couldn't drum up a lot of sympathy for that prick Darden, but falling ass over feet down the stairs had to be a shitty way to die. Drunk or not. Still, something about the timing didn't strike Grif quite right. "A douchebag like him must've had a few enemies."

"Which is the reason I wanted to talk with the two of you." Maggie clicked off her tablet and stood. "Thanks for the information."

"You'll let me know if it turns out this wasn't an accident."

She pointed her stylus in Grif's direction again. "That didn't sound like a question."

"Because it wasn't."

"You do your job, Mr. Bigshot, and I'll do mine." And with that nonanswer, Maggie left the stockroom.

"That's horrible," Carlie Beth breathed.

"Sounds like it was his own damn fault. The guy was obviously an idiot."

"Because he liked me?"

God, Jonah had been lecturing him about women with big boobs and not much else? This reminded Grif why they were easier to deal with. "No. Because he didn't understand the concept of *no.*"

Carlie Beth pushed up from her chair. Grif caught her wrist, and she stared down at his fingers wrapped around the delicate bones. "About that sushi?" he asked.

"I don't think that's a good idea."

"You don't like sushi? We can—"

"I'll be honest with you because it wouldn't take you long to find out the truth. I can eat my weight in tuna rolls, but I don't think we're a good idea."

She lobbed it out there easily, like the simple declaration was enough, but to Grif it was a challenge. He stood and rounded the table, let her tempting scent wrap around him, and looked into her pretty brown eyes. Her pulse was thumping in her neck, and that tell drew his attention downward.

Unable—and unwilling—to stop himself, he stroked a thumb over the proof that her body thought they were an excellent, an arousing, idea. The savvy negotiator in him was tempted to lay out a handful of logical reasons why she should have dinner with him.

But the Steele Shark knew the best way to come out on top of a deal was to force someone to react emotionally while he remained calm. "You haven't forgotten what it was like. In my backseat. On my hood."

She said nothing, but her pulse picked up more speed.

"I sure as hell haven't forgotten," he said, deliberately lowering his voice. Any time she'd come to mind since he'd moved to the West Coast, she'd always been a warm and sweetly wicked memory.

"That was a long time ago. It has nothing to do with now." The sound she made could only be called a scoff. Looked like there was only one effective way to get her to concede, so Grif backed her against the wall and covered her mouth with his. She tasted like the first bite of a homemade apple pie, sugary with just a hint of tart. So delicious he already knew he wouldn't be satisfied with a mere slice. A single kiss and he wanted the whole damn pie.

That didn't happen to him. He wouldn't allow it.

But she wasn't fully engaged, her lips hesitant on his. And that wouldn't do. He released her wrist to cup her jaw and stroke her cheek. Sure enough, her mouth opened to him and the kiss was no longer sweet. In no way innocent.

It became a hot tangle of tongues and heated breath. He wanted to haul her up, have her wrap her body around him, meet him equally. He pushed into her, half surprised at how small she felt against him. But the way she kissed him made her feel anything but small or weak.

Her fingers plunged into his hair and she yanked him closer. So close air couldn't flow between them. And she kissed the holy fuck out of him.

Teeth, tongue, lips—she used them all. And with a seductive skill that made Grif's head go blank. The feel of her short nails against his scalp shot an unreasonable amount of lust into his bloodstream. He wanted those nails, her small but capable hands, all over his body.

Why now? Why her?

Maybe because she was so different. Nothing like the last woman he'd kissed. Carlie Beth was flash and spark. Raw and honest. So different and strangely familiar.

He spanned her ribcage with his palms, was on his way to covering her breasts when her tight hold on his hair suddenly loosened. And unfortunately, she used that newly freed hand to push at his shoulder.

God, they were making out in a stockroom like two teenagers.

His first inclination was to keep going. The way she'd reacted to him made it more than clear he could persuade her, change her mind. But he, of all people, knew both the man and the woman needed to be on the same page.

Using extreme control, he shifted his hands next to Carlie Beth's head, bracing himself against the wall. He hung his own head and blew out a breath that was about a hundred times shakier than he would've liked. "Still think we're not a good idea?"

Before he could catch her, she ducked under his outstretched arms and danced away like a boxer who knew the only way he could beat his opponent was to keep moving around the ring. "I...I don't know what just happened."

Grif stared down at the floor, or where the floor should be if his tented pants weren't obscuring his view of it. "Flash knockdown," he said, half to himself. Because just like a punch that came out of nowhere, she'd momentarily thrown him off his game. His over-the-top reaction to this woman was just a matter of circumstance, happenstance.

"Whatever it was, it's not happening again."

Bull. Shit. Something this hot, this powerful, needed to be finished. He pushed off the wall and pivoted toward her. "Why not?"

Carlie Beth glanced down, and her staring at his dick certainly didn't do a damn thing to cool off the lust still cruising through him. Her gaze flickered back up to his, and she made a sexy little humming sound that made his skin ripple.

"Can't be a chemistry problem."

"I...because...because I'm just not interested."

Under her baseball shirt, her nipples were tight little beads, completely ruining her argument. But Grif knew when it was a good time to push and when it was time to change tactics. So he took a few deep breaths, but didn't bother to turn his back when he adjusted his slowly fading hard-on.

And he grinned when Carlie Beth tracked his every movement.

He'd just taken his hand off his fly when Yvonne poked her head into the stockroom and said, "Oh, my gosh. Did Sheriff Kingston tell y'all about Roy Darden?"

"Yes." Carlie Beth's hands went to her hair, smoothing and fiddling. When she caught him watching her, she dropped her hands to her sides and strolled back toward the showroom as if they hadn't been plastered together a few minutes before. "Isn't it terrible?"

The hell if he would let her avoid him, so he followed and saw her wave a hand toward the items she and Yvonne had been studying when he walked in the gallery. "If you don't mind, can we talk about these pieces later?" Her artwork was spread out on a cloth on the glass counter, everything from a scrolled iron-and-pearl ring to what looked like a belt buckle.

Damn, she was talented.

He ran his fingers over a pair of intricately fashioned bookends—one a dragon's head, the other his tail. No, Carlie Beth was insanely gifted.

"I can just take them and we'll come to an agreement on price later," Yvonne said. "You know I'll be fair."

"You always are." Carlie Beth's smile was genuine and relaxed, and Grif found himself wishing it was aimed at him.

A ring tone that sounded like Taylor Swift's "Shake It Off" came from Carlie Beth's pocket, and her expression immediately closed up. Kissing him like her life depended on it one minute and pulling away the next. He couldn't get a read on her. She clutched her phone and bolted for the stockroom. "Excuse me."

"Something wrong?" he asked Yvonne.

"That was her daughter's ring tone." Yvonne glanced over her shoulder, then turned back to Grif with an expression he couldn't quite interpret. She leaned on the counter as if she was imparting state secrets, and he couldn't help but notice the way her cleavage was put on display. But it interested him about as much as unbuttered grits. Carlie Beth's breasts in a baseball T-shirt, on the other hand, were like a bowl of double cheese grits doused with Tabasco sauce.

And what the hell was wrong with him, comparing tits to grits? Another day in this town, and he'd be turning into a dirty old man like Mr. Greene or knuckle-dragging like that poor son of a bitch Roy Darden.

Returning his apparently addled brain to his conversation with Yvonne, he asked, "Carlie Beth has a daughter?"

"You talk about two peas in a pod. She and that kiddo are so close it's hard to tear them apart."

The muscles in his neck tensed the way they did when he discovered one of his clients had omitted a critical detail, something like yeah, he *was* driving drunk or yes, the girl in his car *was* underage. He'd come to hate that tense feeling because most recently it had been brought on by his own clusterfuck of a life.

Carlie Beth was a mother. With a daughter. Well, that put a different spin on his invitation. He'd just been looking for a little dinner, hopefully topped off with some tasty dessert.

But he had absolutely no interest in getting mixed up with a full meal deal.

CHAPTER SIX

"MOM, IT'S ONE O'CLOCK!"

Carlie Beth lifted her attention from the oak leaf keyring she was shaping to glance at her daughter standing in the forge's doorway. "Okay."

"The party at Miss Joan's new house starts in an hour."

The sudden need to whack the crap out of the leaf's delicate curve with her rounding hammer almost overwhelmed Carlie Beth. Why had she thought Aubrey wouldn't hear about the shindig out at Tupelo Hill, which was now owned by Jonah Steele?

She still couldn't believe he—and Grif, from what she'd heard—had strong-armed the mayor into changing Canyon Ridge's name to Steele Ridge. Now she'd think of Grif every time she wrote her own address. "I hadn't planned on going. I need to finish these keyrings."

Aubrey's mouth dropped open, revealing her silver braces with pink brackets, and Carlie Beth looked closer. Was her daughter wearing lipstick? God, it was bad enough that Aubrey had a sweep of hair the color of Carlie Beth's, but in the past year, her figure had begun to bloom, with the hint of a woman's hips and breasts Aubrey insisted required an underwire bra. As if. Aubrey was emotionally and intellectually mature, but Carlie Beth was in no rush for her to grow up completely. "Did you get into my makeup?"

Aubrey touched her lips self-consciously. "It's not like you wear it often enough for it to matter."

"My tools don't really care how I look." Resigned to a discussion, she set aside her hammer and the keyring already stamped with her initials and identifying symbol.

Aubrey crept closer, cupped her hand to one side of her mouth and surreptitiously pointed toward Austin, who was in the corner working on a custom set of J-hooks. "He does," she mouthed.

Even thinking about the way Austin had acted like an idiot in front of Dave the other day made her feel as if she should register herself as a card-carrying cougar. No, thank you.

If Austin continued to make advances, no matter how subtle, she might have to find him another teacher. And that would be a shame because he'd been working with her for six months now and showed real promise. But blacksmithing was becoming a lost art, and it wasn't a skill learned overnight. If he wanted to open his own forge someday, he had lots of crawling to do before he walked, which he couldn't do if he was busy flirting with her.

"Not funny, Aub. Whatever you have rolling around in your head, you need to put the brakes on it right this second."

At fourteen, everything in a young girl's life was rainbows and unicorns and hearts. Sometimes exhausting for the thirty-four-year-old mother, but Carlie Beth wasn't so old that she couldn't remember feeling the same way herself. She'd had the biggest crush on her eighth-grade science teacher, Mr. George. Lord, how she'd mooned over him, scratching *Carlie Beth George* in a spiral notebook and even naming the four children she just knew they'd have.

Of course, that was way before she'd given birth to her own beautiful but colicky baby.

"You should ask him to the party."

"Everyone in town was invited, including Austin."

"But he won't go if you stay here working. He looks at you like a dog checks out a piece of rawhide."

Ew. Carlie Beth rubbed at her temple, probably smearing ash on her face.

But Aubrey was right, Austin never left the forge before she did. And she was there any time she wasn't working a bigger welding job or hanging out with Aubrey. The poor guy needed a break, one he'd never ask for.

"Fine, I'll encourage him to go," Carlie Beth finally said. "But *not* with me, and you're not going."

And oh, Aubrey's blue eyes could spark hot so fast. "You're kidding."

"Nope," she said. "Don't you have a class project due soon?"

Aubrey tossed her hair and rolled her eyes, somehow pulling off the move with the kind of disgust only a teenager could. "I've been done with that for two days."

Damn.

"I thought you and Brooke were planning to do something this weekend. You mentioned spending the night at her house."

"Brooke will be at the Steeles' party with her family. Why don't you want me to go? Miss Joan is one of the nicest people in the universe."

Absolutely, one hundred percent true. Grif's mom was pretty much an angel with hidden wings. Raising a big family, sometimes singlehandedly when her husband disappeared for weeks at a time. And all the while, she'd worked as the receptionist at the elementary school. All the kids in Cany—dammit, Steele—Ridge adored her. Probably had a little to do with the Jolly Ranchers she'd snuck them when the principal and parents weren't watching. Many a time Aubrey had come home from grade school smelling of watermelon candy.

Any time Carlie caught the scent on the Sack & Snack's candy aisle, it made her uneasy.

"It would probably hurt her feelings," Aubrey

wheedled. "Make her think we don't appreciate what her son did for everyone. I heard if Jonah Steele hadn't basically bought this town that everyone would be out of jobs. Either have to go on welfare or move to Charlotte."

That made Carlie Beth smile. Oh, the horrors of living in a big city. Once upon a time, she'd believed she would move away from her hometown, become a famous artist in a place like Charlotte or Miami or Atlanta. Maybe even Los Angeles.

She shook her head, only slightly able to imagine that life now. After all, she'd traded in that future years ago. She was happy here in her hometown.

Or at least satisfied.

Definitely comfortable.

God, that sounded pitiful.

But she'd had to put down roots for her daughter's sake. Over the years, she might've wanted to rip them free once in a while, if only for a night or two. But it had become clear that excitement and spark weren't in the cards for her.

After all, one of the men to recently show interest in her—however misguided—was apparently lying in the county morgue. And although Dave out at Black Horn was a nice guy, the spark was missing on her side.

But one man most definitely set off her sparks. He'd made that abundantly clear with his mind-and-bone-melting kiss in Yvonne's storage room over a week ago. When was the last time Carlie Beth had felt tempted to let a man touch her like that in a place where they could so easily be caught? Or touch her like that period.

Don't think about that too closely. You might find yourself counting back to—

Carlie Beth scrubbed her knuckles across her lips, but it didn't drive away the taste of his kiss—minty but not cool. *Blistering* was a much better description. Trying to shake off the memory, she drew in an unsteady breath.

Grif Steele was completely off-limits.

Because he was the one who'd changed her dreams of making art for a living.

He would do nothing but tear apart her life again.

Besides, for all she knew, he was back in Los Angeles.

Which meant it also wasn't fair to keep Aubrey from celebrating with her friends, and from what Carlie Beth had heard, today's party would be one for the record books. Which meant it shouldn't be a problem for her to stay out of Grif's sights even if he was still in town.

"Fine, but I need half an hour to get ready." She sighed and began to straighten her tools—hammers on the left side of her pegboard and tongs on the right. "Have you seen my favorite scrolling tongs?" she asked Aubrey.

"Nope. Maybe Austin borrowed them. Hurry and clean up, okay? I'll do your hair and makeup. Oh, and pick out your clothes." Aubrey's smile widened, making it obvious she'd stolen Carlie Beth's favorite—okay, her only—shade of lipstick.

From where Grif stood on the front porch steps, it was clear the sprawling two-story farmhouse and some of the other buildings on the old Tupelo Farm property needed a new coat of paint, but if he knew his mom, she'd have the place marshaled into order in no time. After all, she'd somehow managed to not only move in but also plant whisky barrels of daffodils and those little purple flowers in a week. And that was over and above organizing a community get-together.

He angled away from the house to look across the lawn, where it appeared as if the entire town of Steele Ridge and the rest of Haywood County had turned out for his mom's housewarming party. He shouldn't be surprised. His mom could be incredibly *persuasive* in her sweet, Southern way.

But she rarely had to turn that brand of persuasion on anyone but her own kids. Everyone else tripped over themselves to do Miss Joan's bidding. Hell, who was he kidding? Her kids did, too.

She'd been a giver their whole lives, and it was about damn time someone gave back to her. Both he and Jonah had offered to buy her a house more than once over the past ten years, but she'd always said no, thank you. Until the town had gotten itself into a bind and needed to unload the twenty thousand acres with his mom's dream house sitting on it.

What she would've given to raise her kids in a place this size instead of the three-bedroom ranch-style house with a basement they'd converted into what his mom called the Boxing Ring. That thousand square feet of space was probably the only thing that had saved everyone's sanity, especially on cold winter days when restlessness set in.

And there was his mom, socializing in the crowd. As she chatted it up, her short silver-shot hairdo gleamed in the sunlight. He'd bet all the money in his wallet she would talk to every person before the afternoon was over. She was heading into her seventh decade of life, but she was as active as she'd been when she was younger.

"Ten to one she calls everyone by their name."

He glanced over to find his younger sister Evie standing at his elbow. Her dark hair fell in thick waves over her shoulders, and her blue eyes were warm with amusement. He threw an arm around her shoulders and pulled her in to his side. "Nuh-uh. That's a sucker's bet."

"You know she's in hog heaven."

"Speaking of, she actually let me buy the pig we've got on the pit."

Evie inclined her head toward the farmhouse. "What's she gonna do with this big ol' place?"

Right now, she'd filled it with her grown sons, with a bedroom set aside for Evie's weekend visits from college. "Turn it into a bed-and-breakfast?"

Evie laughed. "Can you imagine how much she'd feed her guests? If Mom had her way, it would be a bed and breakfast, lunch, and supper. Maybe Hog Heaven would be the perfect name." Her face sobered, and she looked up at him. "Do you know if Dad's stopped by?"

Grif's gut tightened the way it did any time someone mentioned Eddy Steele. And if his dad actually showed up, Grif's gut normally tied itself into a noose. "Not since I've been in town."

"Is she upset about that?"

He sighed. "If she is, she hasn't said."

"And she won't."

Their parents had been living this weird lifestyle for years. One day, their dad up and left the house and didn't come home that evening. After a week, their mom had been frantic, and the sheriff organized a manhunt. They'd found Eddy Steele holed up in a ramshackle cabin about five miles outside town. Since that time, he'd come and gone as he pleased. Sometimes he'd paid the bills. Sometimes he hadn't. Their dad's lack of reliability was the reason Britt, as the oldest of the kids, had never left town.

None of them had trusted that their dad would follow through and take care of their mom, but Britt had been the one who'd shouldered the responsibility. He'd acted as if it was no heavier than shrugging on a down coat rated for forty degrees. But Grif knew staying here had cost him.

From where he and Evie stood on the porch steps, he continued scanning the crowd.

She poked him in the side. "Who're you looking for?"

"Do you know Carlie Beth Parrish?"

"Of course." She wiggled her right arm, where an iron snake wrapped three times around her wrist and laid its head against the back of her hand. "She made this in the forge behind her house. Her jewelry is amazing."

"So she's making a living from blacksmithing?" That night years ago, she was just back from her apprenticeship and glowing with the joy and potential of it all. She'd been like a sunrise—warm and promising— in his arms. He couldn't have kept his hands off her even if he'd tried.

No more than he'd been able to keep them off her last weekend.

Her touch had done something to him—lured him in, yanked him around, and laid him flat. But he wasn't the kind of guy who dated moms. That was stickier than the La Brea tar pits.

"Not from the jewelry. Even if tourism was hopping, Yvonne is the only one in town who carries her work. Carlie Beth is in decent demand from land owners, though. Repairs a lot of fences and does other welding work. What's got you so interested?"

"Ran into her the other night at Triple B. When did she get divorced?"

"What do you mean?"

"Yvonne mentioned Carlie Beth has a daughter. Guess she ended up settling down with someone local." Strange, since she'd had such big plans to get her work into galleries all those years ago. And it sure didn't explain why thinking of her with some unambitious good ol' boy burned him up inside. Carlie Beth was the kind of woman who deserved a good life. A successful life.

Maybe he was just mad that she'd apparently settled.

"Far as I know, she's never been married."

"But she has a daughter."

Evie laughed and punched him in the arm. "Aw, Griffy, do I need to give you a basic biology lesson? We all know what Mrs. Van Dyke used to tell us in Sunday school, but"—she lowered her voice—"babies aren't actually dropped from heaven. You see, when a man puts his pen—"

"Shut it, Evie." He did not want to think about what man had put his *pen* close enough to Carlie Beth to get her pregnant.

Fuck, he was an idiot.

Grif looked out over the lawn only to see people flocking around Jonah like he was the winningest quarterback in NFL history. "What the hell is going on with him?"

Her brow wrinkling, Evie rose to her tiptoes to get a better look. "No way."

"No way, what?"

"It looks like people are asking to take pictures with him. Now it'll take a sledgehammer to get Jonah's fat head back in the house."

Grif grinned at his sister. Jonah still bitched from time to time that his place as the rightful baby of the family had been stolen by Evie the Usurper, but the Steele family wouldn't be the same without her quick wit and smart-ass mouth. "I missed you, kid."

"How many times do I have to tell you lunkheads that I'm not a kid? And yes, even though all four of you aggravate me until my hair stands on end, I miss you when you're not home."

Home?

This town hadn't been home since he'd tossed a bag into his fourth-hand Ford Taurus and pointed the damn thing west fifteen years ago. One of the best days of his life was when he'd finally traded in that POS for a Mercedes coupe at the dealership in Beverly Hills.

Catching sight of Maggie in the crowd on the lawn, Grif waved her over to the porch and said to Evie, "Can you give us a minute?"

Her blue eyes narrowed, but she gave him a final hug and took the steps into the yard.

"Cornhole's just about to start," Maggie grumbled. "I don't want to get replaced."

"It'll wait a minute."

"Jonah paired you with Reid."

Grif groaned. "I thought this was supposed to be a laid-back, fun get-together. I wouldn't be surprised if Reid plays corn hole with an Uzi."

"Lucky for you, your partner throws from the opposite board."

"Easier for him to gun me down. And speaking of violence, any more word on Darden's header down the stairs?"

"Why all the interest in a guy you didn't know?"

"I got to know him when he slapped Carlie Beth's ass. Have you found out anything more?"

"Apparently, a couple of Roy's neighbors remember hearing someone knocking on his door earlier that evening."

"Anyone get a look at his visitor?"

"He lived over at Shady Pines. That's the kind of apartment complex where you mind your own damn business, so no."

"Something about this whole thing strikes me as off."

Maggie's pat to his cheek was, in reality, more of a one-two slap. "Remind me to consult you once you get your law enforcement certification. Now, Jonah said you're playing corn hole on the first set of boards under the white oak tree, so you'd better get your ass over there."

A quick stop at one of the beer kegs, then Grif made his way over toward the tree and what looked like two new corn hole boards. They were made from pine and painted with the gray outline of three overlapping mountains. The words *Steele Ridge* were printed below the mountains, and everything was sealed with a glossy lacquer.

Those bitches were gonna play fast.

Grif stooped down and picked up a bag, tossed it in the air, let it drop, and measured its weight in his palm.

Then the force of a sledgehammer rammed him between the shoulders, and he staggered under the blow. He turned to find Reid—aka the sledgehammer— sneering at him. "Who the hell wears country-club clothes to a barbecue?"

Grif straightened his polo collar and took in his

brother's party attire of T-shirt and cargo shorts. "Someone who gives a shit what he looks like."

Reid chuckled. "Hey, if you think a pink shirt and pussy shoes can get it done, then bring it on."

Pussy shoes? He'd dropped a cool grand on his black loafers. Reid had probably stomped into a sporting goods store and tossed down a couple of twenties for those work boots he was wearing. "You do realize we're on the same team, right?"

Reid huffed. "Told Jonah I wanted Britt."

This. This was only one of the reasons Grif didn't belong in North Carolina anymore. Somewhere along the way, he'd acquired a little style, a little class. Unlike Mr. Neanderthal here. "I'm more than happy to trade you to him."

"Aw, don't get your Victoria's Secret thong in a wad, pretty boy. I'm just giving you a hard time."

Yeah, normally Reid was a little rough-edged, bordering on totally inappropriate. But since he'd recently blown out his knee, his asshole quotient had shot into the stratosphere. "Where *is* Britt?"

"Jonah's probably having to pull him out of a treehouse in the woods."

"Is this bracket number one?" A young female voice cut into their conversation.

"Sure is, sweetheart." Reid turned on the charm as they both looked down at the girl with red hair.

Her tentative smile widened, revealing silver-and-pink braces. "Cool. I'm Mr. Britt's partner."

She was a little bitty thing, probably no more than eleven. No way would Jonah have paired her with three grown men, especially not his brothers. Grif said, "Looks like there's been a mistake. Maybe we should walk over and check the pairings. I know Jonah put together a special kids' bracket."

The girl drew herself up tall, but she still didn't come to Grif's shoulder. "I'm not a kid."

He looked closer, noticed a touch of lipstick and blush

on her innocent face. "Maybe not, but…" Spotting Jonah strolling by, Grif called out to him, "Hey, I think this young lady is lost. Maybe you assigned her to bracket one in the ki…uh…youth game."

Jonah glanced their way and said cheerfully, "Hey there, Aubrey. These two morons giving you a hard time?"

Her red-blond brows went sky-high. "They want me to play with the kids."

Jonah's smile took on an evil edge. "Well, all the other boards are booked up, so you'll just have to try to hang with the big boys."

Aubrey's lips also curved into an expression that spelled trouble, and she sighed dramatically. "I'll do my best."

Jonah gave them all a smart-ass salute and walked the other way. A couple minutes later, Britt finally showed up. He and Reid took their places by one board while Grif and Aubrey headed toward the other. "How about a few warm-up tosses?" he asked her.

Those brows rose again. "If you feel like you need it."

By God, he liked this girl. "Aubrey, how old are you?"

She gave him a sassy wink. "Old enough to play with the big boys."

They'd just see about that.

CHAPTER SEVEN

THE GAME STARTED WITH A passable toss by Britt, with his first corn hole bag hitting the slick board, sliding to the back edge, and clinging there like someone sharing a mattress with a bed hog. Not surprisingly, Reid's first throw dethroned Britt's bag through force alone. When their showdown was over, the score was a meager one to zero, with Reid and Grif in the lead.

Grif glanced at Aubrey. "Sorry about that."

"My mom says you shouldn't ever apologize for being good at something."

"Aubrey, I like your style." Oh, yeah, he liked this girl. A lot. Too bad he didn't date moms, because if the kid was this feisty, her mother was probably a crackerjack, too.

Assuming, of course, there was no Mr. Crackerjack.

"You say that now, but you haven't seen me throw yet. Don't forget we're enemies."

Lord, he could never be enemies with a girl this cute. Maybe kids weren't as baffling as he'd thought. His grin was wide as he sighted on the far board, smoothed out his arm rhythm, took a couple of steps and threw. His white bag thunked solidly to the board but missed the hole by a few inches.

She patted his arm in mock-sympathy, much like Evie had done a million times. "Don't feel bad." Then she ignored him, her complete attention thirty feet away. She let her own light blue bag fly and it cut through the air like a knife headed directly where she'd aimed. And damned if it didn't hit the board, careen into his bag, sending it to the ground, and veer into the hole like she'd just hit a bank shot on a pool table.

"Nice luck," he muttered.

"Not luck. Skill."

Yeah, Aubrey's skill became damn apparent over the next twenty minutes. She and Britt were up nineteen to twelve, and Grif could all but see the steam whirling up from Reid's ears. He finally raised his arm and yelled, "Beer break! Grif, with me."

"Back in a sec," Grif told Aubrey.

"Take all the time you need," she said sweetly.

He and Reid stalked over to the keg. "What the hell?" Reid demanded. "I know you don't want to hurt that little girl's feelings, but if you throw this game, we're out. This is a single elimination tournament. And I'll be damned if Britt is gonna beat us. You need to start playing like a man."

"Me throwing the game? You're the one who couldn't make the bag in the hole if it was the size of a goal post."

"Nine of those twelve points are mine," he growled.

On his way back to the game, Grif rummaged through a cooler and scooped out a can of orange soda for Aubrey. He smiled and held it out to her. "Thought you might need something, too."

"Thanks," she said, clicking open the top. "How did you know this was my favorite?"

He'd had no idea, but had chosen it because he'd always loved orange sodas when he was a kid. But he tapped his temple. "ESP."

She giggled and set her drink aside. "Thank you, but I'm still gonna beat you."

Game. On.

It wasn't fair. In fact, it was downright low, but just as Aubrey was about to toss the next time, Grif said, "So tell me about boys."

But her aim was as true as ever, and her bag landed and slid into the hole like Ichiro Suzuki stealing third base. "What do you want to know?"

"Do you date?"

She gave him a look girls must be taught at birth, the one where they cut their eyes to one side in exasperation.

"My advice? Stay as far away from guys for as long as possible. You can't trust them."

"Aren't you a guy?"

"Which is exactly the reason I know what I'm talking about." Yeah, because if he ever got his hands on Carlie Beth again, he couldn't be trusted not to take her on a trip down Memory Lane. A very hot, sweaty trip. "In fact, I should probably sit down with your mom, tell her you shouldn't date until you're thirty. Maybe forty. What's your last name?"

"Uh-uh," she said, tossing again and landing every damn bag in the hole. Twenty-one to twelve. She turned to him and swiped her palms against one another in victory. "Everyone says you're a charmer, but I'm not stupid."

"This is a small town," he shot back, realizing he'd been having so much fun that he hadn't thought about LA or his clients in hours, much less reserved a flight back west. "I'll find out who you belong to."

"Let's hope you're better at that than you are at corn hole." Her grin was so cheeky Grif couldn't help but grab her and pull her in for a hug.

As soon as Aubrey's corn hole game was over, Carlie Beth cornered her daughter near the dessert table, filled with goodies her stomach had been too upset to accept. And that was a shame because Yvonne had brought her famous lemon poke cake. But when Carlie Beth had spied Aubrey and Grif playing corn hole and chatting like they knew one another, her appetite had skedaddled. "It's time for us to get home."

A bite of pecan pie halfway to her mouth, Aubrey froze. "What?"

"I have some projects I need to finish in the forge."

"Mr. Britt and I won the corn hole game."

"Congratulations."

"No, Mom. This is a tournament. I can't leave or we'll have to forfeit. We could win this whole thing, and the prize is a hundred bucks."

Shoot. And that was quite a motivation for a girl Aubrey's age.

But Carlie Beth stood to lose way more than money. "What if I told you that you could have that makeover slumber party you've been begging for?"

"Are you serious?"

As serious as she'd ever been in her life. She might not have a clue how to do makeovers for half a dozen girls who were dying to be full-fledged women, but maybe Randi could help her figure it out. On the cheap. "Sure."

Aubrey's eyes narrowed. "Why now?"

Oh, her girl was no dummy. Sharp as an upholstery tack, as Carlie Beth's mom would say. But Carlie Beth tried to make her shrug casual. "You've been asking for a while. Your grades were good on your last report card—"

"They're good *every* report card."

"—and it's getting closer to the end of the school year, so it's perfect timing."

"Can we order pizza?"

"As many as you want."

"And stay up all night?"

Internally, Carlie Beth winced. She'd need a case of Red Bull to keep up, but that was a small price to pay. "As late as you can stay awake."

"Can I ask Miss May to bake cupcakes?"

When Carlie Beth had become pregnant, her mother had claimed she was too young to be a grandmother.

Instead of allowing Aubrey to call her Grandma or Nana or Mimi, she'd insisted that her granddaughter refer to her the way she would any other familiar adult, adding Miss to her first name. Once Aubrey was born, her mom had been captivated with her in a way she'd never been with Carlie Beth, but she hadn't compromised on the name. "Absolutely, but the decision is up to her."

Aubrey's eyes gleamed with sly avarice. "And we can watch back-to-back movies?"

"I don't see why not." Carlie Beth sensed her mistake as soon as the words were out of her mouth. "But they have to be appropr—"

Aubrey grinned and executed a victorious hair flip. "*Magic Mike XXL,* here we come!"

Carlie Beth grabbed the plate from Aubrey's hand and shoveled in some pie. God help her, if Grif Steele didn't leave town soon, she'd be the size of Dave's barn.

Grif dropped down on the porch swing beside his mother and took a sip of his beer. At least his consolation prize was cold and topped with the perfect head.

She patted his leg sympathetically. "Tough game."

"Reid probably won't talk to me for weeks."

"You say that like it's a bad thing."

Grif laughed, blowing some of the foam out of his cup. "Have I ever mentioned what a smart lady you are?"

She took a sip from her own cup of—if he had to guess—sweet tea. She wasn't a teetotaler, but she wasn't much of a beer drinker. "I managed to raise six relatively intelligent and well-adjusted children, didn't I?"

Grif wouldn't comment on the sixth, the one who was living a life none of them agreed with. Instead, he joked, "You can't be blamed for the faulty one. We'll lay Reid on Dad's shoulders."

She sighed. "Those two stubborn men do remind me of one another."

Why he'd brought up his dad, another family member he really had no interest in discussing, Grif wasn't sure. "You put together a nice party."

"You sure looked like you were enjoying yourself out there playing corn hole. Maybe small-town life still suits you."

Like hell. "Just doing my job."

"As the new city manager, you mean?"

Now he was the one to heave out air. "It's only temporary. Jonah was smart enough that he only agreed to *provide* a city manager. The contract didn't name me specifically."

"But you would be the best choice, hands down."

"You have to say that. You're my mother."

"So?"

"So, you also thought I built the best pinewood derby car the Boy Scouts had ever seen, and that thing was a heap of crap. I've never felt so betrayed in all my life." Which was total bullshit and they both knew it. He hadn't understood real betrayal until the Madison Henry incident a few months ago. While he'd been embroiled in the whole thing, he hadn't had time to feel the deceit, only the shell shock. But once he'd been cleared, the bone-deep sickness over his stupidity had set in and refused to leave.

His mom's eyes went soft, with either nostalgia or sympathy—he wasn't sure which, but was sure he didn't want to know—and she gripped his hand in hers. "You have plenty of self-confidence now, so there's no need for me to stretch the truth. And the truth is this town needs you."

"There are plenty of people more skilled at running a city than I am. I know nothing about it, but I can find someone who does. In fact, I've already done phone interviews with four candidates."

"But you know everything about this community, about these people."

He rubbed at his forehead hard enough to permanently crease the skin. "Why does everyone seem to have forgotten I already have a job? One that's a couple thousand miles away."

"And has that job made you happy recently?"

"It's not about being happy, it's about—"

"Being someone," she said. "You think I don't know why you moved so far from home? You wanted to make something of yourself. And honey, that's admirable, but you always assumed you couldn't be someone here."

"I like what I do." At least he used to before...

"She broke something inside you."

The sun was shining, his beer was cold, and he didn't want to talk about *her*. "I have clients who rely on me."

"Of course you do."

But his athletes spanned the continent from Seattle to Florida, which meant he could effectively run his business from anywhere with cell service, high-speed Internet, and a relatively close airport. Grif sipped his beer and let the thought roll through his mind. "Are you hinting at something?"

"What do you mean?"

"That I could leave LA and come back here?"

His mom tilted her head in that way she had, completely innocent on the outside, but packing a left hook on the inside. "Oh, now there's an idea."

Shit. He'd stepped in that one, hadn't he? But now he couldn't stop thinking about it. When what he should be thinking about was getting his ass back to the city where he'd built a successful business. Where he thought he'd built a life.

With her tea glass, his mom gestured toward the dessert table. "That Aubrey sure is a pretty one. She's always struck me as slightly familiar. Don't you think she looks a little like Evie?"

"No. Evie's hair is dark and Aubrey's is—" As he watched, Aubrey's face transformed into a thoughtful yet predatory expression Grif had seen on his sister's face hundreds of times. Every damn time she knew she had the upper hand with one of her brothers.

His focus shifted to the person Aubrey was giving that look to. Carlie Beth. Their hair was the same color.

No. Fucking. Way.

"What's Aubrey's last name?"

At his sharp tone, his mom gave him disapproving look. "Weren't you just chatting with her?"

"Yes, but I didn't feel the need to grill her about her entire life." Not like he did right this second.

"Well, she's standing there with her mother, just as plain as day. Of course, her last name is Parrish."

When he'd heard Carlie Beth had a daughter, he'd imagined a girl of eight to ten. Not one who was... "How old is she?"

His mom tapped her cheek. "Let's see. She's in eighth grade, so that would make her about fourteen."

Son of a motherfucking bitch.

CHAPTER EIGHT

GRIF SAT AT HIS MOM'S new dining table at the edge of her vast farmhouse kitchen. With the sun slanting in from the windows overlooking Tupelo Hill's backyard, the morning should've been cheerful.

But the coffee in front of him tasted bitter on his tongue.

He'd barely slept last night, but his insomnia had nothing to do with twisting himself into a full-size bed rather than his luxurious king back home. For at least six hours, he'd replayed the one time he and Carlie Beth had been together.

The steam from his cup curled up, reminding him of that hot humid night.

He remembered what Carlie Beth looked like out at the Rockin' Rio, a county-line dive bar that was no longer in business, probably because they hadn't been big on checking IDs. Happiness and confidence radiated from her as she danced to every song, shaking all her assets to a J Lo tune and swaying to Creed's "Arms Wide Open." Her long hair gleamed in the neon beer signs, and he was more than attracted. He was fascinated.

And so damned turned on he asked her to dance and then take a drive with him.

He didn't make an assumption about sex. If it happened, he would be happy. Very happy. But it was enough to have her snugged up against his side as they flew down backroads and she sang along with Destiny's Child on the radio.

When they drove down by the creek, she opened her purse and pulled out a couple of condoms. That was a first for him. The girls he'd been with before Carlie Beth had all relied on him for protection. She seemed so mature in comparison. He'd been blown away. And smug, thinking they were so damn worldly.

And so he'd done what any eighteen-year-old guy would've done. He'd gone for it.

They made love in the backseat of his car. They slid around on the fake leather seats and laughed like crazy. He finally braced his feet against the front seat and hauled Carlie Beth onto his lap. His hands, her ass. His tongue, her mouth. His mouth, her breast. When she orgasmed, her eyes shot wide, as if she hadn't expected something so damn good.

For the second round, he talked her into letting him toss a thin blanket over the hood, and they did it again out in the open. This time slowly, maybe even a little seriously. Her body was so soft, so right under his. When she cupped his face and kissed him, something inside his chest twisted.

But he breathed away the feeling.

All in all, it had been a hell of a send-off. He'd dropped her off at her own car around three in the morning, scooted back by his mom's house to shower and pack. After his mom cooked him a tearful breakfast of pancakes and bacon, he'd thrown a couple bags in his car and headed west on I-40. A little bleary-eyed from lack of sleep, but grinning like a possum from sexual satisfaction and excitement about his future.

That was the day his new life had started.

Now he wondered if he and Carlie Beth had also started a new life the night before.

Grif dropped his head into his hands and stared down at the dark pool in his cup, breathing in the acrid scent.

Think about this rationally, Steele. Do what you tell your clients to do. Don't get emotional. Think with your brain instead of your gut.

Damn hard for him to do lately.

So Aubrey Parrish had a couple of Evie's mannerisms. Girls who did the hair flip probably weren't one in a million, so that proved nothing.

The girl's hair, thick and the color of muted copper, was obviously inherited from her mother. What about her eyes? Why hadn't he looked at them more closely?

Probably because he'd had no reason to at the time. And once his mom had pointed out the likeness between Aubrey and Evie, Carlie Beth and her daughter left the party only minutes later. Which cheered Reid right up since he'd jumped ship over to Britt's team.

But Grif couldn't stop wondering if Carlie Beth had fucked him over. He squeezed his eyes closed, which only intensified the ache behind them. The Carlie Beth he'd known wasn't that kind of woman, but his judgment wasn't exactly accurate these days.

No birth control was fail-proof. And he'd been flying so high that night, it was possible he'd made a mistake somewhere along the way. Put the damn thing on too late. Not used enough care when he pulled out.

But even if...*if*...Aubrey Parrish was his...

Jesus, it was hard to even think the word.

Even if Aubrey was his daughter, it wasn't as if she needed him. Obviously, the Parrish women were doing just fine.

"Grif, what's wrong?"

He looked up to see his mom padding into the kitchen in her chenille bathrobe and a pair of ratty purple slippers. "What happened to the Natori nightgown and robe I bought you for your birthday?"

"Oh, well..." She glanced down and fussed with the tie that looked as if a band of hungry mice had chewed the ends. "I consider that special occasion nightwear, and I don't have many of those these days."

If Reid heard their mom say those words, he'd probably box himself in both ears, but it made Grif unbearably sad. She was still a beautiful, vibrant woman, and yet she had no one to share her life with. "Why don't you divorce him?"

"Why would I?"

"Maybe so you can move on?"

"Have you moved on? Made it past Madison—"

"We're not talking about her."

"We all do things in our own time, including you." She turned toward the coffeepot. "So let's talk about why you look like Eeyore and someone's hidden your tail from you."

He had to smile at that. Winnie the Pooh books had been favorites of all the Steele kids. "Just thinking about work." A big, fat-ass lie. One he'd probably go straight to hell for.

"I'm sorry if what I said yesterday put more pressure on you…"

"But?"

"But I'm not sorry I said it. We need you, Grif."

And apparently, he needed to stay in town, too. Didn't matter what the hell he'd been trying to convince himself of a few minutes ago. He could tell himself all he wanted that it didn't matter if Aubrey Parrish was his kid.

But he'd waded through enough bullshit in his life to recognize it. And that's exactly what he'd been throwing at himself.

Shooting a strained smile at his mom, he pushed himself away from the coffee that had burned holes in his stomach lining. "If that's the case, then I guess I'd better get to work."

"Now, Griffin Steele, you know this isn't exactly on

the up-and-up." Berna Schroder, the county registrar for the past twenty-five years, pushed her glasses on top of her silvery blond hair and peered closer at him over the counter.

"The Steele Ridge city manager should understand the demographics of the people he's serving." He shot her a confident smile.

"*Steele* Ridge, huh?"

Why wasn't Jonah the one fielding all the backlash about that? *Because he has you, sucker.* "Have you heard Jonah's planning to cover all the costs of the name change?"

"I like the return address stickers from that Labelocity place online."

With a few quick taps, he made a note on his phone. "Any particular color?"

Berna's mouth slid up in a little gotcha smile. "Gray would be appropriate, now wouldn't it? So about those birth certificates you're asking for...Why do you need information on the folks too young to even vote?"

"If I know nothing about our citizens, it sure would make it hard to act in their best interests. And children are our future." His smile was starting to feel brittle around the edges, so he shored it up.

"But I don't understand why you need individual birth certificates for all the kids born in certain months of a specific year." This was one of the many problems with a small town. People felt they had the God-given right to not only offer you their opinion, but also wage an argument about why they were right.

He leaned on the counter and scratched his head as if he was bewildered. "Ya know, I'm not a hundred percent sure either, but I read about some newfangled research method that some towns—ones that are doin' real good economically—are using to figure out how well off folks are gonna be in the future." If some of his California acquaintances heard him slide back into his deep hometown drawl, they would've looked at him as if he'd just married his sister. But if Grif was in Rome, then to get what he wanted he was damn well going to put on a toga.

"By looking at a bunch of teenagers and preteens?"

"Told ya I don't understand it. But heck, I'd juggle knives and walk over hot coals to help this town."

In the end, Berna printed out fifty birth certificates.

Soon after, he was sitting inside Louise with most of the pages littering her passenger seat, because the only one he gave a shit about was in his hand. The piece of paper could've erased the "Am I or am I not?" chant that had been playing on repeat in his head for the past sixteen hours.

But it didn't.

Because the little box for Father on Aubrey Laine Parrish's birth certificate was empty.

Which meant there had been no affidavit acknowledging paternity filed when she'd been born. And if he were a lesser man, he would wipe his hands clean and walk away.

Even though that box was blank, one that was filled blasted Grif with the force of a slapshot to the temple. Aubrey's birthday was March 28.

He'd already consulted his Google calendar and determined March 28 was exactly, to the day, thirty-eight weeks after July 5.

The date he and Carlie Beth had steamed up his car windows.

CHAPTER NINE

HOURS LATER, GRIF WAS BACK in his mother's kitchen, unpacking what had to be the millionth box of dishes. Where the hell had she kept all this stuff in the other house? With a gravy boat and serving platter in his arms, he stomped over to a cabinet and shoved them inside.

From the corner of his eye, he caught his mom's warning look at how roughly he was treating her precious items, but it did nothing but stir up the anger that had been simmering under his skin all day. He went back to the box and yanked out a newspaper-wrapped blob. He set it on the countertop and heard a crunch as something inside gave way.

Shit.

He'd temporarily forgotten his mom's new countertops were made of unforgiving tile.

"Griffin Fletcher Steele." His mom marched in his direction, her mouth also unforgiving. "My household goods might not mean much to you, but I would expect you to be careful." She carefully peeled away the paper to reveal a squatty china teapot decorated with winding roses and latticework. A crack trailed up its side and one of its delicate feet was missing.

Not just shit. Triple shit.

"Mom, I'm sorry."

She just shook her head, but he could see the tears quickly overtaking her eyes. And rightfully so. That teapot had been her grandmother's and was given to her when she married. It had always held the place of honor in her small china cabinet.

"I'll—"

"Don't." She pointed at him with the killer Mom finger. When they were kids, he and his brothers had sworn that thing was more powerful than an AK-47. "Don't you dare say you'll buy me another one. There isn't another one of these anywhere in the world."

He started to reach for the bundle of paper and broken fragments, but she elbowed him out of the way. "I'd thank you not to touch it again."

His chest tight with regret and shame, feelings he couldn't completely attribute to a cracked teapot, he turned back to the box to continue unpacking. It didn't matter what was going on with him. He shouldn't take his rage out on his mother. Because she certainly wasn't the one to blame here. Before he could reach inside again, she said, "You know, I don't think I need more help."

"Mom, I said I was—"

"You're obviously stewing over something. I don't suppose you want to tell me what it is?"

His jaw clenched hard enough that it felt as though his molars were melding together.

"Then get out."

"What?"

"Until you deal with whatever's got you all sideways, you're no use to me. Why don't you find your brothers and go outside to find a way to work it off?"

He laughed, but the sound came out strangled. "Mom, I'm in my thirties. Are you seriously telling me to go outside and play?"

She used the AK-47 finger to jab toward the back door. "Be glad I'm not telling you to go outside and play in the street. Now get. And don't come back inside until you can control yourself.

"Yes, ma'am." It took every bit of gumption Grif had not to hang his head and slink outside. He forced himself to look straight forward and keep his shoulders back.

Maybe he should sneak upstairs and change into shorts to take on the sports complex's climbing wall. He glanced back through the screen door to find his mom glaring at him. No, climbing wasn't an option tonight.

If his adversaries only knew his Achilles' heel, they'd sit Joan Steele opposite him at the bargaining table every time.

At the edge of the porch sat a gray metal trashcan Grif hadn't laid eyes on in at least ten years. He walked over and flipped open the lid to expose a jumble of well-used and well-loved weapons. On the top layer, he spotted a red Nerf Centurion, a jumbo-sized slingshot, and a set of cap guns still in their fake leather holsters. He hefted the Nerf and dug around for the gun's magazine. Another exploration to the bottom of the trashcan scored him a handful of spongey ammo.

Oh, yeah. This was exactly what he needed.

He pulled out his phone and sent an SOS text to his brothers. *Need you on Mom's back porch ASAP.*

Less than ten minutes later, Jonah, Reid, and Britt were all at the house.

"What do we need to fix?" Britt asked. "Plumbing or electrical problems? Whatever it is, I'll take care of it."

Of course he would. Martyr Britt.

"Nothing's broken." Grif winced inside, because that wasn't technically true. Not after what he'd done to the teapot. Maybe he could find a way to have it fixed. After he took down his brothers.

"This have something to do with the town manager thing?" Jonah asked. "Man, I know you aren't keen to take this on, but—"

"I can't even think about that right now," Grif interrupted.

"Then why the hell did you drag me away from researching security systems for the complex?" Reid barked.

Grif waved a hand toward the trashcan. "Because of this."

Reid wandered over and peered inside. "What? Did our precious Grif find a snake inside and need a real man to take care of it for him?"

"Funny, Ape Man," Grif shot back. "How long's it been since y'all saw what's inside there?"

While his three halfwit brothers were busy gazing down into the stash of weapons, Grif positioned himself behind a lounge chair where he'd hidden the big Nerf gun. He grabbed it and let loose on them.

Reid spun around, automatically reaching toward his belt for the weapon he was used to carrying.

Predictably, Britt used his surroundings as cover and ducked behind their mom's potted ferns.

Jonah snatched up the trashcan lid and used it like a shield from a medieval video game.

Before they could catch their balance, Grif took off around the side of the house to the sounds of violent cussing. Less than half a minute later, feet pounded behind him and he sprinted for the tree line.

"You're going down," Reid yelled.

"When jackasses climb trees," Grif hollered back. Once inside the protective hardwoods and pines, he scanned for a decent place to lie low and pick them off one by one.

Wait a sec. Maybe low wasn't the answer. High was. He looped the gun's strap over his head and shoulder and rested it against his back. Then he found a sugar maple to climb that provided reasonable access and superior cover.

His brothers took their time, and when they invaded the forest, they assembled themselves into a miniature

V-formation with Reid at the point. He was even using hand signals to command his two ragtag troops.

Okay, *ragtag* was wishful thinking. Both Britt and Jonah looked just as stone-faced and serious about pursuit as Reid. They'd armed themselves well, with Britt carrying the bow and arrow, bad news because he was an ace shot with that thing. Jonah held the slingshot and his shorts pockets were bulging with some kind of ammo. Reid, of course, had found an actual pellet gun. He made the sign to spread out and their little hunting party increased the space between them. With their stealthy movements, they eased right under the tree where Grif was waiting.

His hands itched to pull the trigger, but it wouldn't be much fun if the game was over this quickly. He'd let them wander around trying to find their asses for a few minutes. Then he'd climb down and ambush them from the rear. He twisted in the tree to keep eyes on them, slipped on the bark and almost lost his footing. "Son of a bitch," he breathed, his heart hammering and his hands sweating.

But apparently, his little snafu wasn't enough to catch his brothers' attention, because not one of them glanced back.

Grif adjusted his death grip on the tree trunk and worked to untangle his feet from one another. As he was starting the climb down, an arrow whizzed by his right ear. What the fuck? He probably looked like a clumsy sloth, but he somehow got himself turned around, his feet braced on two different branches, and gazed down at the forest floor.

Nothing.

"I know you're out there."

Again, nothing.

Those three weren't idiots. And as good a soldier as Reid was, Britt could still probably out-silence him. The guy didn't talk to humans unless forced.

If someone was going to make a mistake, it would be Baby Billionaire.

"Jonah, I bet all they left you with was that crappy-ass slingshot. Do you remember when you were a kid and you wanted that blowback air pistol? But Reid got the new one, and you got the hand-me-down. That must've really sucked, man."

Thwap. Something hit Grif dead center in the solar plexus. Not three seconds later, he was hit again, this time in the left temple.

"What the fuck?" he roared, rubbing his head where his skin was still stinging and sported a tiny indention. Then a barrage of blunted arrows and other stinging projectiles came his way, hitting him in the body and face. He hung onto a limb with one hand and tried to bat the bullets away with his other. He caught one and opened up his fist to check it out. "Which one of you assholes is shooting whole pecans?" That had to be what had poked a hole in his head.

"Guess this crappy-ass slingshot isn't so crappy after all," Jonah called.

"Asshole, you're surrounded," Reid yelled, laughter riding piggyback on his words. "You might as well get your ass outta that tree."

For some reason, his brothers' jeering made Grif wish for a magazine full of real bullets. He let loose a battle cry and jumped. He hit the forest floor with a jarring thud, rolled, and came up to a kneel. Then he shot the fuck out of his brothers until his toy gun clicked with the hollow sound that indicated it was empty. And yet, he just kept jacking with the trigger as though the damn gun would somehow reload itself.

With open mouths, Reid and the others stared at him like he'd transformed into Bigfoot.

Jonah shook his head in mock sympathy. "Dude, if I'd known the pressure of managing a metropolis the size of Steele Ridge would push you over the edge, I never would've asked. I guess some people just aren't cut out for that kind of responsibility."

"Responsibility?" Grif tossed aside his now useless

gun when what he really wanted to do was break it apart piece by piece and crush it all into the dirt. "You want to talk about responsibility? I'm pretty sure the ultimate responsibility is finding out you have a kid about fourteen years too late."

CHAPTER TEN

GRIF'S BREATH SAWED IN AND out of his burning throat. *Fuck, fuck, fuck.* He hadn't meant to say that.

"What did you just say?" Britt asked in his quiet, steady way.

Throwing his arms wide, Grif launched himself backward to lie on the ground and stare up into the trees. "Nothing."

His brothers gingerly laid their weapons aside. Slow and easy as if they were afraid he would make a crazy move for real.

They circled around him, looking down with the kind of concern their mom smothered them with when they were sick or heartbroken or otherwise laid out flat. One by one, they took a knee, their focus never wavering from him. If weighty stares alone could compel a man to spill his guts, his brothers would be a crack inquisition team.

"Are you saying you have a kid?" Reid demanded. "How the hell did that happen?"

That almost—almost—made Grif smile for the first time since he'd walked out of the Registrar's office.

Britt shot Reid an amused look. "Even I know the answer to that question."

"You know what I mean."

Unable to stand being at a disadvantage against his

brothers for another second, Grif pushed himself to a sitting position and braced his back against the tree he'd kamikazed out of. "The father section on the birth certificate is blank, but I know. I *know*."

"Look, if you need to go back to LA to handle some personal business, I'm sure everyone in town would understand." Reid hooked a thumb in Jonah's direction. "Even His Highness Baby Billionaire himself."

Now Britt's amused look transformed into a disgusted head shake. "Did you hear what he said? Fourteen years. That would've been some damn fast work on his part."

Reid's attention lasered in on Grif. "Are you saying you have a kid in North Carolina?"

Shit. It wasn't as if he'd be able to keep it a secret from anyone in town, especially not his family, if he decided to do something about all this. "Aubrey Parrish."

Reid rocked back and landed on his ass in the leaves and pine straw. "Whoa." He rubbed his chin and studied Grif. "Carlie Beth always was hot, but I didn't realize you and she had a thing."

"It wasn't a thing," he said. "It was one night."

One hot, sweaty, fun, sweet night. And God, if he let himself go back over those memories again, he might talk himself out of his mad. And by God, he deserved to be pissed at Carlie Beth.

A frown encompassed Britt's whole face. "I thought I taught the three of you better than to go in unwrapped. Hell, Grif, if not for yourself, then for the girl's safety."

"I don't need a fucking lecture about safe sex. And for your information, we used protection."

"What are you gonna do?" Reid asked.

"Hell if I know."

"Did Carlie Beth say something to you yesterday at the party?"

Grif laughed, the bitter sound drifting up to the treetops. "No."

But her behavior the past few times he'd seen her sure

made a hell of a lot more sense now. The way she'd bolted from his mom's birthday party a few months ago. The way she seemed to skittishly avoid him. The reason she was so fucking hesitant to start a little something up with him, even after that synapses-sizzling kiss.

And possibly even more gut-burning was the fact that he hadn't been exactly gung-ho to get busy with a mother.

Not just *a* mother. The mother of his kid.

His.

Goddammit.

"Aubrey sure is a pretty little thing," Reid offered. "Hair like her mom's and from what I saw yesterday, ego like her dad's."

God, Grif didn't know whether to be proud or scared shitless. "I don't know a damn thing about being a parent."

Jonah hooked a thumb to his left. "Just watch Saint Britt. He's got it down pat."

"Think she's dating yet?" Reid mused.

"For Jesus' sake. She's fourteen." Yeah, now that he knew Aubrey was most likely his daughter, asking about guys didn't seem so humorous.

"Hell, at fourteen, I had Susan McMichael's shirt off behind the high-school football field locker room."

Grif's stomach turned into a trash compactor. "If I find out any guy has taken off Aubrey's shirt, I will frog-march his ass out behind the locker room and teach him the lesson of his life."

"Would that really be your place?" Britt asked. "Have you thought that maybe the reason Carlie Beth never told you was because she didn't want you to be involved in Aubrey's life?"

Even though he hadn't been able to get Britt's words

out of his head all night, this morning Grif stood staring at Carlie Beth's small frame house. From the outside, it looked about thirteen hundred square feet. Probably a two-bed, two-bath. Maybe a small third bedroom. Although it was in decent shape, the trim around the windows could use a scrape and paint.

Maybe dressing like he was going into a boardroom had been overkill, but he adjusted his tie before climbing the porch steps. As he strode across the porch, one of the planks gave slightly under his shoe. He could fix that in a couple of hours.

Dammit, he was a decent guy. Responsible. Successful. Why wouldn't she want him involved if Aubrey was his daughter?

The house didn't have a doorbell, so he knocked hard on the storm door. It protected a wood door inset with eight panes of glass and latched with a scrolling iron pull knob. No doubt it was Carlie Beth's incredible work, but now that he knew what she'd done, he didn't want to admire her talent.

Several minutes ticked by.

He damn well knew she was here because a 1970s International Scout, the same thing she'd driven way back when, was parked in the one-car driveway. "Carlie Beth, open up. I need to talk to you."

Still no answer, and Grif's frustration climbed. Then his phone rang. Irrationally tempted to ignore it, Grif breathed and drew it out of his pocket to check the caller. Ice Athletic Wear.

Excellent. He needed a win today.

"This is Steele."

In less than ten minutes, he negotiated the final touches on Ian Brinkmann's endorsement deal. The Brick was about to be a few mil richer and all he had to do was stand around in Ice's sports boxers showing off his junk.

Yeah, that was a big win.

Phone back in his pocket, Grif started to knock on

Carlie Beth's door again, but remembered something Evie had said. Carlie Beth's forge was here at her house.

He jogged down the porch stairs and followed a crushed rock path around the side of the house. And there in the backyard was an ass-ugly gray metal building topped with a darker roof. The smoke curling from a metal chimney told him what he needed to know.

That and the open industrial-size overhead door.

Inside, Carlie Beth was bent over a metal table, her back to him. And a young man, probably in his late teens or early twenties, worked over an anvil, beating the hell out of a glowing piece of metal with a hammer. An old Dixie Chicks song blared from a grimy boombox in the corner. Something about them not being ready to make nice.

That should be his fucking theme song today.

The kid looked up from whatever he was beating on and caught sight of Grif. His face registered surprise, which quickly morphed into a dog-with-a-meaty-bone expression. But he waved in Carlie Beth's direction until he got her attention. She swung around, and Grif's breath stalled.

Why, he had no idea.

She was dressed in a thick—and he assumed fireproof—apron, gloves up to her biceps, and protective goggles. Her gorgeous hair was restrained in a ruthless braid and her face was smudged with black grime. A drop of sweat rolled off her chin and plunked to the hollow of her neck, only to disappear beneath the apron.

It must've been sheer fury that made him want to strip off that apron, rip away those goggles, and plop Carlie Beth down on one of her metal workbenches. The compulsion to yank off her work boots and pull off her jeans shuddered through him.

To hell with the playful lovemaking they'd shared all those years ago. He'd shove between her thighs and go at her hard. Screw her right here among her tools and the grime until she screamed. For mercy.

In surrender.

In satisfaction.

Carlie Beth set aside the tool she was holding and pushed her goggles to the top of her head, leaving pink indentions around her eyes that made her look like an adorable raccoon.

She's neither. So stop being a softheaded ass.

"We need to talk," he snapped at her. "Privately. So you might want to get rid of your boy toy."

"What did you just say?" Her words were slow and full of WTF.

The guy started toward Grif, all bowed up in the way only someone his age would think was smart or remotely intimidating. "Carlie Beth, do you want me to get rid of this—"

"Kid, I've got at least ten years and thousands of miles on you," Grif said, forcing casualness into his tone. "So unless you want your face sitting backward on your neck, I'd suggest you haul your skinny ass out the door and not come back for a good half hour."

"You can't tell me what—"

"Do it, Austin," Carlie Beth said.

The guy tossed his own eye protection on a table and stalked by Grif, glaring all the while. But he wasn't stupid enough to risk a shoulder sideswipe or some other aggressive asshole move.

Once he was gone, Grif turned back to Carlie Beth. Her mouth was drawn tight and her eyes were shooting something way more lethal than the pecans Jonah had pinged him with yesterday. "Do you want to tell me why you just waltzed in here and not only insulted me, but also threatened my apprentice?"

"Probably not any more than you want to tell me why you've hidden my daughter from me her entire life."

CHAPTER ELEVEN

CARLIE BETH'S JAW DROPPED. ACTUALLY released like a well-greased hinge. All these years, she'd protected the truth. Protected her daughter. Protected this man.

Grif's words hit her like bullets of accusation, slamming into her with the force of a hammer to the head. "How did you... Why would you..."

"I bet you were shitting kittens at my mom's birthday party, weren't you?" He wandered through her forge, his crisp moneyed scent trailing him. He finally stopped his walkabout and hefted a swage block. "Interesting how I've been back in town at least once a year for the past ten and hadn't seen you until a few months ago. And I sure as hell never caught sight of Aubrey. I assume that was one hundred percent on purpose."

"Grif, you don't understand—"

"Oh, I understand perfectly. Rather than sharing our daughter with me, you chose to leave Aubrey's birth certificate blank and let her go through life a bastard."

Bastard. The word thudded through Carlie Beth's head with the force of an anvil.

She looked down at the half-finished pot rack in front of her and remembered the hand-forged mobile she'd made Aubrey before she was born. The old baby spoons had clanked together with a pleasant ping.

Bastard.

How many times in the months after Aubrey's birth had Carlie Beth's mother said the same thing? "Is that what you really want, Carlie Elizabeth Parrish, for your baby to grow up without her proper last name? You need to track down whatever lowlife you made the unfortunate mistake of spreading your legs for and make him do right by you."

For a while, Carlie Beth had been able to dodge and duck her mother's snide comments and accusations about the state of her virtue by paying loving attention to Aubrey and taking care of her so well that no one—not even May Parrish—could fault her as a mother. But one day Aubrey was suffering from the croup, and Carlie Beth had been awake for thirty-six hours straight. She was sitting in a steamy bathroom trying to ease her daughter's seal-like barks when her mother barged in and looked down at her.

Her mother stood there, a Bible in one hand and her other on her hip. "What if this baby's come down with one of those genetic diseases? It's probably all the daddy's fault. And you don't know where to find the no-account loser. Maybe you don't even know who he is. Now, you're young, you're broke, and your baby could die."

Something sharp and ugly broke loose inside Carlie Beth, but she came slowly to her feet because Aubrey was finally—mercifully—asleep on her shoulder. "I know exactly who my daughter's father is. And I know where he lives. I would never jeopardize Aubrey's health, much less her life, if I thought he could help in some way."

Her mother's eyes squinted with disbelief. "If that's the truth, then why don't you go ask him for child support? That would sure help Aubrey out."

Carlie Beth stared at the King James version in her mother's hand and fought back the overwhelming need to yank the book from her and slap her with it. The dawning of that craziness was when she'd known she had to tell her mother the truth or she would never let the topic drop.

"If I tell you who Aubrey's father is, you have to swear on the Bible you're holding that you will never tell another soul. Not now, not tomorrow, not on your deathbed. Do you understand?"

Her mother's head drooped. "I knew it. He's in prison, isn't he?"

"No, Mama, he's in Los Angeles," she blurted out and immediately regretted it. Apparently, all the steam had made her loopy.

Her head whipped back up. "Are you saying this baby's daddy is Gr—"

"I told you not to say a word."

"Those Steele boys aren't exactly what I'd consider marriage material, but Joan is always carrying on about how well they're doing. Grif with that big fancy scholarship to play baseball at UCLA. Surely he has more than enough. You need to demand—"

"I will not ask Grif Steele for one thing." After all, what was the purpose in derailing both their futures when she could handle this situation on her own? She waved a hand through the steam hovering in the small room. "Aubrey and I are not suffering. My baby has a clean house, clean clothes, and nutritious food." Maybe Carlie Beth's life wasn't what she'd once imagined, but she was making it on her own, which gave her an incredible sense of pride. "I haven't asked the government for a dime, haven't asked you for a dime, and damn well won't ask him for a dime."

"There's no need to use foul language. But I bet you if Joan knew a thing about having a grandbaby, she would be over the moon. Maybe not at first, but once she got used to the idea. She'd also make sure that son of hers took care of his mistakes."

Ignoring her mother's *mistake* dig, Carlie Beth tried to breathe away the feeling of her heart squeezing at the mention of Grif's mom. Mrs. Steele was one of the kindest, most generous, least judgmental people she'd ever met. She hated keeping something so important from such a wonderful lady, but she had no choice. Mrs. Steele might delight in a grandbaby, but she would not appreciate Carlie Beth extinguishing her son's bright future. All of the Steeles were so proud of what he was doing out west. "I said you're not to tell anyone about Aubrey's father."

"Why in the world would I agree to—"

"Because you love Aubrey almost as much as I do, which is the only reason I put up with your narrow-minded ways. And if you don't keep your mouth shut, I will pack up my car with everything I own, put Aubrey in her car seat, and drive the hell out of Canyon Ridge. And once I'm gone, I can promise you I will never come back."

Her mother had never again mentioned Grif Steele's name, nor had she ever called Aubrey a bastard.

No one would ever call her that again, especially not her own father.

Carlie Beth tore her gaze off the half-finished pot rack in front of her and advanced on Grif until her filthy apron brushed the front of his fancy shirt. "Don't you dare use that word to describe my daughter."

He didn't flinch away from her and the grime all over her. "Don't you mean *our* daughter?"

The reality of what was truly happening to her crashed through her, and although she wanted to crumple in on herself, she couldn't afford to. Not in front of this man. Right now, he was angry that she'd taken something away from him, obviously bringing out the predator in him. If she let him glimpse the seed of guilt she'd harbored over the years, he'd somehow use it to his advantage. Better to soothe the animal than poke at him. "Look, if I'd planned to demand anything from you, I would've done it a long time ago, so if you're worried I'll ask you for something, you can stop."

"I have to assume no one else in town has figured all

this out. Otherwise, you could've never kept it this quiet."

"Only my mom."

"And she didn't chase me down with the business end of a sawed-off shotgun?"

Carlie Beth sighed. "She and I came to an agreement."

"What kind?"

"The kind where she keeps her mouth shut and I don't take her granddaughter to live somewhere else." Even though she'd threatened, it wouldn't have been easy. Carlie Beth probably would've had to give up blacksmithing altogether if she'd moved away. Here, she'd had enough help to juggle and make it work, even if she'd had to put aside art in the name of food.

She'd done everything she could for her daughter. Couldn't he understand that? Suddenly unable to handle the nearness and Grif's expensive scent for another second, she stepped away and busied herself straightening her tools.

"What about *my* mom?"

That pain she'd felt deep inside all those years ago pierced Carlie Beth again. "What about her?" But she knew. Of course, she knew what he was asking.

"Didn't you ever consider she might like to know she has a grandchild?"

"Yes. But how could I have done anything about it? It wasn't like I could confide in her and expect her to keep it to herself."

"Did you hate me that much?" His voice was low and scratchy.

She whirled around to find him standing in the same place, his face a picture of confused pain, making her want to go to him, smooth a hand over his cheek and soothe him. Which was ridiculous. Grif wasn't a man who needed anyone to make it all better for him. He had the big-city life, was living the dream while she'd been here raising his daughter.

"I didn't hate you at all." Sometimes, she might've

resented him, but she couldn't hate the man who'd given her the most important thing in her world. In fact, on her loneliest nights, she'd thought of Grif fondly, sometimes *way* more than fondly.

"Then why the *fuck* would you keep this from me?"

She laughed, a surprised little huff. "You were living in California."

"Last I checked, these two states are connected by things like airplanes, cell phones, and the Internet. It wasn't like I was living off the damn grid in a third-world country."

"If I'd called you a couple of months after you left here, telling you I was pregnant, what would you have done?"

His head dropped and he shoved his fingers into his artfully rumpled hair. "You never even gave me a chance to figure that out."

"The Steele boys might've been a little wild, but you always had a sense of right and wrong. You would've come home and married me."

"Which is exactly what most women would've wanted."

"I'm not most women."

"At the very least," he ground out, "I would've made sure my name was on that birth certificate. Made sure you and Aubrey were taken care of."

"I've taken care of us just fine. And my not telling you was for your own good. You wouldn't be a sports agent now and you probably would've lost your scholarship to college."

The violent tightening of his jaw made it obvious he was holding on to his emotions through sheer force of will. "There was no fucking scholarship."

"What?"

"I lied about the whole thing. If I was ever going to make something of myself, I had to get out of here. And I had to make my family think I had an all-expenses-paid ticket."

She waved a hand at his stylish clothes. "Then how did you—"

"I lied and I hustled. After I picked up my first client, I slammed my way through a couple of degrees at night while I grew my business."

"Do they know? Your family?"

"That I lied about attending UCLA? Yeah, I finally told them. Figured after I made a name for myself that it didn't matter anymore."

"Well, you couldn't have hustled that way here in Canyon Ridge. You probably would've hired on at one of the Christmas tree farms outside of town, making little more than minimum wage." And he'd been so bright, so smart, so ambitious that she hadn't been willing to sentence him to that life. "You should thank me."

"Thank you?" His lip arched up in what could only be called a snarl. "Does she even know I'm her dad?"

The set of his mouth told Carlie Beth it wasn't a good idea to point out that a father and a dad were two completely different concepts. A dad was someone who carried his little girl around on his shoulders, blew raspberries on her tummy, and kissed her boo-boos. A father was a biological concept.

And that's all there was between Aubrey and Grif—biology.

"No."

"What did you tell her?"

"That her father was someone I knew a long time ago, but that he doesn't live here anymore."

"And she just accepted that? 'Sorry, Aubrey, but your dad is a complete douchebag who just can't be bothered to be around.'"

Indignant anger kindled inside Carlie Beth. "I never once called you something so disrespectful. Honestly, after a few questions when she was little, the only time it came up was on special daddy-daughter occasions."

"And who stepped in for those occasions?"

"Grady, Randi's bartender at the Triple B."

"Were you sleeping with him?"

That hot feeling inside her flamed, and something

kept her from telling him Grady was happily married. "Is that any of your damn business?"

"I think it's my business to know the other men who've been a part of my daughter's life."

"God, Grif, it's seriously too late for this."

He moved in close, glared down at her with his now glacial eyes. "That, Carlie Beth, is where you're wrong. Even more wrong than you were to keep my daughter from me. Aubrey is a Steele. You've not only stolen that from her, but you've stolen her from my family. And I think you know that if there's one thing in this world I cannot abide, it's someone doing wrong by my family."

Like an instinctive shield, her eyes squeezed closed. His family? No, she couldn't afford for him to go down that path. Aubrey was *her* family. She slowly opened them again, trying to project sincerity toward him. "If I say I had your best interests at heart, can we pretend this conversation never happened? Just leave well enough alone?"

His laugh was as sharp and cold as the icicles that ringed her eaves every January. "If by *leave well enough alone* you mean me walking away and forgetting I have a daughter—a loving, breathing, beautiful daughter—then you have lost your mind." He reached into his pants pocket and took out his wallet. With the most deliberate movements Carlie Beth had ever witnessed, he opened it up and withdrew a piece of paper with one sharp fold down the middle. He placed it on a small clear space on her worktable and smoothed the crease, but Carlie Beth kept her focus on his face. On his intent and chilled expression.

"What is that?" she asked.

"It's the price of admission."

"What?"

He tapped the slip of paper, which finally drew her attention downward. It was a check. Made out to her. "Entry ticket."

"I don't understand."

"I figured I've missed approximately one hundred fifty-seven months of child support."

"Dammit, I don't want your money." She snatched up the piece of paper and held it out to him. "I never wanted anything from you."

His icy attention never shifted from her face and he didn't reach for the check. "I'm not asking you what you want. I'm telling you what you'll take."

"I don't need your money." She didn't need anything from him. Couldn't afford to.

"Then put it all in a college fund for Aubrey. I really don't give a shit."

"Wh...What are you saying?"

"That I will get to know my daughter."

"Are you trying to bribe me?"

"No." His smile was hard. "I'm telling you that if you don't take the money and give me access to my daughter that I will find another way. And believe me, if I take you to court for custody of Aubrey, you won't win. I've spent too many years spinning stories and negotiating. I always—*always*—come out on top. By the time I get done with you, you will be so broke, so broken, that you won't be able to buy a pack of peanuts in this town or anywhere else. Do you understand what I'm saying?"

Her stomach tightened at the cold determination she saw in his face. "You're blackmailing me."

"Sweetheart," he said softly. "Blackmail is when someone is demanding money, not forking it over. And I think you'll find I've been more than fair in paying back child support. Now, do you want to make this easy and tell Aubrey I'm her dad, or do you want *me* to break it to my daughter?"

"Mom, is what he said true?" a small voice said.

Carlie Beth's attention snapped to the doorway where

Aubrey stood with an expression of sheer betrayal painting her pretty face, her pink-and-green backpack sliding off one shoulder. One glance at Grif, who was standing there looking as if he was torn between hugging Aubrey or hitting Carlie Beth, told her he wasn't about to step in and make this easier for her.

And why should he? She had never once shared the responsibility of parenting.

Grif turned toward Aubrey, but Carlie Beth intercepted him before he could make a move in her daughter's direction. "Don't do this. Not now. Not while you're this angry. Give me some time with her."

"This isn't over," Grif said, his voice low so his words only touched Carlie Beth's ears. As he walked out the door, he laid a hand on Aubrey's shoulder and squeezed it before continuing on.

Aubrey whirled around, her bag thunking to the ground. "Wait! Mr. Steele...Dad...Wait!"

But he kept walking, down the path and around the house. Strolling out just like he had years ago. Only this time it was worse. Way worse.

Because this time he'd purposefully dropped a grenade into Carlie Beth's lap.

Asshole.

"Mom?" Aubrey's shoulders were slumped and her mouth was trembling. Looking as lost as she had the time she wandered off at an art festival in Asheville and became disoriented in a maze of stalls. When Carlie Beth found her ten minutes later, Aubrey had been going from person to person, asking if anyone knew her mommy. In her own five-year-old way, she'd handled it admirably. But another minute and she would've cracked, thrown her little body on the ground, and pitched a wall-eyed fit.

"Baby, we need to talk." Carlie Beth sighed and glanced down, finally looking at what was written on the check Grif had so carefully placed in front of her. The ham sandwich she'd wolfed down for lunch expanded in her gut, and she snatched up the paper to get a better look.

Six.

Hundred.

Thousand.

Suddenly the heat of her forge overwhelmed her. She shoved the check into her apron pocket and rushed for the door. "Let's sit outside," she said to Aubrey, grabbing her hand and pulling her out into the cooler spring air.

Carlie Beth gulped it down the way she'd guzzled ginger ale when she was pregnant. Like it was the only thing that could keep her alive and mildly sane.

They didn't make it to the back porch because Carlie Beth's legs gave out and she sank down on the edge of a brick planter filled with forsythia. She tried to project calm, but that was damn hard when her hands were shaking so badly.

One glance at her daughter and they shook even harder. Tears had not only welled up in Aubrey's eyes, but they'd also escaped, sluicing down her cheeks with a forlorn sluggishness that broke Carlie Beth's heart.

"Is Grif Steele my dad?" This time, Aubrey's question wasn't tentative. It was chock-full of the strength and chill of her father's last name.

"Yes."

"He was so nice when I met him at Miss Joan's the other day. Why would he just pretend he didn't have a family all this time? Didn't he love us?"

Love? What Carlie Beth and Grif had done that night wasn't driven by love. Fueled by exhilaration and attraction? Yes. She reached for Aubrey's hands, squeezed them in hers. "It was complicated."

"Complicated how? What's so hard about spending time with your kid? Plenty of my friend's parents are divorced. That doesn't keep their dads from doing stuff with them. He's obviously nothing like Miss Joan. He's an asshole."

Cringing at Aubrey's use of the word she'd mentally called him just minutes before, Carlie Beth scolded, "Aubrey Laine, that's unacceptable."

"You sound like Miss May."

If the situation weren't so serious, that accusation would make Carlie Beth gouge herself with the pointed end of a mill file. "It's not right to judge someone when you don't have all the facts, when you haven't walked in his shoes."

"Well, if he was a good guy, you would've told me about him a long time ago. After all, his family lives right here in town. I bet he's visited a million times."

Maybe not a million, but often enough that Carlie Beth could've made a different decision many times.

Aubrey scooted closer, the way she used to when she had a stomach ache and wanted the comfort of a storybook and Carlie Beth's arms. Unfortunately, the affectionate movement rustled Carlie Beth's apron, and Grif's check poked up from her pocket.

"Mom, what's that?" Aubrey plucked it out. Carlie Beth tried to grab the paper, but by the way her daughter's mouth dropped wide, the damage was already done. "Wh...Why did he write you a check for this much money? Is this hush money so we won't ever bother him again?"

As reluctant as she was to share Aubrey with him, she wouldn't let her believe her father was truly an uncaring bastard. "No, honey. Exactly the opposite. That's what he considers back child support."

"This is enough for a house. A lot of houses around this town. But why, after all this time, would he..." She trailed off as understanding must've dawned. Aubrey jumped to her feet and glared at Carlie Beth. "You never told him about me, did you? You never even gave him a chance to know me. To love me."

"Please understand—"

"No, I don't understand why you kept us apart. The only thing I understand is that *you're* the asshole."

CHAPTER TWELVE

WHEN GRIF AND REID STROLLED into the sports complex, it was clear that vandals had somehow jimmied the new doors and hit the place like demented spray-painting fairies. This time, they'd painted on the rock climbing wall—initials, dates, some poetry with questionable spelling. Jonah had already repaired the fire damage done to the reception area when the former city manager had tossed a Molotov cocktail inside the building not long ago, but obviously that hadn't been enough to dissuade kids from mucking around inside.

"Pretty soon, this building won't be worth a fraction of what it cost the city to put it up," Grif commented, just to rile Reid.

"I've narrowed it down to three different securities systems. I just need a little more time to decide on the best."

Grif slapped him on the back. "Think of it this way. Jonah's little project is keeping you off the streets and out of trouble."

"The mighty didn't just jump down from a damn truck," Reid grumbled. "The mighty took a header off a cliff."

"Stop your bitching. You know you love stuff like this." Grif quickly gathered up the climbing gear—belay, ropes, and harness—and turned to his brother. "You want a go at the wall first?"

With a scowl down at his leg, he shook his head. "My physical therapist would kick my ass."

"Sucks to be you."

"Ain't that the truth?"

Grif stepped into the harness and rigged himself up because he damn well needed to do something to work off all the anger he was feeling toward Carlie Beth. *You should thank me,* she'd told him. Like she'd somehow placed herself in charge of his future when she'd found out she was pregnant with his baby.

He'd thought women manipulating him and fucking him over was a recent development, but apparently not.

Once he double-checked all his equipment, he reached for the first grip on the wall.

"Aren't you forgetting something, dipshit?"

Yeah, he'd been more than distracted since he'd stomped into Carlie Beth's workshop and threatened to take away her daughter. He *was* a dipshit for that delivery. He'd been pissed and emotional and out of his depth. But he stood by his message, even though he didn't know how the hell he was supposed to go about getting to know his own daughter. So he was giving himself some time to cool off and think about the whole situation rationally.

He looked down and realized he wasn't clipped in, not that big a deal. "I free climb all the time at home."

"I don't give a free flying fuck." Once Reid had him hooked in to the belay system, he said, "Belay on."

"Climbing."

"Climb on."

The city had spent a fortune on the four-story climbing wall. Damn shame it had barely been used. And now it was painted up like a bathroom wall. But if he knew Reid, he'd have the thing cleaned up soon. His military—ex-military now—brother liked things in order. Too damn bad his life was in such disorder right now.

Like Grif had a single bit of room to talk. One thing

he'd told himself he'd never do was walk out on his kids like his own dad had. And yet he had done exactly that, whether or not he meant to. And right now, he hated Carlie Beth for making him anything like Eddy Steele.

Distracted, he missed his next foothold, tried to anchor himself with his hands, but to his damn humiliation, he came off the wall.

From below came Reid's smug-ass laughter. "Told you free climbing wasn't a good idea."

After that, Grif scaled the wall half a dozen times with perfect form and accuracy, but Reid's smirk never disappeared.

Two days after her run-in with Grif, Carlie Beth was a zombie shuffling from a parking spot to Yvonne's gallery. Aubrey had played the petulant silent game for the past forty-eight hours, and Grif had been just as quiet about his plans. With everything inside her, Carlie Beth wanted to rip that HSBC Bank check into teensy pieces and dump them all over Grif's shiny shoes.

But even in her anger, she wasn't that stupid.

He wasn't the kind of man who made idle threats. He would fight her for custody if she tossed his money back in his face.

When Carlie Beth walked inside, Yvonne glanced up and her face immediately creased with concern. "You look terrible. What's wrong?"

Great. Nice to know she wasn't fooling anyone. "I wanted to drop off a few more pieces I made in hopes you could list them on the gallery's website." She'd been in such a fever since her life blew up around her that she'd been in the forge almost around the clock.

"You know I'll take everything you've got. Anytime. I'd give anything to have your kind of talent. In fact, I've been thinking of trying my hand at a little metalsmithing." She patted a catalog lying on the counter that Carlie Beth recognized from one of the big online smithing supply companies. "Not that I'd ever hold a candle to you, but it would be fun to set up a little backyard forge."

"Let me know if you ever want to use mine."

"That's sweet of you, but I don't think me piddling around is a priority today. What's important is why you look like you could use some tea and sympathy."

Yvonne's understanding tone burrowed behind Carlie Beth's eyes, luring forward the tears she'd refused to shed. After the showdown with Grif, she'd thought about talking the situation through with Randi, but she suspected her occasional boss was having her own problems with Blues, Brews, and Books. Carlie Beth didn't want to lay anything else at her door. "I've...uh...Aubrey and I are having some issues."

Shaking her head, Yvonne turned toward the back room where she kept the coffee and tea. "She's getting to that age. I remember I gave my mom and dad complete hell when I was a teenager. If it wasn't ten in the morning, I'd offer you something a little stronger than tea. In fact, maybe that's exactly what you need, a girls' night out. We could—"

"As much as I'd like to blame this on teenage hormones, that would be unfair. This thing with Aubrey is my fault."

"Gimme a sec," Yvonne said, "and you can tell me all about it."

Carlie Beth settled on a stool behind the sales counter and unpacked the new items she'd brought, an array of hooks, candlesnuffers, and keychains.

When she returned from the back, Yvonne placed a mug of steaming tea and a tall glass filled with ice tea in front of Carlie Beth. "I figured you might need one of each."

Carlie Beth smiled even though it hurt her cheek muscles. "You're a good friend."

"You know what they say. Friends help you bury the body. Good friends bring a backhoe." Yvonne settled on another stool with her own cup of tea. "So tell me what's got you so down in the mouth."

She'd held on to the secret for so long, she wasn't sure if she could actually get the words out. Then again, now that Grif knew, she was surprised the news wasn't all over Steele Ridge. Not that the Steeles were gossips like some others in town, but the truth getting around was inevitable. And Yvonne had been such a good friend. If she heard from someone else, her feelings would be hurt and rightfully so. "Aubrey recently discovered who her father is."

Steam from Yvonne's cup curled around her lowered eyebrows. "You mean she didn't know?"

"I never told her."

"Hmm." Yvonne sipped. "So I'm assuming you weren't behind this revelation."

"God, not at all. Aubrey and I have done just fine. We don't need his money."

In Yvonne's place, even Carlie Beth would've been dying of curiosity, but her friend just waited and drank her tea. She wouldn't push, which made it easier for Carlie Beth to finally say, "Aubrey's father is Grif Steele."

"Oh, my. That is a surprise." If she hadn't been studying Yvonne so closely, Carlie Beth might not have caught the subtle tightening of her friend's lips, quickly masked by another sip. Carlie Beth winced inside at the memory of Yvonne sitting with Grif and Jonah at Triple B recently. It had been clear Yvonne was fond of them both. Possibly more than fond of Grif. Attracted. "I didn't realize the two of you ever had a relationship."

Carlie Beth laughed. "I wouldn't call one night a relationship, exactly." Not then. And not now. No matter how many sweaty dreams she'd had about the man since he'd recently returned to town. "Of course, Aubrey is upset."

"And Grif?"

"Pissed." Carlie Beth let the heat seeping through the ceramic mug singe her fingertips. "But determined to be a part of Aubrey's life."

"And how do you feel about that?"

Her laugh was thin. "Exactly the question I've been asking myself about once an hour since he stalked out of my forge after slapping down a check so big I…I…"

"How big?"

"The kind of zeroes normal people never see on a piece of paper."

"Oh my God. I never believed it was true, but now I'm not sure." Yvonne's hand went to her throat as if the tea had burned its way down. "He's trying to buy you off. Just like he did that woman."

"What woman?"

"Don't you pay attention to the news? It was all over the place last fall. Since I knew Grif growing up, I wanted to give him the benefit of the doubt, but with him throwing money around like this, now I don't know."

"And I don't know what you're talking about."

"It's not really my place to—"

"Are you my friend or not?"

"Of course."

The unsettled feeling vibrating through Carlie Beth's body picked up speed. "Then tell me what you're talking about."

"Just Google Grif along with the name Madison Henry." Yvonne leaned over and gave her a reassuring hug. "Hopefully, he was as innocent as he claimed. He was cleared, but you have Aubrey to think of. And a man like Grif Steele? He's obviously powerful. That's one thing. But if he's unsafe, you need to take precautions because he'll be a part of Aubrey's life—your life—forever."

Sitting across from Jonah's makeshift desk at their

mom's, Grif nodded toward the stash of random antique and flea market finds. "This wasn't exactly your style in Seattle."

Jonah kicked back in his chair and propped his bare feet on the desktop, crumpling a stack of papers in the process. If Grif had to guess, they were probably some other way Jonah had dropped a shitload of money on something ridiculous. "I gave Mom my credit card for a few office supplies, and now she won't stop with the decorating. I think she thinks if she decorates, I'll stay. I've told her a million times I'm not going anywhere, that I'm back in Steele Ridge for good."

Another shortsighted promise as far as Grif was concerned.

Then again, Jonah sure did look relaxed. When was the last time Grif had felt that way? The last time he could breathe without feeling as if a mountain wasn't sitting on his chest? "About all this town manager crap..."

"Look, I know this isn't exactly your speed, but dammit, I promised the people here—"

"If we let things trickle along the way they've been going, it could take a decade or more for Steele Ridge to recover from all the stupid decisions that were made. If you're serious about jumpstarting economic recovery, then we need to get people moving in the same direction. Right now, it's like someone yelled 'the sky is falling' and all the business owners are running around like chickens with their heads chopped off."

"We?" Jonah angled his head to stare at Grif. "I thought you were out of here as soon as you could find a random bum to take the manager job off your hands."

"Things have changed."

"Because of Aubrey?"

"Wouldn't something like that change your life?"

Jonah held up both hands and leaned back in his throne-like chair. "Dude, I'm not calling you out on it. I care about Steele Ridge, but I damn well care about my family more."

"I confronted Carlie Beth."

"And you were right?"

With a sort of foggy detachment, Grif watched his right fist open and close a few times. "Yeah."

"I guess it's a little too late to break out the cigars. When are you gonna tell Mom?"

"Soon." Grif rubbed his palm down his pants and was pissed to find the movement left a small sweat mark. How could what was happening in his hometown make him edgier than handling big deals in LA? He'd once believed he understood all the predators and prey there. Now he wasn't sure he understood a damn thing anywhere.

"You don't want her to hear it from anyone else."

True. "Real soon. So"—he blew out a breath, but it did nothing to relieve the tension that had been eating him up for days—"I think I should commute for a while. I can do two weeks here and two in LA."

"You want to be a telecommuting city manager?"

"You damn well know I can get more done in a couple weeks than some schmuck can in a couple months. If you were so worried about the quality of my work, you shouldn't have promised things in that contract that you can't deliver."

"I figured if you balked, I'd have to step in."

"You?"

Jonah's casual slouch disappeared, and he sat upright, his forearms in a classic triangular power position on the desk between them. "I did run a pretty successful gaming company. Without you."

"Yeah, but if you'd wanted to be the CEO of Steele Ridge, you wouldn't have wrangled me into the job."

"Ever consider that was just a ploy to get you back home?"

"Just because you're stuck here doesn't mean—"

"I'm not stuck. This is my choice." Jonah sat back again and studied Grif with what looked alarmingly like pity. "Besides, don't you think LA's taken a big enough chunk out of your soul? After what happened—"

"In the past."

"The interweb is forever, dude."

"I have plenty of clients who never believed a word of it."

"Still, that bitch worked you over—"

"Enough." The word came out harsher than he'd intended, making it obvious he wasn't as over it as he claimed. "I like what I do, and most of my clients are good people. So can we please talk about Steele Ridge now?"

"Fine."

"This town can't compete with businesses or services in Asheville and the other big cities. Why would people wander out to Steele Ridge for a bite of vegan Indian food or whatever-the-hell when they can get it in their own backyards?"

Jonah sighed and closed his eyes. "It sure sounds like you're saying we're fucked."

That made Grif smile. And he knew, without checking the mirror, it was the expression that had often made team management want to call their mommies asking for their blankies and binkies. It was the smile that told people he was going to hand their asses to them. "For a man who owned a mega-company, you sure give up easily."

"Fuck you," Jonah snapped, opening his eyes. "Why do you think I hired you?"

"Because I'm smarter than all three of my brothers combined."

One side of Jonah's mouth lifted and he lazily shot Grif the bird. "Whatever lets you sleep at night."

"All people have been doing since the sports complex went down the tubes is complain and whine. We need to give them something to rally around."

"Like a mascot?"

"Something that makes them feel like they're in control of the way things turn out. I'll be talking with every business owner in town one-on-one. Then we'll host a State of Steele Ridge event for them. Hell, we'll do it up right with booze, food, and fancy clothes. I'll reveal an economic development plan that includes something splashy to entice people to visit the town."

"We could just go ahead and have a big golf tournament."

"No, we need a twist. A hook. Besides, you hate golf."

"Then we'll do e-sports."

"I don't think Steele Ridge is ready to put together an event for a bunch of geeky Jonah-alikes."

"Then we're back to swinging sticks at a bunch of little balls." Jonah smirked. "Like yours."

"Apparently my balls are big enough to make a kid, aren't they?"

"Griffin. Fletcher. Steele." His mom's sharp and surprised voice came from behind him.

At the sound, Grif's balls shrank a couple sizes. *Fuck.* He slowly turned to face the woman he loved like no one else. Right now, her mouth was drawn into a tight bow and her hands were solidly planted on her hips. "Explain yourself."

God, what time was it? Because surely a man should be able to fortify himself with a shot of whisky before telling his mom she was a grandmother for the first time. About, oh, fourteen years too late.

He shot Jonah, who at least had the good sense not to grin, a hard look. "We'll talk about this more, later. But I'll be reaching out to people here in town in the meantime, trying to instill a little confidence in the future of Steele Ridge."

"And you think that's the answer to our problems?"

"I think it's a start." Then Grif stood and followed his mom out of the room, ready to face a five-foot-two firing squad.

CHAPTER THIRTEEN

IN THE KITCHEN, HIS MOM stared him down. "What did you mean by that crude comment? I've tried to understand and support your life in California, but now I find out you have a child out there?"

"No." He couldn't lie to her because this whole thing was about to blow wide open. Whether or not he was ready. "I have one here."

"Wha...What? Who?" Her eyes immediately filled with something he wanted to turn away from. Confusion. Pain. Disappointment.

Even at his age, talking with his mom about sex wasn't the most comfortable thing in the world. But it had to be done. "Aubrey Parrish is my daughter."

"Oh my God. And you never told me—"

"I didn't know." What he wanted to do was turn away and walk out the door. Instead, he wrapped his mom in a hug. "When you pointed out how she resembled Evie the other day, something clicked."

"I never knew you and Carlie Beth..."

Thank God he was looking over his mom's head and not directly into her eyes. "Just once. Right before I left for California."

"Why..." Her voice broke, breaking his heart in the process. "Why didn't she ever say anything?"

"I don't know, but I have to assume she never

planned for me to find out about Aubrey."

"But we're her family. It doesn't get much more simple than that. I should go over there and give Carlie Beth a piece of my mind."

He drew back and held his mom by the upper arms. "No. I need some time to handle all this."

"I have a grandbaby."

No, Aubrey wasn't a baby anymore. The anger inside Grif kindled higher. Did Carlie Beth have any idea what she'd done? How she'd cheated the people around her? How she'd cheated her own daughter?

"I want to get to know her. Better, I mean. Take her shopping and—"

"I'm working on that." Working on it? Hell, he'd bought and paid for it. But now that he'd thrown his weight around, he realized he didn't know jackshit about teenage girls. Nothing more than how he'd felt about them when he was a teen himself. And that sure did nothing to ease his mind.

Besides, when he'd confronted Carlie Beth, he'd done two things an expert negotiator should never do— become emotional and walk out. Now he was second-guessing everything, both his big-dick approach and what the hell to do with the so-called ticket into his daughter's life he'd bought and paid for.

"Mom, I'm staying in Steele Ridge for a little while, so I plan to rent a place in town."

"There's plenty of space here."

"I know." He pressed a gentle kiss to her forehead. "But I need to do this my way."

Rather than handling his messed-up personal life right away, Grif called a real estate agent, telling her he needed to rent a place with both an apartment and a dedicated work space. He'd be damned if he would set up shop in City Hall.

The Realtor showed him the old Murchison building where the five-and-dime had been when he and his brothers were kids. He wasn't crazy about the big windows across the front, preferring to work without people stopping by and ogling him, but it had an apartment upstairs and he didn't have the time or energy to look for something else.

So the next morning, he stood on the sidewalk in front of his new digs and stared at the white banquet table and a metal folding chair he'd had delivered. His assistant would laugh his ass off if he saw this setup. A steep step down from Grif's Robert Brou Wave desk and Eames chair back in LA.

As steep as a North Carolina ridge.

Jesus.

Unfortunately, a scan down Main Street confirmed the compact business area was as lethargic as ever. Shop owners like Yvonne Winters must've stockpiled some savings when things were going well to survive a drought like this.

His phone buzzed and he drew it out of his pocket to find he'd missed half a dozen texts and three calls from his clients. Dammit, his wheelhouse was big-dollar contract negotiations, not small-town economic development. And yet, here he was, paying more attention to whether or not anyone was strolling into the Mad Batter Bakery than he was his own clients.

He was muscling his crappy-ass furniture through the front door when a small voice said, "Mr. Steele... Grif...Da—"

He swung around to face Aubrey, almost taking out the door trim in the process, and she cut herself off mid-word. God, he wasn't ready for this. Didn't know what to say. How to explain. How to damn well act.

Which made him a complete chickenshit. Because Carlie Beth probably hadn't been real ready when their daughter arrived in this world.

But what the hell did Grif know about having a kid?

Nothing, because Carlie Beth had never given him the opportunity to learn. Never given him the opportunity to know his daughter.

And there was a dark, gnawing place inside Grif because of it. No one took away his choices.

No. One.

He understood what it was like to be one in a family of a half-dozen rowdy kids. Where he'd always been slightly lost in that crowd as neither the oldest nor the youngest. Where things had always been a little lean and he'd had to make his own way in this world.

But having his own family was something entirely different.

And he didn't exactly come from father-of-the-year stock. His dad hadn't been a model, emotionally disengaging from his family little by little over the years, then eventually leaving them physically. He hadn't run far, just to some ramshackle cabin outside of town, but it might as well have been halfway around the world.

But Grif did know enough to stop this mental shit and say something. "Hey, Aubrey." Then he realized it was ten o'clock on a school day and he scowled. "What are you doing here?"

Her eyes going wide, she took a step back. "I...uh...maybe this wasn't a good idea." She whirled around as if about to flee, and Grif said, "Wait."

She turned back slowly, as if she were facing a growling dog.

"Aren't you supposed to be in school?"

He expected her head to droop in shame. Instead, her chin angled up and her shoulders squared. "I'm old enough to make that decision for myself."

"Actually, you're not. Unless something's changed radically in the past fifteen years, the state of North Carolina makes that decision for you."

"These are mitigating circumstances."

God, what teenage girl used a phrase like *mitigating circumstances?*

A rush of pride burst inside him. One related to him.

He checked his watch. "Fifteen minutes, and then I'm driving you back to school."

One quick glance at Louise, parked in a spot in front of his newly rented space, and Aubrey said, "In that?"

"Her."

"What?"

"My car isn't a that."

"Your car is a woman?"

"Yes, but we can discuss Louise inside if you'll get that for me." Grif nodded toward the building's door, and Aubrey slid around him to hold it open it so he could get his load inside. Once he had the table and chair braced against a wall, he said, "My car is definitely female. Beautiful. Curvy. And occasionally temperamental." With a couple of yanks, he unfolded the table's legs, then swung it to its feet.

Then he unfolded the chair and offered it to Aubrey with a little bow, which made her giggle. "So to what do I owe the pleasure of your visit?"

Settling into the chair, she said, "That's just a nicer way of asking what I'm doing here."

"Sometimes it's not what you say but how you say it." Rather than pace around the table as he was tempted to, Grif boosted himself up and sat.

"I don't know what to call you."

Her simple declaration pierced his heart. His own dad might've been, and still was, a flaky old bastard, but Grif had always known who he was. He'd never once had to question where he came from, who he belonged to. "What do you want to call me?"

"I've never had a dad."

Pierce? She might as well have placed a shotgun against his chest and pulled the trigger. *Blam!* Part of him wanted to stay pissed at Carlie Beth. But he also understood, at least a little, why she'd made the decisions she had. Aubrey had been her first and only priority. And from what he'd seen, she'd done a damn good job raising her.

"Sweetheart"—damn, he wanted to reach out and touch his daughter's gorgeous red hair, but something held him back—"you've *always* had a dad. We just never got a chance to know one another."

"What about now? Are we going to get to know one another now? Mom said you never stay in town more than four days at a time."

And there'd been a reason for that. It was damn hard to make something of your family name, make something of your older brother's sacrifices, when you were sitting on your thumb in your hometown.

But in LA, he was somebody. Somebody? Hell, he'd been the fucking golden boy of sports agents until his face had been splashed all over the *LA Times*, ESPN, and the sports section of every major news blog in the US last fall.

"Well, seeing as I've already been here longer than that, I'd say things have changed."

"I don't want to be a burden." This time, her head did lower. "I don't want you to hate me."

Screw the fact that he didn't know what the hell he was doing. He did know when someone was off balance and hurting. For years, he'd made a living putting people in that place, and then he'd been there himself.

He slid off the table and took Aubrey's hand. It felt slightly foreign in his, small and fragile. Had his dad felt this out of his depth with his own kids? Maybe that was the reason the old man had bolted, because Grif had never felt this raw, this unsure in his life. And that could make a man want to run—fast and far.

When Aubrey looked up at him, the vulnerability and fear in her eyes twisted a place deep inside him. For as long as he lived, he wouldn't forget the courage it had taken for her to come here and ask for what she wanted.

So he needed to man up and find the balls to deal with this situation. Figure out how to act toward her. Who to be for her.

He gently pulled her to her feet, slowly drew her into his arms in case she wasn't comfortable with him touching her. But she came into his embrace like a magnet. Just *click*, as if they should've been hugging like this every day of her life. Her head tucked under his chin as she clung to him.

"I could never hate you, Aubrey Parrish," he said against her hair, which smelled of a girlie fruit—peaches or maybe mangos.

"Then would you...do you...mind...if I call you Dad?"

And for the first time in his life, Grif Steele fell helplessly in love.

Although Grif realized he would've been strangely happy to have Aubrey hang out with him all day, he drove her to school with the promise that they would see one another again soon. His kid was smart, funny, sweet. And although his heart pinged when she laughed or smiled, he needed some time to figure out where to go from here.

So he returned to his makeshift workspace, the twelve-foot ceilings and worn hex-tile making his crappy furniture look foreign and completely lacking in style. By the time he'd bought a new Steele-Ridge-business-only laptop and a few office supplies and convinced an Asheville furniture store to deliver a king-size bed the next day, all he wanted was an ice-cold beer.

Or six.

But when he walked into the back alley to crank up Louise and head back to his mother's house for the night, he took one look at his car and had the simultaneous impulse to bawl and brawl.

He'd been not thirty feet away most of the day. How the hell had someone done this to his best girl?

Okay, now that he'd spent time with his daughter, Louise might be his second-best girl.

Then he remembered the feel of kissing Carlie Beth—

excitement and comfort all rolled into one—and Louise slid down to third.

And that thought just pissed him off.

Grif circled the car to find both back tires flat to the fucking rim, but that wasn't the worst of it. It looked as if her rear lights had been smashed with a crowbar. And the passenger side door had obviously been pried open. The metal around the lock bowed out obscenely and the paint was a mess of scratches and gouges.

Whoever the son-of-a-bitch was, he'd thankfully left Louise's hood intact. But one glance inside told Grif the bastard hadn't stopped with the car's exterior.

Four words were carved into his seats, easily readable through the windshield. The passenger side read "Go back" and the driver's completed the thought with "to LA."

Shit, that had been his plan two weeks ago. Now he was knee-deep in a completely different reality. He stroked a hand over the car's hood. "Jesus, I'm sorry, Lou." Then he dug out his phone. One call to Maggie and another to Jonah.

Maggie was the first one on scene—collecting evidence, taking pictures, and asking questions. Afterward, Grif sweet-talked her into releasing Louise and letting him send her to the shop. The sooner she was fixed up, the sooner he could drive her again.

By the time Jonah screeched into the alley in his Tesla Model X, the tow truck Grif had called was backing up to secure the Maserati. Jonah jumped out of his car. "What the hell?"

"Apparently, not everyone here is as shit-fire excited to have me around as you are."

His brother strode over and peered through one of Louise's windows. "That is sacrilege."

"You can see why I needed a ride." Grif stuffed his hands into his pants pockets. "I'm having her taken to Charlotte. That's the closest city with a garage I trust to touch her."

"Her seats are toast."

"Yeah." His fingers curled, making fists inside his pockets. "It'll take some time to set her right."

"If you need to borrow mine, I can—"

"I've already talked with one of the car dealerships. They'll drop off something in the morning."

"Rental?"

"No, I bought a car I can keep here. Louise obviously belongs back in LA."

"I don't think that message was for her, dude."

"I didn't figure."

"Who the hell would do something like this?" Jonah turned in a circle as if he might find the culprit right there in the alley.

"Maybe one of the old ladies who wasn't too happy about having to reprint her return address stickers?"

"Can you imagine Mrs. Van Dyke wielding a crowbar? Besides, why come after you? I'm the one who changed the town name."

"As Reid would say, you might want to watch your six."

"Believe me, I'll be watching the sixes of everyone in this family."

CHAPTER FOURTEEN

GOOGLE WAS ABSOLUTELY NOT CARLIE Beth's friend.

She'd clicked on so many links since Yvonne's pity-filled warning about Grif that she was surprised her right pointer finger wasn't broken. How could she have missed these articles? Surely people around here had talked about it.

Something niggled at the back of her mind, someone at the Triple B making comments about one of those damn Steele brothers finally showing his true colors. But she'd turned away and busied herself clearing empties because she'd tried hard for years to stay detached from that family.

And now she knew what all the brouhaha was about. At least she knew what had been smeared all over the news. And she had to talk with him about it.

The drive out to Tupelo Hill felt like it took ten hours instead of ten minutes, and when she knocked on the front door, Mrs. Steele answered. Her eyes were shadowed and her smile was brittle around the edges.

She obviously knew the truth and it had hurt her. "Grif told you. About Aubrey."

"*Someone* had to." His mom's hand flew to her mouth as if to shove back the words. "I'm sorry."

"I'm the one who should be sorry." Carlie Beth's heart ached with the pain she'd obviously caused. "You have to believe my decision had nothing to do with you."

"Why then?"

"He didn't deserve to have his future turned upside down. He was so young, and I knew, even then, that he was made for bigger things."

"What about you? Didn't you have plans? Dreams?"

"Plans and dreams change. I love my daughter and wouldn't trade her for anything." Not for a place in the National Ornamental Metal Museum.

"Being a parent is the most important thing in the world." Mrs. Steele's smile lost some of its sharpness and simply became sad. "And being the parent of an adult means I don't get to butt in. It means I have to be invited in."

And that had to be heartbreaking as well. Carlie Beth was already headed down that path with Aubrey. How would it feel to someday be on the outside of her own daughter's life?

Gut-wrenching.

"I promise to bring Aubrey by soon, but I really need to talk with Grif tonight."

"You'll find him down at the sports complex." She pointed in the direction of the road that ran in front of the property.

But when Carlie Beth pushed through the door into the facility, only a few dim security lights filtered through the gloom.

"Hello?" she called out. "Grif, you here?"

He damn well better not be ignoring her. She knew Aubrey had gone missing from school earlier today and had a feeling he was the reason. When she'd pressed Aubrey about it, she'd clammed up, saying it was between her and her dad.

Her dad. Aubrey was giving her the cold shoulder and calling Grif *Dad*. A man neither of them truly knew.

Carlie Beth wandered through the mostly empty facility. Although the damage to the reception area had been repaired and repainted, it still smelled faintly of smoke from the fire set back in January. Behind that was a huge open space dominated by a four-story rock climbing wall. A running track was elevated to the top level, giving the nonexistent joggers a prime view of below. The outer edge of the building was ringed with weight rooms and classroom-sized spaces. It was too bad the whole sports complex concept had fallen apart. The school district had already negotiated to allow students access when the project went down the tubes.

What would Jonah Steele do with this place?

Calling out for Grif every few minutes, Carlie Beth climbed the stairs to the track. She stepped out onto the springy surface and decided a slow lap around might do her some good. Slow? She probably needed to run in circles until she passed out. But she was already so tired as it was.

Right, left, right. The soles of her shoes bounced along the track, making a soft *sproing* with each step. She calmed her breathing, matching it in time with her footfalls. In, out, in.

Good, Carlie Beth, because you can't afford to go apeshit on a man who might be capable of—

Suddenly, a clattering echoed above her and to the right. Something that sounded like metal pinging off plastic.

"Grif?" she said, her voice too high and breathy for her liking. "Jonah? Is anyone here?"

No answer.

Then a heavy door clanged. A stairwell door, just like the one she'd pushed through to enter the track level. Someone was in here with her. Someone unwilling to answer her.

An uneasy shiver made its way down Carlie Beth's arms, leaving goose bumps in its wake. What if someone was trying to steal stuff? But really, what would he take? There were a few machines in the weight room, but they'd require a moving truck. They weren't exactly the type of thing a person could carry out on his back.

What if Grif had heard her the first time she called out and was…stalking her?

By now, the small amount of calm she'd created on her walk around the track had completely disappeared. So she returned to the stairwell, easing open the door and peering around before stepping inside. She and Aubrey had taken a personal safety class last year. The woman who'd taught it, a member of the Asheville PD, had preached the concept of vigilance until every woman in the class was sick of it.

But still they'd listened.

No sounds came from the stairs, so Carlie Beth quickly made her way toward the first floor, jogging down the steps and skimming her hand along the railing. By the time she was back on the lobby level, her heart rate was tripping double-time. She pushed into the open space and sprinted for the front door. Air. She needed air.

With outstretched arms, she shoved at the main door only to hear it thud into something. Something that sounded a lot like a person. Her breath hitching, Carlie Beth stumbled back, almost losing her balance. But she was able to keep her feet under her and scramble sideways until her shoulder banged into a wall.

The door swung inward, and a big form stepped into the open space. The person was backlit by moonlight, which kept his face in shadow, and for an instant Carlie Beth went as still as a rabbit that had spotted a wolf.

Then she became the wolf.

Since she was shorter than the shadow, she went in low with her elbow, aiming for the crotch. Her trajectory was off slightly and she hit his hipbone instead.

"Dammit," the shadow bellowed as it grabbed for her arm, "don't be stupid and make this worse by making me beat you up. I don't give a damn who you are. I promise, you'll wish I'd just called the police first."

Beat her up? No way in hell. She jerked out of his hold, cocked her elbow and rammed it home.

"Oof!" Just like he was supposed to, the guy stumbled back and folded in on himself, gasping for breath. "You...little...motherf—"

"Oh, God!" She hadn't recognized Grif's voice at first. Violent relief pulsed through her, followed quickly by renewed fear. She scrambled away, her spine bumping the wall and stopping her escape.

"Carlie Beth?" Grif's focus lasered on her, momentarily pinning her in place. "Wha...What're you doing here? And wh...Why the hell did you elbow my balls into my throat?"

He made a move to straighten, and she held out her hands and stepped back into attack position. "Stop! Don't move."

"Jesus, it's me. Grif."

"I know."

Bracing his hands on his knees above the basketball shorts he wore, he glared up at her, his breath still hard and uneven. "What the hell? I didn't mean to scare you. Did I knock you down when I pushed back on the door? I'm sorry I yelled, but I thought you were the kids who've been painting crap on the walls in here."

"Where have you been?"

"What do you mean?" He was able to straighten enough for her to see his T-shirt was printed with a faded Anaheim Ducks logo.

"Were you in this building with me?"

His faced creased with confusion. "You saw me come through that door not two minutes ago."

"Maybe you left to make it look like..."

"Like what?" He reached out, and she skipped out of reach. "Have you lost your mind? I know I was pissed when I came to your house the other day, but you're acting crazy." His tone broadcasted bewilderment, which for some unknown reason made Carlie Beth want to wrap her arms around her knees and bury her head while she cried. So, so stupid.

"I heard a noise."

"What kind of noise?"

Part of her wanted to tell him it was nothing, but she had to confront this. Confront him. And she was certain someone had been in the building with her. "A clang and then footsteps. Someone going down the stairs."

"Are you sure?"

"I know what I heard. I called out, but you didn't answer."

"Dammit, it wasn't me. Why would I ignore you?"

She could feel the lack of blood in her own face. "Because…because…"

He touched her chin, lightly, and she tried to move out of range, but he blocked her with his other arm, without removing his fingers from her face. His expression darkened and his mouth flatlined. "Why are you suddenly scared of me?"

Carlie Beth fought the compulsion to grab his hand and press it against her cheek. Because that would be like a lamb climbing up on a lion's dinner table. She remembered how it felt all those years ago to be the singular focus of his blue eyes, his sexy smile. Grif could make a woman believe she was the only female in his universe. The only thing he cared about.

Maybe he cared too much. So much he was willing to hurt a woman.

Then again, when they were talking with Maggie about Roy Darden, Grif had also said *a man who hits a woman should be taught a lesson.* "I…need to get home."

"Wait a minute. I want to make sure I understand what's going on. You came out here looking for me, but there was someone else in the building? Did you see who it was?"

"No. Maybe it was one of your brothers. Or maybe I imagined it. Anyway, I can see you were about to do something, so I'll just…"

"I was about to use the climbing wall"—his breath fanned across her cheek, skimming her lips and sending a shiver down her back—"but that's not important right now."

She shoved at his chest, suddenly realizing she'd let him get too close. Way too close. She had no physical leverage from this angle. So she attacked in another way. "Tell me about Madison Henry."

Grif stepped back, taking his hand with him. "I'm surprised you didn't ask before now."

"I didn't know."

"Do you live under a rock?"

"This may shock you," she snapped, "but most of the world doesn't revolve around you."

"It's not ego saying that, believe me. But as a guy who hasn't been able to get out from under the shadow of scandal for months, it's unusual for me to come across someone who hasn't seen my face, and her face, splashed all over the media."

"I—"

"And what kind of mother would you be if you didn't ask?" His words were full of bite, but she could hear the pain beneath them. "I mean, you have to wonder if it's safe for me to get to know my own daughter."

A sliver of shame threaded through her. He'd obviously been ripped apart by the press and even after all the damning stuff she read, she had a hard time imagining this man as an abuser. "Look, I'm not even sure why I came out here tonight. We can talk about all this lat—"

"You came because you're scared. But not for the reason you've convinced yourself of. If you were really afraid I would ever hurt Aubrey, you would've been hightailing it the other way instead of coming out here to confront me. You've had exclusive claim on our daughter for her entire life. I'm a threat to that. Tell me, Carlie Beth, is that why you kept her from me?"

"I didn't keep her from you," she insisted. "You make it sound like I hid her away in a cave somewhere and fought you off with sharp sticks."

"Look, I know I acted like a dick when I came to see you, and I'm sorry for that, but you can't expect me not to be pissed. You purposefully kept me in the dark."

"I shouldn't have to remind you that you were

eighteen, just a boy. You wouldn't have known what to do with a baby."

"And you, in all your nineteen-year-old wisdom, had it all figured out?" He advanced on her, and she sidestepped, her back still against the wall. But he simply followed, not allowing her an escape route.

"I was twenty by the time she was born." Like those few months had made her any more ready for a tiny baby.

"I bet you were all round and rosy." Grif's focus shifted from her face downward, and his hands came up to span her waist. Carlie Beth's nipples reacted as if he'd cupped her breasts, immediately going hard and achy. One side of his mouth inched up as his thumbs fanned across her stomach as though he was holding her pregnant belly. "My mom said she craved grapefruit with all her kids."

Trying to ignoring the little fires his touch was setting under her skin, she said, "I couldn't get enough caramel popcorn and fried clams."

Both Grif's grip and mouth tightened. "I missed everything."

Although part of her wanted to lash out, push this man away so he couldn't threaten the safe, comfortable world she'd built for Aubrey and herself, Carlie Beth cupped his flexing jaw. "It wasn't like we were high-school sweethearts. Technically, we weren't even dating. It was a one-night—"

"Don't say stand," he ordered. "I don't want Aubrey to think she was made from some trashy fuck."

The word hit Carlie Beth midchest. "Well, I can't speak for you, but from my side of things, nothing about it was trashy. Or sordid. But it *was* only one time."

"Two times."

"Fine," she huffed. "But it was only one night. And Grif, we weren't in love. We liked one another, sure. But I didn't think a couple of Natural Lights and a night in your car was a good foundation for a family."

Something hardened in his eyes. Carlie Beth wouldn't call it angry or mean. If pressed, she'd have to say it was determined.

Maybe this was the real reason she'd never told him. She'd known he was honorable then. All this animosity coming off him now stemmed from his belief that she hadn't allowed him to do the right thing. And for a man like him, that was untenable.

How was she supposed to push away a man like that?

Grif slid his hands up her body. He wove his fingers into the hair at her nape and used the other hand to circle her neck, with his thumb in the hollow of her throat. And if she'd thought her heart was racing from fear earlier, now it was a NASCAR contender leading the pack.

"Plenty of marriages have been built on less than what we had. We were attracted to each other. We liked each other."

"We didn't know one another."

"Oh, I would argue I knew you pretty damn well." His gaze was locked on hers, pulling her in. Pulling her under. "It only took me one time to know how you like to be touched. Where to put my fingers and my mouth to send you tumbling. To make you scream."

The memories of his hands on her body—in his backseat, on his hood, in Yvonne's stockroom—rushed over her, and every muscle in her body tightened with inappropriate arousal. He was right. She wanted his fingers between her legs and his mouth on hers. She wanted his body inside hers.

So much that she could feel her body readying itself.

Why him? Why now?

The shame she wanted to feel for having an unexplainable craving for this sexy, complicated man simply wouldn't surface.

"What do you want, Grif? What are you trying to accomplish by dredging up the past?"

He blew out a breath and glanced away, allowing her

to regain a sliver of composure. It wouldn't be good to let him know just how affected she was by him. Yeah, right. As if she could hide that after their little rendezvous in Yvonne's storage room.

He damn well knew she was still attracted to him.

"You can't just breeze into town, let the hey-Aubrey-I'm-your-dear-old-dad cat out of the bag, and think she won't be hurt when you leave."

When he turned back, his face was like acid-etched metal in the shadows. "Oh, I'm more than clear on what I want from Aubrey. I want to get to know her better. She's a beautiful young woman. Smart, with a little attitude." He leaned in, his lips so close to Carlie Beth's she could feel his breath feather across them. "The question I don't have an answer to yet is exactly what I want from you. But it's something, Carlie Beth, and you'll know not long after I do."

God, he'd wanted to kiss her. So damn bad his hands were still clenched into fists as he circled the outside of the building looking to confirm Carlie Beth's story. If someone had been in or around the complex when she arrived, there was no evidence of it now.

Damn her for shaking up his emotions. Over the past few days, he'd felt more about her, with her, for her than he had about anything in a long damn time. His system was in overdrive—pinballing from pissed off to protective to turned on.

Yet he hadn't explained a damn thing about Madison because any time he thought of her, how she'd worked him from the first second she met him, he questioned if he was anything but the hick who'd left North Carolina.

After searching the inside of the building and still finding no one, he had to do something to burn off the adrenaline Carlie Beth had stirred up in him. It was as if he was stuck on the top of a razor-wire fence, with one leg firmly planted on the Los Angeles side and the other dangling on the Steele Ridge side. And all the while, his balls were getting sliced and diced.

Almost literally. His scrotum still ached from being used as Carlie Beth's punching bag. But damn if he wasn't proud of the fact that she could hold her own.

Still, Grif's entire nervous system was on overload—from his bruised balls to the near kiss to the sickness about his mess of a life. Even though Reid would have a shit-fit if he ever found out Grif had done a solo climb, right now he needed to be on that wall so bad. That was the only way he could shove away his conflicting thoughts and feelings about a woman he should hate instead of want.

Fuck it.

He put on his gear and prepped to make a solo climb with a grigri—the only assisted braking device he had here. With a glance at the gloves, he decided he wanted the feel of the handholds under his palms, even if the damn things were fake rocks. If he was lucky, one of them would have a sharp edge and slice him up.

At least then, he'd know he should be feeling pain.

Once he took up the slack in the rope and chalked his hands, he stood in front of the wall, considering his path. Straight up was too easy. But if he started down here on the left and made his way to the right, that would provide not only a longer climb but a tougher challenge.

Exactly what he needed to empty his mind of everything—and everyone—else.

Ignoring the low holds, he jumped and grabbed one a foot above his head. He allowed his body to swing there for a few seconds, savoring the stretch in his lat muscles.

Then slowly, so slowly his biceps jumped with the effort, he pulled himself up as if executing a one-armed chin-up.

Fuck, yeah.

Finally, when that arm was close to rebelling, he

arced out and caught a hold with his right foot, distributing his weight more evenly. But now he was stretched at an awkward forty-five-degree angle that didn't make his next move easy.

Grif torqued his torso and rotated his shoulder to touch a rock above him, his fingers just grazing the lip. Not a lot of security, but when had he ever chosen his moves based on security?

Every two or three moves, he took up the slack, once again pulling his belay tight.

He didn't try to take the wall fast. In fact, he drew out each move, each overreach, until his muscles screamed for him to change positions. This was what he needed. Intense focus that made everything else a blur.

When he made it within five feet of the top, he paused to consider his final move or two. There were a couple of easy grips that would have him up and over the wall within seconds. But what was the use of taking the easy way out now? He needed to top off this climb with a bold move.

And there it was, a handhold eighteen inches out of his stretch range. Even if he used his toes, it wouldn't work. If he wanted to make that, he'd have to let go of the wall for a fraction of a second.

Fucking perfect analogy for his life right now, because he sure didn't have a decent grip on any part of it.

He took up the slack from his top rope and readied his body, positioning himself and giving his muscles strict instructions on what they needed to do to make this move happen.

And then he pushed off, feet and hands free of the wall...until...until...his right hand caught his objective. He gripped, grinning to himself as the rest of his limbs swung free because he'd done it.

Now, all he had to do was reach up and—

His fingers slipped apart, compromising his hold and sending a hell of a cramp into his hand. He stretched out a foot to stabilize himself, but the whole thing went pear-shaped, his fingers sliding off the plastic rock. That was when he remembered his last bold move had increased the amount of slack in his rope.

He tried to catch another handhold as he fell, but the only part of his body that made contact with a grip was his chin. The pain from the impact shot up, into his nose and behind his eyes.

That spun him around. And as his brake jerked his descent to a stop, the back of his head rammed into a protruding grip. Stars? No, as his skull took the brunt, what Grif saw were black spots of doom.

He hung there, eyes closed, just waiting for those black circles to stop expanding and shrinking.

Finally, he was able to pull back the lever on the brake and slowly rappel the wall. His last thought as his feet hit the ground and his knees wigged out on him was *I'll never fucking live this down.*

CHAPTER FIFTEEN

FROM SOMEWHERE HIGH ABOVE HIM, Grif heard a guy say, "I fucking told you, you dumbass. If you're dead, I'm gonna kill you and then tell Mom I warned you."

"Reid?" Grif croaked, his throat feeling like he'd gargled with kitty litter. And even though he opened his eyes, he couldn't see much because his silverback of a brother was crouched over him, two fingers pressed to Grif's carotid artery.

Reid's face was a portrait of what an artist would probably call Study in Pissed Off. "Did I tell you or did I tell you not to climb that mother-effing wall off belay? And unless whoever was belaying you just happened to wander away after you took a header, I'm damn sure you didn't listen."

"Old woman," Grif said, closing his eyes again.

"Uh-uh. Keep 'em open, asswipe. If there's anything worse than me walking in here to find that you've gone and killed yourself, it's having you bite it on my watch. For some reason, our mom seems to have a soft spot for you. And I'm not going down for murder." Holding up three fingers, Reid asked, "How many?"

"Dude, six fingers?" Grif blinked a couple of times, just messing with his brother since he could see those three thick sausages perfectly well. "You're a freak."

"Dammit." Reid scrambled for his phone, jabbing at the screen with his big fingers.

With his right hand, Grif tried to push himself off the floor. Big-ass mistake. His wrist gave out below him—and *whomp*—down he went again. That's when he realized his neck and T-shirt were wet with something. If he'd passed out and slobbered all over himself—or God forbid, even worse, pissed himself—Reid wouldn't have to worry about murder because Grif would just kill himself.

He swiped at his throat and came away with a handful of thick stickiness.

Meanwhile, Reid barked into his phone, "We need an ambulance out at Tupelo Hill." He glanced up. "Yeah, looks like he took about a twenty-foot fall off a rock climbing wall."

No way. He wasn't going to get away with that, so Grif said, "I was almost at the top and my brake held."

"What?"

"But I had slack in the rope."

"Fine, the idiot tumbled ten feet."

"And I don't need an ambulance."

"The fuck you don't," Reid growled at him. "If Cash Kingston is on shift tonight, make sure he's in the ambulance...I think he lost consciousness. Not sure how long because he was out when I found him."

"Didn't," Grif mumbled. "Just had my eyes closed."

"How the hell would you know?" Reid barked at Grif, then said into the phone, "Yeah, I'll stay on the line."

"Not my fault," he told his brother.

"That's what they all say when the sugar turns to shit," Reid said. "You think you're freakin' invincible and don't have to climb safe. I tell you what, if this place was mine, you'd not only be on a real belay, I'd have your stupid head in a helmet. You should've been wearing protection. Hell, what am I saying? You shouldn't have been on that wall at all."

"Carlie Beth was here."

"Are you saying you were showing off for a girl?"

"I wanted to kiss her."

Reid snorted. "Looks like you kissed the floor instead."

Grif smiled and the motion shot an arrow into his frontal lobe. "She left and I was frustrated. Decided to take it out on the wall."

"I'm not buying the bullshit you're selling. You came in here ready to climb."

Guilty.

But he might not have felt the need to do it the hard way if he and Carlie Beth hadn't had a run-in. "Something's wrong up there. I grabbed a handhold, but it didn't feel right, almost like…"

"Don't tell me it was loose. We spent hours all over that wall double-checking the things. Sure as hell couldn't trust the shoddy-ass workmanship of the people the city hired."

"Not loose. Slick."

"Sonofabitch," Reid said. "Will you be okay by yourself for a couple of minutes?"

"Yeah."

"You sure?"

"If you don't stop hovering, I'm gonna start calling you Britt."

Reid just glared at him, then hopped to his feet and strode across the room. A second later, light flooded the cavernous room, sending shards of glass into Grif's eyeballs. He clamped his lids shut, but the brightness still seeped through. God, his brain really had been whacked around like a pinball inside there.

But the whole operation was still working well enough to allow him to picture Carlie Beth, all protective mother and sexy woman rolled into one package. Who in the hell would've ever thought Grif Steele would have a psychological hard-on for the mother of a fourteen-year-old daughter.

His fourteen-year-old daughter.

He'd only intended to take a little cross-country drive, get away from the shadow hanging over him for a couple of weeks. How the hell could he have ever imagined he'd roll into his hometown only to be double-whammied with a freaking city job and a family?

Next thing he knew, he'd be sitting in a recliner asking for his pipe and slippers.

What the fuck was he going to do about all this?

Before he could come to a halfway decent conclusion, EMTs swarmed into the building and began giving him the once-over. Peppering him with questions about what happened, checking his pulse and pupils.

"Pulse is one-ten."

His cousin, Cash, shined a light into his eyes. "Pupils normal and reactive."

"I'm fine," he grumbled. But they continued to pester him, checking him over and asking him questions like what month it was and who the president was. "Hell if I wanna discuss politics."

Cash glanced up at the rock wall. "You fell off that?"

"Not exactly." He didn't have the energy to go through it all. And it was obvious they would haul him into the hospital regardless of his story.

"Still, you're lucky."

A pair of boots appeared beside Grif's head, and Grif slowly turned his head to wince up at his brother. "Yeah"—Reid's gruff voice echoed above him—"he was damn lucky."

When Carlie Beth returned home and realized that Grif had distracted her like the slick hustler he was, that he hadn't actually explained about Madison Henry, she immediately went for her emergency stash of white chocolate and Malbec, both wedged into the corner of the over-fridge cabinet. She had a hefty Ghirardelli bar in one hand and her fingers wrapped around the wine bottle neck when something shifted in the darkness behind her.

She spun around and lost her grip on the bottle. It arced away from her in slow motion. Damn, that was going to make a mess. And she needed it badly enough that she'd be tempted to lap it up off the ground.

Aubrey jumped up from the kitchen table and caught the wine just before it crashed to the floor.

The breath whooshed from Carlie Beth's lungs. "My God, you scared me." The second time tonight her heart had tried to escape her chest.

"I'm sorry. I was just waiting for you." Aubrey carefully placed the bottle on the table and eyed the candy bar in Carlie Beth's hand. "It's bad if you're two-fisting it tonight."

With a boneless movement, Carlie Beth plopped into a chair. "Sometimes it would be nice if I were the adult and you were the kid. You know, totally in the dark about my failings and foibles."

"Foibles." Aubrey articulated the word as if it were a mouthful of delicious white chocolate. "I wonder if that can be used as a verb, too. Ladies and gentlemen, the normally graceful Carlie Beth Parrish almost foibled her precious Malbec medicine tonight. And wouldn't that have been a tragesty?"

All Carlie Beth could do was laugh. Her brilliant daughter had come out of the womb with an affinity for making up words. She'd played with them like some other children had shaped clay or put together Legos.

Aubrey went to the cabinet and withdrew two wineglasses, then eyed the wine. "Don't guess I could talk you into giving me some of that?"

"Sure you can."

Her light eyebrows popped up.

And Carlie Beth finished her thought. "When you're twenty-one."

"Great, only seven years to go." She handed over one

glass and went to the fridge to pour herself some grape juice. Although she gave her drink a baleful look, she said, "I guess if it's good enough for the Baptists, it's good enough for me."

Thank goodness Carlie Beth hadn't already taken a drink because she would've snorted perfectly good wine out her nose. "Don't let Miss May hear you say that."

Settling into the seat across from Carlie Beth, Aubrey moved her own glass from place to place on the table as if she were playing a particularly challenging game of chess. "I'm sorry about what I said to you a few days ago."

"You mean the asshole comment?"

One side of Aubrey's mouth lifted in the same way Grif's had that day in Yvonne's storeroom, and Carlie Beth was filled with a combination of pain and pride. "Most moms would've gone crazy and grounded me for saying something like that."

"I think we've already established I'm not most moms. You're entitled to your opinion about the situation, and honestly, you weren't completely wrong. I'm sure I've made a lot of wrong choices over the years—in your life and in mine. But I won't sit here and say I think keeping him out of your life was one of them. Right now, I don't know if it was or not."

"I went to see him…Grif."

Although she already knew, Carlie Beth's heart shrank to half its normal size. She forced herself to take a casual sip of wine, then said, "So did I."

"He told me I could call him Dad."

Forget half-size. Her heart was now trying to figure out if it wanted to run and hide or jump clean out of her chest. "Baby, I don't want you to get hurt—"

"I'm not a baby. You know that because you've never treated me that way a day in my life."

"But you've never had Grif Steele in your life before."

"So are you saying he *is* an asshole?"

Carlie Beth winced into her wine. Was it right to

warn Aubrey about the man when she had no idea what had truly happened between him and the hotel heiress he'd been accused of abusing? The charges had been dropped. But he'd also dropped the subject when she brought it up. "No, I just don't want you to make him into Prince Charming. Everyone has faults." Has secrets. "And this isn't his home anymore."

"He's leaving?" The panic was clear in her daughter's tone.

Carlie Beth set aside her wine and took Aubrey's hand. "His life is in Los Angeles. Just because he knows about you now doesn't change that."

Aubrey's face closed up and she snatched her hand away. "What are you really worried about, Mom—that I'll get attached to him? That he'll hurt me?" With one motion, she drained her juice and clicked her glass back onto the table. "Or that he'll hurt you?"

Several hours later, after being poked, prodded, and sutured, Grif was finally taking the stairs—one at a time—to his new second-floor apartment. Reid was on his left side, hovering like he expected him to take another dive.

"You're starting to piss me off," he grumbled.

"Welcome to my world," Reid shot back. "You've been doing that to me for years."

On the landing, Grif angled his body so his brother wouldn't see his unsteady hand as he inserted his new key and unlocked the door. "I don't care what the discharge papers said, I don't need you to stay with me tonight."

"Not planning to," Reid said, his voice full of cheer that made suspicion crawl up Grif's back.

When he pushed open the door, he immediately understood the source of his brother's peppy mood. Because there in his living room sat big brother Britt.

On a couch Grif hadn't owned when he walked out of the place earlier this evening.

"What the hell?"

"Aw…" Reid mock-sympathized. "You hurt my witty-bitty feelings by saying you didn't need me."

Turning his entire torso so his brain wouldn't go sunny-side up in his head, Grif glared at his brother. "So you sicced Britt on me?"

Britt didn't budge from from his perch on the ass-ugly green, pink, and yellow couch.

"Where the hell did that thing come from?"

"The thrift shop down the street."

Grif glanced at his watch. "At ten o'clock at night?"

"It was actually around eight. But that's the way small towns work, in case you don't remember. Neighbors and friends are willing to go the extra mile for people."

"And of all the choices, you picked furniture that looks like Rainbow Brite puked on it?"

"This isn't LA. I didn't have a choice of Kobe cowhide or Italian leather. It was either this or a twenty-year-old daybed. Besides, this one is a queen-size fold-out. Important when I'll be sleeping on it for several nights."

"Fucking stupid."

"Keep it up, asshole," Reid said mildly, "and Britt'll be your houseguest for a solid month. And we'll go back to the thrift store to pick up a laminate kitchen table and a 1970s RCA TV."

Britt had the balls to chuckle. "They actually had one of those. Bet that thing was five hundred pounds."

Grif rubbed his chin, the stitches bristly under his fingertips and his skin sticky from blood and whatever gel they'd slathered on his skin. Damn, he needed a shower and his bed. "Mom set you up to this, didn't she?" In fact, he was surprised she wasn't the one glued to that couch. That was the kind of mother she'd always been—one who sat up and watched over her kids whenever one of them was sick or hurt. It was a freaking miracle the woman had ever slept for more than an hour a night.

Reid's mocking expression clamped down and went serious in a microsecond. "No. She doesn't know a damn thing."

Now it was Grif's turn to snort. "You do realize she goes to church with the ER triage nurse, don't you?"

"I asked her to keep this little incident to herself for now."

"There's gonna be hell to pay when Mom finds out."

"Grif, this is serious."

He shuffled across to the makeshift kitchen he'd set up. The whole thing consisted of a microwave and an oversized dorm fridge, both new from the local discount store. Damn, what he wouldn't give for his commercial beer chiller right now. Grif stooped to reach into the fridge and grabbed a Two Cocks Roundhead Bitter.

If it wouldn't have hurt his head, he would've chuckled at the irony of his selection.

Before he could reach for the bottle opener, Britt was across the room yanking the beer out of his hands. "Dammit, Grif. I'd expect Jonah or Reid to be idiots about this kind of thing, but not you."

"Thanks, bro," Reid said.

"You have a concussion," Britt said slowly, as if talking to a particularly hard-to-train dog. "Alcohol and head injuries don't mix."

Grif let out a long sigh. "Fine, then I'm hitting the shower. You two can fight over that floral monstrosity." He waved toward the couch. "But if either of you are in my bed when I get out, I'm kicking ass. I don't care if it gives me a fucking aneurysm."

"Dammit, don't blow this off—" Reid started.

Britt grabbed his arm and said, "Let him get cleaned up. I'll talk with him when he gets out."

As Grif carefully made his way toward the bathroom, the front door slammed behind him, sending a pain through his head that had him lunging for the toilet.

And if he'd thought that hurt, the dry heaving that came next was complete brain-blinding hell.

CHAPTER SIXTEEN

IN ALL HONESTY, WHEN HE woke in the morning, Grif didn't remember much about the night before other than Britt hauling his ass off the bathroom floor and threatening to take him back to the ER. But he'd somehow had enough wherewithal to wage a decent negotiation, promising he'd go back if he didn't immediately rouse every time Britt came in to check on him during the night.

He must've passed each test because here he was, in his own bed, sunlight peeking around the shades on the windows facing Main Street. And someone had apparently removed the icepicks from his head during the night because he could breathe without feeling like puking or digging himself into a dark hole and never coming out.

But the crusty blood on his chin itched like crazy, and he couldn't stand the grimy feeling on his skin. And obviously, Britt had allowed a parade of his beloved wildlife into the apartment during the night because Grif would swear a possum had curled up and died in his mouth.

He made his way to the bathroom, grabbed his toothbrush with one hand and used the other to piss for days. Mouth fresher and bladder happier, he eased under the shower, thankful this old building had decent water pressure.

When he'd used up every ounce of hot water, he

pulled on a T-shirt and sweats, then made his way to his so-called great room. Britt was up, his blanket and pillow folded and piled neatly on one end of the couch. His attention was zeroed in on a paper in front of him, what looked like some kind of map with symbols for trees and arrows and other stuff.

"I'm surprised you didn't come in and watch me shower."

Britt didn't look up. "Figured if I heard a two-hundred pound crash, I'd check on you."

"One eighty-five," he corrected.

A grunt was Britt's only acknowledgment. To Grif's annoyance, however, his brother's ass stayed firmly planted on the sagging cushions of his new-old couch. God, he was gonna burn that damn thing the minute he had the energy to drop it out one of the second-story windows.

For now, he shuffled into his makeshift kitchen and popped a K-cup into his Keurig. If he wasn't careful, he'd have a fully functioning apartment before he'd realized what had happened.

That made him wonder what Carlie Beth and Aubrey's kitchen looked like in that tiny house on the edge of town. Had Carlie Beth been able to afford nice appliances or did she make do with secondhand crap? Just thinking about her and Aubrey being forced to get their housewares and appliances at a thrift store or yard sale made his head start throbbing again.

They damn well deserved better than that.

But so far, Carlie Beth hadn't deposited the check he'd slapped down in front of her like a complete bastard. Hell, she'd probably never seen that much money in her life. Growing up, her family hadn't been broke, but the Parrishes had been a lot like the Steeles—working class all the way. Which meant living paycheck to paycheck most of the time.

Evie was the only kid his parents had been able to afford to put through college. Even now, his mom insisted on paying the tuition from her monthly retirement check.

And it was already obvious that Aubrey was college material. He'd make damn sure she never had to worry where her next tuition payment was coming from. But somehow, he and Carlie Beth needed to come to a detente so he could convince her to take money from him. He should've told her last night that he'd never actually fight her for custody. That had been posturing on his part. And stupid because he knew better than to threaten something he'd never follow through on.

Before Grif's coffee finished brewing, Britt stacked his papers so the edges were perfectly aligned, then strolled over to the small kitchenette. He rooted around in the fridge and pulled a couple of things from a cabinet.

"Where did that bowl come from?" Grif asked, grabbing his coffee and taking a life-giving swig.

Britt spared him a glance over his shoulder. "Same place the couch did."

Great. "The whisk and measuring cups too?"

"Yup."

"Something wrong with the discount store?"

"Why buy new when these are perfectly good?"

"Maybe because someone's used them already?"

"I washed them." One of Britt's shoulders rose and fell as he whisked the hell out of an egg, some flour, and a few other ingredients.

"Where do you plan to cook pancakes?"

"There." He angled his chin toward the microwave. "And they're microwave muffins."

"I'm not five. You don't have to cook me breakfast. We could've walked down the street and grabbed something from the Mad Batter."

"Reid's coming by and wanted me to make sure you stayed put."

And now even the least maternal of all his siblings was getting in on the babysitting action. If Jonah showed up too, with a Disney movie and ice cream in hand, Grif would know he'd hit his head hard enough that the doctor had predicted he'd be dead within the day.

Couple minutes later, the microwave dinged and Britt shoved a hot mug into Grif's hands along with a fork. "You can eat it straight out of there or dump it on a plate."

Grif leaned a hip against the counter and dug in. The bite he shoved in his mouth tasted of apples and cinnamon and made him think of Carlie Beth, which woke up a few body parts besides his stomach. "This is actually pretty good," he said around another mouthful.

Britt just nodded and ate his own breakfast.

They were finishing up when the pounding started on his door, setting off aftershocks in Grif's head. There was only one person he knew who knocked like King Kong. "Doesn't Reid remember I had a concussion?"

Sure enough, when Grif opened the door, his brother was standing there, hands on his hips and a scowl on his face. "You look like shit."

Grif glanced over his brother's own sartorial splendor of T-shirt and cargo pants. "You're one to talk."

"No one invited me to breakfast?"

"I didn't realize we were doing brunch the morning after I went to the ER."

Reid's scowl deepened. "Yeah, that's actually why I'm here. We need to round up the troops and talk this thing through. Mom and Evie are going to Asheville to shop today, leaving early afternoon, so we have some time to strategize. You and Britt can pick up sandwiches on the way to the Hill."

"I don't know if you noticed, but your little brother roped me into a damn job, which is why I have that so-called office setup downstairs, which means I need to get my ass to work."

"I'm wondering if someone isn't happy about you taking over as city manager."

"Exactly what I told Jonah when I discovered someone had carved up Louise."

Reid shook his head in pained disgust, probably over Louise rather than Grif. "Figured you'd want to know that when I went up to check the handholds last night, they were still secure in the wall."

"Just say it, I was stupid and reckless to self-belay." Not the first time and probably wouldn't be the last.

"Who knows you climb?"

"Anyone who knew me in high school. It wasn't a secret that I went up to Boone on the weekends."

"Then we've got a hell of a lot of thinking to do, because someone fucked you over."

"Huh?"

"What do you remember right before you came off the wall?"

"That I grabbed a handhold, but my fingers wouldn't stay wrapped around it."

"Anything else?"

"I didn't have a lot of time to think before I was dangling by my top rope."

"Well, the last row of grips? Someone had greased them up good before you got up there."

Carlie Beth had been in the building last night. Would she have...no. It wasn't worth mentioning to his brothers. Regardless of how pissed she was, if she wanted to hurt him, she'd come at him from the front. And he couldn't imagine she'd risk someone else climbing that wall and getting banged around.

"Carlie Beth thought she heard someone running down the stairs last night."

"Then we need her out at the house, too," Reid said.

"You said the holds were greasy—with what? Maybe that'll tell us something."

"Had the consistency of plain old vegetable oil. Which means our perp could be anyone who has three bucks to spend down at Hoffman's Grocery Store."

Carlie Beth looked at the old Murchison building's

front door and blew out a breath. She and Grif had accomplished nothing last night. Nothing except confusing her and turning her on so much she'd stood under a cool shower for a quarter hour after finishing all the wine and the entire bar of chocolate.

But when she tapped on the door, no one answered. So she twisted the knob and pushed it open. "Grif?"

The lack of answer made her realize she needed to stop doing this—just showing up unannounced. She looked around to find the old store empty of everything but a bare bones office setup. Maybe Grif was still upstairs in the apartment she'd heard he rented as well.

"Hey there, Carlie Beth." She swung her focus toward the staircase to find Reid Steele coming down. How a man his size could move so quietly was a mystery. He should've made a noise like a buffalo when he walked. "Looking for your baby daddy?"

Oh my God. He had not just called Grif her…her…

He busted out a laugh. "You look like I just knocked you over the head with the butt of a gun."

"Has anyone ever told you that you're completely inappropriate?"

"All the time." He grinned. "I have to say I can't see what you saw in him. He was a skinny little runt way back then."

Lean maybe, but even at eighteen Grif had plenty of bulk where it counted. Not that she was about to say that to his brother.

"But I met your daughter and have to admit the two of you did pretty damn good work."

"Thank you." For some reason, the backhanded compliment warmed Carlie Beth's insides. "She's a great kid."

Reid's grin faded. "You realize we all want to get to know her better, right?"

"Yes…but…I…This is all new to me."

"No, it's new to *us*. You've known exactly what was what for almost fifteen years now."

And somehow, that simple statement made her feel smaller and more regretful than ever about this situation. But her daughter came first, always. "I asked Grif about Madison Henry last night."

Oh, the happy-go-lucky expression on Reid's face was definitely gone now, and his stance shifted so his weight was on his back foot. On the offensive, ready to fight. "What do you need to know?"

"How much of the story is true."

"Don't make assumptions based on gossip and blog posts. Get the truth from Grif."

"I tried."

"Try again," he said, then sighed. "Look, I'll say one thing. He let her slip one over on him and he prides himself on seeing all the angles, on always having the upper hand. She and that jagoff client of his sideswiped him like he was riding a tricycle on the freeway. Can you imagine how that makes a man like him feel?"

She imagined it made him feel like shit. Embarrassed. Shameful.

Reid reached out, squeezed her shoulder with what felt like affection. "You may not have had a damn thing to do with him for years, but you've always been smart. Tell me you actually believe you have a daughter with a man who beats up women. Tell me that, and I won't press you about letting Aubrey know this family."

"I don't believe it. But...this...It's hard to share her."

"Mom and Evie are doing a girls' thing this afternoon, shopping and all that crap. They'd be over the moon if you'd let Aubrey go with them."

A lump of something she couldn't quite name lodged itself right behind her breastbone. She wasn't much of a fashion shopper, but she and Aubrey had always done girl things together. The two of them. The three of them if Aubrey brought along a friend.

But it was time to let Aubrey get to know her family. "I'll give her a call."

"Why don't you tell her they'll swing by to pick her

up on their way out of town? Probably around noon."

Carlie Beth glanced at her watch. It was almost eleven now. "I'll let her know."

Reid wrapped an arm around her shoulders and pulled her in for a bolstering hug. "You won't regret this, any of it. I promise." Then he released her and strolled toward the front door, tossing a few final words over his shoulder, "By the way, Grif got a little banged up last night. You might want to go upstairs and check on him."

"What do you mean—"

The door shut behind him.

Fine, one thing at a time. She dialed Aubrey's number.

"Hey, Mom."

"Hey, how would you like to do a little shopping this afternoon?"

"Really?" Aubrey's voice perked up. "Could we do a mani-pedi? I mean, I know a mani is wasted on you, but—"

"Not with me. How would you like to spend some time with Miss Joan and Evie Steele?"

The silence from the other end of the phone was somehow both expectant and hopeful. Finally, Aubrey said, "Do you mean it?"

"Reid…um…your uncle…said they'd be by to pick you up in about an hour."

"Oh my God, Mom. I have to hang up now and figure out what to wear!"

"Be sure to text me to let me know when you'll be home."

"Sure thing. I love you!"

"Love you too, Aub."

Carlie Beth slipped her phone into the pocket of her jeans and climbed the stairs. Wondering what the heck Reid meant about Grif getting banged up, she knocked lightly on the apartment door, but when it swung open Britt stood on the other side of the threshold. "Oh, I was looking for—"

"Me?" Grif strolled up behind his brother. Since he'd

returned to North Carolina, Carlie Beth had never seen Grif look anything but *GQ*-groomed. Even last night in his workout clothes, he could've just stepped out of an Under Armour ad. But today, his hair was a rumpled mess of golden brown strands, dark half-moons circled below his eyes, and his chin… It looked as if he'd gone a few too many rounds with someone twice his size.

"What happened to you?"

"Concussion," Britt answered before Grif could. "And he needs more rest." Britt still hadn't stepped out of the way, just stood there blocking her entry to the apartment and her access to his brother. Apparently, he wouldn't forgive and forget as easily as Reid.

Behind his back, Grif rolled his slightly bloodshot eyes. "Dude, you cooked me breakfast. You watched me all night. You've done your mother-henly duty, so you can get back to your cabin in the woods now."

"I told Reid I'd bring you out to the Hill."

"I bet I can find my way out there."

"You're not supposed to operate heavy machinery today. You know what the ER staff said about having slow reactions for a while."

"I'll drive him," Carlie Beth said.

A look of surprise zinged across Grif's face, then he gave his brother a not-so-subtle shove in the back. "See, it's all taken care of, so why don't you go do whatever it is you do."

"But—" Britt glanced at Carlie Beth, then back at his brother. "Do you think this is smart?"

Grif made a grab for some papers lying on what looked like Hattie Martin's old couch and shoved them into his brother's hands. "Get. Out."

The downturn of Britt's mouth made his displeasure clear, but he eased around Carlie Beth and into the hallway. "He hit his head hard last night. Concussion, so don't let him fall asleep on you. He could die."

"For Jesus' sake," Grif said. "I don't make it a habit to fall asleep in the presence of a beautiful woman."

Carlie Beth couldn't help herself. She looked down at her boots, jeans, and years-old button-up shirt. Why hadn't she thought to dress a little more like a girl this morning? Maybe Grif was being a smartass by saying she was beautiful. There was no way she held a candle to the women he dated out west. *Stop. You're thinking crazy crap. He's smooth and you know it. He probably calls every woman he meets beautiful. Even Madison Henry.*

"Have him out at Tupelo Hill by one," Britt ordered.

She was half tempted to salute him, but figured that would win either her or Grif some kind of lecture. "Will do."

Once Britt was gone, Grif shook his head in disgust and waved Carlie Beth inside. "That man needs a life."

"He just wants to protect you."

"Maybe he's forgotten I've been managing pretty well on my own since I left home."

She let that slide even though it was obvious he'd had a hard time managing more than a few things recently. "What happened to your chin?"

"Stupidity on my part. Let's just say that climbing alone wasn't a good idea." He gestured toward a tiny makeshift kitchen. "Want some coffee?"

She shook her head. "Already had my cup"—or three—"for the day. Guess it's too much to hope that you have a bottle of Cheerwine in that fridge?"

He laughed. "I thought only kids drank something that sweet."

Lord, how could two people have a child together and know so little about each other's lives? How could have hidden the truth from him? How could she have pretended he didn't have a damn thing to do with her life? With Aubrey's life?

In her mind, it had made things so much simpler. But she'd been fooling herself.

She wandered around the nearly empty space, wishing Grif had some knickknacks she could pick up and play with to calm herself. To make this easier.

He popped a pod into the coffeemaker and while it did its thing, he took a bottle of fancy fizzy water from his fridge. "This okay?"

"Sure."

Once his coffee was ready, he gestured toward the couch with his cup. "I'd ask you to sit down, but I'm not sure where the hell that thing has been."

"At 1217 Sweet Gum Street."

"Huh?"

"It was Mrs. Martin's."

His laugh was low and so sexy it traveled through Carlie Beth's body, setting all her already shot cells into vibration mode. "Well, guess I don't have to worry about the state of the foldout mattress then. Normally you don't know who's done what on those things."

Carlie Beth couldn't hold back her smile. "I don't know. There was a rumor going around for a while that she and Mr. Martin were swingers."

Grif visibly cringed. "Of all the things I didn't need to know. That is one of the prime reasons I can't live in a small town anymore."

And that killed the ember of hope that had started to kindle inside her, hope that he might still have some affection for this town, but it was clear he thought it was beneath him. Which meant she and Aubrey were, too. She set her unopened water back on the countertop. "Do you hate your hometown so much?"

His chin and eyebrows rose at that. "I don't hate it."

"Maybe *hate* isn't the right word." She mulled it over for a moment. "*Disdain* might be better. You show up once or twice a year, always sporting clothes and a haircut that would cost most people around here several months' salary."

"When did being financially successful become a crime?"

"I'm not saying that. But the way you dress, the way you walk, the way you talk... It makes it clear you couldn't shake the North Carolina dirt off your feet fast enough."

"I wanted something…"

"Better?"

"Different."

"And did you find it?"

"You don't care about that. What you really want to know is whether or not I beat the shit out of Madison Henry and dumped her on the side of the 405."

"I asked you to tell me last night, but you avoided the topic."

"Do you have any idea what it feels like to be accused of that kind of brutality?" He paced around the mostly empty room, stopping to stare blankly at the couch. "To have people—not just random people, but clients and friends—believe you're capable of punching a woman in the stomach, in the kidneys, in the face?"

"Why did she lie?"

He swung around and pinned her with an intense look. "How do you know she did?"

Because she was thinking rationally now. "Because although I was stupid enough to go out with an asshole like Roy Darden once, I don't have a history of getting involved with abusive men."

Grif dropped down on the couch and leaned his head back. No way would she remind him that he'd wanted nothing to do with the piece of furniture. "I met her at a club called Fair Game. Pretty popular place with beautiful women, most of them sports groupies."

Carlie Beth held her breath, afraid to move or reach for her water for fear he'd stop talking. Shut her out.

"So it's not a place I normally pick up women." His chuckle was low and rough, as though his vocal cords had been scuffed with a rasp. "Hell, I'm rarely the one doing the picking up."

Of course he wasn't. A man who looked like him—slick, handsome, successful—would have women elbowing each other out of the way to get his attention.

"But Madison was different. Cool and calm instead of eager. Once I found out her name, I understood. Since her family owns the Henry hotel empire, she wasn't there looking for money or fame. The way she talked, I thought she was a true sports fan. You'd be surprised the number of people who don't know a sweep from a bootleg. We talked all night and she never once looked around as if she was trying to scope out better prey."

"And you were flattered."

"She had me hooked. And before long, we were dating. Looking back, I saw how she made certain our pictures ended up on all the celebrity blogs and let everyone know we were exclusive."

"She was setting you up from the start." And that must've eaten at him like acid afterward.

"You know what they say about hindsight," he said, his focus on the blank wall across from him. "Of course, I took her to parties at my clients' houses and other events."

"Is that how she met Andre Campbell? Couldn't she have gotten an introduction some other way?"

When he turned his head to look at her, his eyes were bleak. "Of course, but then she wouldn't have had a scapegoat, now, would she?"

"How could she possibly know she'd need one?"

"Apparently this wasn't the first time she went looking for a guy to kick her around. The Henry family was able to keep it quiet for a long time, but she has a history of hooking up with abusive men. They say if there's one victim and one abuser in a crowd of a thousand, they'll find one another. She knew what Andre was. She wanted him, targeted him just like she did me."

Risking the ick factor, Carlie Beth lowered herself to the cushion beside him. "What bothers you more—that you didn't see her for what she was or that your client was that kind of man?"

"Both."

"Have you ever hit a woman or child, Grif?"

"Goddammit, have you heard a word I've been

saying?" He twisted and loomed over her, but she didn't flinch.

"Every single one."

"Then why would you..." Lowering his head, he bracketed his forehead between his fingers and thumb. "Because you were trying to prove a point. What are you really asking me?"

"I have to know if you're going to break my daughter's heart because of me. Because you think I'm just like Madison Henry—a manipulative bitch."

CHAPTER SEVENTEEN

ALTHOUGH GRIF WAS GRATEFUL THAT Carlie Beth believed him, believed he'd been a victim, regret and shame mixed into a toxic brew in his stomach. As much as he wanted to reassure her that he'd never do anything to hurt Aubrey, even he knew that was a hollow promise. No way in hell would he ever raise a violent hand, but it seemed that loving someone, being loved by someone, was a fast-track to hurting one another. His parents' marriage was a testament to that.

"Did you fuck me over fifteen years ago? Did you mean to get pregnant that night?"

"Of course not."

"Then why would you think I'd blame Aubrey for something she had nothing to do with?"

"Sometimes people do. And I can't handle the thought of her becoming attached to you and then being hurt when you leave."

"Have I done something to make you think I play with people and then walk away? That's not what I did with you, so if you've somehow rewritten history and made me out as the bad guy, you need to revise your notes."

"Aubrey's whole world is right here in Steele Ridge. And you threatened to take her away."

"I was pissed off." Unable to help himself, he reached

out and twirled a section of her hair around his finger. The golden-red strands were soft and silky against his skin. The scent that rose up was obviously the same shampoo Aubrey used, but on Carlie Beth, the fruity fragrance seemed seductive. Seemed to beckon him to sin.

With her.

"As a parent, you can't go off half-cocked. Throwing out ultimatums because you're mad or hurt."

"I haven't had a lot of practice," he said mildly.

"Don't you dare turn this around on me. Aubrey needs to know who she can trust. Who she can count on."

His grip tightened slightly. "And you think she can't count on me because I don't live two blocks down the street from her? Here's the deal...Right now I *do* live just a few blocks away. Why can't that be enough?"

"Because when you go back to LA, she'll be devastated." Carlie Beth jumped up from the couch, pulling her beautiful hair from his grasp. Her top teeth anchored her bottom lip, and she rubbed her hands down her thighs. Grif had a strange feeling they weren't actually talking about their daughter anymore.

Maybe the thing he'd been avoiding—his bone-deep attraction for this woman—was exactly what they needed to test out. Because the way things were now, they were constantly dancing around one another without a true understanding of where they stood. What they were to one another.

And since Grif had no intention of being excluded from his daughter's life a second time even though he knew squat about being a father, he needed to understand what he and Carlie Beth would be to one another.

Friendly acquaintances?

Occasional friends?

Civil parents?

Passionate lovers?

His heart hitched at that thought.

"I have no intention of abandoning anyone or breaking anyone's heart." Carlie Beth started to speak, but he held up a hand and continued. "I'm sorry I lost control the other day. I treated you like the enemy. I backed you into a corner, which meant you had no other move but to come out swinging. But it's time for us to be on the same side."

"What if I'm not done fighting? If I'm not ready to forgive you?" Her pursed mouth was more challenge than he could resist.

"I think you need to ask yourself why you're really fighting," he said softly as he stood and advanced on her. "Because you think I'm going to hurt Aubrey or because I'm a threat to you?"

"This isn't about you and me—"

"Carlie Beth, I'd be lying if I said I knew what the future looks like. Right now, I can't see past getting to know my daughter and getting this town back on its feet. But until I do both of those things to my satisfaction, I won't be away from Steele Ridge for more than two weeks at a time. Because I'm a man not easily satisfied."

He was damn gratified to see her swallow, which shifted his attention to the pulse jumping in the hollow of her throat. Somehow, she'd caught a hint of his thoughts, knew exactly where this was going.

Although he was still questioning his own sanity, with a slow deliberate movement, he slid a hand around the back of her neck under the heavy weight of her sexy hair and rested his thumb over that fluttering vein. "Did you hear what I said?"

"If I accept your…your apology, will you stop touching me?"

"You can't deny the attraction between us."

"This isn't why I came over here," she said, her voice breathy. "Now that I understand what happened between you and Madison Henry, I can—"

Stroke.

Her skin—warm and supple—felt like heaven.

"Are…are you listening to me?"

Stroke.

God, he wanted to put his mouth right there.

"This isn't about us. It's about—"

Yank.

He pulled her to him and covered her mouth. And if he'd thought her skin felt like heaven, it was a pale comparison to her mouth. Hot, sweet temptation. She tasted of sweet cherry and something undefinable. He wanted to eat her up, just swallow her whole.

But he didn't want to go down this road alone.

Sliding his tongue into her mouth, he angled his head for better access to her sweetness. Oh, yeah. Now they were getting somewhere because she was kissing him back, gliding her tongue along his.

He grabbed her waist and went in deeper, as if he could get inside her body, her mind, her very soul, through this tangle of tongues. But his newly patched-up chin had other ideas, throbbing from the pressure, and he groaned. Five days he had to live with these damn stitches.

Carlie Beth pushed against his shoulder. "Grif? This is hurting you, isn't it?"

What was hurting worse was the growing pressure below the waistband of his sweatpants. So instead of answering her, he just pressed a line of kisses along her jawline and up to her ear. With a flick of his tongue, he played with her lobe and felt her shudder. When he caught it between his teeth, she wasn't pushing anymore, but was holding on to his shoulders as if she'd fall otherwise.

But she was right. He wasn't in any shape to do this up against a wall. He'd be damned if he would chance his legs giving out on him at a particularly critical time and landing them in a heap on the floor. So he released her ear and said, "Come to bed with me."

"This...I...We...shouldn't."

"You said you believed me."

"And I do. But that doesn't mean I'll have sex with you."

He tilted her face up and looked into her soft brown eyes. She couldn't deny she was turned on as hell because her pupils were blown and with every breath she took, her hard little nipples grazed his chest.

"Are you seeing someone?" God, that possibility should've probably occurred to him after that run-in with Roy Darden. Grif's body went into fight-or-flight overdrive with the need to whip the ass of any man standing between him and this woman.

"No, but—"

Relief and possessiveness crashed through him.

"—it's not that simple between us."

He took her hand, pressed a hot kiss to the center of her palm. "Right now, it's about as simple as it gets. One man and one woman with the same need."

"With more to think about than themselves."

"Maybe that's the exact reason we should do this."

A surprised laugh popped out of her. "What?"

He trailed a fingertip over her cheek, under her bottom lip, down her chin, to the fragile bumps of her breastbone, revealed by the open collar of her shirt. "We need to figure out what's between us. Because our lives are connected, will always be connected. When two people have a child together, their lives are forever intertwined."

"Aubrey will grow up."

"What about graduation? Wedding? Babies?"

Carlie Beth's hand went to her throat. "Did you really just make us grandparents?"

Yeah, it would be pretty damn funny if it weren't actually coming, sometime down the road. And to a man who hadn't known he was a parent a few days ago. "The point is that I plan to be a part of Aubrey's life from now on. You and I will inevitably see one another even after she's a grown woman."

"And somehow that led you to the idea that we should have sex?"

God, she made him smile. He eased her hand away from her throat and laced his fingers with hers. "Can you honestly tell me you don't want me as much as I want you?"

"I don't...want..." But her tongue touched the corner of her lips, completely giving her away.

"Oh, you want," he said. "You just don't think you should."

When she didn't protest, he led her toward the door to his bedroom. Carlie Beth stepped inside the room and paused, taking in the big bed with new sheets and a particleboard table covered by a lamp and a stack of books. "I'd be lying if I said I wasn't interested." The words rushed out of her as if they had a life of their own.

With a gentle tug, he drew her into his arms. "Shortcake, we're both adults. You don't have to rationalize this."

The breath she blew out skimmed over his biceps and heated the skin there. Somehow she made the most normal things sexy. "Weren't we just fighting? And I don't make a habit of this. It's hard to have much of a love life when you're a single parent."

"I would say I'm sorry, because you deserve someone to take care of you, but right now? I'm not sorry you don't have a man in your bed." He wanted to be the only man stretching out next to her, lying on top of her, pushing inside her.

Sunlight flirted around the edges of the window shades, just enough to illuminate the room without flipping on the light switch. Perfect for making love.

Perfect for making love with Carlie Beth.

Grif framed her face with his hands and brushed her lips with his. Slow, easy, sweet. Because before he was done with her he'd also give her fast, hard, and dirty.

CHAPTER EIGHTEEN

HER BREATH ALREADY SHORT, CARLIE Beth turned her face away from his kiss and blinked, trying to orient herself. She was actually in Grif Steele's bedroom looking at what appeared to be a multi-thousand-dollar bed. But there was no tablecloth on the pressboard side table and no curtains softened the tall windows with waist-high sills and roll-down shades.

And she was standing here thinking about sex. It wasn't even noon and she was considering having sex with Grif. *Seriously* considering it.

Was she crazy? Or just lonely? She was a thirty-four-year-old mom, but Grif made her feel like a teenage girl who'd been talked into the backseat of her prom date's car. Breathless. Unsure. Giddy. Greedy.

"You're right," she said. "I want you. But this is just between you and me. So if you're trying to use sex to get what you want with Aub—"

He cut her off with a kiss, completely carnal and slightly brutal. The combination pared her world down to one second. One man.

Grif's hands were suddenly busy working on her shirt buttons while he consumed her with his kiss. Before she knew what was what, he had her shirt off one arm and hanging around her other wrist and she realized she'd worn her most comfy undershirt—a white cami with a ripped hem and little stains where she'd spilled some ketchup.

Oh, God.

She sucked at seduction.

Grif's hands stilled. "You froze up on me. If you're scared—"

"No, I'm just horrible at this."

He slipped his hands around her waist, caressing the subtle curve there. "From my perspective, you're damn good at it. But if it's not what you want—"

"Where do the women you date in LA buy their underwear?"

His eyes closed and his face took on a pained expression. "This is bad. Bad bed etiquette to talk about other women."

"Not if the woman brings up the topic."

"It's especially bad then."

"Just answer the question. Where do they buy their bras and panties?"

"I don't usually ask."

"Probably at little boutiques with a single set hanging on each beautiful rack." He snuffled at that, and she had to laugh as well. "Not that kind of rack. The underwear I'm wearing? I bought it at the local dollar store, and it was crammed between a hundred other pairs of plain cotton bras and panties."

"If it reassures you any, I'm mainly interested in what's inside them."

But she still wondered if she was just someone to soothe his bruised ego. A diversion, someone to play with while he was getting back on his emotional feet.

So what? You're a grown-ass woman. Maybe he's just someone for you to play with.

Carlie Beth shook out her arms like a boxer and exhaled. "You're right. Okay, I'm ready."

His laugh was sharp. "You look like you're about to climb into a ring. I don't want you to have to psych yourself out for this."

No, no, no. He couldn't back off now. If he did, she'd be forced to go home and dig through the junk drawer for all her stray C batteries.

She needed this.

She deserved this.

So she reached for his hand and placed it over her pounding heart. "I'm just out of practice."

That earned her a smile, a slow and seductive transformation of his face, making her heart sputter and stall. What would it feel like to be on the receiving end of that smile every day?

Don't do that. There are no expectations here.

"Well, why don't we see what we can do about that?"

He might be fighting the fact that his hometown needed him, but at his very center, he was a giver, a caretaker, although he'd deny it if she said so aloud.

He started to pull her toward him, but she went up on her toes and kissed him, pouring pieces of herself into it that she didn't even know needed to be released. She slid her hands under his T-shirt, savoring the feel of his warm skin, the ridges of muscle, the soft line of hair below his navel.

To hell with worrying about her underwear. Once they were both naked, who cared? She shoved at his shirt, grazing his nipples in the process. She wanted to lick them, lick him.

"Carlie Beth, honey, we're not in any hurry."

"Britt said one o'clock."

"My brothers can wait."

"What if I can't? I want you out of your clothes."

Grif blew out a breath. "How about one thing at a time?" With gentle hands, he reached for the hem of her tank top and slowly eased it up her torso and over her head. She had to fight not to cross her arms over the cotton bra a preteen girl might wear, but she won the battle, pulling back her shoulders as if she was proud of the meager portion she'd been given.

One side of Grif's mouth swooped up and he bent to

press a hot kiss between her breasts. "I like the flower," he said against the fabric.

She glanced down. Oh, God. She really had worn a little girl's underwear embellished with a tiny yellow-centered pink daisy. She'd accidentally pulled on one of Aubrey's bras. Heat burned in Carlie Beth's cheeks, but she wasn't about to let embarrassment derail her now. "It's your turn."

He crossed his arms and grabbed his own shirt. When he would've yanked it up in a violent movement, Carlie Beth slowed him and stretched the neckline so it wouldn't graze his chin as he pulled it over his head.

And oh, Grif Steele was just as much a golden boy as he'd ever been. The hair on his chest and stomach was shades lighter than on his head, and it glinted like old gold in the muted sunlight. His skin had a healthy California tan. Oh yeah, she wanted her hands all over that landscape.

Suddenly impatient, she kicked off her boots and reached for the button on her jeans. "Ditch the sweats."

"Uh-uh," he said, swatting her hands away from her waistband. He toyed with the button, fanning his thumb along the sensitive skin of her belly in the process, making the muscles underneath quiver. Just that light touch had the space between her legs aching.

"Please."

"Please what?"

"Please stop with the teasing."

He leaned into her and pressed a kiss to the side of her neck. "Haven't you ever heard anticipation is more than half the fun?"

"You really think this is better than being naked?"

His hand jerked on her pants, and praise God, the button slipped free. Before he could stop her, she slid her zipper down and pushed the denim over her hips. Because the faster she got out of these things, the faster Grif would shed his own pants.

Grif took over, crouching to ease the fabric down her

legs, placing him at eye level with her pink cotton panties. His voice was rough when he said, "Step out."

She braced a hand on his shoulder and shook off one leg. He didn't bother with the other, just grabbed her around the ankle and widened her stance.

"Oh, you are most definitely a girl, Carlie Beth Parrish." The pure male satisfaction in his words sent another wave of arousal through her system, and it came to shore directly between her thighs, lapping at her and making her wet. Grif's hands remained anchored on her legs, but he leaned in and studied the strip of fabric that covered her.

His breath penetrated the thin barrier, warming her skin, heating her blood until it was all she could hear in her head.

When his tongue darted out and precisely flicked her clitoris, her knees were taken completely by surprise. But she wanted more. He stroked her again through the cotton. The desire for him to rip it aside and plunge his tongue inside her shuddered through her, and her grip tightened reflexively on his shoulder.

"You want more?"

"God, yes."

To her everlasting disappointment, he didn't shove down her panties and slide his talented tongue over her. Instead, he stood, so close that the head of his penis nudged against her clit before coming to rest heavily against her stomach.

"Then we're going to have a lesson."

"What?"

"Well, you seem to have some strange idea that you're not very feminine." He smoothed a thumb across her lips, and she bit down on the tip, making him groan low in his throat. "And even though you're trying to distract me, we're going to show you exactly how wrong you are."

"I didn't—"

"Didn't what? Didn't mean it? You're the kind of

woman who says exactly what she means." Grif glanced around the room. "Damn, I wish I had a mirror. Hmm, we'll have to do this a different way." He took her hand and led her to the middle of the room.

"You have a perfectly good bed."

"It won't work for this." He turned her away from him and released the clasp on her bra. "Take off your panties."

She reached for them, and his heat shifted away. She looked over her shoulder to see him shove down his sweats and reveal his cock, hard and flushed and pointing directly north. Oh, it had been a little too long since she'd set eyes on one of those bad boys.

Definitely too long since she'd seen Grif's.

She also wanted to trace the sexy hawk-shaped birthmark on his thigh. With her fingers. Her tongue.

But he paid no attention to his erection, just nodded at her, reminding her she was still wearing clothes. So she shed the scrap of fabric and kicked it away. She started to reach for him, but he caught her hands, twirled her around and pressed his very impressive front against her back. He lifted her hands over her head and led her fingers over her hair.

"You have the most beautiful hair I've ever seen," he said, his voice husky. "Feel it."

The stands were silky and sensual beneath her fingertips. A totally different experience from when she quickly brushed it out in the morning and pulled it back in a ponytail or corralled it into a braid. Grif pushed the mass over her shoulder so it hung across her right breast.

"Run your fingers through it."

She did as he asked, raking through the strands and letting them fall against her skin. When he kissed the spot at the top of her spine, her body buzzed with the decadent sensation, sending shocks of awareness to all her already aware spots.

He took control of her hands again, drawing them

from her hair to splay across her chest and collarbone. Her skin was pale—dotted with tiny freckles—against his darker hands. If he would just shift his hold down a few inches...

As if he'd heard her needy request, he moved her hands, skimming them over her breasts and teasing her tender nipples. "Grif, I—"

"Touch yourself like you mean it. You don't appreciate your own body."

She did. It got her where she needed to go. Was strong and healthy. But she didn't pamper it, linger over it.

He manipulated her fingers until she held a nipple between each thumb and forefinger, forcing her to squeeze and release until she almost screamed from the pressure it was building between her legs. She rubbed them together, felt her slick response on her inner thighs.

"So pretty and pink," he said, his voice husky and sincere. "I'm going to suck them while I fuck you."

She wobbled at his declaration, but he tightened his arms around her and adjusted her hold so she cupped her small breasts in her palms and stroked her nipples with her thumbs. The erotic sensation of touching her own body was both slightly unfamiliar and overwhelmingly sensual.

Too soon, he swept her hands away from her breasts and used them to trace the curve of her waist. "Does that feel like a woman to you?"

God, she was so turned on she was trembling from it.

"Soft skin, perfect curves." Under his direction, her palm smoothed over her stomach, flirted with the indentation of her belly button. Her pinkie trailed over her hip bone and came to rest in the red hair at the apex of her thighs, making her clitoris throb in anticipation.

Once he'd helped her explore the soft skin of her belly, he drew her hands back to her hips, coaxed them down and back so she covered her own ass cheeks. But he wasn't satisfied with that. He made sure her fingertips edged between them, teasing and tempting.

Near her ear, he said, "Would you let me bend you over right now? Let me slide into you from behind?"

She was shaking so hard, she wasn't sure she could stay upright. Her legs would give out, and she'd be on her hands and knees on the floor. He would cover her, push into her... "Yes," she breathed, using one hand to grab his thigh and steady herself.

But he didn't bend her at the waist. He led her other hand back to the front of her body, positioning her middle finger directly over her clitoris.

"If you keep holding your breath, you'll pass out."

Air burst from her on a laugh.

"Better." As a reward, she supposed, he pushed her finger into her folds. "Close your eyes."

She did as he asked and rested her head back on his shoulder, almost able to hear his smile.

"Now, touch yourself and tell me what you feel." His hands retreated back to her waist, and Carlie Beth was all alone with the most private, most intimate part of her body.

She used her finger to circle her clitoris, absorbing the sensation. "It's small. And hard. Like a little BB."

"Packs more punch."

She varied her motion—side to side, up and down, around and around—until her breath was coming hard and choppy.

Grif's hands clamped down on her waist. "You're not finished."

"Almost," she gasped.

"Push your finger inside your body."

"But—"

"Do it."

She reluctantly abandoned the source of her shaky knees and moved her hand lower. Wet, so wet and hot. How could her body be so hot and not burn up? Slowly torturing herself, she eased her finger inside her body, her muscles clenching.

"How does that feel?"

"Um…"

Grif's hold shifted from her waist and slid up her arms, and over her shoulders. "Do you know how sexy it is to watch you touch yourself? Explore and enjoy every feminine part of your body?" He grabbed a handful of her hair and bent her neck to the side to kiss it. "Your hair." With his free hand, he cupped her breast and pinched her nipple. "Your breasts." Too soon, his hold moved away, but it landed on her rear. "Your ass." Then he covered her hand with his, pushing her finger deeper. "Your pretty pussy."

She moaned and ground the heel of her palm against her clit, seeking relief.

"I want you to tell me what you are."

She shook her head, unsure of what he was asking.

"Say 'I'm a strong...'"

"This is silly—"

With a quick move, he pulled her hands away from her body, holding them parallel with the floor. "Say 'I'm a strong...'"

"I'm a strong..."

"Beautiful..."

Although it made her shrink a little, she said, "Beautiful..."

"Sexy..."

"Sexy..."

"Woman."

"Fine, I'm a strong, beautiful, sexy woman!"

"One who now deserves a reward." As if she weighed a single pound, he took her by the waist and lifted her to sit on the high window ledge. "Spread your legs."

"I'm in front of a window."

"Shade's down." He walked across the room and snagged a box from the top of neat pile. He withdrew a condom and placed the rest of the box near her hip.

Carlie Beth couldn't help herself. When he rolled the latex over his erection, her tongue touched her top lip. Grif glanced up and caught her at it. "Thinking about something?"

"I want that."

"That's handy because I plan for you to have it."

"Between my lips."

Grif stumbled a little, reached out and caught himself on the window frame, and she laughed in delight. Mr. Seduction wasn't immune, and that made her a very happy girl. Then his mouth transformed into a wicked smile and he grabbed her by the hips, pulling her to the edge of the window ledge. "Not today, Shortcake."

Before she could prepare herself, he braced himself on either side of her hips and lowered his head between her legs.

OhGodOhGodOhGod.

It had been so long since she'd had a man's mouth this close to her happy parts, she couldn't even remember the last time. Now, Grif's labored breath was hot against her inner thighs.

She had to fight the need to squeeze her legs together to get him closer. She squirmed on the cool window casing.

His touch, when it came, was a leisurely lick with a brain-blasting tongue curl at the end. And she knew her chances for survival were in the single digits.

But, oh, what a way to go.

Grif repeated that little technique a few more times, and Carlie Beth didn't realize she'd buried her hands in his hair and was pulling the hell out of it until he paused and said, "Palms on the windowsill."

"Huh?"

He reached up and untangled her fingers, then moved her hands to a safer position near her hips. She shifted for better balance, and he hummed his approval because her movement had pulled her shoulders back, making her boobs look as if she actually had something.

When Grif returned to his previously scheduled program, he pushed her knees wide, opened her as far as her position would allow. Then his tongue became BFFs with her clitoris, playing with the sensitive nerve endings there until Carlie Beth thought her bones would simply disappear. As delicious as his attention was, it wasn't quite enough, keeping her right on the edge.

She moaned her frustration.

"Need a little more?"

Crap. She didn't want him to think she didn't like what he was doing. "Um…"

"Because I'll give you anything you want."

His words arrowed directly into Carlie Beth's chest. Anything? How could he do that when she didn't know what the hell she wanted from him?

But before she could form some type of coherent response, he pressed two fingers against the very heart of her. He slid them inside her, what felt like one stingy millimeter at a time. Hooking his fingers, he touched the spot that made her come unglued.

"Oh, yessss."

Then his thumb teased her clit while his fingers worked some incredible sexual magic. It didn't take long. Probably less than a minute if Carlie Beth had the brain cells to clock it. A few pushes, strokes, and circles, and her body simply gave over to him. Her orgasm was a pulsing, shaking, whole-body affair as she rode his fingers, her hips pumping against his hand.

She had absolutely no shame, no sense of propriety at that moment. All she wanted was for the feeling to go on. Forever.

Grif didn't allow her brain and body to become one again. As soon as her orgasm began to wane, he covered her mouth with his and pushed inside her body.

And oh Lord, if his fingers had felt like heaven, this was…was…whatever was above heaven. He braced her ass with one big hand and proceeded to screw her silly.

Long, hard strokes while he took their kiss to a wild tempo. Tongues and teeth and lips in a wild mash of desperation. Her covered her breast and played with her nipple, never breaking stride in either of his other pursuits.

At eighteen, he'd been a sweet and fun lover. Now, he was completely devastating, able to keep her on the edge of sanity from his touch all over her body. Her heart running a hundred-yard dash, she plunged her fingers into his hair, holding him close as she met him kiss for kiss.

When was the last time she'd felt so...so...*much*?

He gave her breast one last thorough caress, then reached between their bodies to lavish slick attention to her clitoris again. Up and down until she was lightheaded and panting for breath.

Between the slide of his tongue along hers, the slide of him inside her, and the glide of his fingers between her legs, the pressure built. A sweet intensity that seemed to make her pounding heart swell, doubling its size.

Unable to control her response, she took their kiss to the next level, nipping at his lips in desperation. He palmed the back of her head and met her challenge.

Within seconds, another orgasm began to ripple through her, like a tide that could never be stopped, too powerful, too elemental to let a mere woman get in its way.

Grif thrust into her with a wild intensity, his rhythm finally hitching. Then he thrust and held, groaning through his own climax. He leaned his forehead against hers, his chest expanding and releasing rapidly as he worked to catch his breath.

Carlie Beth slid her hands from his hair down to his shoulders, savoring the sheen of sweat glistening on his muscles. Although he'd seduced her, he'd been just as affected by what they'd done.

At least physically.

"That was..."

"Yeah, it was all that and about a hundred times more." His smile was endearingly crooked. "And Shortcake, if you're still worried about not being much of a girl after that, I'm not sure I can help you. Because I think you're one hell of a woman."

Chapter Nineteen

BEFORE THE SWEAT EVEN BEGAN to dry on their skin, Carlie Beth was fidgeting in Grif's arms as though she were locked in a carnival ride she no longer wanted to take a spin on. *Dammit.* He wanted to knock his head against the wood trim. Although it had seemed like a good idea in his lust-inspired fog, he was now having second thoughts about his decision to nail her on a windowsill in an apartment bare not only of furniture but sophistication.

Just because he was living in less-than-optimal conditions didn't mean she should be subjected to them. How many times could he be a dick to this woman?

"Carlie Beth, I'm—"

"Oh my God. You're about to say something that's going to piss me off, aren't you?" She shoved at his shoulder and swung her knee over, almost neutering him in the process. He tried to grab her by the waist, but his phone rang from the bedside table, distracting him. Carlie Beth swerved left and in her scramble to escape him, she bumped the window shade, somehow triggering the damn thing to pull and release. As she hopped down from the ledge and ran for the bedroom door, the piece of fabric that had been shielding them from Main Street rolled up with a reverberating snap, and quite literally left Grif standing there with his dick out.

Although he quickly sidestepped, he wasn't fast enough. From her viewpoint on the opposite side of the street, Mrs. Martin, former owner of his skeevy couch, gave him a toothy smile and a coy wave.

Jesus.

Ignoring his still ringing phone, Grif reached up and yanked the damn shade down three times before it finally caught. Whoever invented those piece-of-shit mechanisms should be taken out and shot.

While he did battle, trying to preserve their privacy, Carlie Beth had hauled ass across the hallway to his less-than-elegant bathroom. This was a complete mess. He'd planned to do a few upgrades before he invited a woman over.

Okay, not just any woman. Carlie Beth.

While she did all her washing and flushing and whatever, Grif snatched up his sweatpants and shoved his legs into them. Because something told him Carlie Beth wouldn't come out smiling.

You're a smooth one, Steele. Had he been about to tell her he was sorry?

Yeah, he had, but not for the reason she probably thought.

He dropped down on the side of his bed and shoved his hands into his hair, jarring his already tender head. Holy fuck. That was a mistake. He breathed through the dull pain and tried to think.

What just happened here?

He and Carlie Beth had mind-altering sex. No doubt he'd expected it to be good because even after all these years, he'd remembered how she felt in his arms. But it had rocked him in a way he hadn't expected. In a way that made him feel uncomfortably vulnerable, a place he never wanted to be again.

Still, he blew out a breath and walked across the hall to tap on the bathroom door. "Carlie Beth, you all right?"

"Dandy," she shot back. "Except I seem to be missing my clothes."

She wasn't missing them. They were exactly where she'd left them, lying in a sexy mess on his floor. "They haven't moved."

"I need them."

"Okay." But he simply stood there, letting the silence stretch out. And out. And out.

He'd wait for as long as it took.

"Grif?" she finally said.

"Yep?"

"Do you have my clothes?"

"Nope."

"What?"

"If you want your clothes, you're going to damn well stop acting like a sixteen-year-old virgin and get your ass out of my bathroom."

The sound from the other side of the door was a combo laugh and snort. "I thought you were supposed to be the classy brother."

"Even classy guys don't like to be pushed."

"*I'm* pushin' *you*?" Her voice held the drawling disbelief only a Southern woman could pull off, and it made him grin. God, he lov—

Whoa.

Whoa, whoa, whoa. Grif squeezed his eyes closed to get a grip on what he'd almost thought about this woman. He liked her. He wanted her. He fucking admired her.

There was a lot to admire—her ability to make beautiful art, her resilience and determination, her dedication to being a great mom to Aubrey.

But he was absolutely not back in his hometown to fall in love. Hell, he'd avoided that his entire adult life. Maybe it was just all this kumbaya family stuff that was clouding his perception of reality. He and Carlie Beth needed to be civil and get along for Aubrey's benefit.

And yes, he'd been the one to suggest they figure out what was between them, but he'd never imagined he'd feel…this. Whatever the hell *this* was.

The doorknob turned, and he expected Carlie Beth to poke her head out demanding her clothes or to have wrapped herself in one of his towels. But she swung the door wide, and she stood there, chin tilted up and hands on her perfectly rounded hips, naked as she'd been when she dashed out of his bedroom.

And the sight of her—slight whisker burn on her neck, red hair a mess, and eyes full of feminine challenge—pretty much hit him like a sharp jab to the kidneys. Made his breath stall and his knees unstable.

"Earlier," he said, "I was going to say I was sorry. But not for the reason you assumed."

Now, her arms crossed over her breasts, plumping them up and momentarily distracting him. "Then why?"

He ran a hand along the waistband of his sweats, suddenly self-conscious of how he looked. This wasn't the Los Angeles Grif Steele. That Grif took women out for a nice dinner, brought them home and offered them something smooth and expensive to drink, and made love to them.

"There wasn't a damn thing slick about this."

"Excuse me?"

He turned away and squeezed his forehead, ignoring the pain it caused. "I fucked you on a windowsill."

"Yes." She had the sheer nerve to laugh. Didn't she understand how serious this was?

"And I gave you Perrier and didn't even offer you a mug muffin."

"Oh, God. You are not okay." She darted around him and dragged his hand away from his face. "You re-concussed your head."

"That's not even a word."

With a little frown, she peered at the cut on his chin, then studied his eyes. "Then we screwed a screw loose in your head."

"I'm fine."

"I don't think so because you're not making a bit of sense." She grabbed his hand and began to tug him toward the front door. "I'm taking you back to the hospital."

"Stop." He pulled her into his arms and held her close. Rested his chin on top of her head and sighed. "We aren't going anywhere."

"Why not?"

"One, because you're butt naked."

She looked down and laughed. "Oh."

"And two, because you were right earlier. You're nothing like the women I've dated in California."

When she tried to pull away, he simply held her tighter. "You're sweet and funny and real."

"And they're sour, stoic, and fake." Her tone was just acerbic enough to make him chuckle.

"They're not you."

There was no way to miss the way her breath whooshed in surprise. "What…what was this? What we did here today?"

"I'd be lying if I said I knew." He kissed the top of her head, breathing in her intoxicating sweet fragrance, and tried to ignore the way his heart was beating the hell out of his ribs. "But I think we owe it to ourselves to find out."

When she nodded, a vague movement that told him she needed a minute to breathe and sort through things, Grif slowly released her. Then he picked up his phone and checked his missed call.

"Need some privacy?" she asked.

"It'll keep." He tossed his phone onto the bed. Jamal Harris would just have to wait a little while to discuss the terms of his contract renewal with the Kings. Instead of making the call, he lounged back on his elbows and watched Carlie Beth dress.

She glanced up at him as she stepped into those cute

cotton panties. "Do you know how long it's been since a man ogled me while I put my clothes back on?"

Her words tightened his gut. *Jealousy is stupid*. He gave her what he knew was a strained smile.

"Oh, since about…never."

Her tone was teasing, but her words hit him hard. She'd missed out on marriage, establishing that comfortable relationship that allowed two people to watch each other dress and undress. See everything—the good, bad, strengths, imperfections. "I fucked things up for you, didn't I?"

"What?" That brought her head up, and she almost fell over with one leg stuck in her jeans. Grif lunged forward and grabbed her by the elbow to keep her upright.

"Let's face it. You're in your thirties. At this point in their lives, most women, especially in a place like Steele Ridge, are married with families."

"I do have a family. Aubrey's my whole world."

"But I imagine there've been men who might've been interested in you if you didn't come with a kid."

"Probably, but those aren't the kind of men who would interest me regardless. I'm a package deal. I have been since I was nineteen years old." Her face took on a stubborn cast—eyes narrow and mouth pinched. "But if you're feeling sorry for me, stop. I've dated. Not a ton, because I didn't want to parade a bunch of guys through Aubrey's life. She always, always comes first. And believe it or not, I've actually fielded several marriage proposals. So you can just put your poor-little-unwed-Carlie-Beth crap to bed."

"Several? What does that mean exactly?"

She looked up and to the right. "Let's see…" She touched one pointer finger with the other. "Chuck Canfield when I was eight months gone with Aubrey. Lord, I was bigger than Dave's barn out at Black Horn Ranch."

Motherfucker. Chuck Canfield had been a classmate

of his. And he'd asked Carlie Beth to marry him when she was round with Grif's baby? He should find the guy and—

"Then…hmm…" She counted off another finger. "Aubrey must've been four or five when a guy from over in Cullowhee asked and offered to give her five or six brothers and sisters. It was hard to pass up, but I decided broodmare wasn't a good look on me."

He didn't know whether to laugh or cuss aloud.

Carlie Beth's eyes went a little cloudy, and it was then Grif's gut tightened to the point of excruciating tension. "A few years ago, I was involved with a man. His name was John." The hint of a sigh in her voice didn't do a damn thing to relieve the sick feeling inside him. Because her expression, her tone, said this guy had been important. Meant something to her. "We dated for several months. He adored Aubrey and she thought he hung the moon."

A different kind of jealousy swarmed over Grif. He could've lost his daughter without ever knowing about her. If Carlie Beth had married, Grif would've never questioned Aubrey's paternity.

He tried to shove away the surge of anger trying to consume him at that thought. *Remember, Aubrey said she's never called another man Dad. That has to count for something.*

"We were both in our late twenties, so it didn't take us long to start talking about marriage. On the day we were supposed to shop for engagement rings, he never showed up. Never called. Ever."

"What are you saying? That the douche just bolted?"

One of her shoulders lifted and dropped. "I guess. But not just on me. He worked at one of the landscaping companies. He didn't give notice, didn't resign. Just left on a Friday and never showed up the following Monday."

"Sounds like a real standup guy," he grumbled. The jerk had obviously been a stupid bastard. One that Grif felt strangely indebted to right now. Because it would've been horrible to discover he had a daughter only to find he'd already been replaced.

"Since then, I've been pretty picky."

"Yeah, especially with that prick Darden."

"Hey," she protested, slipping into her overshirt. "One date. I wasn't stupid enough to do it again."

He reached for her hand and drew her down to his lap. When she settled in and rested her head against his shoulder, Grif's heart did something so foreign, he didn't know how to respond. It simply lost its shape and softened. He swallowed twice to reactivate his voice. "I want you and Aubrey to be happy. To be safe and secure. Do you believe that?"

"Is this a hint to cash that check?"

"I was a complete dick about that."

"Yeah, you were."

"But I didn't miscalculate."

Her laugh was warm against his neck, and he wrapped his arms tighter around her, suddenly wanting to keep her there, to stay that way for the foreseeable future. "If I were to deposit something like that, Highland Bank and Trust would sound the alarms."

"I never want the two of you to do without again."

She lifted her head and met his gaze, her eyes both serious and warm. "I've always provided for us." When he started to speak, she pressed her fingertips against his lips. "Do we always have the nicest or fanciest things? No. But in this day and age, that can actually be good for a kid. Some of Aubrey's friends crook a finger and their parents give them everything they want. Aubrey knows the value of a dollar. She thinks before she asks for something. She's willing to work for the things she wants. And I refuse to believe that's a bad thing."

He kissed her fingers in gratitude. "Thank you."

"For what?"

"For being such an amazing mother to Aubrey. I'm

still sorry as hell I wasn't around to help you. But if anyone could do this parenting thing alone, it's you, Carlie Elizabeth Parrish."

Her eyes and mouth widened. "How did you know my middle name?"

He tilted his head. "Carlie *Beth*. It's not much of a stretch." Just that little thing agitated him all over again. He had a child with a woman who was surprised he knew her middle name. "But I also saw it on Aubrey's birth certificate." Which his name was still missing from.

"What's yours?"

"My what?"

She gave him an eye roll. "Your zodiac sign. What do you think?"

He cleared his throat. There was a reason his business cards read Griffin F. Steele, period. "It's a family name. My great-granddad."

She made a little gimme motion with her fingers.

Dammit. He'd given her so little and so far she wouldn't take his money. "Fletcher," he mumbled.

"Say again. I didn't quite catch that."

"Fletcher," he said louder.

Her eyes brightened. "Ooh, can I call you Fletch?"

"Only if you want me to yank down your pants and spank your round little ass every time you do."

At that, her eyes went even brighter. Good Jesus, his sweet little tomboy had a kinky side. And that brought all sorts of interesting scenarios to mind. "Aubrey could call you Daddy Fletch."

That sure blew away his momentary visions of handcuffs and blindfolds. "You know she asked if she could call me Dad."

"Yeah." Her voice was soft.

"Does that bother you?"

"Not on the surface." She pushed out of his lap and paced over to the window where they'd made love. With restless fingers, she worried the edge of the shade. "But I doubt either of you really knows what a dad is."

His laugh was short and sharp. "Other men do it all the damn time." *Other* men. Not him.

The pressure that she pulled forth in him every time they talked about their daughter began to build, but Grif pushed that shit down. If they continued to get pissed and defensive every time they discussed Aubrey, someone would be stomping around all the time. "Just because my dad doesn't have much to do with his kids doesn't mean I'll do the same to Aubrey."

When she turned to look at him, her face was so damn full of bleak heartache, it would've brought him to his knees if he weren't already sitting. "You live two thousand miles away."

"I'm here now."

"Now. That's an important word. What happens when you wrestle Steele Ridge back into shape and stop spending every two weeks here?"

"We don't have to worry about that right now."

"Mothers worry. It's in the job description."

No, this wasn't just about the distance between Carolina and California. Something else was eating at Carlie Beth, because he'd swear she'd believed him when he said he was in for good when it came to Aubrey. He pushed off the bed and went to Carlie Beth to smooth a hand down her hair, down her spine, letting it rest against her lower back. "What's really wrong here?"

She turned into him, burrowed against him as if she couldn't bear looking at him. Something had her hurting, so he wrapped her in his arms, trying to give her reassurance. "Whatever it is. We'll handle it."

"You said you'd fight me for custody if I didn't take that money."

"We've already established I was being a dick."

Her laugh was more of a snuffle. "What…what if she asked to live with you? What if she wanted to leave Steele Ridge and move to LA?"

Her words were like a body slam. Even when he'd done the strong-arm thing with Carlie Beth, he'd never once believed it would come to a legal battle. He was so damn accustomed to using leverage to get what he wanted that he hadn't considered the impact the same strategy might have on Carlie Beth and Aubrey.

Holding Carlie Beth by the shoulders, he drew her away from him and bent at the knees so they were eye to eye. "She won't."

"Los Angeles is exciting," Carlie Beth said, a little hiccup in her voice. "Fast-paced. Sexy. I mean, Hollywood and Disneyland."

"You can't think I would encourage her to move across the country with me."

"Are you saying you wouldn't want her?"

God, could a man win with two women running circles around him? Evie and his mom would say no, just shake their heads in mock-sorrow at his stupidity. "I'm saying I know she belongs here with you."

"What about visits? Would you let her visit you out there?"

This was like a landmine of questions. What was the right answer?

"Would you approve?"

Her face scrunched up so damn adorably that he wanted to kiss her and spank her at the same time. "There'd have to be rules. No women or wild parties while she's there."

He drew back and pretended to pull his phone from his pants. "I'll send myself a reminder text."

"And you can't buy her anything she wants."

"Got it. No shopping, no alcohol, no sex." He rested his hands on his hips and stared at her. "Anything else?"

"You think I'm overreacting."

"Hell, Carlie Beth, she hasn't even asked to visit and you're already blowing up crazy scenarios in your head."

"You can't deny things happen."

No, he couldn't. His life over the past year was a prime example of a situation getting more than crazy. Becoming dangerous. "If any of my athletes are snorting blow or getting baked, I drop their asses. I have enough shit to clean up without representing complete idiots. And I sure as hell wouldn't take my teenage daughter into some orgy."

"They have orgies?"

For. Fuck's. Sake.

"Honestly, I don't think this is something we have to work out today." He smiled, trying to calm her through force of will. "If Aubrey wants to come out and visit me, and I hope she will, I would be very careful about what she sees and does. And I know everyone in small-town America thinks LA is Sodom and Gomorrah all rolled into one. But the truth is, most people are just regular old folks."

Carlie Beth blew out a breath.

"Besides, I wouldn't let her fly out alone the first time. Has she ever been on an airplane before?"

"No. If we get the chance for a little vacation, we always drive."

"Will it make you feel better if I tell you that I'd want you both to come out?"

She cradled her head between her palms, clearly squeezing as if she were trying to keep it from exploding. "I'm never this crazy."

He pulled her back in for an affectionate hug. "Shortcake, Miss Joan would tell you that being a mother and being crazy are the same damn thing."

CHAPTER TWENTY

AFTER GRIF HAD REELED IN Carlie Beth's crazy, they'd slowly finished dressing, which felt so foreign to her. She wasn't used to this kind of intimacy with a man. Somehow, making love with him, letting him undress her and touch her, had seemed less revealing than putting their clothes back on.

Grif's phone rang as he was trading sweatpants for jeans. Carlie Beth couldn't help herself. Through her lashes, she gave his unbuttoned and unzipped pants a thorough looking at.

"Steele," he said into the phone.

A shiver ran through her and she turned away. It wouldn't do to let him see how affected she was by the sexy tone of his voice. Because that was just a small part of what drew her to him. It was his determination and persistence in the face of challenges he hadn't gone looking for—both in the form of this town and his daughter—that really cut her off at the knees. This was a man you could count on in a crisis, in a moment of weakness, and yet she'd never given him that chance.

"Great," he said. "I'll be down in a minute to grab the keys and sign for it."

She finished buttoning her overshirt, half tempted to do it all the way up to the collar for protection. But that wouldn't do a thing to safeguard her from the real threat. Her own feelings. "Sign for what?"

"My new car."

"You have a Maserati yet you felt the need for something new?" Lord, they lived in two completely different dimensions.

"Someone did a number on Louise, so she's in a shop in Charlotte."

"What do you mean did a number?"

"Bashed in her lights, carved up her seats."

"Here in Steele Ridge?"

"Right out back."

"Oh my God. That's horrible. Who in the world would do that?"

"Maybe someone who isn't happy about the job I'm doing as city manager."

"That's just stupid. I mean, who could be worse than Bobby Ray Benton?"

"Thanks," he drawled. "I think."

"You know what I mean."

When they went outside ten minutes later, a man was twirling a set of keys and leaning against a shiny new...

Nissan Quest minivan.

Grif strode forward to shake the man's hand, sign a paper attached to a clipboard, and take the keys. It took less than two minutes, and the delivery guy gave him a salute, got in a car with another person, and drove off.

Looking down at the keys in his hand, Grif said, "Guess I should listen to Britt on this one and let you drive."

"Th...that?"

"I guess we could take your Scout, but I'd really like to see how this thing rides."

"Didn't you test-drive it?"

"Nope." He handed over the keys, but her feet remained stuck to the sidewalk. "Never even looked at it."

"You bought a tricked-out minivan, but you haven't driven it."

"I read all the reports online. It checked out, and I pulled the trigger."

"You bought a minivan?"

He waved toward the—of course—steel-gray van. "I think that's pretty apparent."

Still knocked sideways by his choice of vehicle, Carlie Beth marveled over the shiny new family ride Grif had apparently paid cash for, poking at buttons every time they stopped for a red light.

"What are you doing?"

She shot him a sly smile. "Looking for the eject button."

When he reached across from the passenger's seat and took her hand in his, Carlie Beth's heart pressed against her breastbone. What was this? What in God's name were they doing?

They pulled up in front of the sprawling white farmhouse, and Reid was standing on the porch, his back propped against a column. They stepped out of the van, and he lifted his arm as if checking his watch, but he was actually scowling at Grif. "Maybe my watch stopped, but I thought I told you to have your ass...uh...your butt out here at one o'clock."

Grif pocketed the car keys. "I'm here now, so stop your worrying. Otherwise, I'll start calling you Britt."

"This is serious shit."

With a hot glance in her direction, Grif told his brother. "It's not the only serious thing going on in my life right now."

Reid pinned Carlie Beth with a dissecting stare. "Britt's gonna shit a llama," he muttered, probably not expecting her to catch his words.

She tried to angle away from Grif, but he caught her hand again, making it clear something was going on between them. "Stop it," she said in a low tone. "You don't need trouble with your brothers."

His smile was crooked as he lifted her hand and gave it a smacking kiss. "I've always got trouble with those three halfwits."

Reid just shook his head and eyeballed the van. "Carlie Beth, you get a new ride? If I'd known you were looking to get rid of the Scout, I would've been happy to take it off your hands."

"It's not mine," she said.

"Rental? Yours in the shop?"

"Nope." Her own grin went wide and wicked. "The van is your brother's."

Not watching where he was going, Reid rammed his knees into one of the brightly painted Adirondack chairs near the front door. His stupefied gaze swung between the minivan and his brother. "You? You bought a soccer mom car?"

Unfazed, Grif lifted a shoulder. "It's got good shit inside it."

"Uh-huh." Reid nodded absently. "Like a place to hang your purse and store your tampons."

Carlie Beth frogged him in the shoulder. "Hey, you make it sound like girl stuff is bad."

"Nah." Reid waggled his eyebrows at her. "I like girl *stuff* just fine. Girl cars, not so much."

"Remind me you said that when you want to stash your beer in the cooler built into the floor," Grif said mildly.

Reid's eyes telegraphed interest. "It's got hiding places?"

"I thought that might get your attention."

"You're still never gonna live this down."

"Probably, but I also bought a custom Harley."

Reid's teasing expression went serious as he held open the front door. "Sure sounds like you're settling in—apartment, wheels"—he shot Carlie Beth a quick glance—"and things."

Hmm…one of those *things* apparently being her. Grif's only answer was a small smile that somehow conveyed the message for Reid to stay out of his business.

"In here." Reid led them into the kitchen where Jonah

and Britt were sitting at a massive farm table made from a slab of wood set on metal legs. Britt was poring over some papers, muttering to himself and making little notes in the margins. Jonah was engrossed in something on his phone—from the sounds of it, a shoot-'em-up video game. The table's top was gorgeous, a slab of pecan with swirls and character. Carlie Beth drew away from Grif and leaned over to get a look underneath. The craftsmanship definitely took a dive when it came to the table's supports.

"Mom's newest purchase," Jonah told her. "Some dude over in Buncombe County made it."

"Jason Krieg."

"That's the one."

The craftsman was one heck of a woodworker, but he shouldn't touch metal with a ten-foot pole. Carlie Beth looked pointedly at where Jonah had his bare feet propped on the table surface. "You put much weight on this thing, it'll collapse."

"If that's the case, then Reid shouldn't even look at it." Jonah hooted and swung his legs down. "Mom fell in love with the wood."

She squatted down to get a better look at the underside. Yeah, those joints were not up to snuff. "Think she'd want a sturdier support?"

"You offering?" Reid asked.

"Well, I'd hate to find out one of the Steele brothers met an undignified end by being crushed under this thing."

"You'd do that for my mom?" Grif asked her.

What he didn't realize and she didn't want to admit to herself was that there were a lot of things she'd do for this man. Do for his family.

After all, Aubrey was one of them. No matter how many years Carlie Beth had tried to deny it.

"This is inferior welding. Besides, it's ugly," she said, trying to make her smile look calm and confident. "Can you ask your mom if she's okay with me making her something new?"

"I doubt I have to, but sure."

"Now that we have Mom's interior decorating all set, can we please talk about why someone was trying to kill Grif last night?" Reid dropped into a chair, but he was careful not to touch the table itself, which made Carlie Beth's smile widen.

Until his words registered.

"What? What do you mean tried to kill him?"

"After the ambulance picked up Grif last night, I went up and checked all the handholds. Every damn one of them across the top was greased up like a pig at the county rodeo," Reid said, sending a hard look Grif's way. "It wouldn't have mattered which one you grabbed hold of. Your ass was coming down."

"I was wrong to climb by myself," he admitted. "But in my defense, up to this point, the worst the kids have done is clog up the toilets and paint some questionable haiku on the walls."

"Limericks," Jonah mumbled, his eyes still glued to his phone screen. "Haiku has three lines with a total of seventeen syllables. Limericks rhyme. You know, 'There once was a girl from Nantucket.'"

The sound of the front door opening and *snicking* closed came from the foyer. "I know at least a couple of you boneheads are here," a woman called out. "Because your cars are here."

Britt scowled at Reid. "She sounds pissed. Tell me you called her."

"I was going to after we talked about all this."

When Carlie Beth looked, the sheriff was standing in the dining room doorway, her face like a sudden storm sweeping over the mountains. "Someone want to fill me in on what happened out here last night and then tell me why the hell you didn't call my people?"

Grif rubbed at his forehead, pushing at his hair so he looked like a rumpled little boy. Then he tilted his face to give Maggie a clear view of his chin. "Can you keep it down a little? My head's still tender."

Although concern touched Maggie's eyes, her hard look didn't falter a bit. "And whose fault is that, you idiot?"

Looked like Grif's little sympathy play wouldn't appease his cousin. Good for Maggie.

Reid stood and offered Maggie his chair. "Mags, can we get you some coffee or iced tea?"

She strode over and glared at him, somehow appearing to be on his level even though she was inches shorter. "Cream and two sugars. And make it fresh. I don't want anything left over from your breakfast."

"Jonah, go make Mags some coffee," Reid ordered.

Jonah's only response was a lazy lift of his middle finger.

So Reid stomped into the kitchen while every other person at the table wore a little smirk. This family. They were tough cookies, but it was obvious they loved one another. The tightness in Carlie Beth's chest that she'd had since she realized she'd have to share her daughter loosened a little more.

Maggie pointed at Grif. "Other than Britt, I expected you to be the smartest of the lot, and yet I hear you were climbing that damn wall like a deranged monkey."

"I was doing a pretty damn good job. Would've made it over the top if I hadn't slipped."

"The point is you did slip."

Reid came back in carrying a single cup of coffee and set it in front of Maggie.

Britt frowned at him. "That's it? No one else gets any?"

"If I wanted to run a diner, I'd rent a place on Main Street."

Maggie took a sip from her cup and choked. "Don't complain. He did you a favor. This is instant. Now, why the hell didn't anyone think I needed to know what happened to Mr. Numbskull last night?"

Reid propped a shoulder against the wall. "We've had some petty vandalism in the sports center recently. A little graffiti before Baby Billionaire ever bought the place. And you know about the fire a few months ago. A few mishaps since."

"Why haven't you mentioned the building vandalism before now, especially after what happened to Grif's LuLu?"

"Louise," Grif corrected. "And we didn't say anything because it was stupid stuff—jacking up some of the equipment, stuffing paper towels in the toilets."

"But nothing that hurt anyone?"

"Have you ever had to muck out a flooded bathroom?" Jonah said. "That's not without pain. Believe me, when we catch those kids, we'll—"

"Call me immediately," Maggie ordered. She took another sip of her coffee and grimaced. "The ER folks tell me Grif had something on his hands when they admitted him."

"I didn't realize it at the time," Grif said. "Just thought I didn't have a good grip on the handhold, but apparently, there was something slick on it."

"Like motor oil?" Maggie asked Reid, leaning forward intently.

"Definitely an oily consistency, but not as dark," Reid said.

"Why all the questions?" Grif asked, pulling Maggie's attention from his brother.

"Because you were hurt, and under normal circumstances, I wouldn't put it past one of you to sabotage the other."

Reid pushed away from the wall. "Hey—"

Maggie held up a hand. "But I don't buy that you'd actually risk killing one another. Was this oily stuff all over the wall?

"No," Reid said. "I found it on every handhold within three feet of the top. Someone didn't want anyone to make it over."

"You asked about motor oil," Carlie Beth said to Maggie. "Roy Darden was a mechanic. Do you think they're related? That someone purposefully meant to hurt Grif?"

"Doubtful," Grif said. "Would be pretty hard for a dead guy to come back and get revenge on me. But Mags, what about the person Darden's neighbors spotted the night he died?"

She sighed. "Our best witness never actually saw anyone, just heard the knocking. When we questioned him again, he swore up and down alien raccoons frequently visited Darden."

"In other words, total dead end."

"Yep," she said. "And not relevant. So I need to find out what was on those handholds last night. If Reid hasn't completely screwed things up, I can get a sample and send it off to the Western Regional Crime Lab."

"Isn't that where all the law enforcement agencies from around here send stuff?" Reid commented.

"Usually," Maggie said. "Which means they're normally a little backed up."

"Even though it's probably just those jackass kids," Reid said, "I don't like the idea of leaving this swinging in the wind."

"What about private labs?" Grif asked Maggie.

"The couple here in Carolina are a little faster, but they're pricey."

An unexplainable feeling of foreboding came over Carlie Beth, and she gripped Grif's forearm. "Something about this scares me."

When he looked at her, his expression held a question. As if he was also trying to figure out what the heck was going on between them and why they were feeling so pulled toward one another. He blinked and whatever it was disappeared.

Grif gave her a slow and thoughtful nod. "Carlie Beth's right. Maggie, get me those lab names. I'll foot the bill to have this oil checked out."

CHAPTER TWENTY-ONE

WHEN CARLIE BETH ANSWERED THE knock at her front door a few days later, her heart went into overdrive at the sight of Grif standing on her porch holding a bouquet of flowers in each hand. Those, combined with his killer smile and casual outfit of perfectly faded jeans, a pair of well-used hiking boots, and crisp plaid shirt folded back at the forearms, about did her in. The stitches he still sported in his chin and the sexy scruff on his face from being unable to shave gave him a total tough-guy look.

That *did* do her in.

"I…um…Hi." Her voice came out breathy.

His smile went wider as he took in her cut-off jean shorts, tank top, do-rag, and eye-blinding purple painted toes. "Hi, yourself." His attention remained on her feet.

"It's called Royal Pain."

"Every time I think I have you figured out, you surprise me."

"Is that a good thing?"

He shifted a bouquet to his other hand and pulled her in for a soft kiss that left her off balance. "That, Carlie Beth Parrish, is a very good thing."

"Mom, who—" Aubrey drew up short and darted a look between them, her gaze taking in their closeness and Grif's hand wrapped around the back of Carlie Beth's neck. "Oh…"

The awkward tension wove around them for a few seconds before Grif crashed through it. "How would you two feel about an outing to Asheville?"

Carlie Beth glanced down at herself. "Oh, but I was just cleaning the—"

"Mom," Aubrey said through her teeth. "The bathrooms will wait."

"But I'm not dressed."

Grif and Aubrey shared a look that insinuated they wanted to both shake their heads at her. "Does she have clothes in her closet?" he asked Aubrey.

"Are we talking fancy or casual?"

"Definitely casual," he said, passing the pink, yellow, and orange daisies to Aubrey. "For you."

Aubrey's eyes went soft and dreamy. Her first flowers from a boy. From her father. Which made Carlie Beth's heart go soft and dreamy. He was doing more than paying lip service to being a dad. He was trying and, from the looks of it, succeeding.

Aubrey raised up on tiptoe and pressed a kiss to Grif's cheek. "I'll see what I can do."

Her smile was the size and strength of the sun as she headed for Carlie Beth's room.

"How did you know daisies were her favorite?"

"The same way I knew sunflowers were yours. Sometimes I forget the sheer power of knowledge in a small town." Grif eased past her into the house and held out the other bouquet to her. "How do you feel about dinner and little sightseeing?"

"I don't want to confuse Aubrey."

His easy smile disappeared. "I'm not trying to confuse anyone. She's my daughter and I want to spend time with her."

"Then why don't the two of you go and I'll—"

He caught her arm. "Is it her you don't want to confuse, or yourself?"

"Yes."

"I'm not trying to complicate or muddle things, but I

do want to spend time with both of you. But this is a no-expectations outing. A little dinner and fun."

"Mo-o-o-o-m!" Aubrey called from down the hall.

He took Carlie Beth by the shoulders and turned her around with a swat on the—

"Did you just pat my ass?"

A tinge of pink crept into Grif's cheeks, which just charmed the heck out of her. "Sorry. Probably brought back bad memories of Roy Darden."

"Not even remotely the same."

Twenty minutes later, Aubrey had not only changed her own clothes, and done her makeup and hair, but she'd made Carlie Beth presentable in knee-high leather boots and a cute dress she hadn't remembered she owned. While Aubrey brushed her hair, she caught Carlie Beth's gaze in the bathroom mirror. "What's going on between you and…" She took a deep breath and swallowed. "…Dad?"

Carlie Beth's skin burned hot and cold, not only because she was being put on the spot, but because Aubrey calling Grif Dad made it sound as if they were actually some type of family. And she had no idea what they were. "I don't know."

"Are you dating?"

Was windowsill sex considered dating? Carlie Beth could readily admit to herself it was the best so-called date she'd had in a long damn time. "We're…talking."

"Is that a euphemism?"

Squeezing her eyes closed, Carlie Beth breathed. "Please tell me that was rhetorical."

When she opened them again, Aubrey's expression was serious. "I know I was kinda rude the other night, but I really don't want him to hurt you."

She grasped her daughter's hand and tried to give her a reassuring smile, hopefully masking her trembling lips. "Don't worry about me. The most important thing is for the two of you to get to know each other better."

But dear Lord, the drive to Asheville, with Carlie

Beth riding shotgun and Aubrey sitting behind her in Grif's new soccer mom van, felt entirely too much like a true family outing. They even squabbled over who was entitled to control the radio. Aubrey voted for Taylor Swift while Carlie Beth argued in favor of Creed. In the end, Grif persuaded them that the driver was the only person with the power over the dial, so they sang along to Springsteen for the forty-minute drive.

Grif glanced over at Carlie Beth. "I booked us on one of the comedy city tours, but now that I'm replaying our last conversation about"—he glanced in the rearview mirror—"stuff, I'm rethinking that."

"I know I came across as prudish the other day, but I'm pretty open with Aubrey. She's been begging to go since some of her friends went on one. It'll be fine."

By the time they boarded the tour bus in front of the French Broad Food Co-op, both Carlie Beth and Aubrey were antsy with excitement.

"I feel like a tourist," she told Grif.

He took her hand. "That's the whole point."

An hour and a half later, they'd laughed so much that the muscles around Carlie Beth's ribcage ached. The tour had been a little ribald, pretty informative, and highly entertaining. She said to Grif, "If you were thinking of starting something like that in Steele Ridge, I hate to tell you the whole thing would be about ten minutes long, if that."

"Actually, I'm trying to get an idea of what Steele Ridge can offer that Asheville and other towns can't. That's our sweet spot." He grinned at Aubrey. "So for dinner, should we go tourist or local?"

"I say tourist," Aubrey told him.

"Tupelo Honey Café it is."

Once they were inside the famous Asheville restaurant, Grif flashed a smile at the hostess and a table for three miraculously opened up even though a line of people snaked down the sidewalk outside.

"You live a charmed life, you know that, right?"

Carlie Beth said to him as the hostess led them to a table near a window and flashed an I'd-be-happy-to-be-dessert smile at Grif.

The most entertaining part of the entire situation was Aubrey's glare at the attractive twenty-something woman. "You're scoping out my *dad*."

"Oh." The hostess had the grace to tuck her chin in embarrassment. "Sorry about that." She quickly passed around menus and scurried from the table.

"Aubrey," Carlie Beth scolded.

"What?" Her tone was mild as she studied her menu, but she darn well knew what she'd done.

"That was rude."

"So is eye-frisking a man who's with two women."

"If I'd realized a fourteen-year-old was such good personal security, I would've imported Aubrey to LA years ago."

Aubrey looked up and trained her narrowed eyes on Grif. "Do a lot of women hit on you?"

He shot a panicked look at Carlie Beth and she gave him a subtle head shake. No, she hadn't mentioned a word to Aubrey about Madison Henry. That was something he'd have to do when the time was right.

This was probably the only time Carlie Beth had ever seen him fiddle with his clothes, first tugging at his folded sleeves and then brushing a hand down his shirt front. She gently pulled his hand away from his collar before he completely mangled it. "Los Angeles is a big city," he said finally.

Aubrey pulled out her phone. "Hmm...population of LA County is ten million and gender split is fifty-one percent women and forty-nine percent men. If you assume one out of each five hundred, then we're talking over ten thousand women."

"I don't even know that many women."

"You don't have to know them. You just have to come into contact with them."

He propped an elbow in the table and cradled his

head in his hand, angled toward Carlie Beth. "I can't win this, can I?"

"Nope." A surge of affection so huge welled up in Carlie Beth that it threatened to drown her, simply crash over her head and take her to the bottom. So she avoided Grif's scrutiny and fumbled for her menu. "Should we order?"

A few seconds later, she looked up and caught sight of a familiar face in the line outside the restaurant. Dave was standing—arms crossed and mouth drawn—staring directly at Carlie Beth. He'd told her several times that he wasn't a fan of the city, so what was he doing in one of the busiest parts of Asheville?

Aubrey caught the line of Carlie Beth's gaze and looked over her shoulder. Her eyebrows went up, but she waved at Dave, and he grudgingly returned the gesture.

When she turned back to the table, Aubrey said, "Wow, Dave is having a night on the town. Wonder if he has a date?"

From the way he was standing apart from the other people in line and scowling toward Carlie Beth, she doubted it. Still, she gave him a tentative wave as well, but he turned away and melted into the crowd.

"Who was that?" Grif asked.

"Just a friend from home," she said, shaking off the apprehension that Dave might've followed them from Steele Ridge.

When the waiter approached the table, Aubrey asked for the Southern Belle grilled cheese, Grif went for the shrimp and grits, and Carlie Beth simply pointed at something on the second page. "Oh, and one of those bacon Bloody Marys, please." Lord knows, she needed some fortification.

Once the waiter was gone, Grif said, "So I had an ulterior motive for bringing you to Asheville. It was a spy mission."

Aubrey giggled. "Oh, like Mata Hari."

"More like corporate espionage. Steele Ridge needs something that no other town has, something really big to attract tourists to Steele Ridge. Maybe an event that would benefit from my contacts in the sports world."

Aubrey's face went slack at that. "Are you saying famous sports players might come to Steele Ridge?"

"Nothing's for sure right now."

"If you tell me Ian Brinkmann is coming to my hometown, I will just die."

Grif shot a look Carlie Beth's way. "I'm scratching him off the list for any future event."

Aubrey clutched at his arm and bounced in her seat. "Are you serious? You know the Brick?"

"Maybe."

"Oh my God, my dad knows the hottest hockey player in the history of the world. Wait until I tell Brooke. She'll just die."

Not long ago, Grif's and Aubrey's easy back-and-forth would've put Carlie Beth on edge. Made her feel defensive and territorial. But today, it simply felt like a normal family dynamic.

Unfortunately, they weren't a normal family.

Not a true family at all.

On their way home from Asheville, Aubrey dozed in the backseat and Grif glanced at Carlie Beth, his expression as full of affection now as it had been at the restaurant earlier. "I know I've said this before, but you raised a great kid."

"Yeah, but she's not perfect. So be careful about all those stars in your eyes. After you left the forge that day and she figured out I'd never told you about her, she called me an asshole."

"Whoa. Miss Joan would've been pulling out the Ivory soap if I'd done that at Aubrey's age. Half the time, I think she'd give all her kids a good mouth-washing now if she thought she could catch us."

"I know what it's like to be infatuated when you first realize you're a parent. It's easy to want to be a friend and sweep the little things under the rug."

"So are you telling me not to let her snow me?"

"I'm reminding you there's a difference between a parent and a friend. And it's easy, when you don't see your child every day, to overcompensate when you're with her." Although it would be hard on Aubrey—and not only her—each time Grif got on a plane to fly west, it was actually a better deal than a lot of kids from divorced families had. "I've never had to share her before."

"I don't want to take her away from you. I'm sorry I ever threatened you with that. I was just so...so..."

"Surprised?"

"I was going to say hurt."

It seemed impossible that she could hurt such a self-assured, sophisticated man. But she reached for his hand and he threaded his fingers with hers. The comfort, the rightness, of his touch flowed over her. "She could stay with you sometimes when you're in town, if you both want."

"Really?"

"The only catch is that the rules have to be the same no matter where she sleeps. I have friends whose kids ping-pong not only between two houses but between what are essentially two lives. I don't think that's good for anyone."

"I started to ask Aubrey something at the table earlier, but I wanted to pass it by you first."

"What's that?"

"I'm putting together a nice reception, something where I can introduce the Steele Ridge business owners to plans for economic improvement. Would you be okay if Aubrey helped me organize the reception? I know she's not old enough for a real job, but I'd pay her and she'd get some good experience."

"Thanks for asking me," she said as they pulled up in front of her house. "But it's really up to Aubrey."

"What's up to Aubrey?" The sleepy question came from the backseat.

Grif got out and came around the van to open Carlie Beth's door. She couldn't hold back a grin when he slid open the side door—*shoop*—to hand Aubrey out of her seat.

Grif Steele driving a family vehicle. It still boggled the mind.

"I was asking your mom if she thought you'd like to help me put together a reception event. Catering, AV setup, that kind of thing. You do a good job with that and it could give you a leg up if I ever organize something with sports players."

Aubrey's eyes popped wide and she looked over Grif's shoulder to catch Carlie Beth's attention. "Really?"

"As long as your schoolwork doesn't suffer, it's up to you."

Aubrey tilted her head in disbelief. "When has my schoolwork ever suffered?"

"Then I guess there's your answer."

With a flying leap, Aubrey jumped out of the van and wrapped her arms around Carlie Beth. "You are the best mom in the whole world."

Behind Aubrey, Grif stood there grinning like a complete lunatic at the two of them wrapped up in one another. Before he could brace himself, Aubrey released Carlie Beth and swung her attention to him, clinging to him like bull nettle. "And you're the best dad in the whole world."

His grin faded to an expression that could only be described as two-by-foured.

Aubrey gave him a smacking kiss on the cheek, then did a complicated dance step toward the front door. "I have tons of ideas. Gotta go write them down!"

Once the front door slammed cheerfully behind her, Grif stood there in the front yard, his arms limp by his sides and his jaw slightly unhinged. Poor man had just been Aubreyed. "Nobody warned me about teenagers."

"Unfortunately, you don't even get an Ikea-type instruction booklet with them."

"Someone should write one."

"They're like Transformers. By the time you think you understand them and can document the whole thing, they've mutated. When Aubrey gets excited about something, there's no stopping her. She's a force of nature."

His head shake was a vague movement, as if he were just waking from a particularly confusing dream. "I wonder where she comes by that?"

"Well, you've got nurture or nature."

His blue eyes cleared of their fog and took on a predatory intensity that made Carlie Beth's pulse flutter in her throat. "I'm splitting my money between them." In that way he had, Grif slowly advanced on her, one side of his mouth tilting up, until her spine hit the van's side mirror. "Is there anything you can't do? You make cool art with your bare hands. You make single parenting look easy. You make my heart beat like I've just run the length of Malibu."

"I can't be trusted with white chocolate or Malbec."

His hands went to her hair, lifting the thick mass and letting it drift through his fingers. "And I apparently can't be trusted with you."

When his mouth met hers, it was hot and avid, like he was making a statement and asking a question at the same time. If only she could decipher what they each were.

She knew her statement and question.

I want you and *where are we going?*

But the power of his kiss was only one reason she didn't say either of them aloud. She feared an answer as much as she craved it.

When Grif's hand covered her breast, her thoughts whooshed away. Her nipple tightened as he rolled it between his fingers.

His hips pushed against hers, making the level of his arousal more than obvious.

Carlie Beth smiled against his lips.

He slid over to kiss the corner of her mouth, her

cheekbone, her earlobe and growled, "Something making you particularly happy?"

Knowing they were in shadow, that Aubrey wouldn't be able to see them even if she were staring out the front window—which she wasn't because she was too busy making lists—Carlie Beth eased her hand down Grif's torso and rubbed the heel of her palm along his erection until she could cup his balls through his jeans.

"Fuck," he groaned.

She laughed, slightly amazed at how wicked she sounded. "Not tonight."

"This having-a-teenager thing has its complications, huh?"

"You haven't seen the half of it." She rubbed again, tracing the width and length of him.

With his teeth set, he grabbed her hand and interrupted her exploration. "What are we doing, Carlie Beth?"

That stopped her cold. "You're asking *me*?"

"Isn't that obvious?"

"The girl is the one who's supposed to ask that question."

His brows drew together. "Uncertainty goes both ways."

"What do you want us to be doing?"

"I could make a crack about that being obvious." He glanced down at where he was still hard behind his zipper. "But I won't, because this is serious."

"Grif, I'm not asking you for anything. Not for myself, anyway." Still, a ray of hope was forming inside her.

His expression went thoughtful. "Maybe that's the problem. Maybe you need to be selfish for once. Let me take you out. An adult date this time. Wine, dinner, and dessert, if you want. Say yes." Then he kissed her again, his lips gentle, the lust still there but banked.

"I never turn down dessert." But Carlie Beth was worried that what she really wanted was her very own hazelnut cream cheese puff.

CHAPTER TWENTY-TWO

ALTHOUGH GRIF HAD GOOD INTENTIONS of treating Carlie Beth to that promised wining, dining, and desserting, apparently the citizens of Steele Ridge had a completely different idea of how he should spend his time. This was the third time this week that he'd come downstairs to find people lined up outside the door of his workspace.

He needed to get window coverings sooner rather than later. Hell, if push came to shove, he'd settle for butcher paper or aluminum foil. But neither of those would save him right now so he simply unlocked the front door and let the line parade in.

And damn, he'd meant to make a call to the private lab to see if they had any results about that oil for him yet. He made a quick note on a Post-it and slapped it on a stack of papers.

Betty Jane Cuddleford eyed the still-pink scar on his chin with suspicion before looking around his barren office and giving a sniff. "Griffin Steele, if you're not going to do the proper thing and keep an office at City Hall, the least you could do is hire a secretary and decorate this place a little."

A table, crappy chair, and paper every-damn-where. Not exactly a decorating scheme that commanded respect. But he smiled at the woman, putting a little teeth behind it. "But not out of the city coffers, I assume."

Her penciled-in eyebrows disappeared under the poufy hair. "If the Steele brothers have enough money to buy off this town, I assume you have enough to spare to take care of it yourself."

Hell, maybe he should call his assistant and have him fly in. He'd have this whole damn place whipped into shape within forty-eight hours. Then again, Grif needed him doing exactly what he was doing—holding down the fort on the other coast until things were more settled here.

"What can I help you with, Betty Jane?"

She frowned at his use of her given name and adjusted her purse more securely on her shoulder. "Well, I wanted to talk with you about the state of the benches at Barron's Park. See, my book club likes to meet over there on Wednesdays, and last week ElmaSue almost landed in the dirt when she sat down on a bench and it collapsed under her."

What Grif judiciously refrained from pointing out was that ElmaSue Smith was three and a quarter if she was a pound. "That sounds like it's right up the Parks and Rec director's alley." He picked up the phone. "Why don't I call her and let her know you'll be over to discuss the situation?"

Betty Jane sniffed again, and Grif was half tempted to offer her a bottle of allergy meds. "That girl, she's from Chicago."

Grif waited for her to go on, but apparently she thought that cryptic sentence explained everything. "So I understand."

Betty Jane huffed. "You can't possibly believe she'd understand a dad-burned thing about running Southern parks and such."

He was pretty sure a bench was a bench was a mother friggin' bench. "What would you like me to do about this situation?"

The older woman's eyebrows played hide and seek again. "Well, fix it, of course." When she turned, a cloud of lavender-scented perfume rose around Grif, and he was the one who suddenly needed a dose of Sudafed.

A few hours later, the line had finally dwindled to nothing, but only after three complaints about noisy neighbors, one woman frantic because her cat had been missing since Sunday, and a man who wanted to lobby for legalized prostitution inside the Steele Ridge city limits.

When the door swung open once again, Grif looked up from his makeshift desk with a snarl.

"Whoa," Aubrey said. "You've got your mean face on."

He rubbed a palm over his forehead. "Sorry."

"Long day?"

"Why are people crazy?"

"Why is the sky blue?"

"Pretty sure it has something to do with light, some part of the atmosphere, and reflection or refraction."

She swung her backpack off her shoulders to wedge it in a corner. When she turned back to him, her grin hit him like the sun he'd just been talking about. Carlie Beth had been right when she called their daughter a force of nature. "When I was a little girl, I used to wonder about my dad. If he was handsome. If he was nice. If he was smart like me."

He leaned back in his chair. "And?"

"Don't be coy," she said. "You know you knock number one out of the park. As for number two, most of the time. And three? You somehow got all those people to finally leave you alone, didn't you?"

"By the grace of God." He glanced at his phone. "Is it really already after three o'clock?"

"Yep. I would've been here sooner, but I figured you wouldn't okay me skipping out on school a second time."

"Your mom and I agreed you have to abide by the same rules no matter which of us you're with."

"She lets me stay out until one in the morning and eat all the pizza and chips I want."

"You realize I make a living from confirming truth and rumors, right?"

She shot him a wicked grin. "It was worth a try."

"No, never negotiate from an inferior position. You should always know what the person on the other side of the table knows. Bluffing rarely works."

"Does that mean I shouldn't *ever* lie?"

Damn. Sticky ground. Like fly paper. "I feel like I should plead the fifth."

Aubrey laughed and Grif saw so much of Carlie Beth in her that it took his breath. How could he have lived without these two for the past fifteen years? And how the hell would he juggle them with the rest of his life now that he knew about Aubrey? He was starting to dread the flight that would take him back to LA.

The front door opened again, and Grif momentarily toyed with the idea of stabbing himself in the eye with a pencil, but then he realized that although he was tired, he'd also enjoyed fixing things for the crazy citizens of this town. When he heard the familiar jangle of Louise's key fob, he looked up to find the garage owner from Charlotte. "You brought her back?"

"We did what we could to the exterior, but I can't get my hands on new seats for a few weeks. Figured you wouldn't want me to keep her all that time."

"What is it with men thinking cars are women?" Aubrey muttered.

The garage owner shot her a superior smile, then looked back at Grif. "I took a good look at those gashes in the upholstery to see if I could figure out what someone used to carve them up."

Grif laughed. "Like a forensic analysis?" Maggie would eat that shit up when he told her about it.

"One of my guys used to be a stocker at a grocery store. Says he's opened more boxes of beans than you can shake a stick at. He's pretty sure your vandal used a box cutter."

Grocery store. First the oil and now a box cutter.

Maybe Grif should round up his brothers and go shake down the manager at Hoffman's Grocery. "Thanks, man."

"Oh, and I had my upholsterer do a little patch job on the seats to hold you until the other ones come in." He handed Grif an invoice.

Without glancing at it, Grif said, "Just use the card on file."

"You got it, and I'll give you a holler when the seats are on their way."

Once the garage owner was gone, Aubrey said, "You didn't even look to see what he charged you."

"I know what he quoted," he said.

Aubrey snatched the piece of paper off his desk. "Holy shi—"

He gave her a hard look.

—taki."

"Nice save." He strolled to the front window to gaze out at Louise. "Want to take a ride?"

"Can I drive?"

"You're gonna keep trying, aren't you?" He looped an arm around Aubrey and led her toward the door.

"Can you blame me?"

"Not a bit." He unlocked the car and opened the passenger door for her, trying like hell not to look at the stitched-up seats that made Louise look like an automotive interpretation of Frankenstein's monster.

When he slid into the driver's seat, he could feel the threads against his back. But he couldn't worry about ruined leather when there were way more important things at stake than Louise's upholstery.

They were on the outskirts of Steele Ridge when Grif asked his daughter, "So how would you feel about me dating your mom?"

Grif and Aubrey had been so busy putting together

the State of Steele Ridge reception that Carlie Beth had barely seen either of them.

This afternoon, Grif called with an apology, promising he hadn't forgotten that he asked her to go out with him. "How a town of less than ten thousand people can be this chaotic, I have no idea."

"Tell you what," she said, "I'm having Yvonne and Austin over for dinner tonight. Why don't you come, too? Even if you don't have much time, you can eat a meal that you didn't nuke in the microwave."

"What time?"

When she hung up the phone, she realized she'd smiled and laughed more in the past couple of weeks than she had since she was a kid. All because of Grif.

And when Aubrey came home, she was grinning too, giddy over the event and spending time with Grif. "Mom, he knows Dean and Sam."

How could she compete with a man who was acquainted with the *Supernatural* actors? A little piece of Carlie Beth still wanted to be jealous that Grif was so much cooler than she was, but she just didn't have the heart to give it any attention. So instead, she wrapped her daughter in a hug. "How do you feel about all this, Aub?"

"You mean the suddenly having a dad thing? Or the having-a-dad-who-knows-famous-people thing?"

Carlie Beth nodded against her daughter's hair. "How would you have felt if you found out your dad worked in a factory or was a farmer?"

"Don't get me wrong, his social circle is amazing. But I wouldn't have cared what he did as long as he was Grif Steele."

"He's a good man, but he still lives thousands of miles away."

"He asked me if I minded if he dated you."

Her heartbeat picking up speed, she asked casually, "And what did you say?"

"That he better treat you right."

Carlie Beth pulled back and looked directly into Aubrey's eyes. "It's normal for kids from divorced families or, in our case, never-married families to hope their parents will get together. Like it will finally make everything in the world right."

With a sigh, Aubrey said, "Mom, my world was totally right before I found out about Grif. Would it be kinda cool to have a mom and dad who, you know, live in the same house and"—a sly smile transformed her face—"sleep in the same bed? Sure. But I'm not a kid. I know things will either work out on that front or they won't."

Her little girl, the Zen philosopher.

The doorbell rang at ten until six, and Carlie Beth ran her arm across her sweaty forehead and said to Aubrey, "Can you grab that?"

As she pulled a pan of lasagna out of the oven, Carlie Beth wondered how Joan Steele had cooked for six kids, four of them boys, for all those years. Because Carlie Beth was a fine cook, but a single casserole seemed to take more out of her than working in her forge all day. She sat the steaming dish on the stove and raced for the fridge. Why did people show up early? Didn't they know that made the hostess freak out and want to steal away with a bottle of Malbec?

Calm down, Carlie Beth. A dish of pasta isn't going to make or break your chances with Grif Steele.

When she heard footsteps on the kitchen floor, she swung around with a smile on her face. Worked hard to keep it from faltering when she realized the early guest was Austin instead of Grif. Her apprentice was spit-shined. Hair damp and combed back. Rumpled but freshly washed khakis, thin dress shirt, and—was that?—she blinked. Yes, and a clip-on tie. On the right side of his chin, a piece of toilet paper clung to a spot he'd obviously cut shaving.

"These are for you," he said, a shy smile touching his lips as he held out a bouquet of fluorescent pink carnations.

"How sweet," she said. "Thank you."

Her phone buzzed on the counter. "Can you get that, Aub, while I put these in a vase and get Austin a drink?"

"Iced tea or soda?" she asked him.

His Adams apple shifted up and down. "I don't guess you have a beer."

God, sometimes she felt a thousand years old, but she gave him a sympathetic smile. "Not for a nineteen-year-old."

"Tea then."

She poured him a glass, then went to the sink to handle the flowers.

Austin cleared his throat and said, "Dave told me he saw you with Grif Steele in Asheville the other night."

"Which makes me wonder what Dave was doing there anyway."

"Said he was there to pick up some feed."

Weird. There was plenty of grass in his pastures and a perfectly good feed store in town.

"Mom?" When Carlie Beth glanced at Aubrey, she found her daughter's expression as forlorn as it had been when she was ten and she'd thought Carlie Beth had forgotten her birthday. But this time, Carlie Beth didn't have an after-school surprise party planned. "What's wrong?"

"He said he can't make it."

"Oh." A block of disappointment sat right down on Carlie Beth's chest because honestly, there was only one *he* in their lives now. "Did he say why?"

"Just that something came up."

They stood shoulder to shoulder at the sink. A little rude to exclude their guest, but this wasn't anyone else's business. "Things happen," she whispered. "Don't get all upset."

Lowering her voice too, Aubrey said, "But he promised..."

"And don't assume this means he can't be trusted to keep his promises," she said. "He's spent a lot of time with us, which makes it easy to forget he's a very busy man. He's working two jobs right now."

"So you don't think he's dissing us?"

"I think we shouldn't make this a bigger deal than it is. We shouldn't start reading anything into it. Girls have a habit of that, but guys tend to say what they mean. If he said something came up, it was important, okay?"

Aubrey eyed the retina-searing carnations Carlie Beth was stabbing into a vase. "Those are...Wow."

"Yeah. Hey, do me a favor and go move the other flowers off the dinner table, okay?"

"Don't want to make Austin's flowers feel inferior?"

"Men have strangely fragile egos."

Aubrey rolled her eyes. "I'm starting to think they're more trouble than they're worth."

Although Carlie Beth was half tempted to echo her daughter's opinion, she said, "Some of them are totally worth the trouble."

"I'll remind you of that when I bring home my first bad boy." She grabbed the vase and headed for their small dining room.

Carlie Beth cleared her throat and turned to face Austin.

"Everything okay?"

"Just a little girl talk," she said cheerfully.

He glanced toward the door Aubrey had just disappeared through and chuckled. "Kids, huh?"

Carlie Beth squelched the need to shake her head at him. He seemed to have forgotten he was only five years older than her daughter.

He set his tea glass on the countertop. "Can I help with anything?"

"How are you at chopping vegetables for a salad?"

With a boyish grin, he said, "If I can work a drill press, surely I can handle a paring knife."

"Second drawer on your left."

Carlie Beth turned to grab the pile of produce, but

when she swung around again, Austin was mere inches from her. "Oh!"

Before she could step back, he grabbed her by the shoulders and kissed her. Oh. Lord. Have. Mercy. She tried to wiggle away, but either his nervousness or his fervor had him gripping her like a hawk with a mouse.

She shoved at his shoulder and said, "Austin!" against his lips. When she finally pried his hand and mouth from her, he stood there panting, his eyes dilated and a little wild.

"Carlie Beth, I love you."

Then came the sound of a low cough and Carlie Beth whirled around, so damn relieved to see her friend standing in the kitchen doorway. She had saved the day, the night, the whole year. "Yvonne!"

"I'm sorry. No one answered the door, so I just..." The other woman was cradling a cake pan, which hopefully held her lemon poke cake. Lord, it was shaping up to be a wine, white chocolate, *and* lemon poke cake kinda night.

"No, it's fine," Carlie Beth babbled. "We were...I was..."

Jesus, her pulse was erratic and not from Austin's kiss. How was she supposed to handle this? Maybe avoidance was her best bet. She held out her hands for the cake pan. "Why don't I take that and put it in the other room. Austin, would you get Yvonne a drink?"

She grabbed the pan and bolted. When she rushed into the dining room, Aubrey glanced up. "Mom?"

"Next time I think it's a good idea to have people over for dinner, remind me of tonight."

"Why? What happened?"

"Austin kissed me!"

Aubrey's mouth went slack. "Did you mean for him to?"

"What do you think?"

"Poor Austin."

"I don't know what to do. He's a nice kid, but..."

"But there's no way you're interested. He has to know that."

"By the way his tongue was…Never mind."

Aubrey made a gagging noise. "Definitely TMI."

Yvonne poked her head in the room and smiled at Aubrey. "Hey, kiddo. Can I help with…Carlie Beth, you look a little flustered."

"Just…the heat from the oven. Let me get the food on the table and we can all sit down." When she returned to the kitchen, Austin had cut the carrots into long slivers, thin enough to see through. His cheeks were red and he wouldn't meet Carlie Beth's gaze. "Austin, about what happened before Yvonne walked in—"

"Forget it."

"We…we work together. Actually, you work for me and—"

"I get it," he said. "Why settle for a local guy when you can get busy with a California bigshot?"

Carlie Beth hated the thought of having to send Austin to another blacksmith, but if this behavior persisted, she'd have to consider it. She tore lettuce into jagged pieces and tossed them in a bowl along with the paper-thin carrots. The bell pepper would just have to suck it up and go back in the fridge. "Grif Steele has nothing to do with this. Any relationship other than teacher and apprentice between you and me would be completely inappropriate."

Austin avoided her direct statement. "I'll carry the salad."

Needless to say, dinner was awkward, with Carlie Beth and Aubrey trying to make extra small talk while Austin picked at his food and sulked. And if that didn't say everything there was to say about whether or not he was ready for a romantic relationship of any kind, nothing did.

Yvonne ate her last bite of lasagna and put her fork aside. "That was delicious. Thanks so much, ladies."

His plate still half-full, Austin pushed away from the

table and mumbled, "Just remembered I have to be somewhere."

"Before dessert?" Aubrey said.

"I'm allergic to chocolate."

"Let me walk you out," Carlie Beth offered.

"I know the way." Then a few seconds later, the front door opened and closed.

"It's not chocolate. It's lemon," Yvonne said, finally making Carlie Beth happy for the first time since she'd heard Grif wouldn't make it to dinner. "What are you going to do about that, Carlie Beth?"

She laughed. "Eat it."

With a raised brow, Yvonne drawled. "Not the cake. The kid."

"Give him a little time to get his pride back together. It'll blow over."

"What if it doesn't?"

She sighed. "Guess I'll deal with that when I have to. But enough about my problems. How're things going at the gallery? Any uptick in business since Grif Steele took over as city manager?"

With a nod, Yvonne said, "A little, but I'm hoping it's a good sign. I've actually gotten a few requests for axes lately. One person in particular is interested in a Gotland style. Think that's something you could work up for the gallery?"

Hmm. Not her normal type of work, but maybe for the handles, she could reach out to the woodworker who'd made Miss Joan's table. "Let me put some coffee on and we can chat about it over cake."

By the time the coffee was brewed, Aubrey excused herself from the table with a big piece of Yvonne's cake, saying she had some homework to finish.

Yvonne watched her carry the plate from the room. "Do you ever regret having her?" she asked Carlie Beth.

Carlie Beth almost dropped a mug of coffee in front of Yvonne and sat her plate down with a clink. "What do you mean?"

"With the quality of your work, you could've been huge, showing in galleries all over the world."

"Who says I won't still do that?"

Yvonne's laugh had a condescending edge Carlie Beth had never heard before. "I love my gallery, but I can't say it's ever been a jumping-off spot for major talent."

"I'm happy with my life."

"Of course you are." With a slow drag, Yvonne raked her fork tines through the frosting. "Since the gallery is right there on Main Street, I can't help but notice she's spending a lot of time with Grif."

"She's helping him with the State of Steele Ridge reception."

"That doesn't worry you?"

"No, why should it?"

"Madison Henry."

Indignation scrawled up Carlie Beth's back, stiffening her spine. "You said yourself he was cleared. He and I discussed the situation and I believe every word he said."

Yvonne nodded, but it didn't convince Carlie Beth she was convinced. "What about money?"

"What about it?"

"Not to be crude, but he has a lot more of it than you do."

"So?"

"So girls Aubrey's age like things—clothes, makeup, cars."

"I've already told him he's not allowed to go overboard with her."

"Then I'm sure it'll be fine." Yvonne scooped up a bite of cake and chewed. When she smiled, a tiny piece of lemon glaze clung to her lips, quivered there, then dropped to the table. "Now, about those ax heads."

Still unsettled by Yvonne's comments, Carlie Beth deliberately took a breath, scooted her plate to the side, and reached for paper and a pencil. "Tell me what you have in mind."

CHAPTER TWENTY-THREE

"IT'S WHAT?" GRIF ASKED THE guy handing him the report. The private lab he'd hired to test the slippery stuff on the climbing wall grips had finally come through.

"A quenchant."

"Never heard of it."

"It's basically an oil or polymer used to temper metals."

Then what the hell was it doing smeared all over fiberglass climbing holds? "And where would I buy something like that?"

"Lot of online suppliers. Best I can tell this is something called Sure-Quench." The guy pointed to a line on the lab report.

Griff read the quenchant description aloud. "Often used by knife makers or other craftspeople who work with metal." He pinned the guy with a stare. "Would that include blacksmiths?"

"I'm no expert, but I'd say yes."

"Motherfu—"

"I take it this isn't good news."

"Not really."

"Good luck to you, man."

It was a little after eleven when Grif pulled up in front of Carlie Beth's house. He sat there in Louise's less-than-comfortable seat for a few minutes just thinking. Or at least trying to, because the buzzing in his brain made it hard to be rational. His heart hadn't stopped thumping in a sick rhythm since he left the lab in Charlotte. Because who the hell in Steele Ridge but Carlie Beth or her apprentice would use quenching oil?

Maybe she didn't believe he was innocent of all the abuse accusations. Maybe she didn't believe a damn thing he said about anything.

That thought ate at his gut like a pint of mountain moonshine.

But he needed to know the truth, so he shoved his door open without giving a crap that he pushed it to the limit of its hinges and it protested. But before he could make it to Carlie Beth's porch, the front door swung open and she was squinting at him.

"Grif? I thought you couldn't make it. Dinner was over four hours ago. Do you want to come in?"

"No. Yes. No."

"Let it never be said that you're not a decisive man. There's still lasagna and cake."

"I'm not hungry." The words came out sharp.

"Okay. Not looking to force-feed you. You're obviously in a pisser of a mood. Something go wrong with the event? It's a school night, so I don't want to wake up Aub—"

"I'm not here to chat with Aubrey. I'm here to talk with you."

She nodded, a hesitant motion, and pointed toward the small porch swing. "We can sit out here."

Grif tried not to notice how damn cute and rumpled she looked in her shorty pajamas. When she sat on her wicker porch swing and pulled her feet up, he averted his gaze so he wouldn't be seduced by the sexy line of her hamstring. Instead of taking the space beside her, he leaned against the porch rail and trained his attention over her head. "Tell me about hardening steel."

"What? Why?"

"Just humor me."

"Okay. Oils and fats have been used for hundreds of years to harden metals. Of course, blacksmiths back in the day didn't completely understand why that was. But now, you could read all the ins and outs of heat transfer in academic papers. If you cool too rapidly, the metal, especially steel, can distort or crack. But basically the quenching oil controls the heat transfer, tempering the metal, which reduces that likelihood."

"So an oil is always used to temper metal?"

"No, some people prefer water."

"What about you?"

"What about me what?" She grabbed the chain holding up the swing, causing it to lose its smooth track. "Why would you wake me up in the middle of the night to talk about—"

"It's only eleven-thirty."

"When you have a kid in school, it's the middle." She stared at him as if she'd never seen him before. As if he couldn't possibly understand the rhythms of being a parent. Goddammit.

"Carlie Beth, what do you and Austin use in your forge to cool and harden metal?" He swiped a hand across his eyes, hating himself for the way he was pushing her, but knowing he had to. If she'd been the one to—damn, he didn't want to think it. Her apprentice also had access to everything in her forge.

"Now I know exactly what this is about." She put her feet down on the porch and the swinging came to an abrupt stop. "You got the lab results back."

"Yes."

"What was it?"

"Quenching oil. Apparently a kind often used by blacksmiths."

"And you think Austin…I know he's acts a little territorial around me, but he's just a kid with a crush. Besides, I don't let him temper anything yet—"

"Hell."

Sudden understanding—and hurt—filled her eyes.

She jumped off the swing and squared off with him. If the human eyeballs could mimic death-ray lasers, Carlie Beth's would've laid him out flat in a smoking pile of ash. "All this getting to know Aubrey. All this family time. All this"—her hand waved between them below waist-level—"between you and me was complete pretend, wasn't it? The whole time, you were just trying to keep us close while you figured out who has it in for you."

God, when she said it like that, it sounded bad. And it was bad. But her anger didn't mean he could simply drop this. "Do you or do you not use quenching oil in your forge?"

She was glaring so hard at him that her teeth were actually bared. "I don't know why you even bothered to ask because you won't believe what I have to say anyway." She stalked toward her front door and yanked it open so hard that it bounced off the siding. "So why don't you go find out for yourself?"

Although he wanted to follow her, explain himself, he didn't for two reasons. One, because he heard the deadbolt engage approximately three-quarters of a second after the door closed behind her. And two, because she hadn't answered his damn question.

Still, he stood there on the porch for a few minutes, head down, and rubbed at the back of his neck. None of this shit would be happening if Jonah hadn't fucked with that contract. Right now, Grif would be home...

Yeah, he'd be home in his professionally decorated LA apartment, still in his office, probably with his phone superglued to his damn ear. On the West Coast, it was too early for his clients to be out stirring up trouble in the nightclubs. So Grif would still be dealing with the daily shit—contracts, deals, hustles.

Somehow, that didn't sound so damn attractive anymore. Truth be told, it hadn't for months. But coming back home, finding out he had a daughter, getting involved with Carlie Beth was making him face that truth head-on.

What was happening to him?

Rather than answer his own question, he stepped off the porch and strode around the side of the house. He tried the the forge's door, but it was locked. He was reaching for the overhead's handle when someone said, "What the hell do you think you're doing?"

Grif turned to find Austin standing there trying to look big and tough. And Jesus, if he'd thought Carlie Beth's look earlier was a killer, this one would've sliced him open and pulled out his guts.

"I asked you a question and I expect an answer." Whoa. True, Grif hadn't exactly been a charmer when he met the kid before, but this was more than simple territory marking. This was *you're a fucking douche and I'd as soon shoot you as look at you.*

"I need to get something from the forge."

"Carlie Beth know you're out here?" Subtext: *asshole.*

"She's the one who suggested I come out here." Okay, maybe *suggest* was pushing it. "Can you please unlock the door?" It took every bit of self-control Grif had not to get chest to chest with this guy and show him which dog was the alpha.

Austin pulled out a set of keys and pushed by Grif to open up the forge. Once the lights were on, he said, "Now what do you want?"

"Carlie Beth have a quenching tank?"

"Yeah."

"Where is it?"

"Are you here for a blacksmithing lesson?" Austin's hostile expression took on a cocky are-you-effing-kidding-me slant. "If so, we do those tours on Neverdays at ten and two."

Okay, enough, young pup. Grif got right up in the guy's

personal space. "Where's the fucking quenching tank?"

Austin's chin angled up, but then he used it to motion to his left. "Over there by the coal forge."

Yeah, like Grif knew what a coal forge was.

"That vat." Austin pointed to a large bucket near a metal table with a lip surrounding it. Yeah, he should've known because the coal forge was littered with chunks of what looked like black rock. "You know, with the liquid in it."

It was wrong to want to coldcock someone this bad, so Grif tried to eighty-six the feeling. Then he realized he hadn't brought a damn thing to put a sample in. "You got a cup or something?"

Carlie Beth's apprentice sneered, "Maybe you'd like some crumpets with that?"

Grif surged around and grabbed him by the shirt. "What is your problem?"

"You're my problem, you slick big-city asshole. You stroll into town acting like Carlie Beth should fall at your fancy-shoed feet."

Grif glanced down at his expensive loafers. What the hell did people have against his damn footwear? Maybe it was time to invest in a new pair of hiking boots. "How is it any of your business what's between Carlie Beth and me?"

"She's too good for you."

Yeah, that was probably true, but that hadn't ever stopped Grif from going after what he wanted before.

"And she deserves better."

Ah, so the possessiveness wasn't about Carlie Beth being his teacher, his mentor. He actually thought he had a chance with her. "You realize you're closer to Aubrey's age than Carlie Beth's, right?"

"Age doesn't matter."

Grif leaned forward, took a good look at the guy's chin. "Maybe not, but I figure she might want a man who's shaved more than once in his life."

Total asshole thing to say, but every one of Grif's buttons had been pushed tonight.

Austin covered his chin. "You fucked everything up. She would've noticed me if not for you strutting around town."

Grif took a deep breath, trying to keep his shit together. In fact, when he got all this oil crap settled, he'd swing back by and invite Carlie Beth's apprentice out for a beer. Shit, or maybe just a soft drink. "I'm sorry if you feel like I've wronged you in some way, but Carlie Beth and I have history. In the form of a fourteen-year-old daughter. Neither you nor I can do a damn thing about that. Now, I need a cup."

The guy shot him one last glare before stomping across the room and coming back with a battered Solo cup. "Get it and get out."

CHAPTER TWENTY-FOUR

THE GUY AT THE PRIVATE lab thought Grif was a complete nut job when he called him up around midnight asking to bring in another sample. At first he said no way in hell, but when Grif had offered him a cash bonus to meet him and run the test ASAP, the lab dude had changed his mind, apparently deciding a nut job with money to burn was okay.

So here it was, seven thirty in the morning, and Grif was sitting outside Carlie Beth's house after wrestling a dolly holding his forgive-me-because-I'm-a-dumbass gift to the foot of her porch steps. But when the front door opened, it was Aubrey who walked out.

"Dad?" She drew back a little and studied him. "What are you doing here so early and why do you look like you slept in your clothes?"

"Is your mom up?"

"Yes, but she wasn't in a great mood, so—wait a minute, y'all had a fight, didn't you?"

"It wasn't a fight exactly. It was more of a—"

"It was something because she forgot to put coffee in the basket and ended up brewing a pot of hot water."

"Maybe she was—"

"And she drank half a cup before she realized it."

"Oh." Yeah, that was pretty damn bad. Maybe he

should've hit the Mad Batter and picked up a box of pastries before coming here.

"I thought I heard people talking last night."

"Your mom and I had a little discussion."

"So I didn't dream the door slamming."

He sighed. "No."

Aubrey slumped down beside him on the porch swing. "I knew it was going too well."

"What's that mean?"

"You know, that we were kinda getting our groove as a family. And you and Mom were...um...dating or whatever."

Yeah, with the way he'd screwed things up, they might not be *whatevering* again. He took his daughter's hand, sad that he hadn't held it when she was a baby. When she was learning to walk. Learning to ride a bike. "I missed a lot. I don't want to miss out in the future."

"What're you saying?"

"I can't make any promises," he said. "Because relationships take two people. But I can promise you regardless of what happens between your mom and me, I'm in your life for good now. And as your parents, we'll learn to do it together."

Aubrey rested her head against his shoulder, and everything in Grif's world simply slipped into alignment. "It would be great if the two of you would *be* together, but I'll love you both however it works out." She seemed to realize there was a big wooden stump near the porch steps and laughed. "Is that what I think it is?"

He'd called around for hours trying to find something that would say "I'm sorry" to a blacksmith. He'd gotten lucky—damn lucky—when he woke Randi up in the middle of the night and she mentioned Carlie Beth had been pining for a sturdier anvil stand. "Stupid?" Shit, he should've gone for the traditional—chocolate, more flowers, jewelry.

Aubrey's smile dominated her face, and she hopped off the swing to give him a quick hug. "No, perfect.

Which means there's still hope for you, Grif Steele." She jumped nimbly off the porch and waved as she headed down the sidewalk.

"Aubrey?" Carlie Beth's voice came from inside. "What are you doing out there? You need to get to school." The storm door swung open and she poked her head outside. Her forehead scrunched, and then she spotted Grif and it scrunched even more.

Before she could close the door, he lunged off the swing and caught it. "Hey, I came by to talk with you about—"

"I know you took a sample from my quenching tank," she said. "Austin told me after you left with it."

"If you'll listen to me—"

"You had it tested, didn't you? Did you also figure out if it was Austin or me who dumped it all over your stupid climbing wall?" Her eyes, with faint violet circles underneath, made her look fragile, but the stubborn set of her lips said she was pissed. And rightfully so. She held out her wrists. "Maybe you should just cuff me. Make a citizen's arrest and have Maggie haul me off."

"You could've just explained that you use mineral oil instead of a specialized quenching oil. I know neither of you messed with those handholds."

"But you had to have proof, get confirmation. You couldn't take my word for it."

"Carlie Beth, I'm sorr—"

"Did you really think I would hurt you? Slice up your car? What reason would I have…" Her gaze snapped to his. "Oh my God, this wasn't about me. It was about you."

"About me being an idiot."

"No, about you being scared. Because I pose a threat."

"Listen to me. I know it wasn't you."

"Not that kind of threat. An emotional one. You might not be scared of being physically hurt, but Madison Henry really pulled one over on you. And I lied to you way before she did." Now her shadowed eyes just looked miserably sad.

"But you did it for what you thought were the right reasons." He caught her hand and drew her outside.

"I thought you didn't trust me, but the reality is you don't trust yourself. All this time, I've been terrified you'd up and leave. And you've been terrified you might be tempted to stay."

The truth of her statement hit Grif in the gut. He'd spent so much time fighting what was in front of him that he was risking something way bigger than his professional reputation. He was risking his chance at a future. One that made him feel happy and needed instead of just important.

She'd been worried he would leave, which meant she felt something for him. Something big enough to have her running scared, too.

She butted her head against his chest, no doubt able to hear how hard his heart was beating. "Why did you have to come back home?"

"Maybe the universe knows where we're supposed to be and who we're supposed to be with much better than we do."

"What's that supposed to mean?"

He was pretty sure it meant the universe had decided she was the woman for him. But he wasn't ready to admit that to himself, much less say it aloud.

His heart full—of regret, hope, and, he half-feared, love—he kissed her. She tasted of coffee and faintly of sweet lemon. And her lips under his were soft and held what he hoped was a first hint of forgiveness. Her skin felt so damn right against his, and he dove in to the kiss, trying to sort out his feelings.

God, he wanted her naked and under him. Wanted to drive her up and push her over. Wanted to hear her whisper the three words that would send him with her.

Wanted it so desperately that he almost didn't recognize himself.

A casual whistle—a jaunty little tune that sounded like *Grif and Carlie Beth sitting in a tree*—drifted through the air. Carlie Beth shoved away from him and wiped her mouth with her hand. "I can't think when you do that."

They both glanced toward the sidewalk. There stood one of the town's longtime postmen, shoving envelopes and flyers into Carlie Beth's mailbox and watching them make out. He lifted his hand in a friendly wave and meandered his way down the street.

"Oh, God," Carlie Beth groaned. "This'll be all over town by lunchtime."

"We're adults. We're allowed to kiss one another in public."

"You don't just kiss. You make a woman forget who she. Where she is. I do not want my neighbors talking about how Carlie Beth Parrish orgasmed on her front porch in broad daylight."

Now that sounded like a challenge. "Make-up sex can be excellent." He reached for her, but she danced away, almost tripping in her haste. With a quick lunge, he grabbed her wrist and kept her upright. "Careful there."

She must've caught sight of his peace offering because she asked, "What is that?"

Crap, the guy he'd bought it off had assured him she'd be ecstatic. "Are you saying you don't know?"

Her hip cocked out, which also pushed out her breasts. To hell with the neighbors. He could have her screaming inside ninety seconds if he could just get his hands—

"Uh-uh. I don't know what just went through your mind, but by the look in your eyes, it was dirty."

"Dirty is good." He pulled her toward him. "Very, very good."

"The way you do it, I totally agree. But that's totally off the table, so explain to me why there's an oak stump at the bottom of my steps."

"Because I already bought you flowers."

"Makes total sense." But her doubtful expression said otherwise.

"I wanted to say I'm sorry and easy girl gifts aren't special enough for you."

"I like flowers. And candy. And stuff."

He pointed at the stump. "Which would you rather have—a box of chocolate or a chunk of wood to mount your anvil on?"

She took the porch steps two at a time, knelt beside the stump, and ran her hands over its surface. By the possessive nature of her touch, he had his answer. "This is mine?"

"Do you like it?" He followed Carlie Beth and shook his head at himself. When was the last time he'd felt like a fourteen-year-old kid, totally unsure of how to win over a woman?

Probably when he'd been fourteen.

She glanced up at him over her shoulder. "If I take this, does it mean I have to forgive you for even entertaining the idea that I would try to hurt you?"

"If there's one thing I know, it's the value of the perfect bribe."

She came to her feet and propped her hands on her hips. "You don't play fair."

"You're right, Shortcake, I play to win."

She probably should've held on to her mad for a little longer, but Carlie Beth had never been particularly good at all those girl-guy games. They were exhausting and wasted time that would be better spent making things from metal. Eyeing the stump, she asked Grif, "Will you help me get it to the forge?"

But he grabbed her hand. "Before you get distracted playing with your new toy, I want to settle this between us. I'm sorry I doubted you. Will you forgive me?"

He was right. This was serious, and if they were going to go forward in whatever capacity, co-parenting or more, they needed to trust one another. "I'm a grown woman. I can handle the fact that you and I are still circling one another. But Grif, you can't do something like this to Aubrey. She is so infatuated with you right now, it would crush her to have you doubt her. Do you understand what I'm saying?"

"I don't want to hurt either of you. This is all so damn new to me."

She went up on her toes and pressed a soft kiss to the corner of his mouth. "We all just do the best we can."

"Maybe I'm not cut out to be a dad."

His words held such a hollow misery that she lifted her hands to his face and smoothed them over his cheeks, savoring the scratch of his scruff against her skin. God, the combination of sexual attraction and bone-deep emotion she felt for this man might do her in. She held him still until he met her gaze. "Do you want to be Aubrey's dad?"

"I *am* her dad." The way he said it, all macho and offended, made her smile. Because he didn't just mean he was biologically responsible, but that he cared. Really cared.

"Then you'd better reconcile yourself to being a big ol' screwup sometimes. No one has an inside track on this parenting thing."

"It's like the ultimate cosmic joke, isn't it?" Grif curved his hands around her waist.

"I want you to know that I'm committed to being Aubrey's dad. Carlie Beth, I love that kid." He huffed a small laugh and shook his head. "Our kid. A month ago, I couldn't imagine having one. And now, I can't imagine life without her."

Oh, how she loved this man... Carlie Beth's brain went blank. Simply empty.

But it didn't stay that way for long because the reality slammed through her. She'd fallen in love with Grif Steele. Her baby daddy. Fifteen years after the deed was done.

The pressure on her chest threatened to completely suffocate her.

Carlie Beth breathed, trying to keep the tears that were creeping up on her from escaping. He'd done her in, simply sent her over the edge and made her heart fall at his feet.

What was she supposed to do now?

Because his promise to be a father to Aubrey wasn't a commitment to be *her* true partner and lover. And she needed a little space to figure out how to deal with that.

"Carlie Beth?" Grif's voice seemed to come from down the road. "Are you okay? You went as white as a plumber's crack."

That shocked her out of her little panic attack and she coughed out a laugh. "I'm fine, and as long as we're all trying, everything will fall into place," she said, hoping it was true. "And now that we've kissed and made up, can I please take my new anvil stand out to the forge?"

The smile that crossed Grif's face was so real, so full of relief that Carlie Beth knew they could make this work. She'd once believed career, money, and ego were everything to him, but the man standing before her valued people and relationships. Valued her.

"Right after this," he said, and then he put his mouth on hers.

This kiss was different from any they'd shared before. It was full of messages that Carlie Beth tried to interpret. Instead of frantic passion, it tasted like simple affection. Contentment even.

And oh God, was there anything in the world more attractive than a man who honestly liked you?

Grif's kiss was slow and thorough and devastating in its simplicity. When he finally drew back, she wasn't sure she could remember her own name.

But she knew that she needed this man. Needed him every day for the rest of her life.

CHAPTER TWENTY-FIVE

WHICH WAS A CONCEPT CARLIE Beth couldn't think too hard about right now, so she forced her mouth into a shaky smile. "I need to remember I like that last part of kissing and making up."

"Don't worry. I'll be around to remind you."

Would he? Would he really?

He tilted the dolly holding the tree stump and headed for the backyard. When she didn't immediately follow, he glanced back over his shoulder. "Thought you couldn't wait to get this into your forge."

"Just thinking of all the ways I'm going to use you. *It*, I meant use *it*."

"Hey, I'm willing to be used. All in the name of art, of course." Then he winked at her. Winked. From any other man, it would've been a cheesy gesture. But somehow, Grif made it look sexy and suave.

This man would kill her yet.

They rounded the house into the backyard, and Carlie Beth's smile wasn't shaky anymore. It was so broad, it could've juiced up Steele Ridge's power supply for a year. But when they approached the forge, it faltered. "It's not locked. Austin has his own key, but he's never forgotten to lock up after himself."

Grif's expression turned sheepish. "He might've been distracted last night."

"Why?"

"Because I came out here and we kinda…"

"Locked horns like idiots? So help me God, if you've cost me the best apprentice I've ever had, I will…I don't know what, but it won't be pretty."

"I'll apologize to him, too."

She hoped that was even an option. Austin had been in such a state when he stomped out after dinner last night. And he'd been absolutely right about Carlie Beth being head-over-heels for Grif. She couldn't change that.

And wouldn't even if she could.

Grif edged her away from the door and lowered the dolly. "Let me check it out."

His words almost stopped her heart, making her realize that if Austin left the place open, all her tools and projects could be gone. But if that were the case, surely she would've heard something last night. And who in Steele Ridge would do something like that anyway? "I'm sure everything's fine—"

"If you won't agree to stay right here, I'll lock you in your house."

"You've lost your mind. I guess that's what you'll say to Aubrey when she wants to date."

His eyes went squinty and mean. "That's a conversation for another time. But I can definitely see the appeal of cleaning my guns when boys come calling."

He had her so off balance that Carlie Beth didn't immediately follow him when he slipped inside the forge. They really needed to discuss what he was thinking. He kept dropping little pictures of the future into their conversations, but she wasn't sure what to make of them.

She grabbed the door and the hinges squeaked, immediately giving her away.

"Don't come in here," Grif ordered, his voice as hard as titanium. "Go get your phone and call Maggie."

"What's—"

"Now."

She might've admitted to herself that she was in love with this man, but if he thought he would become the boss of her, he was out of his ever-loving mind. Carlie Beth swung the door wide and stalked inside. Austin had remembered to turn off the lights, but the windows on either side of the building let in sunlight, illuminating Grif's back where he was crouched over something on the floor.

"What did they take?"

He glanced up and pinned her with a stare she couldn't interpret. "I said to get the goddamn phone and call Maggie."

"Don't you have your cell phone? Why should I—" Her words were cut short when she strode forward and caught a glimpse of what Grif was shielding on the floor. Thin white fabric. "Austin was wearing that shirt last night." That's when she noticed the ladder not far away. "Oh my God, Grif. Is he hurt? What happened?" She hurried forward, but Grif swung an arm out, stopping her forward progress.

"Don't touch anything."

"Is he conscious? Emergency services will want to know." He was right. She had to get the phone because if Austin was hurt, she had to get help right away. "We need to give him CPR!"

Grif swiped a hand across his eyes and hung his head. "Why couldn't you have listened and stayed outside?" He shifted slightly so Carlie Beth could see Austin's full form. "We're too late for CPR."

Carlie Beth's already shallow breaths stuck in her lungs. Because the fall from the ladder she'd been imagining was nothing compared to the scene on the floor of her forge.

Her apprentice was sprawled, blood crusted around a puncture wound on his temple and arms extended from his sides, with railroad spikes rammed through both his palms and his throat.

This wasn't an accident.
It was murder.

Grif had tried like hell to get Carlie Beth off her own property once Maggie and her deputies showed up on the scene. But the damn woman wouldn't leave. Just stood there and watched while the place was photographed and picked over. Watched when they carried her apprentice's body out in a bag.

Of course, the town grapevine was working like a champ, and people started to gather on the sidewalk in front of her house within fifteen minutes of the 911 call. Thank God that contingent included his brothers and they handled crowd control.

Once Maggie's people had cleared the scene and there was nothing else to gawk at, folks began to meander away. But they would gossip over beer and dinner and dessert.

Although he'd hated to bring her into the ugliness, Grif had called his mom and asked her to come sit with Carlie Beth. But she hadn't been able to talk her into moving farther than a brick planter in the backyard. When Grif walked out of the forge and caught his mom's eye, she immediately stood and reached for Carlie Beth's hand. "Sweetheart," she said, "why don't we go pick Aubrey up from school and take her out to my house?"

The dazed expression on Carlie Beth's face cleared slightly and she scrambled for her phone. "Is it that late already?"

"Last bell will ring in ten minutes, and I don't think you want her to come home to see…"

When Carlie Beth's gaze rose to meet his across the lawn, the complete devastation in her eyes tugged at something deep in Grif's chest. Why couldn't he have shielded her from this? He wanted to wrap his arms around her, comfort and protect her, yet after what he'd found in her forge, he felt dirty. Unworthy.

Like he'd somehow been responsible for what had happened to that boy. Jesus, what if he'd been the last person to see him alive before…

Before whoever had done that to him.

This was personal. That much was obvious. Someone had brought death and terror into Carlie Beth's home. And fuck-all if Grif would let someone get away with that. He fortified himself with a long, slow breath, then walked across the grass to Carlie Beth and his mom.

"She's right, Shortcake. You need to pick up Aubrey and go back to Tupelo Hill. Get to her before someone tells her what happened here today."

"I…I don't know how to tell her."

Grif took her hands, turned them palm up and looked at the lines and whorls there. So damn capable. But even these hands couldn't handle everything alone. "We'll talk with her together, if that's okay with you."

Without a tug from him, she slid her arms around his waist and rested her head against his chest. When he wrapped her in a hug, it became more than clear to him that he never wanted to let her go. Above Carlie Beth's head, he met his mom's speculative look. He nodded once and that seemed to satisfy her.

He wasn't sure what they'd just communicated, other than the fact that he would never let Carlie Beth handle life alone ever again. He tightened his hold and kissed the top of her head, letting her apple scent soothe him. "Give me a half hour to meet you out there."

"What are we going to do about it?"

We. That had to be one of the most powerful words in the world. So as much as he might want to tell her that she'd be staying out of this situation with Austin's death, he knew that was a lost cause. "We'll be having a big Steele family powwow this evening."

She looked up, and her beautiful eyes were glossed with tears that unmanned him. "Will it scare you to death if I say I don't know what I'd do without you right now?"

"No," he said, his voice husky. "Because I don't know what I'd do without you, either."

"Sweetheart," his mom said, "we need to leave now to get Aubrey."

With obvious reluctance, Carlie Beth backed out of Grif's hold. "Half hour?"

"Count on it."

CHAPTER TWENTY-SIX

CARLIE BETH FELT LIKE A sleepwalker trudging up the sidewalk toward the middle school's front door. Even more so when the final bell rang and kids streamed by her chattering and laughing.

Didn't everyone understand the world had changed today?

"Mom, what's wrong?" Aubrey said the second she spotted Carlie Beth. "You look bad."

Carlie Beth forced a little laugh, but it was hollow and tinged with panic. "Wow, thanks. Why don't you let me carry that?" She took Aubrey's backpack and led her toward the car where Joan was waiting for them. If Aubrey didn't have her bag, she wouldn't have access to her phone, which meant no texts or social media updates about Austin's death before Carlie Beth was ready to break the news.

When Aubrey spotted her grandmother, her face brightened. "Are we doing something with Miss Joan?"

"We've been invited out to her house for…" Carlie Beth's brain didn't have the wherewithal to make up a decent lie.

"Supper?"

"Yeah."

Aubrey stopped in the parking lot and turned to Carlie Beth. "You know I love Miss May, right?"

If there was ever proof of a benevolent God, this was it. A girl who loved a woman who so often acted uncharitably. She reached out and pushed a strand of Aubrey's hair behind her ear, mostly to settle herself. "Absolutely."

"Do you think Miss Joan would mind if I called her something more…I don't know…grandmother-like?"

Oh, this had been such a horrid day. And as always, without even realizing it, Aubrey had managed to bring a ray of sunlight back into it. Carlie Beth hugged her daughter hard. "Why don't you ask her?"

When they climbed in Joan's car, Aubrey settled into the backseat. "Miss Joan?"

"Yes, sweetheart?"

"I was wondering…" Aubrey glanced at Carlie Beth and must've seen what she needed because she continued, "…would you mind if I called you something else? I mean, all the kids around town call you Miss Joan, but since I'm your…" She faltered again.

Joan turned to face the backseat. "Since I'm your grandmother, you mean?"

"Yes, ma'am."

She took Aubrey's hand and squeezed it. "Did you have something in mind?"

"I thought maybe Grammy."

"I've always wanted to be a Grammy," Joan said, and the smile she shined on Carlie Beth made it clear she'd forgiven her for keeping her granddaughter a secret all these years.

As soon as they made it out to Tupelo Hill, Joan ushered Aubrey inside and told Carlie Beth, "Why don't you enjoy the front porch for a few minutes while my granddaughter and I rustle up a snack for everyone?"

What Carlie Beth really felt like doing was crawling under the covers, with Grif curled around her, and never coming out again. But that wasn't an option right now, so she settled onto a swing big enough for a family of five, savoring the feel of the thick cushion under her.

She gave it one push and let the momentum rock her, the chains squeaking slightly with each back and forth. But it couldn't soothe away her troubled thoughts about Austin. Why would someone kill him? She couldn't imagine he'd brought it on himself. At heart, he'd been a good kid with a love for alternative music and a talent for working with his hands.

Maggie had made it clear she would contact Austin's parents, but Carlie Beth would follow up with a phone call of her own. Although he had legally been an adult, he was still their child, and they'd entrusted her with him. The guilt of that alone was eating her up.

Within a few minutes, Britt's truck pulled up and three of the Steele brothers stepped out, momentarily distracting her from her circling thoughts. But the only brother who did it for her—mind, body, and heart— wasn't here yet. Britt, Jonah, and Reid trooped up the porch steps. Britt gave her a nod and went inside. But Jonah and Reid came toward her, neither of them smiling. Jonah sat on her left, and Reid flanked her on the right, setting the swing in motion again with his weight. He wrapped one beefy arm around her shoulders and pulled her in to his side.

It felt nothing like being in Grif's arms, which was a combination of comfort and pure stimulation. Reid's hug was like a big brother's and she soaked in his strength and steadiness.

"You gonna be okay?" he asked.

"I'm a tough girl."

He patted her shoulder. "Death makes us all pussies."

Jonah snorted in clear disgust. "Someone needs to install a filter between your brain and your mouth."

"Shit," Reid muttered. "I mean…"

But Reid's social incompetence was exactly what Carlie Beth needed. "I get what you're saying. I'm just sick over having to tell Aubrey. We have to live in that house and I have to work where…" Carlie Beth swallowed down her sudden nausea. "I just don't want her to be scared."

Reid said, "Do you trust Grif?"

"Of course."

"And he told you we'd handle this, right?"

"What does that mean exactly?"

Before he could answer, Grif came driving up, not in Louise but in the minivan. And even as shell-shocked as Carlie Beth was, that made her smile. When Grif got out and pocketed the keys, his gaze arrowed on his brothers. "I'm five minutes late and you two boneheads move in on my girl?"

"She finally figured out she prefers a real man. You know, one who can't pluck his eyebrows while looking into the reflection coming off his shoes." With that trademark grin, Reid yanked Carlie Beth closer, almost suffocating her in the process.

"Better than having to pluck my ass hairs," Grif said mildly.

That cracked them all up, a much-needed moment after the day they'd had, and Grif was smiling as he strolled across the porch and hooked a thumb at his brothers. "Move before I have to hurt you both."

Reid gave Carlie Beth a squeeze and pushed off the swing, making it sway wildly. Once his brothers disappeared inside the house, Grif settled beside her. "Sorry about those two."

"I think they're sweet."

With a snort, Grif leaned his head on the back of the swing. "Not a word I'd ever associate with my brothers."

She'd been so shaken by Austin's death that she hadn't considered that the situation had also thrown Grif off balance, but now she could see the exhaustion lines around his eyes and mouth. Needing to provide the comfort he so obviously needed, she ran a hand down his chest to rest against his heart.

His thoughtful, protective heart.

It thumped reassuringly against her palm.

"Do you know what I see when I look at you and your brothers?"

He gave her a mock glare from the corner of his eye. "You shouldn't be looking at my brothers."

"I see four men who were raised right. You take care of your mom. You take care of each other. For God's sake, you take care of this town. A town three of you haven't lived in for years."

Grif covered her hand with his bigger one, pressing it closer to his heart. "It's home."

His simple statement made emotion clog Carlie Beth's throat. "I see four men who protect the people and things they care about."

"Damn right. I know some people think we're a big bunch of arrogant assholes. But if Jonah, Reid, and I hadn't left, we wouldn't be able to help people around here the way we can."

"You're right."

"And the best way I know how to take care of people is to keep doing what I'm good at."

"You mean being a sports agent." What he didn't realize was that his gift wasn't winning big deals for big money. It was solving problems and taking care of people, making sure they had an advocate in their corner.

"It's made me a pretty well-off guy."

"Do you love the work?" Because she couldn't imagine a world where she didn't love what she did.

He blew out a breath and stared at the porch ceiling. "I'm damn good at it."

Carlie Beth knew in some ways they were both avoiding the reality of Austin's death. But this was a conversation they needed to have. She needed to have. Because she needed to understand just how much she'd jeopardized her heart by loving a man who loved a different lifestyle.

"Mom?"

Carlie Beth refocused on the front door to find Aubrey leaning out, looking at her and Grif with hungry eyes. Eyes hungry for a real family. "Yeah, baby?"

"Grammy has cookies ready."

"Grammy?" Grif asked.

Aubrey dipped her head slightly. "She said I could decide what I wanted to call her."

"Think the cookies can wait a few minutes?" He scooted over and patted the empty spot he'd made between Carlie Beth and him. "Your mom and I need to talk with you."

Eyes sparking with excitement, Aubrey let the front door crash closed behind her and she dashed over to squeeze between them. The emotion that had threatened to choke Carlie Beth a few minutes ago swamped her. Simply cut off her ability to draw a full breath because her daughter looked so happy.

And they were about to snuff out that light.

She took her daughter's hand. "Aub, we've got something serious to tell you."

"I knew it!" She threw her arms around Carlie Beth. "You're getting married."

Looking over her shoulder, Carlie Beth caught sight of Grif's *oh shit* expression. Oh shit because they were about to destroy Aubrey's excitement? Or oh shit because marriage was not on his to-do list? Ever.

She pulled Aubrey's arms from around her shoulders and looked into her eyes. *Like a Band-Aid, Carlie Beth. Just rip the damn thing off.* "Austin is dead."

Eyes wide, Aubrey jerked back, almost head-butting Grif in the process. "What?"

Grif took Aubrey's hand. "Your mom and I found him in the forge this morning. We didn't want you to hear about it from someone else."

Her eyes dull, she asked, "What happened?"

Now Grif shot Carlie Beth a look that said he was out of his depth.

She pushed off the swing and took a deep breath before facing her daughter. "Someone killed him."

"Killed?" Aubrey's panicked gaze darted between Carlie Beth and Grif. "You mean on purpose? Like...m-murder?"

She'd been hoping to avoid that word, but she nodded once.

"In our backyard?" Aubrey asked.

Carlie Beth knelt in front of her daughter, placing both hands on her knees. "I know this is scary, but—"

"Someone came on our property and took Austin's life." Aubrey's volume went up with each word. "Who the hell do they think they are? We should hunt them down and—"

"Whoa, whoa there," Grif cut in on her tirade. "There is no *we*. You need to know what happened, but that's the extent of your involvement in this situation, young lady."

For the first time, Carlie Beth witnessed her daughter turning on her father. "Are you really *young lady*-ing me? You don't get to do that. Who gave you the right to act like you can tell me what to do? Austin was my friend. I cared about him. And someone needs to do something about this."

Although he looked taken aback at the force of Aubrey's anger, Grif said quietly, "Someone will."

"Just not me."

"You're a girl," he said. "This isn't your fight to fight."

"So you'll just let Sheriff Kingston deal with it?"

Grif swallowed. Yeah, Aubrey had him there. Because Carlie Beth knew there was no way on God's green earth the Steele brothers would walk away from something like this. "That's not for you to worry about."

Aubrey jumped off the swing and glared at Grif. "You...you...don't think anyone else can possibly fix things the way you can. You know what? We did just fine without you." She whirled around and stormed back into the house.

"She didn't mean that," Carlie Beth said quietly. "She's just scared and upset."

"But she's not wrong." His heart felt bruised from the force of his daughter's anger. "I could go back to LA and the two of you could return to being the tight little family you were before I bullied my way into your girl world."

She ran a light hand down his arm and linked her fingers with his. "How do you like it when you feel helpless?"

"Not at all," he said. "But I'd rather her be angry with me than risk her safety."

"Welcome to the Catch-Twenty-two of parenthood." She tugged on his hand. "Now, your brothers are waiting for us inside."

"Maybe you should—"

"If you're about to suggest I go help your mom and Aubrey in the kitchen, stop right there. Leaving a fourteen-year-old girl out of the loop is one thing. But this is my home and business we're talking about."

"Fine." But it wasn't fine. He wanted to take her and Aubrey upstairs to one of the four bedrooms and lock them up like Rapunzel.

His brothers were already inside Jonah's office, and Reid was busy screwing a massive whiteboard into the wall.

"Mom's gonna have a shit-fit," Grif told him.

"That's too bad," he muttered back. "Because we have a killer to catch."

Britt drummed his fingers on the arm of the chair he was seated in. "Forgive me for stating the obvious, but isn't that Maggie's job?" Both Grif and Reid glared at their older brother. "Just trying to keep you out of trouble."

"We don't need a conscience right now, Tarzan," Reid said, looking around the room at each of them. "Okay, what do we know?"

"Austin was killed on my property," Carlie Beth said, her voice small and thin.

Reid was busy scratching out completely illegible words on the whiteboard.

"Dammit, we can't read a word of that." Jonah bolted out of his chair and snatched up a dry erase marker. "Besides, you're making a list and this calls for a mind map. You reason and I'll write." He printed *Austin Burns* on the board and drew a circle around it.

"The kid was working late last night," Grif said. "And I talked with him out at the forge."

Reid paced from wall to wall. "What time?"

"About midnight."

"What did you talk about?"

Oh, hell. He hadn't told his brothers about the lab report yet. Grif blew out a sigh. "The oil on the climbing wall turned out to be a quenchant."

"What the hell is that?" Reid demanded.

"It's used to temper metal," Carlie Beth explained.

"So you use it in your forge?"

"No." She didn't glance at Grif, which just made him feel like more of an asshole for even thinking she could've been the culprit. "I use plain old mineral oil."

Jonah drew some more circles around the new info.

"Do you know if Austin had any enemies?" Reid asked. "Anyone who'd want to get back at him for something. Ex-girlfriend, maybe?"

"He never mentioned anyone," she said. "In fact, he…"

"He what?" Grif asked.

"Well, he came to dinner last night and when he left, he wasn't too happy."

"Because of me?"

"Apparently, he developed a little crush on me over the past few months. He…uh…" Carlie Beth's face wore a wash of pink.

"What did he do?"

"He kissed me."

"That little—"

Carlie Beth raised her brows at him. "Surely you remember what it's like to be nineteen and full of yourself. Oh, wait. You were eighteen and full of yourself."

Reid rolled in his lips like he wanted to add to the conversation, but for once, he showed some restraint. "Mags is gonna come talk to you both."

"That's fine," Grif said. "Because we know neither of us did it."

"Lot of other weird stuff going on around here lately," Britt drawled, nodding toward Jonah's map about the quenching oil. "Grif's fall off the climbing wall."

Jonah sketched more circles. "And someone messing up Louise."

Yeah, that still made Grif's stomach hurt. "The vandalism out here at the complex."

"Any other crimes that y'all can think of without us having to ask Maggie?"

Carlie Beth raised her hand as if she were in a grade-school classroom. "What about Roy Darden?"

Reid's eyes narrowed as he looked at her. "His death was ruled an accident."

"That was before all the rest of this shit went down," Grif said, a bad feeling creeping over him.

"Hey, guys," Jonah said. "I think this mind map is working."

"You come up with something?" Reid asked.

"Yeah, but you're not gonna like it." Jonah's body was shielding the whiteboard as he wrote and drew another circle. When he stepped back, all the other circles bore arrows pointing to the big oval in the middle. And inside there were two words.

Carlie Beth.

CHAPTER TWENTY-SEVEN

SON OF A BITCH. GRIF stood in the middle of Jonah's office just staring at all the circles, hoping he would see a connection that his little brother hadn't. But the Baby Billionaire hadn't become richer than sin because he was an idiot and overlooked things. He'd made a stack of cash because he was so fucking smart he made other people look like slobbering idiots.

Carlie Beth wrapped a hand around Grif's biceps.

"He's right," she said.

"Reid, we need security now. Yesterday."

"I've got some guys I can call to patrol the house."

"Jonah, can you take some pictures of the board? There's no way in hell we're leaving Maggie out of this. We need all the help we can get. We have to catch this bastard before he moves on Carlie Beth."

"You don't think—" she started.

"The only thing I'm thinking right now is that I want you and Aubrey safe." He hadn't planned for them to return to their house tonight regardless, but now, they wouldn't be returning there for the foreseeable future. "You'll be sleeping at my place tonight."

Carlie Beth looked up at him. "Have you forgotten that you have one bed and a sofa we already determined is questionable?"

Damn.

"You can stay out here," Jonah said.

"I don't want to put your mom out."

Grif took Carlie Beth by the shoulders and turned her toward him. "You're not going back to your house. If y'all need some of your stuff, I'll pick it up." And first thing tomorrow morning, he was going out and buying a houseful of fucking furniture. He wanted his family with him. Under his protection. "I don't want you back in your forge or out on any jobs alone until we figure out who this guy is. You so much as step outside onto the porch, and you'd better have one of us with you. Same goes for Aubrey."

"What about school?"

"I'll send her with a damn bodyguard if I have to." The thought of someone putting their hands on his daughter made his blood boil through his veins.

"I still can't believe someone is hurting people because of me."

"We'll figure it out." He sealed his words with a kiss, one full of promise. Carlie Beth's mouth was so sweet, but he tasted heartache on her tongue. "Finding this guy is my top priority. Nothing else."

"Ah...Grif?" Jonah went to the closet and pulled out two suit bags with the name of an Asheville formalwear store on them. "Did you forget about the State of Steele Ridge reception this week?"

"Dammit. I can't think about that right now. The last thing I have time for is town politics."

"You'll lose any ground you've made with the business owners if we don't follow through on this," Jonah said. "Besides, it'll give you a chance to scope out all the people who might have it out for you."

"We decided this"—he gestured toward the whiteboard—"was about Carlie Beth."

"Nothing happened before you hit town."

"Nothing happened before you *bought* the damn town, you mean." He spared a glance at the black bag in his brother's hand. "So help me God, if you tell me you rented me a tuxedo from off the rack I will—"

"Mom called your tailor. Don't worry, no one else has sweated his balls off in your tux. This one was made to order." Jonah shot a pointed look at Carlie Beth. "And please tell me you have a date."

Her mouth opened and she backed up several steps. "Uh...no. No thank you," she told him. "I don't do dress-up events. Besides, I don't have anything to wear."

Grif said, "I'll buy you—"

Carlie Beth shot him a look hotter than the coals in her forge. "Money's already gotten you in trouble once. Besides, I haven't been asked."

Ah, so his beautiful tomboy wanted to be romanced, did she? What a hell of a time for it, amid all the chaos right now. But he was more than happy to give her what she wanted. So Grif took her hand and bowed over it. "Would you do me the honor of accompanying me to the State of Steele Ridge reception?"

"Is this like a real date?"

He smiled up at her, knowing damn well his expression was both smug and wolfish. "This, Carlie Beth Parrish, is absolutely a real date."

CHAPTER TWENTY-EIGHT

GRIF WAS FORCING HIMSELF TO stay busy—finalizing his economic development plan for the city—so he wouldn't storm into Maggie's office and demand to know what was going on with the investigation into Austin's death. That hadn't, however, kept him from calling her multiple times a day.

His ear was still ringing from the frustrated lashing she'd given him. "Dammit, Grif, stay out of my investigation and do your own damn job before I'm tempted to commit murder myself."

Fine. It was time to pick up Aubrey from school anyway. And he'd only agreed to let her go back on the conditions that she was never alone and that he would be the one to drive her to and from. He grabbed a jacket to protect against the rain that had blown into town. Which meant when he arrived, the carpool lane was so backed up that the parking lot was a snarl of cars, trucks, and SUVs.

He'd been shortsighted on the minivan purchase. He should've bought something with all-wheel drive. "To hell with it," he muttered to himself and turned the wheel to hop a curb and drive over a patch of newly sprouted grass and back onto the asphalt. A glance in the rearview told him he'd probably be paying for some new flowerbeds after the next school board meeting.

What the hell ever.

As he got out and hurried toward the building's glass doors, he saw Aubrey wave from inside. He raised his hand in return, but realized her gesture hadn't been for him when she pushed open the door and ran toward a red Subaru.

How many times had he told her not to go anywhere alone and to stay inside that building? And hadn't he made it clear to the principal that he'd have his ass if anything happened to Aubrey while she was on school property?

"Aubrey!" Grif bellowed. But with all the rain and traffic and people, his words were swallowed up. His damn Gravati loafers didn't have the best traction, but he when he saw his daughter lean inside the car's open window, he put on an extra burst of speed, internally cussing his choice of ineffective footwear.

Closer now, he shouted again, "Dammit, Aubrey, get the hell away from there."

Yeah, that reduced the noise level around him a little, and his daughter glanced up, her eyes going wide. "Dad, I—"

Grif yanked open the driver's door and grabbed an arm.

"What're you doing?" Aubrey called.

Still glaring at his daughter over the top of the car, he wrestled the driver out of the car. "Let me see your face, you son of a..."

That's when he realized the arm he held seemed small, and he glanced down at the person he'd manhandled onto the sidewalk. *Shit.*

Aubrey raced around the front of the car. "Have you lost your mind?"

Apparently. He released Yvonne's arm so quickly that she stumbled to the side and smacked her hip against the open door. He tried to catch her, but she shifted away, her eyes full of distrust.

"God, I'm sorry. I thought..."

Yvonne rubbed at the spot above her elbow where he'd grabbed her and gave him a sickly smile. "After hearing about what happened to Austin, I just wanted to check on Aubrey. I never meant to scare either of you."

His hand shaking, Grif rubbed a palm across his forehead. "Let me see your arm. I pulled you out of there pretty hard. Maybe I should drive you to the clinic."

"I'm fine."

Aubrey scooted by him to wrap her arms around Yvonne, then turned a glare on him. "I'm not stupid. I knew it was her."

"Still, I told you to stay inside."

"You may not remember this," Aubrey said, "but my mom and I aren't princesses you can lock up in some tower. We took care of ourselves for a lot of years just fine without you."

"Those years are over. Forever."

Carlie Beth was a wreck. Had to be because she was basically trapped out at Tupelo Hill. Ha. Trapped on twenty thousand acres. Not that she had access to more than a handful of them.

Or maybe she was a wreck because she had nothing to wear to a formal event. Who did that kind of thing in Steele Ridge?

No, that was probably the wrong question.

People hadn't done that kind of thing in Canyon Ridge. But times had changed with the Steele Brothers taking charge.

No one in this town would ever be the same again.

Especially not Carlie Beth.

She was picking through the meager wardrobe of dresses she'd had Grif pick up for her when there was a knock at her door.

"Come in."

Aubrey walked in and eyed the outfits strewn across the full-size bed. "None of those are nice enough."

Carlie Beth wanted to roll her eyes the way her daughter did sometimes, but she restrained herself. "I know, but shopping isn't in the cards today."

"I hear we have visitors!" A teasing feminine voice came from the hallway and Evie poked her head inside the room. Although she wore a smile, her troubled eyes made it clear Joan had already filled her in on what had happened to Austin. Evie came farther into the room and studied the pile of clothes. "What's up?"

"I'm no longer allowed to go to the State of Steele Ridge reception." Aubrey shook her head in disgust. "Plus Mom has a date with Dad, she has nothing to wear, and we can't shop."

Evie waved them across the hallway. "C'mon over to Evie's House of Fashion and we'll see if we can hook you up."

When she opened the double doors to the closet, Carlie Beth and Aubrey both stood there gaping. Although filled from side to side on two rows, the space was immaculately organized.

"It's color coordinated," Aubrey breathed, her admiration clear.

Evie turned to Carlie Beth and must've caught her puzzled look because she said, "I worked part-time at La Belle Style in town before I started my nursing clinicals. The owner, Brynne, hooked me up with clothes." Her smile was slightly chagrined. "And Grif takes me shopping a couple of times a year when he flies me out to LA to visit."

"You've seen where he lives?" Aubrey asked.

"Yep, and it's nothing like Steele Ridge."

The slightly sick feeling Carlie Beth had been carrying around all day flared. Here she was, stressed about a little dress-up event and Grif probably did this kind of thing every day of the week.

"His condo is in Westwood," Evie elaborated. "Very modern and slick."

Again, nothing like Carlie Beth's decor of retro real-life.

"I can't wait to see it," Aubrey said. "Maybe this summer."

With cheerful efficiency, Evie began to pull dresses out of the closet one by one, laying them over the bed and hanging them from the window trim. She motioned Carlie Beth forward and held a shimmery green dress against her. "Hmm. Pretty, but so cliché."

Then she chose a short red thing that Carlie Beth was pretty sure would show her underwear.

Evie shook her head. "Definitely washes you out."

Thank Jesus.

Maybe Evie had a denim skirt. The thought made Carlie Beth chuckle.

"Mom," Aubrey said in a warning tone, "whatever you're thinking, stop." She told Evie, "I never let her go shopping without me. The one time I did, she came home with a stack of jeans from the boys' section and shirts she bought from the tractor supply store."

"I'll have you know I bought that gray hoodie I love in the girls' department."

"See what I mean?"

"Ooh, I've got it," Evie muttered and reached for a waterfall of fabric that at first glance looked black, but when she pulled it from the closet, it changed in the light, becoming a flash of bronze.

"He is going to swallow his tongue," Evie said.

Aubrey laughed. "That sounds kinda gross."

Carlie Beth got a good look at the dress's neckline and backed away. "Uh-uh. No. I don't do"—she waved a hand up and down—"that."

"This is the dress," Evie insisted. "I got a deal on it at the boutique. Haven't even worn it yet. See, the tags are still on it."

"Then save it for a special occasion," Carlie Beth said. "You know what, I'll just tell Grif—"

"Strip," Evie ordered.

"Excuse me?"

"Don't make me wrestle you to the ground. A girl doesn't grow up with four brothers without learning a few tricks. Now, down to your underwear."

Evie's blue eyes were filled with determination, and Carlie Beth knew she could either drop her pants or risk not making it out of this room alive. So she reached for her T-shirt and pulled it over her head. And knew immediately what Evie's tongue cluck and Aubrey's groan were about.

"I happen to like wearing a sports bra."

"It's a good thing you can't wear a bra of any kind with this dress."

Yeah, probably not, since the dress would show her belly button.

Once she extricated herself from her bra, Carlie Beth ditched her pants and Evie unzipped the dress. While Aubrey supervised from her perch on the bed, Evie held the dress for Carlie Beth to step in. And oh, what was this made of? The fabric was cool and sleek against her skin, eliciting a shiver as Evie lifted the dress and hooked the bodice around her neck, leaving at least half of her back bare. The skirt swept the floor like something from a fairytale.

Well, a slightly wicked fairytale.

"Come look in the mirror," Evie told her.

"Mom, you look amazing."

Carlie Beth shot her daughter a smile. "Thanks." Then she caught her reflection. Even with her hair in an anti-glamorous ponytail, the sight of herself in this beautiful, shimmery dress stole her breath. "It's gorgeous, Evie."

Evie stood behind her, also reflected in the mirror, and grinned. "No, *you're* gorgeous. One shot and he's a goner."

Aubrey bounced on the bed. "I just met him, so I'd like him to stay alive a little longer."

"We'll do CPR," Evie told her.

The mention of the lifesaving technique made Carlie Beth's chest tight with grief for Austin. His parents had been devastated. Although it was tough, she tried to remember that death always, always gave the living a gift. This time, it was a reminder to grab life and hang on to it.

Watching Evie and Aubrey together, Carlie Beth felt a bittersweet ache. How had she never realized how much her daughter needed a family? One bigger than the two of them.

Carlie Beth twisted her torso to get a look at the side of the dress and a breeze wafted across skin it shouldn't have been able to waft across.

Aubrey laughed and fell back on the bed, and Carlie Beth looked down at herself to find, sure enough, that her left boob had popped clean out of the so-called bodice. Quickly, she pulled the fabric, what there was of it, over her breast. "See, this won't work. One reach for an appetizer and I'll send Mayor Hackberry to the hospital from a morality stroke."

"That's why they invented this." Evie opened a dresser drawer, grabbed a small box, and waved it like a magic wand. "Boob tape!"

Aubrey lost it again and Carlie Beth stared at the box. "You can't be serious."

"Look in that mirror again," Evie demanded. "And tell me what you see."

"It's beautiful," she admitted. "But if I have to corral my boobs, it's also going to be a royal pain in the..."

Now, Evie's grin was knowing and wicked. "I know someone else who's a royal pain, but he also knows clothes. You in that dress will take away all the syllables in that man's vocabulary except for *uh* and *ah*."

A heavy knock came at the bedroom door, and Carlie Beth patted her chest to make sure her breast was back under wraps.

"What do you want, Reid?" Evie called.

"Security called up," he said. "Someone's here to visit

Carlie Beth. Yvonne Winters from the gallery in town. Do you want to see her?"

The reality of the situation hit Carlie Beth. Reid's security people were screening her visitors. This was insane. "Of course," she called out. "She's my friend."

"Send her up," he said from the other side of the door.

A few minutes later, he knocked again. "Yvonne's here."

When Evie opened the door, Reid caught sight of Carlie Beth. His jaw worked as if he were carrying on a conversation, but not a single word came out.

Evie nodded with satisfaction. "What did I tell you? That dress is a man-killer."

"Wow," Reid finally said. "I…uh…ah…You clean up real nice there."

Evie pushed at his shoulder. "And Mom wonders why you're single? Yvonne, come on in."

Reid pointed at his sister. "Don't forget what I told you about locking your French doors." As he started to close the door, he winked at Carlie Beth. "If my brother is too stupid to see what he's got right in front of him, remember I'm the better-looking one anyway."

Knowing he was being a total tease, Carlie Beth gave him a saucy toss of her head. "Don't think I won't."

Yvonne took two steps into the room and stopped cold, staring at Carlie Beth. "Wow."

"That's two wows now," Aubrey said, hopping up to give Yvonne a hug.

But she was so busy making a slow circle around Carlie Beth that she didn't notice. "You…that's…gorgeous. And crazy sexy."

"Which means Evie shouldn't have had it in her closet in the first place," Reid said before pulling the door closed.

Evie just said, "Brothers!"

"I don't think I understand all this brother-sister thing," Aubrey said to Evie. "It seems like y'all can't stand each other."

Evie plopped down on the bed beside her and gave her a shoulder nudge. "That's called affection."

"Y'all don't need any enemies, then."

"Oh, don't you worry," Evie said. "If anyone messes with one Steele, you'd better believe the rest of us will be hot on that person's trail."

Aubrey's mouth twisted downward. "I'm not a Steele. Not really."

"Bullshit," Evie said, with no apologetic shrug for the curse word. "You're as much a Steele as any of our kids will be one day. My babies won't have the last name Steele. Unless I hyphenate. Which could be pretty cool. Regardless of your last name, you're a Steele where it counts." She poked Aubrey's chest. "Right here."

Before Carlie Beth could spiral down the rabbit hole of what to do about her daughter's last name, another knock came at the door. "Girls!" Joan called. "I have cookies ready!"

Aubrey and Evie jumped off the mattress like it had bedbugs.

"Hey," Carlie Beth protested. "What about me? And the dress?"

"You do not say no to my mom's brown-butter-and-pecan-chocolate-chip cookies," Evie said. "Not ever. Yvonne can get you out of it. But I'll need to help you dress a half hour before Grif is supposed to be here because that tape can be a little tricky. Make it an hour and we'll do hair and makeup, too."

"That's good," Aubrey said. "All she has to do is bathe."

Once they raced each other out the door and, by the sounds of it, down the stairs, Yvonne asked, "You're wearing that to the reception?"

"Too much?" Half-embarrassed for being caught looking so girly, Carlie Beth bent her head and reached for the catch at the back of her neck.

"No! Here, let me help you with that." Yvonne shooed Carlie Beth's hands away and released the hooks. Carlie

Beth held the bodice against her chest while Yvonne worked on the zipper. "Sorry, this one's being cranky." The back of her hand grazed Carlie Beth's spine, sending a shiver over her skin before the zipper finally gave way. "Must've had a piece of fabric caught in it."

"I'll be more careful when I put it on later." Because she wanted to wear this dress in the worst way. And even more, she wanted Grif to see her in it. Which also meant digging through her things for the very best pair of panties she could find.

With her back to Yvonne, Carlie Beth stepped out of the dress and quickly pulled on her clothes. They were friends, but they weren't shopping friends and it felt uncomfortable to be stripped down to the skin in front of her.

Adjusting the hem of her T-shirt, Carlie Beth turned to find Yvonne standing in the middle of the room with a thoughtful expression on her face. "You okay?"

She nodded, the movement slightly jerky. "Yeah, it's just, you know. I just keep thinking about Austin."

Carlie Beth rushed forward and grabbed her friend's hands. "Oh, God. Me, too."

Yvonne squeezed her fingers. "I wanted to make sure you were okay. That you weren't blaming yourself."

Why would she think Carlie Beth would blame herself? "You know it wasn't an accident, right? They think someone…someone killed him." Because a person didn't fall, knock into a worktable, and have steel spikes tumble down hard enough to pierce skin.

And probably muscle and bone.

Carlie Beth shuddered.

Dropping Carlie Beth's hands, Yvonne said casually, "Did Aubrey happen to mention the little scene after school earlier?"

Her shudder froze halfway down her spine. "No. What happened?"

She wandered across the room, ran her fingers over the other dresses Evie had taken from her closet. "Oh, it was nothing."

"If it were nothing, you wouldn't have mentioned it."

"When Grif picked her up, he got a little... sideways...with me."

"What do you mean?"

"I was chatting with Aubrey, just to check on her, too. He lost it. Opened my car door and dragged me out." She pushed up her shirt sleeve to display a bruise above her elbow.

Although her stomach felt uneasy, Carlie Beth said, "If you were in your car, that means Aubrey was outside the school. We told her several times she wasn't to leave the building without her dad."

"I didn't realize that. No wonder he was so upset." Yvonne pushed down her sleeve and smiled, but the expression was obviously forced. "If Austin was murdered, if there's someone else dangerous around town, the sheriff should let people know."

"They're still investigating."

"You look a little shaky, Carlie Beth. You're sure you're up for a date with Grif tonight?"

A date she was hopeful would end with another visit to Grif's bed because she needed to feel his arms around her. Needed him. She plopped down on Evie's mattress, feeling it sink beneath her. "I don't know what this thing is."

"I know that look." Yvonne sat beside her and gave her a bolstering hug. "I've worn it myself."

"What look?"

"That puppy-dog-mixed-with-preteen-girl mope one second and high-on-life sparkle the next."

With a wince, Carlie Beth said, "Is it really that obvious?"

"It's clear you're getting in deep."

"Maybe over my head."

"Just promise me you'll be careful, with Grif and Austin's death." Yvonne patted her shoulder with a light, sympathetic touch. "It would break my heart to see you get hurt."

CHAPTER TWENTY-NINE

THE GOOD NEWS WAS THAT Grif wouldn't have to kill his brother, because the tux fit perfectly. Possibly better than the three Grif had hanging in his closet in LA. Not that he would admit that to the Baby Billionaire.

Even though Grif knew he looked good, he stood on his mom's front porch and shot his cuffs. Then he adjusted the line of his pants. Then he went for his bowtie.

"So help me, if you start fiddling with your bra next, I'm fucking outta here," Reid drawled.

Grif looked over to find his brother at the far end of the porch. "What're you doing out here?"

"Just keepin' an eye on things." Reid rubbed his chin. "I was able to get feet on the ground out here and I'm working with a company on a security system. But that isn't something they can just run out here and toss together. Not the kind I want."

"You trust the guys you have making the rounds on the property?"

"Enough to bet my life on."

Yeah, but he was also betting on Carlie Beth's and Aubrey's lives. "I tried like hell to pump everyone who came through my office today, and believe me, there were plenty of them."

"Anything pop?"

"Not unless you think the PTA is getting even with Carlie Beth for missing the last bake sale. Good news is no one else seems to have made the Carlie Beth connection with everything that's been going sideways in town."

"Yeah, we wanna keep it that way." Reid strolled over and adjusted Grif's bowtie. "You fucked it up." Then he sniffed. Sniffed again. "Man, you smell better than a two-bit whorehouse after the Avon lady leaves."

Grif looked up toward the sky just as he'd done a million times before when his brother said something completely offensive, but God had yet to get around to striking down Reid. "I'll take that as a compliment."

Suddenly, Reid grabbed his wrist and wrapped his thumb around the inside.

"What the hell?" Grif tried to pull away, but Reid was a strong son of a bitch.

"If I had to guess, I'd say your pulse is in the low hundreds. Someone's either tachycardic or nervous."

"What are you—the date monitor?"

A big shit-eating grin spread across Reid's face and he leaned a shoulder against a porch column. "I've seen her, and she looks hot."

"If I didn't know you were yanking my chain, I'd lay you out right here on Mom's porch. Let her find your chewed-up ass after the coyotes got ahold of it."

Reid's face took on a serious expression, one he wore once the joking took a hike. "Don't do Carlie Beth wrong. She deserves a hell of a lot better than that."

"I know she does. I'm working on it, okay?" Which was the main reason his hands weren't steady. "You are staying here tonight, right?"

"Like I got anywhere else to be?"

"Jonah'll be back after the reception, but I plan to talk Carlie Beth into going back to my place. But Aubrey—"

Reid clapped him on the back so hard, Grif had to take a step forward to keep his balance. "Don't worry about her. Not a damn thing'll happen to her with me around."

Brotherly affection welling up in him, Grif grabbed Reid in a headlock. "She's a hell of a kid, isn't she?"

Reid halfheartedly punched Grif in the side. "Yeah, bro, she's a Steele through and through."

And Grif planned to make that legal. He released his brother with a playful shove and went inside. His mom came out of the kitchen, wiping her hands on a dish towel. "Well, don't you look handsome?" She straightened his tie.

Once she was done with her fussing, he handed her a box, one crammed packed with protective cushioning.

"What in the world?"

"Your teapot. Good as new." The porcelain restorer had been worth every penny, and his mom's soft expression told him that he was forgiven.

"You're a good boy. Now, did you bring Carlie Beth flowers?"

Pure panic streamed through him. *Fuck, fuck, fuck.* But he said, "This isn't prom."

"Griffin, flowers are always appropriate."

With a glance at the stairs to be sure they were empty, he blew out a breath and reached into his interior coat pocket. "What if I told you I brought something else?" When he pulled out the black velvet box, his mom's eyes glistened.

"I would ask to see it, but I'm sure I'll get a good look later."

"About that," he said, "Carlie Beth and I need a little time alone. Reid assured me he'd be here all night."

"You don't worry about a thing. Evie, Aubrey, and I already had a movie night planned." His mom's smile faded. "But honey, how are you and Carlie Beth going to manage between here and LA—"

"I'm still working on that."

"I'm proud that you're taking your responsibilities seriously, but I want you to be happy, too."

He kissed her cheek. "Mom, just like you don't see

the ring first, you don't hear the words first either."

Her smile returned. "I'll run up and get Carlie Beth." She headed for the stairs.

After showing his mom the ring box, his nerves were back full force. He wandered over to the fireplace and rearranged the poker, broom, and shovel so they stood nice and straight in their own places. Everything in its place. Wouldn't it be nice if his life would fall back into place? It would if Carlie Beth said yes.

When he heard footsteps on the staircase, he turned and wham! Awe hit him square in the chest.

Good God, he should've asked Reid for a Kevlar vest to wear under his tux.

Carlie Beth was slowly descending the stairs. He vaguely registered that his mom, Evie, and Aubrey were hovering behind her. But Carlie Beth was the epicenter of his universe.

The dress she was wearing gleamed in the light, flashing black one second and bronze the next. The skirt wasn't tight but had a slit over her left thigh. Obviously, the designer had realized it wasn't necessary for walking, but it was damn sure necessary for Grif's enjoyment. Carlie Beth's shoes were strappy black sandals with thin heels. He'd never once seen her in anything like them, and the sight of her slender ankle made his skin flash hot.

But the part of the dress that almost stopped his heart was the strip of fabric that came from her waist and circled around the back of her neck. With every step she took, he caught a peek at the curve of her breasts.

He wouldn't survive an evening of speeches and small talk with the city council members and business owners while Carlie Beth was in the room.

When she stepped off the final tread, she wobbled a little in those sexy shoes, charming him. Reminding him she was his Carlie Beth. He caught her elbow to steady her, but his heart was beating so loudly in his ears that he couldn't string together a sentence to tell her how gorgeous she looked.

"I think," Evie said in a singsongy voice, "an I-told-you-so is in order here."

The tentative smile Carlie Beth had worn on her way down the stairs faltered. "I shouldn't be wearing these shoes," she muttered. "I feel stupid."

"Griffin," his mom said sharply, yanking him out his sexual stupor.

He cleared his throat and said, "You look beautiful."

"You don't have to say that."

As he leaned in close to her ear, a tendril of hair from her updo brushed his cheek, and he whispered, "I can't say what I'm really thinking because there are other people in the room, and I doubt you want Aubrey hearing how I want to shove my hands under your skirt, rip off whatever sexy panties you have on under there, and fuck you against my mother's living room wall."

Color rushed into her cheeks. "Oh. Well, then."

But he did kiss her, right there in front of their daughter, his family, God, and everyone. It was sweet and innocent as far as kisses went, but it made a statement. Made a claim.

"You not only look beautiful. You *are* beautiful. Inside and out."

The pink in her cheeks depended. This was a woman who needed to be complimented more. To be reminded just how much of a woman she was.

And he planned to do that every day for the rest of his life.

He looked up to catch their daughter watching them closely. He wished he could reassure her that everything was going to turn out fine, but that was a conversation for later. After he and Carlie Beth had things settled between them. "Aubrey, you're staying here tonight."

"Are you sure I can't go to the reception?"

"Your mom and I will both feel better with you here, and she's staying with me tonight."

"Oh."

Carlie Beth shot him a wide-eyed did-you-really-just-tell-her-that look. But he knew she was always upfront with Aubrey and he wasn't about to change that. "Do you feel okay about that?"

"As long as Mom does."

"I promise she'll be as safe as you are out here."

"Does Reid have security at your place too?" his mom asked.

"Nobody's getting through me," he told her before turning to Carlie Beth. "You ready?"

She took an audible breath and nodded.

After hugs all around, he took Carlie Beth's hand and led her out the front door. She looked up, a smile lighting her eyes. "You brought Louise."

"I figured this called for something a little fancier than the van." He laughed and pointed at the car. "But I had to drape towels over the seats. I didn't want you to snag whatever you were wearing."

She stopped right there in the driveway and turned to him. "Not once in all the chaos over the past few days have I said thank you."

"For what?"

"For all the things you've done. But if I listed them all, we'd be standing here all night. So the short list is…Thank you for being thoughtful, for looking out for Aubrey and me, and for being an all-around good man."

Now, he could feel heat filling his face. "I'm just being me."

"And that's what I'm most thankful for." The kiss she gave him was sweet and simple, filled with a sweet and simple message that inflated his heart.

They could do this. They could damn well make this relationship work. He just needed to get them through this reception first.

It was an education, watching Grif sleekly weave his

way through the crowd in the ornate city hall lobby. Even though everyone was dressed up—tuxes, suits, and pretty dresses—he was like a beautiful shark swimming through a pool of minnows.

Because her feet were protesting from being forced into the insane shoes Evie had insisted were the only ones that would do the dress justice, Carlie Beth was hanging back, leaning part of her weight on a cocktail table near the buffet and people watching. A few stopped by to grab a plate and chat. Everyone complimented Aubrey's work with the caterer, who'd provided everything from tiny cornbread and peach tarts to delicate cheese straws.

Wearing a caftan the color of plums with tiny silver bugle beads at the neckline, Jeanine from the bakery swept by and said something that sounded like, "Friends are like boobs. Some are real, and some are fake."

Carlie Beth chuckled at the strangely profound soundbite.

That's when she noticed Dave standing on the other side of the room, sipping a beer and glaring into the crowd. She traced his line of sight to find Grif in conversation with Brynne Whitfield, the owner of the boutique Carlie Beth's dress had come from. Dave must've caught her scrutiny because he turned toward her, wearing an expression that was a twist of anger and agony. And the way he was strangling the neck of his beer bottle hinted that he wanted to do the same to her. He started in her direction, but Lord, this was not the time or place for him to throw a hissy fit. So she shook her head, pointed at Grif, and mouthed *I love him.*

His face tight, Dave slammed his beer down on a nearby table with enough force to rock it, sending two wine glasses tumbling to the floor. He never glanced at the broken shards at his feet, but simply stepped through the mess and stalked out of the reception.

After his exit, people near the front door parted like something out of the Old Testament, and in walked an eye-blindingly beautiful couple. Jonah still had his scruffy look going on, but his hair was tamed and his tuxedo reminded Carlie Beth that although he was lean, he was a big guy. As big as any of his brothers.

Baby Billionaire indeed.

But the woman on his arm made every junior-high insecurity threaten to rise up inside Carlie Beth. The blonde was a head taller than she was and strolled in her peacock-blue heels as if they were an extension of her body. And if Carlie Beth had been concerned her dress might be a little too provocative for Steele Ridge, she shouldn't have worried because Jonah's date was wearing a strapless sheath that hugged her very obvious assets.

She was like a real-life Jessica Rabbit. The kind of woman who set off sexual pings in every person in the room regardless of his or her gender preference.

Jonah drew his date toward Carlie Beth and said, "Carlie Beth Parrish, I'd like to introduce you to Genevieve D'Artois."

This was one of those situations where she wished people had been trained to call her Elizabeth. But the reality was, she was a Carlie Beth, not an Elizabeth. She reached out to shake the other woman's hand, expecting a limp, bored touch. But the woman's grip was surprisingly firm and her smile was genuine, if a million and three watts.

"It's great to meet you," Jessica…er…Genevieve said. "Jonah's told me all about you."

Carlie Beth shot him a quick look. Really? Because she'd bet her favorite cross pein hammer he hadn't said a word to anyone about Genevieve. "It's wonderful to meet you, too. Do you live here in North Carolina?"

Genevieve laughed. "Oh, no. This is my first trip to the state. I live in San Francisco."

Interesting. "Well, welcome to the boonies."

"It's a beautiful area. Jonah's promised me a full tour of Steele Ridge, the sports complex, and his mom's house tomorrow."

Even more interesting that she wasn't staying with Jonah out at Tupelo Hill. Then again, maybe he was sleeping over somewhere with her.

Carlie Beth felt a big warm hand skim her back and looked up to find Grif standing there. When he stroked his hand down the sensitive skin of her inner arm, she couldn't hold back a little shiver, which made him flash her a secret smile that said he'd be caressing way more than her arm later.

Jonah made introductions again between Grif and his date, but didn't offer up any additional information about Genevieve.

When it came time for Jonah and Grif to make speeches, Carlie Beth and Genevieve stood next to each other and watched the two most handsome men in the room. Grif outlined a short but punchy economic development plan that hinged on a multiday pro-am tournament where registrants would be teamed up with big-name athletes to compete in a variety of sporting events from kayaking to rock climbing. Assuming it was a success—a guarantee with Grif in the driver's seat—the event would be held once a year and would be the cornerstone to attract tourists back to Steele Ridge.

Genevieve leaned toward Carlie Beth. "Are they all this panty-incinerating?"

It would be silly to pretend she didn't understand. "Each in his own way, yes."

"But your knickers only catch on fire for Grif."

Carlie Beth had to laugh at that, especially after his early comment. She discreetly waved a hand in front of her warm face. "He just does it for me."

"Jonah told me you two have a daughter."

Obviously, they were close if he'd shared that. "Yes, she's fourteen."

"Between the two of you, I bet she's a knockout," Genevieve said, simply and genuinely as if she weren't aware she was one of the most beautiful creatures on Earth.

"She's definitely coming into her own. Pretty, yes. But brains, that's her real gift. That kid is so smart, sometimes I have no idea what she's talking about."

"Jonah also told me you're a blacksmith."

Carlie Beth laughed and ran a hand down her skirt. "Which is the reason this dress feels so awkward tonight."

"I can see where full skirts could get in the way," she said. "Do you have any of your work for sale? I'd love to have a look before I leave town."

"I'm exclusively at Triskelion Gallery on Main Street. Tell Yvonne I sent you." Scanning the room, she looked for her friend. "In fact, she should be here tonight, but I haven't seen her yet."

"I'll be sure to stop by the gallery." Genevieve smiled and Carlie Beth had the unexplainable urge to hug the woman, just because she was so darn nice. Not at all what Carlie Beth had expected.

People around the room clapped, which made Carlie Beth realize the speeches were over. Sure enough, Grif and Jonah strolled up.

"Did I see you two whispering back here instead of paying attention to my brilliant economic development overview?" Grif asked.

"Aubrey will be thrilled to meet Ian Brinkmann," she teased. "Maybe you can put her on a team with him."

"Maybe I should think up another plan."

Jonah wiggled his eyebrows at Genevieve. "Now that all the handshaking and glad-handing is done, what do you say we get out of these clothes and go have a little fun?"

Interestingly enough, Genevieve's eyes sparked with a competitive gleam. "You are so on."

"Later, y'all," Jonah said cheerfully and took his date's arm to hustle her out of the room.

Carlie Beth just stared after them while Grif laughed, a low choking sound. "Do you think they're off to perform some kind of bedroom Olympics?"

"I don't know what to think," she said honestly. "Other than with the Steele brothers back in town, it'll never be the same again."

When Grif finally got Carlie Beth back to his apartment, the first thing she did was pull off her heels. The moan of pleasure she released as they came off was like a woman riding a good, long orgasm. He could honestly say this was the first time a woman stepping out of her shoes had given him a semi.

"Oh, my God," she said, low and breathy. So damn sexy. "That feels sooo good."

Jesus, forget the semi. His dick was full-on hard.

His chest expanded with the breath he took as he tried to rein in a little control. But he'd been half-crazed all night watching her in that dress. A flash of thigh here, a glimpse of breast there. "Want me to rub your feet?"

"You would do that?"

"Uh…it's not that big a deal."

"You don't understand. It's a very big deal. To a woman, a foot rub is like a confession of…"

He approached her and curved a hand around the back of her neck. "Of what?"

The pulse in her throat was pumping, which made him feel powerful. And predatory.

"I actually had a good time tonight," she said. "If you don't count the shoes."

"Next time, you can go barefoot."

Her eyes flared with what he hoped like hell was hope. Hope for next time. "Have I mentioned how much I like you, Grif Steele?"

That hope inside him deflated a little. *Like* wasn't nearly what he wanted. And he was a man used to getting what he wanted.

One way or another.

He tilted Carlie Beth's chin up, and her breath came faster, making her breasts rise and fall. They'd been playing peek-a-boo all night and he wanted to feel them again his chest. Against his mouth.

He released her to shrug out of his suit coat and let it fall to the floor. "Do you remember what I said earlier?"

"You said a lot of things." Her smile was witchy and she, honest to God, looked at him through her lashes.

"The one about putting my hands under your skirt."

"I think you used the word *shove.*"

And by the smoky expression in her eyes, word choice was important to her. "And did you like the sound of that?"

"You have no idea."

He grabbed at her skirt, not giving a damn if he ripped it. He'd buy her a replacement. He pushed the material up to her waist, revealing a pair of rose-colored lace panties.

"Hold your skirt," he ordered.

"Grif, I—"

"Do it."

She grasped the fabric, scrunching it in her hands while he went down on his knees in front of her. He could smell her—warm, wet, woman.

"And," she panted, "you might've used the word *rip.*"

"Seems like a waste to destroy something so pretty." He hooked his fingers into the sides and stroked the soft skin of her hips until she squirmed. He yanked the scrap of lace down to her ankles and off one foot. Before he could get his mouth on her, her skirt floated down and she sidestepped him. "What the hell?"

"Who said we're going to do this your way? You didn't give me a chance to tell you what I wanted to do to you when you walked in looking so handsome in that tux. I want to undress you. I want to run my hands all over your amazing body. And then I want to go down on my knees and—"

"Now." His brain exploded with the memory of her comment last time about putting her mouth on him, and he grabbed her hand and took off toward the bedroom. Damn, he wanted her out of that dress and in his bed. "I swear," he growled. "I'm getting more furniture soon if I have to have someone else pick it out."

"Something wrong with your bed?" She cast a glance at it.

"No, but I want to have plenty of options, and we've already determined the windowsill is dangerous." He reached for his shirt studs, but she batted his hands away.

"My turn." Her touch burned through the tux shirt, through his T-shirt, straight into his chest. Into his heart. Once she had the studs released, she went for his cuff links, making his head spin with her teasing strokes on his inner wrist.

She circled him, her dress making a swishing sound, reminding him she was bare underneath. Totally bare because there was no damn way she could be wearing a bra.

Maybe that windowsill would work in another way. He would brace her hands on it, bend her over, and push up her dress. Then he'd push into her from behind and drive into her while they pretended to watch the languid traffic on Main Street.

She slowly slid his shirt down his arms, her fingers trailing over his forearms until he was shaking from it. She tugged his T-shirt from his pants and scraped her short nails over his lower back, making Grif's hips surge forward in response. When she pushed the fabric up his back and pressed an openmouthed kiss to his spine, he reached out to brace himself against the wall.

She eased her hands around his sides as she dragged her tongue along his spine. When she reached his pecs, she pinched his nipples.

"Fuck me," he breathed.

"Oh, don't you worry." She laughed. "I plan to."

She toyed with him, pinching in the front and nipping in the back, until Grif couldn't tell which way was up. He reached for the hook on his slacks, and her hands immediately left his chest and stilled his. "No, sir. I'll get to that in a minute. Be patient."

God, in negotiations, he'd been known as the King of Patience. He could outwit, outwait, and outlast anyone at the negotiating table. Yeah, he was a fucking survivor.

Carlie Beth shoved at his T-shirt, pushing it up his torso. Grif lifted his arms, and she skimmed the fabric up, tickling his underarms. His breath chuffed in and out so hard he was about to hyperventilate. He couldn't stand it anymore, so he ripped the damn shirt over his head.

"Turn around," she murmured against his back.

He whipped around and she settled her mouth over his left pec and took his nipple between her teeth while her fingertips played with the other. She did that until his head was about to explode. Finally, she looked up at him, her eyes lazy and self-satisfied, and pushed him against wall. "You're going to want to brace yourself for this."

She unhooked his pants as if she'd done it a million times and released his zipper. The instant relief made him lightheaded. When she shoved his boxer briefs and pants over his hips, he said, "Thank you, Jesus."

To hell with what she wanted, he had to shuck these damn pants. He pushed them the rest of way down and stepped out of them. Then he reached for Carlie Beth's dress.

She huffed a little laugh. "What about 'my turn' are you having a hard time getting through your head? Now, get your back against that damn wall and let me put your dick in my mouth."

Well, that stole the breath from him like a mule kick to the midsection.

Carlie Beth rucked her skirt up almost—almost—high enough for him to get a glimpse of heaven, then she went to her knees in front of him.

My God, was there anything else in the world that made a man feel like this? Both powerful and vulnerable.

Carlie Beth trailed her tongue slowly from his balls to his tip, humming to herself as she went.

The caveman in Grif wanted to grab her hair, yank her head back, and push himself inside her warm mouth. The barely leashed civilized guy inside him dug his fingers into the drywall and waited.

Her tongue circled the head of his dick and he knocked his head against the wall. Once. Twice. Three times.

And then she took him in. Her mouth was hot and agile. The slide and suck made colors expand and recede behind his eyelids. She kept up that satisfied humming sound, sending vibrations though his dick into his belly, making it bunch and jump.

He stood like a freaking statue, just trying to keep control, until she released him and said, "You're being awfully polite."

His jaw was so tight he could barely grind out words, but he gritted, "It's called staying in control. Believe me, this is what you want."

"What would you do if you lost control?" Her tongue touched that place on her top lip, and Grif would swear he heard synapses popping in his brain like cheap guitar strings. The caveman took over.

He grabbed Carlie Beth by the arms and pushed her flat on the ground. His breath heaving, he positioned himself over her in the opposite direction, lining his cock up with that beautiful mouth. "This."

She moaned, opening her lips, and he pushed inside.

His mind full of nothing but animal impulses, he fucked her mouth with jerky thrusts, careful to hold his weight off her with his arms. And the sounds she made deep in her throat said she was enjoying every second of it.

Her legs came up and her knees released so that every pretty pink fold was on display. Wet. So fucking wet. He wanted…

When she took him deeper, his thoughts scattered and his balls tightened. Oh, God. If he didn't get control soon, this would all be over. He needed to be inside her. Now.

He pressed a kiss to her hipbone, then tried to pull away from her mouth, but she grabbed his ass and urged him deeper. "Shit, I'm gonna. I need to…"

She slipped her fingers between his butt cheeks and Grif lost every shred of control he'd held on to.

His orgasm slammed through his body with the force of a plane crash until he was completely drained and his biceps were shaking from the effort of keeping his body poised over her. "Fuuuuuuck."

Chapter Thirty

WELL, YEEHAW. CARLIE BETH COULD feel herself grinning from one ear to the other as Grif rolled to the floor on his back, his arms splaying out on either side of his body. His delicious chest was moving like he'd just run the fastest sprint in history.

"You're happy with yourself, aren't you?" he puffed out.

"So much I'd put those damn shoes back on and do a jitterbug."

"You're crazy."

She shifted to her side and stroked a hand down his thigh, the hair soft against her skin. Interestingly enough, his penis reacted.

Grif raised his head and looked down at it. "No matter what it says, it's gonna take me a minute to recover from that."

A feeling of power surged through her, making her smile go wider. "I can wait."

"As Toby Keith would say, 'I'm not as good as I once was, but I'm as good once as I ever was.'"

"You listen to Toby Keith?"

"Along with the Arctic Monkeys. I'm a man of varied musical tastes."

And a man of varied female tastes, but she tried not to think about that too closely.

Grif sat up and took her hand. "How about we move to the bed for the next round?"

"That would be a nice change of pace."

He drew her to her feet, his body hard yet safe against hers, as if she could lean her head against his shoulder and never worry again.

"But first, I'm damn well going to get that dress off you." He quickly unzipped her and unhooked the clasp at her neck.

She caught his hands. "Be careful."

"I won't tear the dress."

"No, I'm worried about my skin."

"Huh?"

"I'm…uh…kinda trapped. Evie had to use some special tape to keep my boobs in there."

His laugh echoed in the sparse room, and he caught her by the waist and fell back onto his mattress. "Are we talking painter's tape, Scotch tape, or duct tape?"

"Something very sticky."

"You glued your breasts into a dress for me. Carlie Beth, I love you."

They both stilled, their bodies stiff against one another. Carlie Beth's heart was slamming against one of her tape-trapped boobs. "I…uh…"

"Well, shit." Grif's voice was low and full of disgust.

"I know what you meant. It's just a turn of phrase. It's fine." No, it wasn't fine and she needed space. She tried to scramble away, but he wrapped her tight in his arms.

"Nothing about tonight has gone the way I planned for it to," he said. "I have a bottle of Armand de Brignac in the fridge. Candles." He slapped the mattress. "A set of Milos sheets."

She had no idea what Milos was, but she rubbed her hand over the linens. "They're nice."

"When I see you in that dress, I say something crude. And hell, once we got back here, I did several things that were crude."

Yeah, those crude things still had her wet and achy beneath her skirt. In fact, she was pretty damn proud of everything they'd done. Proved she wasn't just a blacksmith and mom.

She had serious seduction skills.

Grif slid out from underneath her and said, "Can you please work on getting that dress peeled off yourself while I grab something from the other room?"

"What? Why?"

"Because if I'm going to do this naked, then you're damn well going to be naked too." He stalked out of the room, and Carlie Beth admired the way his butt flexed with every step.

Still off balance from those three words he'd said and what they really meant, she sat at the edge of the mattress and slowly began to peel her bodice away from her breasts. Good Lord, Evie should've provided a bottle of Goo Gone.

Normally, Carlie Beth would've just done the rip-it-off-quick thing, but not happening this time. By the time Grif strode back in the room, his fist curled around something, she had one side unstuck and was working on the other.

"Oh, Shortcake," he said, crouching down in front of her. "That looks painful."

Her skin was pink where the tape had been, and he leaned in to kiss her breast. Light, barely there touches of his lips not quite at her nipple. It tightened in response, and she worked the other side down. Grif moved over and gave her other breast the same gentle treatment. "Doesn't matter how fucking hot that dress is, I don't want you taping yourself into clothes for me."

She laughed. Oh, if it inspired the kind of response he'd displayed earlier, she'd hog-tie herself into sexy clothes once a week. "It doesn't hurt."

He worked her dress off her hips and tossed it aside. Yes, Carlie Beth would definitely be handing Evie a check because her dress would never be the same again.

Besides, she'd die if Evie ever wore it now, after Grif had his hands all over it. Under it.

Grif swept her body with a quick look that set her nerves buzzing, but his attention quickly returned to her face. He shifted onto one knee like kids did around the coach after a Little League game.

Then he held out a box.

A black box.

A black velvet box.

"Carlie Beth Parrish, will you marry me?" He opened it to reveal a ring that had to have been custom made. A wide, silver-colored band with a trio of channel-set diamonds.

A slightly hysterical laugh tumbled out of her. Of all the things she'd been expecting, this wasn't one of them. The power she'd felt earlier drained from her, replaced with a confusing stew of uncertainty and fear and hope. "Why?"

"Why should you marry me? There are a hundred reasons—"

"No, why are you asking me? I know Austin's death has us all on edge, but Maggie will get to the bottom of that. If you're worried about Aubrey and me, I've told you time and time again that we're fine. If it's because—"

He pressed his fingers against her lips. Not in a sexy way, but in a shut-up way. "I can't say those things don't matter, because they do. But I'm asking you to marry me because what I said earlier wasn't some off-the-cuff turn of phrase. I meant all three words. I love you."

And oh, how she loved him. But if she'd known all this would happen when she'd spotted Grif in Triple B a few weeks ago, what would she have done? Would she have dashed headlong toward him or run like she'd wanted to?

"Have you forgotten your work is in California?"

His eyes shuttered a little. "I tell you I love you and you're talking logistics?"

"Logistics are important."

"What about 'love conquers all'?"

"How did that work out for your parents?"

He visibly flinched, and she immediately regretted her words. She was lashing out because she was scared. Probably more scared than she'd been when she found out she was pregnant with Grif's baby. Because that, she'd known she could handle on her own. Had, in some ways, wanted to. This? When it involved two people, she no longer called all the shots.

"I think you care for me." His was face immobile in the shadows. "I don't think you sleep with men you don't care about."

"So says the man who knocked me up."

"Why are you doing this?"

As much as she wanted to jump out of this bed and run like hell, she couldn't. She owed him better. After all, he'd given her the most precious thing in her life.

Now she had to tell him how she felt. For better or worse.

She leaned into him and rested her head on his shoulder. "Because I am scared all the way down to my toes."

"How many times do I have to tell you that I'll take care of you and Aubrey? The whole point is you don't have to do this by yourself anymore."

His skin was warm against her face, and she couldn't help but press a little kiss to his collarbone. "That's not what I'm afraid of. I can do it. I have done it. Grif, we don't need your money, but we need *you*."

"You have me. I'm moving back to Steele Ridge."

Oh, God how she longed to believe that was what he truly wanted. But if he made this sacrifice, then decided he'd been wrong and walked away, she'd wasn't sure she'd survive it. She lifted her face and looked at him straight on. "I'm scared that you only think you love me because of the circumstances. Learning about Aubrey and someone targeting people I care about has brought out all your protective instincts."

His mouth tightened, triggering a matching response inside her. "I can't sign an affidavit or a contract, Carlie Beth. All I can give you is my word. Yes, I'm worried about finding the person who killed Austin. I can't even express how much I appreciate that you're the mother of my daughter, but that's not why I fell in love with you." He intertwined his fingers with hers as if he would hold her hand forever. "You're beautiful, in a sexy dress or jeans. You're talented, with fences and artwork. You're smart, with business and people. You're strong, in life and"—he drew their hands up to her chest—"in here. I'd be crazy *not* to be in love with you."

His expression was so serious, so sincere and heartfelt, that the tension inside her began to fade, bit by bit. God, being loved by this man would be…intense, sometimes overwhelming, and downright amazing. Her heart was reaching out for him, but her brain was still gun-shy. "Do you really think we can make this work?"

"I don't know," he said, shocking her again. Lord, this was one seesaw of a conversation. "Because I'm greedy. I want it all. And I'm not willing to marry a woman who doesn't love me back."

"What?"

"I put myself out there." He glanced down at the ring box and snapped it closed, and Carlie Beth gasped. *No. No, no, no.* She wanted that ring. "And you said nothing."

"I didn't say no."

"But you didn't say I love you."

"Yes, I did."

One side of his mouth quirked up. "Are we really going to have this yes-I-did, no-you-didn't conversation while I'm down on one knee ass naked?"

Okay, so maybe her thoughts hadn't actually made it out of her mouth, and his leg was probably numb by now. She grabbed his hand and tugged. "Come up here, please." Relief rushed through when he did it without setting that precious ring box aside. Once they were lying on their sides facing one another, she took a deep breath. "I think I fell a little bit in love with you the night we were together all those years ago. You were so charming, so optimistic."

"So cocky, you mean."

"Maybe a little. But it looked good on you. Still does." She smoothed a hand over his cheek and made sure their eyes met. "When I learned you were back in town for more than a visit, I panicked. Still, I wanted you. But I fell in love with you for reasons that have nothing to do with this." She waved a hand down their bodies, and Grif's eyebrows rose. "Okay, maybe a little to do with this. Really, it's about the man you are. Passionate, funny, dedicated. And a snazzy dresser." She flashed him a smile. "Most important, you accepted Aubrey. Maybe that shouldn't factor in, but to a mom, it does. I can't love a man who doesn't love my daughter."

He turned his head to kiss her palm. "You never have to worry about that."

"Grif Steele, I am so in love with you, I'm infected right down to the bone."

He laughed and pulled her closer. "Only you could make that sound like a good thing."

When he came in for a kiss, though, she avoided his lips and looked at the box resting between them. "Aren't you forgetting something?"

"Mercenary little thing, aren't you?" Grif flipped open the box, and the ring once again caught her breath. Most women would ooh and ah over a delicate setting with a big diamond. But Carlie Beth wasn't most women. The three diamonds shimmered in the shadows of the room. Because of the way they were set in the metal, she wouldn't have to worry about knocking them loose. "It's titanium."

"It's perfect."

"Do you know how hard it is to pick out a ring for a woman who can make her own jewelry?"

"I don't work with precious metals."

"Then let's put this where it belongs." He slipped the

ring from the box and slid it on her finger. And it fit perfectly. Only Grif would get something like that just right.

She pushed her hands into his hair and lined up their mouths, feeling the ridge of his erection growing between them. "Now that we have that settled, what do you say we put something else where it belongs?"

"I think I can manage that." And with one slick move, he rolled her over, wedged between her legs, and slid home.

CHAPTER THIRTY-ONE

WRONG. THEY'D ALL BEEN THE wrong ones. That schmuck Carlie Beth dated back when Aubrey was younger, John Something-or-Other. Roy Darden. Austin Burns.

Possibly even that asshole Grif Steele.

Because the strongest love in the world was the one between mother and child.

Why had that truth been unclear for so long?

No longer.

Never again.

The balcony on the back of the house offered up a small challenge, but the French doors leading into an upstairs bedroom were unlocked. Sloppy of the Steeles. But perfect.

It was a sign. This was right. The right move.

The right time.

There was just enough moonlight to navigate the room. Only one girl—Evie with her long dark hair spread over the pale duvet—occupied the bed. Which meant Aubrey was somewhere else. Not ideal, but a little inconvenience wouldn't stop what Carlie Beth had started.

Out in the hallway, a quick pause revealed no threats. No sounds or movement.

Luckily, Aubrey was in another bedroom at the back

of the house, one that also had French doors and a balcony. Another sign.

When the girl woke, she was groggy. "Wha... Mom?"

"Aubrey, your mom's been in an accident. I need you to come with me."

She seemed to shake off a little of her confusion and jumped out of bed. "I have to tell Evie and Grammy and Uncle Reid."

"Kiddo, they're already gone."

"They... they wouldn't leave without me."

"They aren't used to you being here. Raced out before they remembered. But they called me and asked me to come get you." Step one, quietly open the French doors. Done. Step two, get the girl on the balcony.

"Why are we going this way?" Aubrey glanced around, confused and still half-asleep. But not dazed enough. "I need to get dressed."

"Aubrey, your mother could die. Now, stop asking questions and come with me!"

Fear flashed in Aubrey's eyes and she grabbed the phone off the bedside table. "Please take me to her."

A firm grip on her elbow and she dutifully went outside. "Give me your hands and I'll help you climb down."

"I still don't understand—"

"Do you want your mother to die?"

The girl let herself be lowered over the side, and once they were both on the ground, she looked around. "Where's your car?"

She simply wouldn't go without causing problems, would she? Shouldn't have been a surprise. The brat had always been trouble. Way more trouble than she was worth. If Carlie Beth hadn't gotten herself knocked up—

"This is scaring me," the little bitch whined. "How are we—"

One well-aimed blow to the temple cut her off mid-sentence. Thank Jesus. Kids were nothing but a distraction.

It was a pain in the ass to drag her a half mile

through the woods, but every ache and pain would be worth it once Carlie Beth's daughter was out of the picture.

And out of her mother's heart.

The tiny whirling stars at the edges of Carlie Beth's vision refused to be blinked away after Grif had put his mouth, hands, and fingers all over her. In her. She shivered, half from her cooling skin and half from the recent erotic experience.

"You okay?"

"You're very...thorough."

"I don't like to leave anything to chance." He played with her hand, rubbing his thumb over the ring he'd given her. "Especially when it comes to giving you pleasure."

"You ever go to Vegas?"

His forehead crinkled. "A few times. Why?"

"You win every time, don't you?"

He laughed. "Bet it all on black, baby. Bet it all on black." His laughter died away, and he said, "What I said earlier about logistics? I know it's an issue. But I would never take you and Aubrey away from your home."

"What if you lose clients?"

His arm moved against hers with his shrug. "I'm cutting down my client list significantly anyway. I'll only work with the athletes I really believe in. I want plenty of time for my family. And this city manager gig is starting to grow on me."

"Are you serious?"

He laughed and gave her a smacking kiss above her left breast. "If anyone can run multimillion-dollar careers and a town, it's me."

"You don't have to do this for Aubrey and me."

"I'm doing it for all of us. But I've been wondering

something. What about..." He paused and shook his head, obviously trying to decide if he should continue his question.

"What about what?"

"How do you think Aubrey would feel about little brothers and sisters?"

The air whooshed from Carlie Beth's lungs even as something low in her belly tightened. She'd thought that train had left the station. "Don't you care what I think?"

His grin slashed across his handsome face. "Of course. But I figured if the idea wouldn't fly with Aubrey, then it would be off the table."

She rolled the idea around in her brain. Lord, she hadn't had a baby in fourteen years. Could she do it all over again? Was she too old?

No, that was ridiculous. Some women were just having their first babies at her age.

Babies.

"You said brothers and sisters. Like multiples."

"I come from a big family."

"Your mother is a saint."

"True."

"This has been a lot tonight. The ring, the proposal, the I-love-yous. Can we table this one for a little while?"

Although his expression didn't change, she could see the disappointment cloud his eyes.

"I'm not saying no," she hurried to add. "I just need to mull it over a little to figure out how many babies I can give you and still stay sane. I love my work."

"And you're damned good at it," he said, the smile back in his eyes. "But think about it this way. I missed all those late nights and diaper changes with Aubrey. Don't you think it should be my turn?"

Well, when he put it that way...

The sound of Grif's cell ringing came from across the room, and Carlie Beth started to get up to grab it.

"Leave it," he said.

"What if it's a client?"

"They can wait." He tried to roll her under him, but she scooted away and grabbed his pants to root around for the phone. "A long, long time."

One look at the screen and her body went cold. "It's Reid."

Grif lunged off the bed and grabbed the phone from her limp hand. "What happened?" he barked.

Carlie Beth heard Reid say, "Aubrey's missing."

Grif couldn't have given a shit less that he was probably ripping out Louise's entire undercarriage on the backroads out to his mom's place. As long as the car made it for long enough for him to find Aubrey and beat the ever-lovin' fuck out of the guy who'd taken her, it was fine. Even though he was driving like a bat directly out of hell, it still took them seven minutes and Carlie Beth spent every one of them curled into herself like an armadillo trying to avoid being roadkill.

He snagged her hand, her fingers like individual icicles against his. "We're going to find her."

"How could this happen? You and Reid assured me. Promised me she'd be safe." Her voice rose in both volume and pitch with each word.

"Reid's got security combing the area around the house. Something will lead us in the right direction."

She turned away from him and looked out into the night, but he could see her pale face reflected in the window. He'd let her down. After just telling her he'd always take care of her and Aubrey.

Obviously, that had been a crock of shit.

When they pulled up and came to a neck-snapping stop, his mom's house was lit up like someone had taken a torch to it. Reid was standing on the front porch barking into his phone while three of his security guys patrolled around the house.

Carlie Beth slammed out of the car and raced up the stairs to beat at Reid's chest.

Reid said, "Keep me posted" into his phone, then just stood there and let Carlie Beth whale away on him.

Grif caught his eye over Carlie Beth's head, and Reid shook his with the message: *Let her do it.*

Finally, she wound down and rested her head against Reid's chest, and her sobs wrenched Grif's heart. "How could you let this happen?"

Grif pulled her off Reid and into his arms.

"Did you fall asleep?" Grif asked his brother.

"No. I was downstairs, making another round of the house. When I went back upstairs to check on the girls, Aubrey wasn't in her bed and the balcony doors were open."

Carlie Beth looked up, her face streaked with the mascara she'd worn earlier. "I made sure they were locked before I left. Double-checked the deadbolt."

"Yeah, well, Evie's doors weren't. That's how the dickhead got in. I told her to lock that goddamn door." He smothered a sigh. "It's my fault. I should've gone in there and made sure she'd secured it before I did my walk-through downstairs. Someone snuck in before I got back upstairs."

"Where are Evie and Mom?"

"Inside. Evie's blaming herself."

Grif held Carlie Beth by the arms so he could look into her face. "I need you to go inside. Reid and I will—"

"You are out of your fucking mind if you think I'm going to sit around and wait while someone has my baby."

Her use of the F-word hit Grif like a slap across the face. But he understood, so he nodded once, then asked his brother, "What else do we know?"

"Looks like the guy used a four-wheeler to come in on one of the hiking trails. Maybe he left it in the woods so we wouldn't hear it and then hoofed it the rest of the way to the house. I'd need a battalion of guys to patrol all this acreage."

Damn Jonah for having to piss a long stream of money at the city. Who needed twenty thousand acres?

"Can we follow the trail in your truck?"

"Already did. The tracks end at the county road. Whoever it was might've had a truck stashed and driven the ATV up onto a trailer, but it's doubtful because there were no other tire tracks on the side of the road."

"Which means he took Aubrey somewhere on the ATV?" Carlie Beth said. "Oh my God, she could be anywhere out in the woods. He could be holed up in some—"

"Don't jump to conclusions and panic," Grif said, shooting Reid a gimme-something-we-can-work-with look.

Reid took a deep breath. "I think it was someone Aubrey knew, because there was no sign of a struggle in her bedroom."

Carlie Beth looked Reid up and down. "A man your size could've just picked her up and thrown her over his shoulder."

"Yeah, but a human body is awkward to carry, especially if—"

"If what? If she was dead weight? If she was de—"

"It all leads back to you." Grif held her by the arms, trying to pull her out of the spiral of crazy they could both get caught up in if they didn't keep their heads on straight. "What are we missing here? Who are we missing?"

"We went over all this before. If I've offended someone so badly that they're killing people I care about, it's slipped my mind."

"Wait a minute," Grif said. "People you care about. What about Roy Darden? He wasn't exactly a loved one."

"I went out with him one time."

"Jesus," he breathed. "What if up to this point, this whole thing hasn't been about people you care about, but people who care about you?"

"I don't understand."

"Remember that guy you mentioned who disappeared on you?"

"John? So?"

"So what if he didn't just take off?"

Reid rubbed his hand across his hair, messing it up even more. "You think whoever grabbed Aubrey has been systematically getting rid of people who love Carlie Beth?"

"It fits."

"How does this help us figure out who has Aubrey?" Carlie Beth's voice was full of the panic and misery Grif felt deep in his gut. Apparently her knees finally gave out because she slumped to the wood porch. "Oh my God, Maggie. Why haven't we called the sheriff?"

"I did that before I ever called Grif," Reid told her. "She's got her people out all over the place."

What was Grif missing? There had to be a piece of information he'd overlooked. The oil. "I never got a call back from the last store around here that sells quenching oil." He pulled out his phone and hit redial for the supplier he hadn't been able to get a hold of yesterday. A long shot, but having the phone in his hands kept them from shaking so damn much.

After four rings, the call connected. "D'ya know what time it is?"

"Is this Bill Smithfield?"

The man grunted what Grif assumed was a yes.

"I'm Grif Steele from Steele Ridge. I called yesterday asking about anyone who'd recently bought quenching oil from you. Did you get that message?"

"Yeah." The old guy snorted, coughed, and spit something on the other end of the line. "Went through my records, but then the wife cooked ham and collard greens for dinner and—"

"Sir," Grif tried to keep his voice steady, but he was so close to losing his shit. "I need to know *now*. This is a matter of life and death." He glanced down at Carlie Beth to see what little color she'd still had in her face completely disappear. "Did you sell quenching oil to anyone recently?"

"Yeah, about three gallons to some gal who owns the gallery there in town."

CHAPTER THIRTY-TWO

"LET'S GO." GRIF BARKED AND grabbed Carlie Beth's hand to yank her off the ground. "In Reid's truck. Now."

"What did he say?" She kept pace with him as he ran toward the driveway with Reid right behind.

"I think she has her at the forge."

"She?"

He shoved her up into the truck and was only halfway in the cab himself when Reid fired it up and tore down the driveway. Grif asked Carlie Beth, "Have you ever had any strange interactions with Yvonne Winters?"

"You think Yvonne took Aubrey? Killed Austin?"

He nodded at Reid, who grabbed his phone and quickly gave Maggie the update.

"Yeah, I think she was listening while you and I were talking with Maggie about Darden's death. That's when she got the idea to grease up the climbing grips, and Smithfield just confirmed she bought several gallons of quenching oil not long ago."

"She's talked on and off about trying her hand at blacksmithing. Maybe she was just..." She must've caught something in his expression because she trailed off. "She...she warned me about you when you first found out about Aubrey."

"Warned you how?"

"She's the one who told me about Madison Henry."

"Anything else?" Reid asked as he navigated down the narrow backroad toward the edge of town where Carlie Beth's house was.

"Just a little speculation about Austin's crush on me at dinner the other night." She paused and looked at Grif, her expression full of apology. "And she mentioned that you might try to lure Aubrey away from me, promising her nicer things."

Hell. "And this was right before I came storming up, slinging accusations at you."

"Yeah."

Carlie Beth shook her head as though trying to dislodge a thought. "This is probably nothing…"

"No such thing as nothing," Reid said. "Spit it out."

"When I was trying on Evie's dress, Evie and Aubrey went downstairs for cookies, so Yvonne helped me get out of the dress."

"And?"

"Nothing exactly. Just a feeling. I was uncomfortable being in my underwear in front of her."

"Has she ever touched you?"

"Girlfriends give each other hugs all the time."

"You know what I mean."

"Just a strange little brush on my back. And she had trouble with the zipper, but Evie and you didn't."

God, how he wished they could go back to earlier tonight. Although it hadn't gone down like Grif had planned, even their argument was so much better than this gut-twisting fear.

Reid pulled the truck to the side of the street about ten houses down from Carlie Beth's. "We'll walk the rest of the way."

"No," Grif said. "We run." When they approached Carlie Beth's house, he caught sight of light coming from the forge's window. "They're in there. I know it."

Carlie Beth darted forward, but Grif and Reid each caught her by an arm. "No. We scope it out first."

"I have to—"

Grif stopped and cupped her face in his hands. "Please listen and be logical. I know you're frightened. I'm so fucking scared I can't see straight. But letting your emotions put you and Aubrey in even more danger isn't the way for us to handle this. Do you hear me?"

She nodded, but tears gathered at the corner of her eyes. Grif pulled her in for a hard hug and whispered, "I will not lose you and I will not lose Aubrey. Nobody is taking either of you away from me."

The Taylor Swift song Grif had heard the day at the gallery came from Carlie Beth's pocket, and she clawed it out. "Aubrey, baby, are you okay?"

He pointed at the phone and mouthed *speaker*. Carlie Beth immediately hit the button and held the phone out in her palm.

"Mom?" Aubrey's shaky voice, tiny like a little girl's, made Grif feel as if an icepick was being slipped between his ribs and up into his heart.

"I'm here. Are you okay? Has she hurt you?"

Apparently Yvonne had the same speaker phone idea they did, because she said, "What do you mean you're here?"

Carlie Beth's eyes went wild and her gaze darted from Grif to Reid and back to Grif. "I…ah…I'm here at the house. I thought—"

"You thought what?" Yvonne's tone was sharp and brittle, like cheap crystal shattering on a tile floor. "Tell me, Carlie Beth, how much does your daughter's life mean to you?"

"Everything. You know that."

"Then prove it."

"How?"

"If you come into the forge, I'll let Aubrey go." The line went dead and it took every shred of control Grif had not to lean over and heave on his shoes.

With a hand as unyielding as his last name, Grif gripped Carlie Beth's wrist. "Wait for Maggie and her people. You can't do this. It could be a trick."

As if she were in the eye of a hurricane, Carlie Beth was finally calm inside. She *would* get her daughter the hell out of there. No matter the cost.

God, she, Grif, and Aubrey had been so close. So close to being a real family.

She rose on her toes and kissed Grif hard. Hard enough that she could feel his teeth behind his lips. When she dropped back to her feet, she said, "I have to do this. If she'd asked for you, you'd make the same choice." He couldn't deny it. She could see the truth in his eyes.

Carlie Beth touched Grif's face, capturing his attention once again. "I want you to know how much I love you, but our daughter needs me. If…if I don't—"

"Do not even fucking say those words."

"I want you to know I asked for an amendment to Aubrey's birth certificate for paternity determination, just in ca—"

He gripped her around the waist and gave her a kiss that matched the fierceness of hers, cutting off words she knew he didn't want to hear. If sheer will could solve problems, they'd come out on top every time. "I love you."

She let her hand trail slowly off his face and hurried around the house to the backyard. With a steady finger, she dialed Aubrey's number.

Yvonne answered with a "Yeah?"

"I'm ready. Will you please send Aubrey outside?"

The laugh from the other end sent chills over Carlie Beth's arms, and they settled in a cold knot in her stomach. "I'm not stupid. You come in and she gets to leave."

"Do you promise?"

"What, are we in fourth grade? Do you want me to pinkie swear? Just come to the fucking door." Again, Yvonne disconnected.

From her side vision, Carlie Beth caught sight of movement on her right. Holding handguns they must've gotten from somewhere in Reid's truck, Grif and his brother had been joined by a group of deputies. Maggie was waving Carlie Beth back, but the stoic expression on Grif's face gave Carlie Beth the last bit of strength she needed.

She jogged up the path toward her forge and knocked on the door. "Yvonne, let me in." It swung open just enough for Carlie Beth to squeeze her way inside. She immediately reached for Aubrey and shoved her behind her. "Go."

"Mom, I can't—"

"Do it right this second, Aubrey Steele."

"Mom, come with—"

"Go and I'll be right behind—"

"You're not going anywhere until we have a little chat." Her eyes red and her short hair standing every which way as if she'd pulled on it, Yvonne let Aubrey slip out, but blocked the door before Carlie Beth could follow.

Carlie Beth faked a sidestep, hoping to lure Yvonne away from the door, but she wasn't having any of it. Instead, she pushed Carlie Beth's shoulders, making her stumble back.

"So you went and married him," Yvonne said, staring down at Carlie Beth's left hand.

"No."

"But you will."

"Yvonne, you got what you wanted. I'm here talking to you, but you really don't want to keep me from leaving—"

"I got what I wanted?" Yvonne's laugh was edged with mania. "I've never gotten what I wanted." She took a step, but Carlie Beth matched her with a backward shuffle.

One, two, three. Carlie Beth kept moving. She knew every inch of her forge and would dance this twisted tango all night if that's what it took. If she kept Yvonne talking long enough, surely Grif and Maggie would come to her rescue. "What do you mean? You're a successful business owner. You have respect and people here love you."

"Do you have any idea how long I've loved *you*?"

How could she have known when she hadn't even realized her friend—former friend—was gay? "I—"

"Been in love with you? Do you know how long I've waited for you to look at me the way you look at that slick bastard you're fucking?"

Assuming the best answer was no answer, Carlie Beth bit her lip and edged her way around the coal forge. If she could circle back to the door without Yvonne realizing she was luring her in that direction, everything would be okay.

"Do you know what it feels like to do without the one person in the world who's your other half? Who would complete you?"

She hadn't realized until recently, but she'd been living that way for the past fifteen years. Telling Yvonne that sure wouldn't help this situation, so she held out a raised hand to keep her at bay. "I'm sorry I didn't recognize your feelings."

"What kind of friend are you?"

Apparently a blind one. Or maybe just a trusting one. "We could still be friends."

"Friends? You want to be friends? Where the hell has that gotten me for years?" Yvonne screeched. From the worktable, she snatched up a pair of scrolling jaw tongs, the ones that had gone missing recently. *Oh, God.* The ones with jaws that matched the wound on Austin's temple. With short, sharp movements, Yvonne thrust them toward Carlie Beth's face to make her point.

With every jab, Carlie Beth scooted back a little.

Aubrey's phone rang in Yvonne's hand, and with wild eyes, she tossed it on the anvil and attacked it with the tongs—*wham, wham, wham*. Bits of plastic and electronic guts jumped like crickets and rained down on the floor. Lip curled and teeth bared, she glared down at the only piece left—half of the back cover. "I don't want them to call me again!"

Carlie Beth's heart was like a trapped animal in her chest. *Stay calm and keep her talking. That's the only way you'll get out of this.* "Then what do you want?"

"What I've always wanted," she cried, advancing again, the tongs waving wildly in her grip. "I want you to love me."

"Carlie Beth!" Grif's panicked yell came from just outside the door. "Are you okay?"

"Dammit, Grif, get away from there." Maggie's voice was commanding, but Carlie Beth thought she heard a thread of fear in it as well.

She tried to get words past her tight throat, but the first two were silent wheezes. Finally, she was able to respond. "Everything's fine. Just—"

"Shut up, you stupid bitch!" Yvonne lunged forward.

Carlie Beth was hemmed in by two metal worktables, and couldn't dodge the blow to her shoulder. Holy God, the pain exploded through her. It was then she realized Yvonne was subscribing to the if-I-can't-have-you philosophy of relationships.

How could this be happening? How had she missed that Yvonne was a crazed lunatic?

Maybe the same way Grif had missed that Madison Henry was an abuse-seeking psycho. Because they both believed people were who they said they were. Because that's what growing up in a small town taught you.

But living in this small town had also taught Carlie Beth to fight to make her own life because no one was going to simply hand it to you. And sometimes it wasn't as pretty as people liked to believe small-town life should be.

Regardless, it was her life, she loved it, and she damn well wanted it.

Which meant she couldn't wait for someone else to take care of this situation. If she could just make her way over to—

Thud. The tongs connected with her thigh, washing her with a vicious, nauseating pain. She breathed through it in shallow gasps.

Yvonne rested the tongs on her shoulder. "That's how you make me feel every time I see you with that man."

Say something back. Maybe if you keep her talking, she'll let up on the whacking.

"What...what if I could learn to love you?" She shuffled left a couple of steps, her leg protesting.

Yvonne's eyes narrowed as she seemed to consider Carlie Beth's words. "Learn to love? Bullshit. Two people are either meant to be together or not. And I love you, have always loved you, enough for both of us."

"That's..." She couldn't say *nice.* "I didn't realize. I'm sorry."

"You're sorry?" Little flecks of spit were gathering at the corners of Yvonne's mouth and her eyes looked like one of Dave's spooked cows—wide, white, and rolling from side to side. "Sometimes *sorry* just doesn't cut it. Tell me, do you think your rich lover will take your daughter to Los Angeles after you're dead? She'll probably get out there and whore around with a bunch of men just like you've done."

A bunch of men? The only thing that kept Carlie Beth from laughing in Yvonne's face was the shit-fire crazy in her eyes. Two more steps. Just. Two. More. Then she could reach...

One. Two. She angled her body toward Yvonne, so she could reach for the rounding hammer behind her. "I know Aubrey is in good hands with her father. With the whole Steele family," she said, pushing confidence into every word. Yeah, she was antagonizing Yvonne, but they were playing to win now.

Yvonne made a sudden move, and expecting another blow with the tongs, Carlie Beth jumped to her right, only to have Yvonne's fist connect with her temple from the left. *Pop*. Things flashed in Carlie Beth's head that shouldn't have. But still she wrapped her hand around the hammer on her worktable.

She opened her mouth and let out a loud, long yell like the self-defense instructor had taught in class. Yvonne's eye flew wide at the sound and she stood still, giving Carlie Beth an opening. She brought the hammer around with every ounce of strength she had in her body only to have Yvonne dodge and avoid most of the blow.

"You bitch, you don't love me! You can't love me and hurt me at the same time."

God, the irony.

From outside, Maggie yelled, "Grif Steele, don't you dare—"

The forge's door slammed open with such force that it bounced off the metal wall, diverting Carlie Beth's attention for a second. Just enough time for Yvonne to lurch forward, arcing the heavy tongs down toward Carlie Beth's head, leaving her left side unprotected. As Yvonne bent her knees, Carlie Beth brought the hammer up and around, catching *her* temple this time.

The sound of the steel hammer head connecting with flesh was like a melon dropping to the floor—thick and dull.

The tongs fell from Yvonne's grip and she lurched sideways, hitting the worktable with her shoulder, then thudding to the floor.

Hammer still firmly in her grip, Carlie Beth backed away, but kept watch on Yvonne even as Grif leaned over and felt for a pulse. "Maggie," he yelled, "Yvonne's down!"

Carlie Beth's stomach contracted, spasming with the

need to vomit and forcing tears from her eyes. Her leg throbbing, she stumbled toward Grif without turning her back on Yvonne. Because she would never get caught off guard again.

Never.

She made it to Grif and collapsed into his arms just before those stars detonated in her head again.

CHAPTER THIRTY-THREE

JESUS WILLIAM CHRIST. AFTER GRIF had scooped up Carlie Beth and rushed her to the hospital, he hadn't closed his eyes for the rest of the night. He just sat in that uncomfortable-as-hell chair and stared at her, half-afraid the doctor had made a mistake, saying she was sleeping, but that she was actually in a coma.

At one point, Aubrey had pulled her chair closer, given him a comforting hug, and said, "She's tough. Don't worry."

At about three in the morning, he'd finally talked Aubrey into letting Reid take her back to Tupelo Hill, hoping Carlie Beth would be awake by the time Aubrey returned to the hospital. But it was now ten and Carlie Beth still hadn't opened her eyes. God, what did he have to do to get a miracle around here?

The door to Carlie Beth's room eased inward—proving without a doubt that the person entering wasn't a medical professional—and Maggie walked in. "Hey," she whispered. "Has she woken up yet?"

Barely sparing his cousin a glance, he shook his head. How could he have let Carlie Beth go in there last night? That crazy bitch Yvonne had almost killed her.

He took a small bit of satisfaction in knowing that the woman was in this very hospital on another floor, handcuffed to the bed and in a true coma. A very small and mean part of him wished she had died on that damn floor last night.

The door opened again and in came the first wave of his family, with Aubrey leading the pack. Evie held a small travel bag, and his mom was hugging a tub of cookies that would've provided snacks for every daycare in North Carolina for a year. Aubrey's forehead was creased in worry, and Grif held out his hand to her. She rushed to him, filling him with such a painful joy his throat went tight, and he pulled her down in his lap.

The only thing better than her head on his shoulder would be when her mom opened those beautiful brown eyes.

"Grif, we need to talk," Maggie whispered. "We searched Yvonne's house and the gallery."

"Don't tell me you need some other kind of proof to hold her. She beat the shi...crap...crud out of Carly Beth."

"*Crap* is fine, Dad," Aubrey told him.

"Oh, no," Maggie said. "Ms. Winters won't be going anywhere but prison for the rest of her life. Come out into the hall."

"If you have something to say, do it in here." At Carlie Beth's gritty words, Grif shot out of the chair, almost dumping Aubrey on the floor in the process.

"Mom!"

"Hey, baby."

Aubrey leaned over to hug Carlie Beth, but stopped herself. "I don't think I should touch you."

Carlie Beth blindly reached for her hand. "I don't hurt here. How about this?"

Maggie said, "I'll just wait outside for you, Grif."

"There's something you don't want somebody to hear, and I'm betting it's me," Carlie Beth said. Her voice sounded as if someone had scratched sandpaper over her vocal cords, so Grif reached for the water pitcher.

"Shortcake, can you take a sip?"

Her eyes finally cracked open. "Bedside service?"

"You scared the crap out of me."

"Why? You told me you'd never let anything happen to Aubrey or me."

"I let you walk in there with that psycho stalker."

Carlie Beth's small smile was aimed at his mom. "Oh, he thinks he can let me do things. Is this a bad sign?"

"Love is a tightrope, sweetheart. Remember that."

Carlie Beth's focus shifted to Maggie. "Tell us. We're all family."

The word *family* cruised through Grif like a fine port—warm and intoxicating. He hadn't fucked everything up last night—the botched proposal, letting Carlie Beth and Aubrey down, almost losing them both.

They were a family, wedding or not. And no one was ever going to take these two away from him.

"We went through Yvonne's things," Maggie said. "We found a crowbar with flakes of blue paint on it that we suspect she used to vandalize Grif's car."

"That's all?" he asked. "What about the quenching oil?"

"Oh, we found that and plenty more. Carlie Beth, how long would you say she'd been carrying the pieces you make?"

With a small wince, Carlie Beth said, "Around three years, I think."

"And how many items would you estimate you've placed with her in that time?"

"I don't know offhand. I'd have to look back over my inventory records. Maybe a couple hundred. Some small things like wall hooks. A few more elaborate pieces like a special order chandelier for one of her customers."

The look Maggie aimed Grif's way told him he wasn't going to like her next words a damn bit. "That's about the number we found stockpiled in her house. All signed with CEP and marked with a bird in flight symbol—a hawk, maybe?"

"What? Are you saying—"

"That she didn't sell a single one of your items as far as we can tell."

"But…but she said Ian Brinkmann bought something, and that iron chandelier I was commissioned for supposedly sold for over a thousand dollars. Good Lord, that witch paid for Aubrey's braces."

"Unfortunately, we have to take everything in as evidence right now."

"And I thought I was starting to do well." Carlie Beth's laugh was hollow and Grif carefully brushed her hair back. He wanted to kiss away her pain, but a room full of people and a big goose egg on her temple didn't exactly encourage intimacy.

Maggie gave Carlie Beth a nod. "Again, real sorry about that. But, girl, you have some nerves of steel. Let me know if you ever decide to give up blacksmithing for law enforcement."

"Oh, hell no," Grif said.

Maggie waved on her way out, and Carlie Beth's smile was real now. "I don't know if you know this about me, but I'm kind of a badass."

"You're a bruised badass."

Evie stepped close to Carlie Beth's bed. "I am so sorry. This was all my fault. I'll understand if you never want Aubrey around me again."

Carlie Beth did a little eye roll that said she'd heard this kind of drama before and Grif held in a grin. She told his sister, "It wasn't your fault. It's a crazy woman's fault. Plain and simple."

"Reid's at home right now, probably ripping out those doors and framing in the whole thing. If I know him, he'll take my windows away, too."

His mom skimmed a hand over Carlie Beth's feet, covered by the sheet. "Sweetheart, we're just going to leave these things and let you have some time with your family."

Carlie Beth held out her arms to his mom. "I hope you're all my family now."

"Good," his mom said, giving the love of his life a gentle hug. "Then get yourself out of this hospital as soon as possible."

"I will."

Once his mom and Evie left, Carlie Beth closed her eyes. "I can't believe I knocked her out."

"Knocked her out? She hasn't regained consciousness since they hauled her in here last night."

"I'm not sure that makes me feel better."

Aubrey bent closer to the bed, near Carlie Beth's left hand. "Mom, what's this?"

Grif couldn't hold back a smile. When they'd brought her in last night, the nurse had tried to take the ring off her finger, but Carlie Beth had curled her hand into a fist and mumbled something that sounded like *Not in this lifetime.*

"It's an engagement ring." Her forehead wrinkled. "At least I think it is."

"Oh yeah," he told her. "I'm adding a wedding band to that. The jeweler told me he could solder the two together if we want. And I definitely want."

"You're getting married? The two of you?"

"That's the plan." He took his daughter's hand and they stood on either side of Carlie Beth, making a circle of three. He kissed the back of Aubrey's hand, then smoothed his lips against Carlie Beth's.

And soaked in the sweet taste of home.

Enjoy an excerpt from Adrienne Giordano's
Living FAST, the next book in the Steele Ridge series:

BY ADRIENNE GIORDANO

SOMETHING DREW RANDI'S GAZE AND Brynne glanced over her shoulder to find Reid Steele, the most perfectly chiseled hunk of man she might have ever set eyes on, entering the Triple B. Reid had gone to school with her sister and even back then he was a hottie. Now, he'd been back in town for a few months, since his stint with the Army ended. Between the dark hair and muscles, a Reid sighting sent every female hormone in town fluttering.

Brynne's included. Except she only wanted to look. Looking was harmless. Looking didn't require the gutting, soul-sucking, emotional annihilation of relationships.

Besides, she'd sworn off men for the next five years.

Particularly ones like Reid. From the time she was ten and Reid sixteen, she'd been watching her older sister roll through boys while Reid did just as much rolling with the girls.

In the backseat of his car.

At least that's what Brynne had heard. And looking at him? All that swagger and cool confidence, she didn't doubt it.

"Ladies," he said as he strode toward them and settled onto the bar stool next to Brynne.

"Hi, Reid," she said. "Nice work with the ducks."

He slid off his sunglasses and his deep blue eyes—stormy ocean—zoomed in on her, traveled over her face, settling on her lips, and the usual nagging insecurity poked at her. Stupid ex-husband. They'd met as sophomores in college after she'd come so far in slaying her childhood demons. College had been paradise. Newly confident and shedding weight, little by little, Brynne had enjoyed freedom from her insecurities and then...New York, where her kind, amiable Kurt turned into an aggressive and highly critical up-and-comer. He scrutinized her appearance daily, sometimes hourly, until she was afraid to leave the house without his appraisal.

At least until he dumped her.

She lifted her fingers to her lips. The lipstick. She'd tried a new shade today, hadn't liked it and rubbed it off. Maybe she'd gotten some on her face.

No. She'd checked. Five times. She dropped her hand, forced herself to be still. To not step back or run from the blast of Reid Steele's focused attention. The man was so darned intense. Totally unnerving.

"Thanks," he said. "Always ready to please a woman in distress."

At that, Brynne snorted and Randi mockingly fanned herself. Such a man.

"What can I get you, Reid?" Randi asked.

He snagged the menu from the holder on the bar. "I'll have a beer to start. Whatever's on tap. And you know I'm digging your Gouda burger. I'll have one of those, too. Medium rare."

"You got it."

Randi set a beer in front of him and wandered off to

the kitchen, leaving Brynne alone with the hunk of all hunks. Great. What would they, the chubby girl and the beefcake, possibly have to talk about?

He pushed his sunglasses and keys off to the side and swiveled to her, once again storming her with all his attention. Fighting the urge to make herself smaller, she threw her shoulders back and sucked in her stomach.

"So," he said, "I...uh...need a gift for Evie."

Evie. Yay. Neutral ground. Plus, Brynne loved Evie. She only got to see her on weekends since she was away at school, but even with their four-year age difference, they'd immediately clicked when Evie started working at the shop.

If Brynne remembered correctly, Miss Evie had a birthday coming up.

"I was in your shop the other day," Reid said. "You weren't there."

"I have part-timers that help out."

"I couldn't figure out what to get her, but I'll tell ya, it smelled good in there."

"It's potpourri," Brynne said. "Made by a friend with neroli oil. If customers like it, I'll start carrying it in the store."

"My mom goes for all that stuff."

Ah. Potential sale already. "I'll give you some to take to her. She can be my test case."

She set her purse on the bar, snatched her iPad out and tapped at the screen. "I have Evie's wish list in my customer file."

"Her wish list?"

"Yes. If customers see something they like, they tell me and I add it to their file. Kind of like a bridal registry."

Reid scrunched his face. "A what?"

How cute was he? She entered Evie's name into her customer file and...yep. Birthday next month.

Beside her, Reid shifted and she glanced back to see his insanely haunting eyes sliding down her body, landing, if her guess was correct, on her butt.

She bolted upright, casually angling sideways and hiding the ginormous continent known as her rear. The one her ex-husband insisted would get smaller if she lowered her fat intake.

Forget him. She cleared her throat, drawing Reid's gaze back to her face. "You must be getting ahead of your shopping."

The comment was met with silence. And a straight-faced look of bewilderment.

"Uh, getting ahead?"

What was she missing here? She rolled one hand. "Evie. Her birthday is next month."

"Shit," Reid said.

Oh, my. "I thought that's what you needed a gift for."

His lips quirked and he ran his hand over his face before hitting her with the full-wattage I-am-*the*-man smile that had probably taken out half the female population on the Eastern seaboard.

"Busted me," he said.

"Sorry?"

"I…uh…saw you outside. Wanted to say hello."

Well, that was neighborly, but, really, she didn't even know him. Sure, she knew of him, everyone in this town knew the Steeles. But he certainly didn't know her and didn't need to go out of his way to say hello.

She cocked her head and the corner of his mouth lifted. "I used Evie as an excuse. To talk to you."

Okay. What was she supposed to say to that?

"Alrighty," he said. "I've definitely lost my touch because I'm hitting on you and you don't even know it."

Hitting on her? The man who induced flash-mob panty drops was hitting on *her*? Even if men weren't the scum of the earth, who'd have guessed Reid Steele, master of the orgasm—if the rumors were true—would even notice her.

Not plain-old Brynne. Her normal truckload of makeup and big hair helped, but she still couldn't compete with her sister's natural beauty and sculpted bones.

A flaming ball of heat rushed up her throat and she whirled away before her face flooded with color. "Um." She stuffed the iPad back into her purse. "There's a bracelet Evie wants. They're like bangles, but they have different charms you can add."

"Bangles?"

Without looking at him, she held her wrist up. "This. Sterling silver. How much did you want to spend?"

"Whatever. If that's what she wants."

"Yep," she chirped. "That's what she wants. You can keep buying her charms." Still refusing to look at him—*five-year plan, five-year plan, five-year plan*—she tapped a note into her phone. "I can set one aside for you when I go back to the store. Shall I wrap it for you?"

Reid dug into the back pocket of his jeans, and his T-shirt stretched across his chest and—wow—the guy was ripped.

And then ripped some more.

Total man candy.

He slapped his wallet on the bar. "Wrapping it would be good. How much?"

"Eighty-five. Plus tax."

His eyes widened. "Holy hell, my sister thinks all her brothers are billionaires. Let's bill that to Jonah."

She stared back at him, mute. Dear God, what was wrong with her? He'd made that damned crack about hitting on her and now she was totally thrown.

Reid let out a huffing laugh. "I'm going down in flames here. Brynne, I'm kidding. It's a running joke in my family. Bill everything to Jonah." He waved it away. "Never mind. I don't have that much cash on me. I'll stop in and you can run my card. That work?"

She put her phone back into her purse, went to move the purse to a stool, knocked over the cup of straws Randi had on the edge of the bar, and decided she wanted to die right then.

They both reached for the cup, their fingers tangling together and—wow, he had awesome hands. A little rough at the fingertips and work-hardened and enough to make a girl's skin go hot.

She snapped her hand back.

Reid righted the cup and replaced the straws that had spilled out.

"Thank you."

"Brynne?"

"Yes?"

"Do I make you nervous or something?"

ACKNOWLEDGMENTS

This series wouldn't have been possible without the amazing friendship I have with two incredible women. Adrienne Giordano and Tracey Devlyn, how can I even begin to say thank you for all we've shared since 2009? I was damn lucky to sit down at that table with Theresa Stevens eight years ago. (Um...and thank you for finally, finally letting me KILL people!)

As always, I wouldn't be able to squirrel away during the intense times when I hate my book and need to make it better if it weren't for the support and understanding of my husband and son. Y'all keep me going when I'm not sure I can make it. Thank you for reminding me it's like this with every book.

Major kudos to the amazing editors who are taking the Steele Ridge ride with us. What we're asking of you is a challenge, but you've met it and more! So some deep genuflecting to Gina Bernal, Deborah Nemeth, and Martha Trachtenberg.

And to my sister, Brandi Prazak...Who knew we'd hurt, maim, and kill so many people together, if only in the name of fiction? Thanks for always giving me the medical means to beat up my characters.

And to my super-fan groups, the Sass Kickers and the Dangerous Darlings, thank you for supporting my work and making me smile all the time. I can't imagine traveling this writing road without y'all.

Finally, thank you to all the readers who are already in love with this series and the Steele brothers. Adrienne, Tracey, and I wanted to bring you something bigger than what one author could create on her own. And don't worry—we're not finished yet!

KELSEY BROWNING is a *USA Today* bestselling author of sass kickin' love stories and co-authors Southern cozy mysteries. She's also a co-founder of Romance University blog, one of Writer's Digest 101 Best Websites for Writers. Originally from a Texas town smaller than the ones she writes about, Kelsey has also lived in the Middle East and Los Angeles, proving she's either adventurous or downright nuts. These days, she hangs out in northeast Georgia with Tech Guy, Smarty Boy, Bad Dog and Pharaoh, a (fingers crossed) future therapy dog.

FIND KELSEY

Facebook: facebook.com/KelseyBrowningAuthor
Twitter: twitter.com/kelseybrowning
Goodreads: goodreads.com/kelseybrowning
Pinterest: pinterest.com/KelseyBrowningAuthor
Instagram: instagram.com/KelseyBrowningAuthor.

Join Kelsey's street team, the Dangerous Darlings
facebook.com/groups/dangerousdarlings

or her fan group, the Sass Kickers
facebook.com/groups/sasskickers

Made in the USA
Middletown, DE
15 November 2019

78762964R00205